Louis N. Boudrye

History Records of the Fifth New York Cavalry, First Ira Harris Guard

SALZWASSER
VERLAG

Louis N. Boudrye

History Records of the Fifth New York Cavalry, First Ira Harris Guard

Reprint of the original, first published in 1865.

1st Edition 2022 | ISBN: 978-3-75258-849-1

Verlag (Publisher): Salzwasser Verlag GmbH, Zeilweg 44, 60439 Frankfurt, Deutschland
Vertretungsberechtigt (Authorized to represent): E. Roepke, Zeilweg 44, 60439 Frankfurt, Deutschland
Druck (Print): Books on Demand GmbH, In de Tarpen 42, 22848 Norderstedt, Deutschland

HISTORIC RECORDS

OF THE

Fifth New York Cavalry,

FIRST IRA HARRIS GUARD:

ITS

ORGANIZATION, MARCHES, RAIDS, SCOUTS, ENGAGEMENTS AND GENERAL SERVICES, DURING THE REBELLION OF 1861 - 1865,

WITH

OBSERVATIONS OF THE AUTHOR BY THE WAY,

GIVING

Sketches of the Armies of the Potomac and of the Shenandoah.

ALSO,

INTERESTING ACCOUNTS OF PRISON LIFE

AND OF THE

SECRET SERVICE.

Complete Lists of its Officers and Men.

BY REV LOUIS N. BOUDRYE,
CHAPLAIN OF THE REGIMENT.

ILLUSTRATED WITH STEEL PORTRAITS AND WOOD CUTS.

SECOND EDITION.

ALBANY, N. Y

1865.

TO THE BRAVE BOYS

OF THE OLD FIFTH,

who

have

so often displayed unsurpassed

Patriotism, Fortitude

and Valor in the

trying vicissitudes of

Military Life; and who,

on so many bloody Fields

of Battle, have heroically up-

borne the Starry Banner, and have

vindicated its authority in the pres-

ence of its enemies, are these

His- toric Records of their

NO- BLE DEEDS

DEDICATED by their

CHAPLAIN.

HEAD QUARTERS, Fifth N. Y. Cavalry,
Near Staunton, Va., *June 5th*, 1865.

REV. LOUIS N. BOUDRYE,

Chaplain, Fifth N. Y. Cavalry,

Dear Sir: We, the officers of the Fifth New York Cavalry, desirous to possess true and full Historic Records of the Regiment, since its organization, do respectfully request you to prepare the same for publication in such form, that ourselves and the men of this Command may be able to procure them.

Pledging you our assistance in the accomplishment of this difficult labor, we remain

Respectfully Yours,

(*Signed*).— A. H. WHITE, Col.; T. A. BOICE, Lt. Col.; E. J. BARKER, Major; H. A. D. MERRITT, Major; O. W. ARMSTRONG, Surgeon, and others.

CAMP Fifth New York Cavalry,
Near Staunton, Va., *June 6th*, 1865.

Col. A. H. WHITE, Lt. Col. T. A. BOICE, and others,

Dear Sirs: I cheerfully undertake the "difficult labor," which you request me to perform for several reasons, viz: first, because you request it. Second, because I believe it to be the duty of every regiment to prepare a correct history of its services in this war, for future reference. Third, because my services as chaplain of the regiment, for nearly three years of its active campaigning, have afforded me an ample opportunity to know its character and history. A diary of all the remarkable events of that period, written during the lull of battle; — in the halt of the march; — through the respite of hospital labor; — in the loneliness of the prison (where I was confined three months), and during the quietness of the camp,— will be invaluable in this enterprise. I pledge myself to search out diligently, and to state faithfully, the *facts* of our eventful history. Hoping that among these records in future days, we may spend many happy and profitable hours, living over again some of the glorious experiences of our military life,

I remain, Very Respectfully Yours,

LOUIS N. BOUDRYE,

Chaplain, Fifth N. Y. Cavalry

ILLUSTRATIONS

STEEL PORTRAITS.

WOOD CUTS.

LIST OF TABLES

CONTENTS

CHAPTER I.

CHAPTER II.

CHAPTER III.

CHAPTER IV.

CHAPTER V

CHAPTER VI.

CHAPTER VII.

CHAPTER VIII

CHAPTER IX.

CHAPTER X.

CHAPTER XI.

CHAPTER XII.

CHAPTER XIII.

CHAPTER XIV

CHAPTER XV

CHAPTER XVI.

CHAPTER XVII.

CHAPTER XVIII.

APPENDIX.

CHAPTER I.

Our Cavalry Deficient at Bull Run.— This Arm Recruited.— Organization of the Fifth New York Cavalry.— Hon. Ira Harris lends his Name and Influence.— Early History of Regiment.— On Staten Island, New York.— Flag Presentation.— Speech of Senator Harris.— Regiment Leaves the State.— In Baltimore.— In Annapolis.— At Camp Harris.— *July* 26*th to Dec.* 31*st*, 1861.

The first battle of Bull Run clearly demonstrated the importance of the cavalry arm of the service, and that the enemy's cavalry, including his notorious Black Horse, was far superior to ours. Fully aware of our deficiency the authorities went directly to work to reënforce this weak arm and to invigorate it with new life and discipline. Recruiting officers at once appeared in every section of the loyal north, whose calls were made for cavalrymen, who would be expected to take the field against the proud chivalry, whose success, thus far, had made them more defiant and confident than before.

On the twenty-sixth of July, 1861, the secretary of war authorized Col. Othniel De Forest, of New York city, to raise a regiment of cavalry for the field service. With earnest zeal the colonel began the work assigned him, and by the last of September he had gathered on Staten Island, New York, the nucleus of a fine cavalry brigade. From this assemblage of recruits Col. De Forest organized the Fifth New York Cavalry, known as the First Ira Harris Guard, in honor of Senator Ira Harris, of Albany, under whose patronage the organization was commenced and completed. New York City had contributed liberally of men, though whole companies and parts of companies were raised in Essex, Wyoming, Allegany, Tioga and Orange counties. A few men were also obtained from the states of Massachusetts, Connecticut and New Jersey. No bounties were then paid to recruits, and a bounty of only one hundred dollars was promised to be paid by the United States, at the expiration of term of service.

On the first of October, on Staten Island, New York, the field and staff of the regiment were mustered into the service of the United States for three years, by Capt. L. S. Larned, of the United States army. The muster took effect from that date. The regiment was now quartered in common, or A tents, furnished by the United States, and the place where the boys received their first lessons in discipline and drill was called Camp Scott, after the old veteran, who, at that time, was closing his active military labors. The first and second battalions received their horses during the month of October, and began to be instructed in *mounted* drill.

October 31st. The regiment was inspected for the first time by Lt. Col. D. B. Sackett, of the United States army. The last company had now been mustered in, and the command stood with a strength of 1,064, besides the officers. On this day of inspection the regiment was also mustered in for pay, preparatory to receiving its first remuneration from the government, which came on the sixth of November. At that time the government had not yet learned to deal in paper money, and the boys received their pay wholly in gold and silver, though it was the last time they were cumbered with the precious metals.

Monday, November 11*th*, was a memorable day for the regiment, which was then presented with two beautiful flags, one by the common council of the city of New York, and the other from the hands of Misses Kate Harris and Mary F. Blake. A stand had been erected in the centre of the plain, at Camp Scott, in front of which, at the appointed time, the regiment was formed into a hollow square, the officers, some thirty in number, in full dress uniform, advancing to the front, Col. De Forest occupying the centre of the group.

At the unfurling of the colors, Senator Harris, who was present, arose on the stand, and spoke as follows:

Col. De Forest, Officers and Soldiers of the Ira Harris Guard:—I am here to-day to perform a most pleasing service. It is one of the proudest moments of my life. To-morrow,[1] many of you will depart for the seat of war, there to take part, actively and successfully, I trust, in the great encounter in which our country is now engaged with treason and rebellion. The rest of you will soon follow. Before you go, I desire to place in your hands and commit to your keeping a most sacred deposit — one which I am sure you will be ready to defend with your hearts' best blood. Look upon that standard. Behold these stars and stripes. As the star of Bethlehem has been, for ages, the great centre of religious hope, so these stars and stripes are the emblem of all we hold dear as Americans. Upon these the patriot rests his best hopes. They are the great beacon-

[1] The regiment did not go as was expected.

light of oppressed humanity throughout the world. And yet these stars and stripes — so precious in the eyes of every true American — and now tenfold more precious than ever before — were, a little while ago, at Fort Sumter — in one of the states represented by these stars, basely, ignominiously *shot down.* This outrage was committed, not by a foreign foe — this could have been endured — but by the coward hands of traitors. This was too much to bear. At their country's call, hundreds of thousands of patriotic men have gone forth to revenge the insult and suppress this most atrocious rebellion — the most atrocious that the world ever saw. Hundreds of thousands more are ready to go whenever their country needs them. Neither men nor money shall ever be wanting until this great rebellion is utterly extinguished. This is the great and noble errand upon which you go. I think I know the men to whom I speak. They are brave men — they are patriotic men. I trust and believe there is not one of you who would not pour out his blood like water, to save his country from destruction and dishonor. How gladly would I go with you. Did my circumstances permit, I would march with you to-morrow, and share with you the perils and the glory of the patriot soldier. But though I cannot go, I rejoice that my name and honor are to go with you. I know they will be safe in your hands. Col. De Forest, as the representative and leader of this noble band of men, I commit this standard to your hands. Keep it — stand by it — defend it, even with your life. Let it be rent and marred in the intensity of the conflict to which you go, but let it never be dishonored by the polluting touch of a traitor's hand. And I ask you — both you and the men of your command — now and here, in the presence of this large assemblage, to record your vow, that, God helping you, this banner shall not pass from your hands until it shall wave in graceful triumph over the very grave of treason. And, colonel, I have yet another equally delightful office to perform. The duty has been assigned me of presenting to you this other flag. It comes from delicate hands. It is the united gift of love and patriotism. Take it with you, and, when far away upon the tented field, let it be to you for a memorial of the loved ones you leave behind you. And when you come to meet the foe in battle, let it, with talismanic power, nerve your arm to strike heavier, deadlier blows in your country's cause. And now, colonel, officers and men, farewell! I shall watch your movements with the intensest interest. Whatever my humble efforts can accomplish for your welfare or comfort shall be done. But the life of a soldier is no holiday life. I know you will endure hardships as good soldiers — that you will brave even death itself in a cause so glorious. Some of you will fall in battle. Oh, it is a glorious death thus to die. Some of you — most of you, I hope — will live to return. But come not back, I charge you, until you come covered all over with glory, to receive the plaudits of a grateful country.

To this profoundly impressive address, which was frequently interrupted by cheers from the whole regiment, Col. De Forest made a very touching and appropriate response. This was followed by an outburst of enthusiastic cheering.

November 18th. The regiment took its departure from the state, and after a pleasant journey by rail road without accidents, reached Baltimore on the 19th. During their stay in the Monumental city the 3d battalion drew horses and equipments, and on the 25th the regiment made its first march, from Baltimore to Annapolis. During their stay here most of the men were quartered in St. Mary's College and yard. On the 28th they left this capital and pitched their tents about three miles from the city, and named the place Camp Harris.

CHAPTER II.

Discipline and Drill. — First Bivouac. — At Harper's Ferry. — Winchester. — Its Appearance then. — First Capture made by the Regiment. — Col. Turner Ashby (Rebel) in the Valley. —Fight with him at Harrisonburg. — Gallant Conduct of the Fifth. — First Casualties. — Cavalry towing Infantry across a River by hanging on the Horses' Tails. — Battle of Front Royal. — The Flanker Stonewall Jackson. — The Regiment Engaged. — A Portion of it cut off. — Great Daring. — Belle Boyd, the female Rebel Spy. — Letter of Charles H. Greenleaf. — How Gen. Banks saved his army.—Result of Retreat.—*Jan. to May 26th*, 1862.

The winter at Camp Harris was not spent in vain. Under the instructions of a thorough disciplinarian, and of excellent drill masters, the regiment had become versed in the tactics of war. Horses as well as men had learned the "certain sounds" of the bugle, and were masters of evolutions and dispositions required of them. Thus the foundation of a career destined to be important and glorious was laid, and the command was only waiting for the opportunity of practicing in the field what it had learned in camp, and of achieving what had been fondly hoped by its friends. That time soon came. The last day of March, 1862, found them breaking up their winter quarters and preparing for the realities of field service. On that day the 1st and 2d battalions marched to Annapolis Junction, and entered into their first bivouac. The first April they were at the Relay

House, and on the 2d at Harper's Ferry. Until the ninth April the battalions were separated from each other, and sent from one post to the other as though the authorities did not know where they were really needed. They alternated between Ellicott Mills, Washington and Harper's Ferry, until at length the whole regiment bivouacked together amid the rough scenes of the John Brown raid. On the 10th Cos. F and L escorted Maj. General Rosecrans to Winchester, Woodstock, Paris, and returned again to Harper's Ferry.

During a heavy rain, which made the roads almost impassable, and the weather uncomfortable, the regiment marched, on the 20th April, to Winchester. This was then a beautiful town. "Grim visaged war," with her fire and sword, had not yet desolated the fine public buildings, nor destroyed the beautiful shrubbery and foliage of the streets. But Winchester was then as rebellious and aristocratic as it was beautiful. Thoroughly loyal Union families were there, but they were like angel's visits, "few and far between." It is true it cost something to be loyal there, but the virtue of loyalty is a possession well worthy its expense.

The regiment remained not long to luxuriate in this pleasant locality, but moved on the 22d to Strasburg, where it remained two days, moving to Woodstock on the 24th. On the 26th the men received their pay from the government, and were prepared to march to New Market the next day. On the 29th, while on a scout, they captured four prisoners. This was the first capture the regiment ever made, and, at that time, it was considered a *big thing*.

May 2d. Co A made a reconnoissance from Harrisonburg toward Port Republic, running into General Jackson's camp. In the skirmish and flight that followed, they had one man captured, the first man ever lost from the regiment in an engagement.

May 3d. The regiment advanced to Harrisonburg, and reported to Brig. Gen. John P. Hatch, commanding cavalry in the valley. On the 5th the whole force fell back to New Market and bivouacked.

May 3th. Col. Turner Ashby, a young dashing Rebel officer, with a force of picked cavalry, had been playing mischief with our outposts for several weeks. His exploits had been so daring, quick, and so generally successful, that he had made himself a great name, and become a terror to our forces. During the day it was reported that Ashby with his men was coming down the pike from Harrisonburg. In the afternoon a detachment of the Fifth New York was sent out to check any advance that might be made. Within about five miles of Harrisonburg, they encountered the redoubtable Ashby. Our men all eager for a fight, fell like a whirlwind upon the enemy, and using their sabres with terrible effect, soon scattered and turned them back in confusion. And now commenced a scrambling race. Clouds of dust arose from the road, which almost entirely enveloped both the pursued and the pursuers. Occasionally the Rebels rallied, but were swept away again, and finally chased into the suburbs of the town, badly defeated. The conflict cost them 3 men killed, 5 wounded and 7 prisoners, besides several good horses captured. On our side we lost Asahel A. Spencer, Co. E, killed, who was the first victim of the regiment, offered to the God of battles. William Mills, Co. I, was wounded. Sergeant Wm. H. Whitcomb, Co. M, was captured, but escaped through dint of Yankee ingenuity. "The Rebels had stripped off his arms and were using the indecorus language with which the Yankee prisoner is usually saluted," when he informed them that they had been pursued by only a dozen Yankees whom they might all capture by dashing back upon them. They charged back, were scattered, and some of them captured by our boys, and Whitcomb escaped. Adjutant Hasbrouck was here captured and taken to Richmond.

One correspondent says of the affair: "The brilliant charge, of which you were informed by telegraph, has established beyond a cavil the reputation of the Ira Harris Guard. Hereafter the Rebels will not forget that there is cavalry in this division capable of driving back their mounted guerrillas in confusion and consternation; capable of using the sabre, the proper instrument of the trooper, in close hand to hand conflict. This is the first time that we have heard from this body of New York cavalry, and they have made a good report of themselves, and done honor to their state."

Another writer says: "I asked one of the prisoners, if he thought our boys could fight well. He said: 'Only that *regular* cavalry; they fought like devils.' That regular cavalry was the glorious New York Fifth."

After returning from this successful encounter, some of our men, while bathing in the river near New Market, were attacked by bushwhackers, and two men of Co. I were killed and one of Co. L captured.

The day following this affair, the news was received of the evacuation of Yorktown, and the army was in a great jubilee of rejoicing. Consolidated bands visited Generals Banks, Williams and Hatch, and made the town echo with patriotic music. They also visited and serenaded the Fifth

New York in honor of their gallant charge yesterday. As that had been the first cavalry charge of the war, where sabres were used, and with such signal success, the affair created much comment at the time in military circles.

On the 12th the whole force fell back to Woodstock, and continued as far as Tom's Brook on the 14th, at which time quite a skirmish was fought at Woodstock by our cavalry. As our army fell back, its rear was closely followed and frequently attacked by Ashby's force. Consequently a strong guard was required. On the 21st, Gen. Hatch, with about 150 of the Fifth, made a successful attack upon this force, driving them many miles, killing, wounding and capturing several and returning without the loss of a man.

Meantime, Co. H, which had been detached with Brig. Gen. Sullivan in the Luray Valley, during the last of April, had fought several spirited skirmishes with the enemy and now rejoined the regiment. While in the Luray Valley they had witnessed a curious modus operandi, where a force of our infantry and cavalry was hard pressed by the enemy on the bank of the Shenandoah river, which was so high as to be unfordable. As a last resort the cavalrymen plunged into the stream, swimming their horses, and towed across the infantrymen who clung to the animals' tails.

May 23d. Gen. Banks had been lying securely a few days in and about Strasburg, when he was unexpectedly informed by messengers of the Fifth N. Y. Cavalry, that a sudden attack had been made by the great flanker, Stonewall Jackson, upon Col. Kenly's force at Front Royal. Companies B and D had been sent to Col. Kenly during the afternoon arriving just as the Rebels began to pour down the valley and the hills upon this devoted garrison. The cavalry was immediately ordered to charge the enemy. Quickly obeying the order, a splendid charge was made with great force. Had bravery been sufficient to win, the Ira Harris Guard would have again succeeded, but, greatly outnumbered, flanked and almost surrounded, with a large number killed, wounded and captured, the remnant was driven back upon our main force which was now retreating at a rapid rate. In this charge fell the young and brave Lieutenant Dwyer, Co. B, mortally wounded. Capt. A. H. White, Co. D (afterward Colonel), and Adjutant Griffin, while gallantly leading their men, fell into the enemy's hands.

Gen. Banks, in his report to the war department, says: "Information was received on the evening of May 23d, that the enemy in very large force had descended on the guard at Front Royal, Col. Kenly, First Md. Regiment, commanding, burning bridges and driving our troops through Strasburg, with great loss. Owing to what was deemed an extravagant statement of the enemy's strength, these reports were received with some distrust; but a regiment of infantry, with a strong detachment of cavalry and a section of artillery, were immediately sent to reënforce Col. Kenly."

Meanwhile preparations were made to fall back to Winchester as rapidly as possible. Col. De Forest with six companies of the regiment and Col. Tompkins with an equal number of his regiment—the First Vermont, with a detachment of Zouaves d'Afrique (Gen. Banks' body guard), and a section of Hampton's battery, were ordered to cover the rear and to destroy stores not provided with transportation at Strasburg. But before this could be accomplished the enemy had pushed a force between our main army and this rear guard. Swift and desperate charges were made, but

O. De Forest
Colonel 5th N.Y. Cav

a junction could not be effected and our men were threatened with annihilation. Middletown and Newtown Cross Roads were the scenes of fearful encounters, but the noble band was beaten back every time. At length, breaking away from the enemy, this guard took to the fields toward the Little North Mountains, hoping, by a circuitous route around the enemy's flank, to be able to join Gen. Banks at Winchester, where Col. Tompkins with some artillery joined him next day. Col. De Forest, encumbered with a train, was not so fortunate, but was compelled to pass over the rugged mountain roads for several days, reaching our army at last by way of Cherry Run and Clear Spring, and bringing in with him a train of 32 wagons and many stragglers. Gen. Banks, after a hasty and disastrous retreat, fell back into Maryland at Williamsport and Falling Waters. Belle Boyd, the noted Rebel female spy, was undoubtedly instrumental in causing our defeat. It was afterwards ascertained that she was the bearer of an extensive correspondence between Rebels outside and inside our lines.

The following letter from one of our brave boys, will show how Gen. Banks saved his army from utter destruction at Strasburg:

WILLIAMSPORT, MD., May 26, 1862.

Dear Father and Mother: You have probably heard by this time of the three days' fighting from Strasburg and Front Royal to Martinsburg. Our company and company B were ordered to Front Royal in the mountains, twelve miles from Strasburg, last Friday, and when we got within two miles of our destination we heard cannonading. The major[1] ordered the baggage to stop, and our two com-

[1] Maj. P. G. Vought, commanding Detachment.

panies dashed on, and found several companies of our infantry and two pieces of artillery engaged with several thousands of the enemy. Just as we arrived on the field, Col. Kenly, who had command of our forces, rode up to me, and ordered me to take one man and the two best horses in our company, and ride for dear life to Gen. Banks' headquarters in Strasburg for reënforcement. The direct road to Strasburg was occupied by the enemy, so I was obliged to ride around by another, seventeen miles. I rode the seventeen miles in fifty-five minutes. Gen. Banks did not seem to think it very serious, but ordered one regiment of infantry and two pieces of artillery off. I asked Gen. Banks for a fresh horse to rejoin my company, and he gave me the best horse that I ever rode, and I started back. I came out on the Front Royal turnpike, about two miles this side of where I left our men. Saw two men standing in the road, and their horses standing by the fence. I supposed they were our pickets.

They did not halt me, so I asked them if they were pickets. They said no. Says I, "who are you?" "We are part of Gen. Jackson's staff." I supposed they were only joking. I laughed, and asked them where Jackson was. They said he was in the advance. I left them and rode toward Front Royal, till I overtook a soldier, and asked him what regiment he belonged to. He said he belonged to the Eighth Louisiana. I asked how large a force they had, and the reply was "twenty thousand." I turned back and drew my revolver, expecting either a desperate fight or a southern jail; but the officers in the road did not stop me, and I was lucky enough not to meet any of their pickets. But if it was not a narrow escape, then I don't know what is. When

I got out of the enemy's lines, I rode as fast as the horse could carry me to Gen. Banks, and reported what I had seen and heard. He said I had saved the army.

In less than an hour the whole army was in motion toward Winchester. After I left Front Royal to take the dispatch to Strasburg, our two companies of cavalry, who were covering the retreat of infantry and baggage, were attacked on three sides by about three thousand of the enemy's cavalry. Our boys fought like devils, till nearly half of them were killed or wounded, and then retreated to Winchester. Capt. White, William Watson, Henry Appleby, and nine or ten men of my company are killed or taken. William Marshall is all right, except a slight sabre cut in the shoulder.

We had a fight at Winchester, got licked and retreated. Our company and company E were ordered to cover the parrot gun battery, and bring up the rear. We rode all the way from Winchester to Martinsburg, with cannon shot and shell flying around us faster than it did at Bull Run. We crossed the Potomac last night. It was so dark that we could not find the ford, and had to swim our horses across. We have got our batteries in position on this side, and the rear of the army is crossing.

From your son,

CHARLEY H. GREENLEAF,

Co. D. Fifth N. Y. Cavalry.

Thus ended this famous retreat. It cost the government about 50 wagons, which were either abandoned or destroyed, about nine hundred European rifles left at Strasburg and large quantities of medical and hospital stores, including surgeons' instruments, destroyed and abandoned at

Strasburg and Winchester. The army was considerably demoralized. Discouraged with their defeats many of the boys took advantage of their sojourn in Maryland to take *French* furloughs, though some of them afterward returned to their commands.

CHAPTER III.

Rebel Army Crossing South of Blue Ridge.— Successful Advance on Martinsburg.— Services and Sufferings of the Cavalry.— Cavalry Battle of Orange Court House.— Fifth New York Boys.— Terrible Dealers in Hardware.— Reconnoissance to Louisa Court House.— Gen. Stuart's Adjutant General and Important Dispatches from Gen. Lee Captured.— Reconnoissance through Snicker's Gap and to Berryville.— Capture of a Rebel Camp, one Stand of Colors and much Spoil.— Charge on a Sutler's Shanty.— Sword Presented to Gen. J. P. Hatch.— Interesting Correspondence.— *May 31st to December 31st*, 1862.

With the valley cleared of the Yankee army, the Rebels began to throw their forces across the Blue Ridge to attack our main army in front of Washington, leaving only a strong picket line at the foot of the valley, opposed to our army in Maryland. It soon became necessary to advance across the river, and ascertain what was in our front. The regiment, which had been divided in the retreat, now advanced from Harper's Ferry and from Williamsport. The former column met the enemy at Charlestown, and drove him; and the latter advanced on Martinsburg, drove the pickets through the town and captured several prisoners, a wagon, muskets, ammunition and an American flag. They also recaptured several of our officers and men lost at Front Royal, among them Adjutant Griffin. Several engines and cars were also captured from the enemy, who appeared to have been taken wholly by surprise. This encouraging advance took place the last day of May. On the fourth of June the regiment advanced to Winchester, where its fragments were reunited. However, companies B and D, which had distinguished themselves at Front Royal, were detached from the regiment, to serve on a battery.. (See register of companies). Not much was accomplished during the month.

On the sixteenth the regiment received pay, marched to Middletown on the twenty-seventh and to Front Royal the thirtieth. This march was continued to Flint Hill, the fifth of July, and on the sixth, at Sperryville, a squad of Rebel cavalry was encountered and a fight ensued, our boys scattering the enemy. The regiment was here joined by Major Gardner, who had been detached with Companies C, F, G, and L, on the 19th of June.

July 8th. The regiment marched to Gaines' Cross Roads, advancing on Culpepper Court House on the twelfth, where it had a skirmish with the enemy, drove them through the town and captured fifteen prisoners. The sixteenth the boys enjoyed an all-day march through an all-day rain, to Rapidan Ford. The next day they marched into Orange Court House, expelling, after a short skirmish, the enemy that was in town. Being the first Union troops that had ever visited this place, they were objects of excited observation. But to the intense satisfaction of the people, they left on the eighteenth, and returned to Rapidan Ford. While on pickett at Barnett's Ford, a large portion of Company A was captured.

This was a season of great suffering among our men and horses for want of rations and forage, especially the former.

Being almost constantly on the move, and most of the time on the extreme out-posts, it was not possible to bring them supplies. Of the cavalry in general, one correspondent makes this remark :—" They picket our outposts, scout the whole country for information, open our fights, cover our retreats, or clear up and finish our victories, as the case may be. In short, they are never idle, and rarely find rest for either men or horses." And he might have added, "are often sadly in want." During the remainder of July no force of the enemy was encountered, but the regiment was almost constantly on the march, having passed and bivouacked by the following places:—Sperryville, Woodville, Culpepper Court House, James City, Wolftown, and into the Luray Valley, by way of Swift Run Gap, to Luray, Woodville again, and back to Culpepper Court House near which they bivouacked until the 1st of August. On this day they marched to Raccoon Ford. At this place was concentrated quite a force of cavalry, under Gen. Crawford, preparatory to an important movement. During the month Gen. Hatch was removed from the command of the cavalry in this department. Gen. John Buford succeeded him.

August 2d. Gen. Crawford with the 1st Vermont, 1st Michigan and the 5th New York advanced at an early hour to reconnoitre the force and position of the enemy about Orange Court House. Scarcely a Rebel appeared until the column approached the town. Without opposition the advance entered the town, whose streets they found deserted, while a stillness like that of death seemed to reign all around. But suddenly volley after volley broke the stillness, and proclaimed the presence of a heavy force of the enemy. On reaching the suburbs of the town, a strong flanking party, consisting of Cos. G and H, under command of Capt. Hammond, was ordered around to the left toward the Gordonsville road, whither they dashed off with spirit, under their gallant leader.

The main column encountered a heavy charge of the enemy in the street, which, at first, drove our fellows back a little. Rallying from the first shock, they now dashed back upon the enemy, and a fierce conflict from pistols and carbines followed. Shots flew in every direction, killing horses and men alike. The fight was furious in the narrow streets; and just as the enemy's column began to waver, Capt. Hammond, who had fought the enemy at the depot, and was now partially surrounded, with drawn sabres charged upon the rebels in his front, crying as he flew forward, "give them your hardware, boys!" And they did the work most heroically. Tremendous were the blows they dealt, and the street was strewn with unhorsed men whose heads displayed fearful gashes from the Yankee sabres. Lieutenant Penfield, Co. H, with a thorough knowledge of sabre exercise, with a long, strong arm, and a courageous heart, did terrible execution in this fray. The enemy could not stand these "hardware" dealers, and fled in the utmost confusion, leaving their dead and badly wounded in our hands. The great number of these only showed how determined and gallant had been our attack. Fifty prisoners were captured, including a major, a captain, and two lieutenants.

During this fight, Col. De Forest had a very narrow escape with his life, and was indebted for his preservation to bugler Bohrer, of Co. I.[1]

---

[1] See Register of Co. I.

This engagement clearly proved our superiority over the enemy's cavalry, which, in this instance, consisted of their best Virginia regiments lately under Col. Ashby.

Heavy reënforcements having been received by the enemy, and our work having been accomplished, our cavalry fell back to the Rapidan, where the Rebels ceased pursuing. Here were rested our victorious squadrons.

On the 4th the regiment marched to Culpepper and to Madison Court House on the 5th, bivouacking near the town. From Wolftown to Stannards on the 7th we formed a line of pickets; and on the 9th was fought the memorable battle of Cedar or Slaughter Mountain. Only a few of the regiment were engaged in this battle, one of those being killed. A slight skirmish was fought with the enemy on the 10th as they fell back toward Gordonsville.

August 11*th*. The regiment marched to Culpepper Court House and found the town full of our wounded from the battle of the 9th.

August 12*th*. On a reconnoissance to Barnett's Ford on the Rapidan and back to Culpepper. Paid off on the 15th and marched to Mitchell's Station on the 16th, preparatory to a swift move on the enemy's lines.

August 17*th*. Detachments of the Fifth New York and First Michigan, Col. Broadhead commanding, marched out early on a bold reconnoissance to Louisa Court House, where they captured Gen. Stuart's Adjutant General and several very important dispatches. Gen. Pope in his report speaks of this affair as follows:

"The Cavalry expedition sent out on the 16th in the direction of Louisa Court House, captured the Adjutant General of Gen. Stuart, and was very near capturing that officer himself.[1] Among the papers taken was an autograph letter of Gen. Robert E. Lee to Gen. Stuart, dated Gordonsville, August 15th, which made manifest to me the disposition and force of the enemy and their determination to overwhelm the army under my command before it could be reënforced by any portion of the army of the Potomac."

Having spent a night in chasing through the confederate lines, our men returned to their own side of the Rapidan. Gen. Pope's army was falling back across the Rappahannock, and the regiment marched to Barnett's Ford on that river, and held the crossing.

August 20th. The regiment advanced to Kelly's Ford, and took part in a general engagement. They were ordered to support a battery, which was exposed to a fearful fire. The colonel encouraged his men by a short address, and they did their work well.

On the 22d we marched to Fayetteville, continued the march to Warrenton the next day, and on the 24th participated in a severe engagement at Waterloo Bridge. Our men suffered from the Rebel batteries which were brought to bear upon them. During the fight a shell took effect in our ranks killing instantly three horses belonging to the three officers of Co. I but fortunately only a few men were hurt.

On the 27th Cos. I, K, & L, were detached as orderlies and escort of Gen. Heintzelman; the balance of the regiment was made escort of Gen. Pope. On the 28th Company M was detailed escort of Gen. Banks, and the main body of the regiment marched to Bull Run Bridge and camped.

---

[1] His belt was captured.

August 29th. To-day commenced what has generally been known as the second Battle of Bull Run, better named Groveton. The Rebels were in overwhelming force, driving Gen. Pope before them. Our lines fell back, and on the 30th the conflict was renewed on the field of the first Bull Run. The field though hotly contested, was again won by the enemy, and though not panic-stricken we were compelled to retreat. Gradually on the 31st our forces fell back toward Washington.

September 1st. Generals Kearney and Stevens distinguished themselves on the bloody field of Chantilly, and both lost their lives. The regiment reached Fairfax Court House.

The retreat was continued and the regiment camped at the Arlington House on the 5th. The Rebel army now moved into Maryland, and on the 17th and 19th was fought the memorable battle of Antietam.

October 8th. Lt. Col. Johnstone with one hundred and ten men went out with the brigade on a reconnoissance to the Rappahannock, returning, without meeting the enemy, on the 11th.

October 15th. Another expedition went out under Maj. Hammond, marching the first day to Chantilly, then on to Aldie, White Plains, and back to Centreville on the 19th. During this expedition skirmishes were fought at Leesburg, Upperville and Thoroughfare Gap, ending with a running fight from Haymarket to Warrenton whither we drove the rebels.

On the 20th the regiment was ordered on picket at Chantilly, where it continued patrolling and picketing the country until the twenty-eighth, when it went to Centreville, and next day to Manassas Junction and back to Chantilly.

October 30*th*. We patrolled to Pleasant Valley, and closed the month by picketing by detachments at Pollock's Church, Anandale and Centreville. This work was very dull, and yet very wearing. The weather was becoming cold and unpleasant, and picketing and scouting were not very desirable. However, the month of November was wholly devoted to this work, so that there was scarcely a day of rest. The journal of movements runs as follows: on the first to Centreville; second to Bull Run battle field and picket; third to Gainesville; fourth to Buckland Mills; fifth to New Baltimore and have a fight; sixth to Buckland Mills; seventh to Gainesville; eighth through Hopewell Gap, after a skirmish; ninth to Aldie and Middleburg; tenth to Hopewell Gap; eleventh through Thoroughfare Gap with a fight, and to Aldie; twelfth to Middleburg on patrol; thirteenth to Hopewell Gap; fourteenth to Aldie, where we rested on the fifteenth. Such was the cavalry service in those days. On the sixteenth we had a skirmish at Upperville, and returned to Hopewell Gap next day, and on to Chantilly the eighteenth. Here we met with a little rest, the monotony of which was broken by an expedition to the Blue Ridge and into the Shenandoah Valley and back. This expedition, in command of Gen. Stahel, commenced its march November 29th. The men of the Fifth New York Cavalry were commanded by Capt. Krom, Company G. In Snicker's Gap a Rebel picket was captured. On arriving at the Shenandoah river at Snicker's Ferry the Rebels annoyed our men and prevented rapid crossing, by firing from the houses beyond the river. Capt. Krom, with his men, dashed across the river, though the water was deep and the current swift. On reaching the bank the Rebels were furiously charged and driven. Our men pursued them at the utmost speed of their horses for about three miles, when they came upon the Rebel camps, which the enemy attempted to defend. Their effort failed. Our men being reënforced, the enemy was beaten and fled, leaving in our hands one captain, two lieutenants, thirty-two men, one stand of colors and several wagons, one of them filled with tents, and others with provisions. Several ambulances also were taken laden with articles which had been taken by White's men, in a recent raid into Poolsville, Maryland. Sixty horses and fifty head of cattle were also captured in this gallant charge. The expedition returned on the 30th through Leesburg, Goose Creek, Broad Run to Chantilly.

December 1st. To our old duty again on picket until the 4th, near Chantilly. On the 10th we picketed at Centreville, and did the same duty on the Bull Run battle field, on the 12th. Marched to Chantilly the 13th and picketed till the 28th. Being relieved from this duty, we were immediately sent on a scout to Union Mills and Fairfax Station, spending the night at Fairview.

December 29th. Stuart's raiders came through our lines and passed near our camp on their return. The regiment was sent in pursuit. We followed them about six miles, but found their force too strong for us to attack. On the 30th we returned to Chantilly on picket, and ended the year by falling back to Fairfax Court House, where the boys, actuated by mischief and with a desire of having something with which to celebrate the coming New Year, made a charge upon a sutler's shanty, which resulted in the capture of much spoil and in a general victory.

The following correspondence will explain itself:

2D CAVALRY BRIGADE, 3d Army Corps,
Near Fort Scott, Va., December 3d, 1862.

To Brig. Gen. JOHN P HATCH:

General: The accompanying sabre is presented to you by the officers of the First Vermont and Fifth New York Cavalry.

We have served under you while you commanded the Cavalry in Virginia—a period of active operations and military enterprise—during which your courage and judgment inspired us with confidence, while your zeal and integrity have left us an example easier to be admired than imitated.

We, who have passed with you beyond the Rapidan, and through Swift Run Gap, are best able to recognize your qualities as a commander.

Accept, therefore, General, this testimonial of esteem, offered long after we were removed from your command,—when the external glitter of an ordinary man ceases to affect the mind, but when real worth begins to be appreciated.

On behalf of the Officers of the Fifth New York.

ROBERT JOHNSTONE,
Lt. Col. 5th New York Cavalry.

Oswego, N. Y. Dec. 15th, 1862.

To the Officers of the Fifth New York and First Vermont Regiments of Cavalry:

Gentlemen: A very beautiful sabre, your present to myself, has been reeeived. I shall wear it with pride, and will never draw it but in an honorable cause.

The very kind letter accompanying the sabre has caused emotions of the deepest nature. The assurance it gives of the confidence you feel in myself, and your approval of my course when in command of Banks' Cavalry, is particularly gratifying. You, actors with myself in those stirring scenes, are competent judges as to the propriety of my course, when it unfortunately did not meet with the approval of my superior; and your testimony, so handsomely expressed, after time has allowed opportunity for reflection, more than compensates for the mortification of that moment.

I have watched with pride the movements of your regiments, since my separation from you. When a telegram has announced that "in a Cavalry fight, the *edge of the sabre* was successfully used, and the enemy routed," the further announcement that the Fifth New York and First Vermont were engaged, was unnecessary.

Accept my kindest wishes for your future success,—sharp sabres and a trust in Providence, will enable you to secure it in the field.

Very truly, my friends,
Your obedient Servant
JOHN P HATCH,
Brigadier General.

CHAPTER IV.

Mosby, the Guerrilla.— His men.— Picketing against him at Chantilly. — Building Winter Quarters at Germantown. — Description. — Mosby at Fairfax Court House. — Fight at Chantilly. — At Warrenton Junction. — Congratulatory Order of Commanding General. —Fight at Greenwich. — Capture of a Howitzer. — Gallant Conduct of Lieut. Barker.— *Jan. 1st to June 14th*, 1863.

The campaign of 1862 had ended, and the two great armies had constructed their winter quarters facing each other, along the line of the Rappahannock, the Rebels occupying the south bank above and below the heights of Fredericksburg, and the Federals stretching their camps for many miles on the northern shore above and below Falmouth. Between this line and that of the defenses of Washington lies a vast territory, which abounds in creeks, marshes, deep, sombre forests, with only here and there a village or settlement. A little to the west runs the chain of the Bull Run Mountains, with their ravines and caverns. This is a very fit hiding place for guerrillas and bushwhackers, who, in considerable numbers, infest the country, and commit their depredations on our lines. These guerrillas consist mostly of farmers and mechanics, residents of this region of country, who are exempt from the Rebel conscription. They generally follow their usual avocation during the day, and congregate at certain localities at night ready for any work proposed by their leader, though each is often found to act quite independently of the rest. Their commander-in-chief is John S. Mosby, who, as a Rebel soldier who had known him from childhood up informed the writer, had always been a sort of guerrilla — deserting from his home in mere boyhood — fighting duels as a pastime — roving the country far and wide in search of pleasure or profit — and finding now his chief delight in the adventures of guerrilla life. Under such leadership this guerrilla force has become very formidable, and a strong picket line was necessary at some distance from the defenses of Washington.

January 1*st*, 1863. The regiment celebrated this anniversary by marching from Fairfax Court House to Chantilly, and was there posted on picket, to guard against the incursions of Mosby and his gang. The peculiar nature of the force opposed to us requires special pains in the picketing. The main reserve, established from one to two miles from the line of videttes, is so situated as to be within easy striking distance of each picket relief — at least when this can be done — so as to render speedy assistance in case of an attack on any portion of the line.

The boys will not soon forget the dreary, dangerous hours they spent along this picket line. In fancy they will see themselves shivering around a miserable fire among the pines, compelled often to sit or lie down in snow or mud. In this plight they hear the summons to be ready to stand post. Mounted upon their shivering horses, the poor fellows with nothing cheering but their courage, go out to sit in the saddle for two hours, facing the biting wind, and peering through the storm of sleet, snow or rain, which pelts them in the face mercilessly. Happy if the guerrilla does not creep through bushes impenetrable to the sight, to inflict his cruel blows. The two hours expired, relief comes and the vidette returns to spend his four, six, or eight hours off duty as best he may.

January 5th. At a post called Frying Pan, the pickets were attacked by guerrillas, and quite a number of men were captured. The nature of the country is such as to afford the enemy the greatest possible advantage. Deep ravines, skirted by massive foliage summer and winter, give him shelter, while his knowledge of every road and footpath gives him a fine opportunity to escape with his booty in case of pursuit.

January 6th. Several men were captured and one wounded on picket near Cub Run. The guerrillas are very active. The utmost vigilance on our part cannot secure us perfectly from their depredations. The only way to rid ourselves of this plague would be to scour the entire country with a large force, arrest every male inhabitant able to carry a musket, and burn to the ground every building, including houses, where these bushwhackers reside or find refuge. To so stern a punishment, falling upon innocent and guilty with like terror, the government is not willing to resort. If the war is to continue long this would prove to be true policy, saving the lives of many of our brave boys.

January 10th. From the Chantilly mansion, owned by one of the Stuarts, the regiment moved to Germantown, pitching camp on a pine-covered knoll. The streets are laid out quite regularly by companies, a space averaging about 25 or 30 feet being occupied by each company. The men construct stockades of logs about 3 feet high, on which they place their tents, called A tents, on account of resemblance to that letter. Chimneys are made of stone, or of bricks found in the remains of destroyed houses in the neighborhood, and sometimes of sticks of wood carefully laid in mud, which is by no means very inferior mortar. With this material the crevices of the stockades are also well plastered, making the soldier's cabin quite tight and warm, if he is not too idle to supply himself amply with fuel. In front of the tents is a street which has to be corduroyed or it will become impassable for mud, and just across the street are the stables for the horses. These are usually covered with a thick thatching of pine boughs, which afford a tolerable shelter for the cavalryman's trusty friend.

January 11th. The regiment went on a scouting party to Brentsville, and returned by way of Bristoe Station and Manassas Junction.

January 12th. A false alarm aroused the entire camp, which consists of a brigade of cavalry, composed of the First Virginia (Union), Eighteenth Pennsylvania and Fifth New York regiments of cavalry.

January 13th. Another false alarm disturbed our usual rest; and before quieting down again we were sent on picket, to remain about five days. We were relieved on the 17th.

January 17th. Sergt. Maj. Gall and 1st Sergt. Bryant, Company G, went to Buckland Mills with a flag of truce.

January 20th. Companies E and G went on picket at Frying Pan, dismounted, that they might be the better prepared for guerillas should they appear.

January 24th. The same companies were ordered out on a scouting party to Herndon Station, and captured a sutler's wagon, which was being smuggled into the Rebel lines, and some prisoners.

January 26th. Mosby made an attack on the 18th Pa. on picket near Chantilly Church, capturing 11. The Fifth N. Y. was sent in pursuit of the guerrillas. Having reached Middleburg, Maj. Hammond, in command, ordered a charge through the town, which was executed handsomely and with entire success, resulting in the capture of 25 prisoners and the scattering of Mosby's men. The entire party, save one man captured, returned safely to camp, after a journey of 34 miles.

January 29th. We resumed picketing this morning, only a small portion of the regiment remaining in camp.

January 30th. The regiment was relieved from picket until further orders. The object, doubtless, is to give us other work to do.

February 2d. We were ordered out on a scout. Passed through Centreville about sundown. Followed the pike over the Bull Run battle field, by Gainesville and New Baltimore, arriving at Warrenton, as the town clock struck 12 of the night. No force of the enemy was found in town. One hundred muskets were captured and destroyed. Patrols were sent to Waterloo Bridge and Sulphur Springs. The country appeared to be clear of the enemy. Having accomplished the object of our scout we returned to camp, after a cold, dreary journey.

February 9th. The regiment was again sent out to scout the country. At Bristoe Station companies F and H, with Capt. Penfield in command, were sent to Warrenton. On their way at New Baltimore they encountered quite a force of the enemy, with which they had a spirited skirmish, which was repeated but with less energy at Warrenton, next day. The main body of the regiment on the 10th drove in the enemy's pickets near Spotted Tavern, where they captured two prisoners.

February 11th. The regiment moved to within four miles of Falmouth, and then turned northward through Stafford Court House. It pursued its journey through Dumfries, Wolf Run Shoals, Fairfax Station and Court House, reaching camp on the 13th, after a very fatiguing journey.

February 18th. Company G was sent on a scout to Herndon Station.

February 21st. Received orders to resume picket duty.

February 25th. During the night the 18th Penn. lost twenty men and thirty horses on picket, by Mosby.

February 26th. Major Bacon, with one hundred and fifty-one men, started on a scout, passing through Centreville. Not being able to cross the Bull Run bridge, he returned to Centreville, where were rendezvoused other cavalry.

February 27th. The whole command under Col. Wyndham moved to Bealeton Station and thence to Falmouth. The going was horribly muddy, many horses giving out by the way. This was the most remarkable feature of the expedition. After resting ourselves and animals for a few days at Falmouth, the expedition returned to camp by way of Stafford Court House and Wolf Run Shoals, arriving March 3d, very much exhausted.

March 1st. Capt. Farley with seventy-two men was sent on a scout to Aldie, and returned without meeting the enemy.

March 9th. About three o'clock A. M., Mosby and his

gang, led by Sergeant J. F Ames,[1] formerly of company L, of this regiment, having safely passed by the pickets, entered Fairfax Court House. Without scarcely firing a shot, they captured fifty fine horses and about thirty prisoners, including Brig. Gen. Stoughton, and Capt. Barker, Fifth New York Cavalry. The brigade was sent in pursuit of the dashing party, each regiment taking different routes; but they returned at night unsuccessful, the Fifth New York having gone to Herndon Station. Such a raid, five or six miles within our lines, resulting in such a heavy loss to us, reflects very uncreditably upon some of our military leaders, while it shows how wily a foe we have to contend with. It is thought that not a few of the inhabitants of the region are more or less engaged in the business of giving Mosby important information, which lays the foundation of his success.

March 12*th*. We sent two hundred men on picket, averaging the number from the different companies.

March 14*th*. Maj. White with first battalion went out at night as a reserve for the pickets. We are almost constantly on duty. One small brigade of cavalry is doing the duty that one division should do.

March 15*th*. We moved our camp a little below Fairfax Court House on a fine elevation, which overlooks the surrounding country. Before night snow and hail began to fall, and a terrible night was experienced. The mercury at 5 P. M. stood at 28° 30′

March 18*th*. The regiment went on picket for 24 hours.

---

[1] Ames, after deserting to Mosby, was called Big Yankee. He became efficient for the Rebels and was finally killed.

March 23*d*. Went out on picket again. About 5 P. M. Mosby made an attack on the pike, introducing himself by shooting the first vidette he came to through the head. The main reserve being alarmed, formed and pursued this force about three miles. Here a barricade of trees is thrown across the road, back of which the guerrillas had formed themselves. Our column was stopped by a fire of carbines and pistols, and by a flank fire from the woods. At this inopportune moment the Rebels made a charge, which broke our column. Our boys were then driven back furiously. Some horses giving out, the hapless riders were captured. By the heroic exertions of Major White and the arrival of the reserve from Frying Pan, the boys were rallied and the Rebels again driven back, and pursued for eight miles. But they escaped after inflicting upon us very serious injury. For some reason the regiment never acted with so little concert, and was never so badly beaten by so small a force, supposed to be about eighty strong. Every one felt mortified at the result of this day's work, and resolved to retrieve our fortunes on some more fortunate occasion.

March 25*th*. Maj. Gen. Stahel took command of this cavalry division, composed of three brigades. The third brigade is composed of the 1st Virginia, 18th Pennsylvania and Fifth New York.

March 27*th*. We went on picket with Maj. Bacon for 24 hours.

March 30*th*. Picket duty again with Maj. White.

April 2*d*. Maj. Bacon went out again with the regiment on picket. The three regiments of the brigade do picket duty by turn, being on duty one day and off two.

April 6th. We sent out one hundred men for picket.

April 12th. The 3d brigade paraded for muster, under orders from Col. De Forest, who was assigned to the command as acting brigadier general, the seventh inst. His command appeared well on parade. He rides his horse beautifully, and presents a very soldierly bearing.

April 17th. The 18th Pennsylvania was transferred to the 2d brigade, and the 1st Virginia, with which we were so often associated in 1862, was transferred to the 3d brigade.

April 18th. Our brigade made a reconnoissance to Catlett's Station.

April 21st. The regiment received the new and beautiful flag, ordered for us by the city of New York, in November, 1862. For some reason unknown to us, it has been long delayed.

April 27th. Gen. Stahel, with the 2d and 3d brigades and a light battery of four guns, moved out about 6 A. M. on a reconnoissance. As each regiment wended its way from its camp to Fairfax Court House, the place of concentration, presenting the appearance of a vast serpent, winding its folds through its accustomed path among the hills, the morning sunlight fell with magical effect upon the scene, producing an impression which the beholder does not soon forget. The force moved on to two miles beyond Middleburg.

April 28th. The regiment being detached, moved out two miles, sent patrols to Upperville, and rejoined the division, with which we moved to Rectortown, Salem, White Plains, and back to Middleburg. Thirty-five prisoners were captured, mostly guerrillas of Mosby's gang.

April 29th. The division moved east of Aldie and

bivouacked for a few hours. After dark we moved back to our camps at Fairfax Court House, arriving after midnight. The boys made the old hills ring with shouts of delight on returning to their tented homes.

May 1st. Col. De Forest, with the 3d brigade, moved to Bristoe Station. The command had two days' rations.

May 2d. The regiment was ordered to reconnoitre as far as Rappahannock Station; and having accomplished its task, returned to Warrenton Junction.

May 3d. At an early hour the 1st Virginia cavalry, while feeding and watering their horses, were surprised by a force of Rebels, consisting of detachments of the Black Horse Cavalry, Mosby's and other guerrilla forces, with Mosby commanding in person. Our boys, being thus dismounted, fled to a house near by, where they fought with terrible earnestness, but to great disadvantage. All efforts of Mosby to make them surrender were in vain. Finding that he could not intimidate them with bullets, he ordered the torch to be applied, and the house was set on fire. At this critical moment, the Fifth New York, which had bivouacked in a grove at a short distance from the scene of action, with Maj. Hammond commanding in person, descended like an avalanche upon the guerrillas. Mosby was heard to exclaim, "My God! it is the Fifth New York!" A hand to hand encounter now took place, where Yankee sabres were used with fearful effect, and soon the Rebels broke and fled, entirely demoralized and panic-stricken. Gen. Stahel, in his dispatch to Gen. Heintzelman, says: "The Rebels, who fled in the direction of Warrenton, were pursued by Maj. Hammond, Fifth New York Cavalry, who has returned and reports our charge at Warrenton Junction as being so terrific as to have thoroughly routed and scattered them in every direction. I have sent in 23 prisoners of Mosby's command, all of whom are wounded — the greater part of them badly. Dick Moran (a notorious bushwhacker) is among the number. There are also three officers of Mosby's. The loss of the enemy was very heavy in killed besides many wounded, who scattered and prevented capture. I have no hopes of the recovery of Maj. Steele,[1] of the 1st Virginia. Our loss is one killed and fourteen wounded."

Templeton, a Rebel spy, was killed. In the *Richmond Sentinel* of May 16th, we find this interesting notice of the fight:—"About the 1st of May, near Warrenton Junction, Mosby, with his company, fell in with the First Virginia regiment, so called, which has been a long time looking for him. A fight ensued, which resulted in the capture of the whole regiment. As Mosby was making off with his prize, however, the First Vermont[2] and Fifth New York beset him and recaptured the Virginia Yankees. Mosby's loss was small, and he wants to know whether the First Virginia is looking for him again."

The following Complimentary Order was issued:

HEAD QRS. STAHEL'S CAVALRY DIVISION,
Department of Washington,
Fairfax Court House, May 5, 1863.

SPECIAL ORDERS No. 30.

When soldiers perform brave deeds a proper acknowledgment of their services is justly their due. The commanding

---

[1] He was a noble officer and a splendid soldier. His wound proved mortal. His funeral services were attended with military honors, Sunday, May 31st.

[2] The First Vermont was not engaged.

general therefore desires to express his gratification at the conduct of the officers and men of Col. De Forest's command, who were engaged in the fight at Warrenton Junction, on Sunday, May 3d, 1863. By your promptness and gallantry the gang of guerrillas who have so long infested the vicinity, has been badly beaten and broken up. The heavy loss of the enemy in killed, wounded and prisoners, proves the determination of your resistance and the vigor of your attack.

Deeds like this are worthy of emulation and give strength and confidence to the command.

By command of

MAJ. GEN. STAHEL.

HENRY BALDWIN, JR., Major and A. A. G.

This order was followed by another of similar import by Maj. Gen. Heintzelman, commanding the department.

May 8th. Capt. McMasters, with six men, was attacked and pursued by a squad of the Black Horse Cavalry, while on his way from the picket lines to Fairfax Court House. One of his men was captured, and another, Sergt. Murphy, Company C, was drowned while endeavoring to ford Bull Run.

May 11th. A scouting party of the regiment went to Rappahannock Station. They saw a few Rebels, but had no encounter with them.

May 13th. The pickets were driven in by the enemy, with some confusion. Bands of guerrillas like so many ravenous beasts and birds of prey, hover around our lines, attacking wherever an opportunity offers plunder.

May 15th. We were ordered to Kettle Run, a little

south of Bristoe Station, and we camped along the rail road.

May 17*th*. A scouting party, under Capt. Hasbrouck, went to Brentsville, and toward Dumfries, and returned without meeting any force of the enemy.

May 25*th*. While the main portion of the regiment was picketing along the rail road a sufficient number of men remained in camp to care for it. To-day the camp was moved about a half mile north into a piece of woods, with a clean, grassy field just in front.

May 30*th*. Between seven and eight o'clock A. M. the cavalry pickets and reserves were startled by artillery firing, just below them on the rail road. A train laden with rations and forage had passed on its way to the Rappahannock, but a few moments before. It was soon ascertained that the guerrillas had carefully unfastened one of the iron rails, in the woods, and by means of a wire fastened to it, and extended at some distance from the road, a man had drawn the rail out of place just as the engine was approaching it, and thus stopped the whole train. A mountain howitzer had been placed in position, which immediately plunged a shell through the train. The infantry guard on board the train fled in confusion, leaving the whole ground to the Rebels, who destroyed the train by fire. But the cavalry had been aroused, and detachments of the First Vermont and Fifth New York, each in separate routes, commenced a vigorous pursuit of the enemy. Mosby, who commanded in person, did not anticipate so sudden an attack as was made. The detachment of the Fifth, after going about two miles, came within range of the howitzer, which sent a shell, that exploded in the midst of the solid column.

Fortunately no one was hurt, except that Lieut. Boutelle, Company A, was suddenly dismounted by the killing of his horse. The nature of the ground was unfavorable for a cavalry charge. The enemy, however, showed no disposition to fight but fled toward Warrenton as rapidly as possible, firing an occasional shot, but without inflicting injury. Eagerly the boys spurred on their chargers, and were soon joined by the Vermonters, who added fresh excitement to the pursuit. The Rebels, finding themselves too closely followed, and knowing that something desperate must be done, suddenly turning at the head of a narrow lane, brought their artillery into position and commenced firing. "That gun must be silenced or captured," cried Lieut. Barker, of Company H, "and who will volunteer to charge it with me?" About thirty brave men promptly responded, and suiting the action to the words, "charge, boys!" he rushed furiously forward at their head, but fell severely wounded before a murderous discharge of grape and canister, which killed three men and wounded several others. But before the piece could be reloaded the surviving comrades were crossing sabres with the gunners over the gun. The conflict was a fierce one, but of short duration; the boys in blue retaking the twelve pound howitzer, which had been captured by the Rebels from the lamented Col. Baker at Ball's Bluff. Among the enemy's wounded and captured was a Capt. Haskins, formerly in high rank in the British army, who had run the blockade and espoused the Rebel cause. He received his death wound as follows: Having wounded Geo. H. Jenkins, private of Company F, he roughly cried out, "Surrender, you damned Yankee." "I will see you damned first," was Jenkins' characteristic reply, at the same time lodging a pistol ball in the captain's neck. The Rebels were completely routed, and pursued as far as the jaded condition of our horses would permit. In the correspondence of Mr. George H. Hart, we find the following quotable sentence: "The troops fought gallantly, and the Fifth New York ably sustained its claim to the title of the Fighting Fifth; nor were the First Vermonters behindhand."

This engagement has been known as the battle of Greenwich, from a little village near by, bearing that name.

June 10th. Adjutant Gall, with a small party, encountered a squad of Mosby's men at Middleburg and captured Lieut. Turner in command.

June 14th. The regiment returned to camp at Fairfax Court House, from Kettle Run, and awaited further orders.

CHAPTER V

Gen. Lee Invades Maryland and Pennsylvania.—Breaking Camp at Fairfax Court House.—Fidelity of the Horse.—March over Bull Run Battle Field.—Reorganization of the Cavalry Corps.—Kilpatrick in Command of the Third Division.—Cavalry Battle of Hanover, Pennsylvania.—Battle of Gettysburg, Third Day.—Attack on Rebel Train in Monterey Pass.—Battle of Hagerstown.—Battle of Boonsboro'.—Attack on Rear Guard of Rebel Army at Falling Waters.—The Invaders Expelled from Free Soil. *June 19th to July 14th,* 1863.

The disastrous battle of Chancellorsville had been fought and Gen. Lee resolved upon a grand invasion of the northern states. His intention was fairly understood in the early days of June. It now became necessary to concentrate as large a force as possible to meet and drive back the invaders. Consequently General Stahel's cavalry division was detached from the defenses of Washington, to be incorporated into the great Army of the Potomac.

June 19th. Orders for breaking up camp were received and the work immediately commenced. Surplus baggage, which always accumulates during winter quarters, was put into parcels and sent to our northern homes, by express, or boxed up to be sent to Alexandria for storage, under the charge of the quartermaster of that post. This done, our tents were soon struck and sent to the rear with the baggage, and we were left to bivouac as best we could, until the orders to march should be received. To the young soldier this was a new era in military life. His tent now is bounded only by the far off horizon, and covered by the canopy of heaven. Rolled up in his woolen blanket or rubber poncho, having sought the shelter of a leafy tree (if such a desirable spot was accessible), he lies down with a stone, or, perhaps, his saddle for a pillow, while his faithful horse stands as a watchful guardian by his side. It is often the case, that a cavalryman has nothing to hitch his horse to but his own hand, and though the animal will walk all around him, eating the grass as far as he can reach, yet it is worthy of note, that an instance can scarcely be found where the horse has been known to step upon his master.

June 21st. The regiment moved with the division about noon on the Little River turnpike. Passed through Centreville, and over the Bull Run battle field, the aceldama of America. Evidences of the terrible conflict of the past are still visible on every hand. Unexploded shells and pieces, solid shot, broken muskets, and remains of gun-carriages, graves, and bones of unburied heroes, tell their sad stories as we pass. A skull is kicked along by the horses as they move over the muddy way! No one seems to care much about it, for worse sights have so often been seen before.

After passing through Gainesville, we bivouacked near Buckland Mills.

June 22d. The line of march was resumed with the early sunlight, passing through New Baltimore, and arriving at the beautiful village of Warrenton about noon. No force of the enemy was here encountered, as had been expected. Small scouting parties were sent out in various directions, and the division bivouaeked for the afternoon and night in the fields adjacent to the town.

June 23d. Journeyed back to Fairfax Court House after making quite a halt at Gainesville to issue rations, and rest our animals. It was after midnight when we arrived.

June 24th. Division moved about 3 P. M. toward Leesburg, stopping for the night about one mile beyond Drainesville.

June 25th. The mareh was resumed at an early hour. A little beyond Broad Run the column turned to the right, striking the Potomae a little below Edward's Ferry, where we forded. On reaching the Maryland shore, the 3d brigade with a section of the 9th Michigan battery and one brigade of infantry, was sent to Poolsville, and thence by Monoeacy Ford to Licksville, where we bivouacked.

June 26th. This force moved on to Adamstown, Jefferson, Birkinsville, through Crampton's Gap, where the infantry and artillery remained, though the cavalry moved on near Rhorersville, where we spent the night.

June 27th. The brigade moved at 4 P M. to Birkinsville, Middletown, Frederick City, and three miles and a half north on the Emmettsburgh road, where we bivouacked with the remainder of the division, at daybreak.

June 28th. Gen. Pleasanton reviewed the division, and reorganized the entire forcc. We are now the Third Division of the Cavalry Corps, Army of the Potomae, with the gallant Kilpatrick in command. The first brigade eonsists of the 1st Vermont, 1st Virginia, 18th Pennsylvania and 5th New York, Brig. Gen. Farnsworth commanding. Brig. Gen. Custer commands the 2d brigade, composed of Miehigan regiments.

Gen. Buford commands the first division and Gen. Gregg the second division; the whole force forming the most efficient cavalry corps ever organized on this continent. To-day Gen. Meade superseded Gen. Hooker in the command of the Army of the Potomac.

June 29th. At 10 A. M., with its new commander, the division moved to Pennsylvania, passing through Walkersville, Woodsboro', Ladiesville, Mechanicsville, Taneytown, and finally Littlestown, Pa., where we were received with the greatest demonstrations of joy by the people. A large group of children, on the balcony of a hotel, waving handkerchiefs and flags, greeted us with patriotic songs, while the men made the welkin ring with their cheers. How different was such reception from that we had been accustomed to have given us by the inhabitants of Virginian villages!

June 30th. The column moved early to Hanover, where we were again enthusiastically received by the citizens, who furnished refreshments liberally to the troopers, as each regiment entered and passed through the town. This enjoyable state of things continued until about 10 o'clock; and while the Fifth was receiving the attentions of the people, the sudden report of a cannon was heard from one of the neighboring hills. At first this was taken as a friendly salute for our troops, but the deception was soon removed by a fierce charge of Rebel cavalry under immediate command of Gen. Stuart, upon the unsuspecting column in the street, sending terror to the people, especially to the ladies and children, who were paying their compliments to their defenders. With his accustomed coolness and bravery, Maj. Hammond, in command of the regiment, quickly withdrew from the street to the open field near the rail road depot, ordered the boys into line and led the charge upon the Rebels, who then possessed the town. The charging columns met on Frederick street, where a hand to hand conflict ensued. For a few moments the enemy made heroic resistance, but finally broke and fled, closely pursued by our men. They rallied again and again but were met with irresistible onsets, which finally compelled them to retire behind the hills under cover of their guns.

In less than fifteen minutes from the time the Rebels charged the town, they were all driven from it, and were skulking in the wheat fields and among the hills of the vicinity. The dead and wounded of both parties, with many horses, lay scattered here and there along the streets, so covered with blood and dust as to render identification in many cases very difficult. Meanwhile, Gen. Kilpatrick, who was several miles beyond the town, at the head of the column, when the attack was made, arrived upon the field, and took personal charge of the movements. These were ordered with consummate skill, and executed with promptness and success. His artillery, well posted on the hills facing the Rebels, and well supported, soon silenced the guns of the enemy, and compelled him to retire in the direction of Lee's main army. He left not less than 25 dead in the streets and fields, and his wounded by far exceeded this number. We captured 75 prisoners, including Lt. Col. Payne, who commanded a brigade, and one stand of colors, the flag of the 13th Virginia cavalry. This was the trophy of Sergt. Burke, Company A. Our entire loss was nine killed, thirty-one wounded and a few prisoners. Among the killed was Adjutant Gall, who fell while gallantly charging the enemy in the street. The fatal ball entered his left eye, and passed through his head, killing him instantly.

The citizens of Hanover, who so nobly cared for our wounded in the hospitals during and after the battle, and assisted us in burying the dead, will long remember that terrible last day of June.

The brave boys, who had so valiantly defeated the enemy, though taken by surprise, built their bivouac fires and spent the night on the field of their recent victory.

July 1*st*. At 11 A. M. the 1st brigade moved to Abbottstown, to Berlin, and pursued Rebel cavalry from this place to Rosetown, capturing several prisoners, and returned to Berlin at midnight and bivouacked.

July 2*d*. The division moved to within two miles of Gettysburg, thence to New Oxford and Hunterstown, where we fought till dark. This was the extreme right wing of our army, while engaged in that great conflict, which decided the fate of the Rebellion and saved the Republic from ruin.

July 3*d*. During last night we moved from the right to the left flank of our army, about 2½ miles from Gettysburg, near Little Round Top. The remaining portion of the cavalry corps was left to attend to Stuart and his troopers, who still threatened our right. Kilpatrick's work was with infantry. His division, however, was reënforced by Gen. Merritt's regular brigade of the first division. About 10 A. M. Kilpatrick sent out his skirmishers upon the Rebel right flank and rear. The design was to create a panic, if possible, and force the enemy back upon his trains. About 3 P. M., during the most terrific cannonade ever known upon this continent, a large force of Rebel infantry was seen advancing, with the evident intention of sweeping away the cavalry, and of then turning our position on Little Round Top, occupied by our artillery with infantry support. To defeat this design of the Rebel chief, became Kilpatrick's all animating theme. Quickly making the best possible disposition of his command, he ordered Gen. Farnsworth to charge these serried ranks, which must be broken. Placing the Fifth New York in support of Elder's Battery, which was exposed to a very hot fire, and ordering the First Vermont, First Virginia and Eighteenth Pennsylvania, into line of battle, he led them gallantly on to the unequal contest.

Though this charge was not entirely a success, its well directed blow prevented the flank movement, which prisoners asserted, was the intention of their leader, and thus the cavalry added another dearly earned laurel to its chaplet of honor, *dearly earned* because many of her bravest champions fell upon that bloody field. Gen. Kilpatrick, in his official report of this sanguniary conflict, says: "In this charge fell the brave Farnsworth. Short and brilliant was his career. On the 29th of June a general, on the 1st of July he baptized his star in blood, and on the 3d, for the honor of his young brigade and the glory of his corps, he yielded up his noble life."

During this charge a shell passed through the body of Daniel Hurley, Company C, killed a horse, and afterward exploded, wounding John Buckley of the same company, and several others. Elder's battery was handled with his usual skill, and with wonderful effect, silencing two or three times a Rebel battery that *could not be seen*, a thing but very seldom accomplished.

Before the sun went down on that day of carnage, it was evident that the Union arms had been victorious, after three days' almost incessant fighting, and our tired and nearly worn-out boys that night rested quietly upon the fields so dearly won.

July 4th. Having gathered his troopers together, Kilpatrick addressed them a few words of cheer, assuring them that their noble deeds would not be passed by unrequited, and that he trusted their future conduct would be but a copy of the past. Having received orders to intercept the Rebel trains, which were known to be on the retreat southward, the whole division was moved to Emmettsburgh, to Monterey Springs and to the summit of the South Mountains, where the train was encountered, passing through the gaps. The night was pitchy dark, and the rain fell fast, before the train guards were met. For some time they kept up a desultory fire upon us, but finally yielding to our superior skill and determination, a train of 200 wagons, mostly loaded with plunder from the stores and granaries of Pennsylvania, fell into our hands, and about 1,500 prisoners, among whom were several wounded. Most of the wagons were destroyed.

July 5th. Moved to Smithburg about 8 A. M., and sent the prisoners to Boonsboro' About sundown we shelled the forces of Gen. Stuart approaching us from the mountain passes. This done, we marched to Cavetown, and thence to Boonsboro', where we bivouacked and rested.

July 6th. Moved to Hagerstown and held the place in advance of Gen. Stuart. His approach was met with determined resistance, and a heavy battle was the result. Had not Gen. Ewell's corps come down upon us we could have managed the cavalry alone, though they were compelled to fight desperately, as this was their only way of retreat. Charges and counter-charges were frequent during the day. One reporter says, "Elder gave them grape and canister, and the Fifth New York sabres, while the First Vermont used their carbines."

In one of these charges, made in the face of a very superior force, Capt. Penfield, at the head of his company (H), had his horse shot down under him, and, while struggling to extricate himself from the animal, was struck a fearful blow of a sabre on the head, which came near proving fatal. Thus wounded, with the blood running down upon his long beard and clothes, he was made a prisoner. It was here the gallant Captain Dahlgren lost his leg while leading a charge.

Before the heavy infantry force which was now attacking us, we retreated to Williamsport, fighting all the way. From Williamsport, having joined Gen. Buford, we fell back to Timball's Cross Roads.

July 7th. The division moved to Boonsboro' and bivouacked.

July 8th. The Rebel cavalry under Gen. Stuart, supported by Hood's infantry, attacked our pickets along the Antietam Creek, and drove them in with some confusion.

About noon a furious battle was raging near Boonsboro' Buford and Kilpatrick united their respective divisions in the work of repelling this attack. Over the broad plains, it was a splendid sight to witness the manœuvrings of these cavalry chiefs. The struggle was desperate—Stuart fighting for the safety of the Rebel army, and our boys for the South Mountain pass. About sundown, after a brief consultation between Buford and Kilpatrick, their bugles were ringing with the order for a concentrated and united charge; and with a wild shout those invincible squadrons fell upon the enemy, driving his broken lines from the field, which he left strewn with his dead and dying. With the laurels of another glorious victory, our boys returned to their bivouac, and sought the repose they had so well earned.

After the battle Col. De Forest assumed command of the brigade.

July 10*th*. The regiment moved to Jonathan Doub's house and bivouacked.

July 11*th*. We moved out two miles, drove in the enemy's pickets, and returned to our bivouae.

July 12*th*. Gen. Kilpatrick moved his division to Hagerstown, and, after a skirmish with the enemy, oeeupied the place.

July 14*th*. At 4 A. M. the division moved in pursuit of the retreating Rebel army, which, it was ascertained, was crossing the Potomac as rapidly as possible. The third division swept away what vestiges of it remained at Williamsport, and, following it down the river, struek the rear guard, under Gen. Pettigrew, at Falling Waters. The battle was short, but disastrous to the Rebels. Many a poor fellow never gained the long looked-for Virginia shore. One brigade of infantry, two battle flags, and two pieces of artillery fell into our hands. Gen. Pettigrew was mortally wounded. In the charge made upon the Rebel earthworks, constructed to protect this important crossing, the 6th Michigan cavalry, Major Weber commanding, covered itself with immortal honor. By the boldness of their eharge, and by the destructive fire of Pennington's battery, these remains of the once boastful invading army, were made to feel that they could fight us at much better advantage upon their own soil than upon ours.

As the last foot of the invaders disappeared on the southern shore of the Potomac, our boys built their bivouac fires and rested themselves and their weary animals near the scene of their victory

CHAPTER VI

Lee's Invasion, a great Failure.— He is not Pursued very Vigorously.— Reasons Why.— We Recross the Potomac.— The Gun-Boat Expedition.— Battle of Culpepper Court House.— Lee flanks Meade.— We Retreat from the Robertson and Rapidan Rivers.— Kilpatrick Surrounded at Brandy Station.— His Brilliant Charge.— Battle of Buckland Mills.— The Armies Swing like Pendulums.— Skirmish at Stevensburg.— Several Days' Fighting at Raccoon Ford.—Change is the Soldier's Life.— Excitement about Reënlisting as Veteran Volunteers. —Building Winter Quarters.— *July* 15*th* to *December* 31*st*, 1863.

The enemy was now fairly expelled from the free states which he had insolently entered a few days before. His losses had been immense in men and *material* of war. He had failed in every important minutiæ of his plan. Instead of weakening the Union cause as he fondly hoped by the pomp and promise of his entry into Maryland, he had increased our numbers and strengthened our hands in the good work. He was now returning *to his own place*, with a demoralized and beaten army, whose ranks had been thinned by desertions and by unprecedented casualties in battle. He had barely escaped annihilation. To pursue him as closely as possible, harrass his rear and do him all further damage in our power, was the course adopted by the commanding general; the main body of the Rebel army escaping as best it could through the valley towards Staunton and

Gordonsville, their cavalry meanwhile taking possession of the gaps in the Blue Ridge to prevent flank movements. Our pursuit was not as vigorous as it would seem it might have been. But it must be remembered that our infantry had made many forced marches, describing in its route a line resembling the circumference of a circle, while that of the Rebel army was like the diameter. Our cavalry had not only defeated the Rebel cavalry in many battles and skirmishes, but it had met the solid columns of their infantry also, as at Gettysburg. Consequently our movements were not as rapid as they might otherwise have been, owing to the fatigue of our men.

July 15*th.* The division moved up the river to Williamsport, swung around to Hagerstown, and bivouacked for the night at Boonsboro'; men and horses came to their rest with a wonderful relish.

July 16*th.* "Boots and saddles" at an early hour, and the whole division was soon in the saddle, where we might be said *to live, move, and have our being*, and we were again on the march. We revisited Rhorersville, recrossed Crampton's Gap, and bivouacked near the Potomac at Berlin. Before night the first brigade moved to Harper's Ferry and bivouacked in the yard of the ruined arsenal.

July 17*th.* This morning we crossed the Shenandoah on the new wire bridge, passed around the foot of Loudon Heights, and followed the Potomac to opposite Berlin, where we were joined by the second brigade, which crossed on pontoons. The division then moved to Lovettsville, Wheatland, Purcelville, Va., and halted for the night.

July 19*th.* The division moved to the following places :—

Sniekersville, Bloomfield and Upperville, where we stopped and rested.

July 20th. The 5th and 6th Michigan, with the 5th New York, under Col. Town, of the 1st Michigan, marched to Ashby's Gap, expelled therefrom a force of the enemy, after a brief skirmish, and occupied the Gap. The Fifth New York returned to Upperville. From this time until September, the headquarters of the third division were near Warrenton, while picketing was performed by the regiments in rotation, along the line of the Rappahannock, opposed to Stuart's cavalry, whose headquarters were at Culpepper.

September 4th. To break the monotony of picketing, and to subserve the cause, a most novel scheme was now undertaken, known as Kilpatrick's Gun-boat Expedition. The object was to destroy a part of the Rebel navy (?) anchored in the Rappahannock, near Port Conway, opposite Port Royal. This peculiar warfare, which required *dash* and boldness, was waged by the troopers with complete success, and they returned to their old bivouac fires, to enliven the weary hours with stories of the long march down the river, and their successful attack upon the gun-boats of the enemy.

September 13th. A grand advance of the Union army had been ordered by its chief, in which the cavalry was to take a prominent part. Accordingly, at an early hour, Gen. Pleasanton moved his corps, crossing the Rappahannock with Gregg's division at Sulphur Springs, Buford's at Rappahannock Bridge and Kilpatrick's at Kelly's Ford. The enemy's pickets were easily driven before this mighty host, and dispositions were made to attack Stuart at Culpepper, a naturally strong and fortified position. Pleasanton.

P. Vail N.Y.

John Hammond
Col Comdg
5 NYVC

with the first and second divisions, moved directly on the enemy from Brandy Station, where they had concentrated. Over the plains they moved on, sweeping everything before them, until within a mile of the town, where they were checked by the stubborn and determined resistance of the Rebels. Not long had this equal contest continued, when Kilpatrick's artillery was heard thundering in the enemy's right flank and rear, on the road from Stevensburg, whither he had led his swift squadrons. Under this well directed fire the enemy fell back into the town; and, before he had time to reform his broken line, and in spite of a heavy fire from his artillery, the Fifth New York and First Vermont, with detachments from other regiments, charged into the streets of the town, capturing three Blakely guns, and throwing the boast of the chivalry into a perfect rout. They hastily retreated in the direction of Pony Mountain and Rapidan Bridge, whither they were pursued closely by our victorious boys. Several prisoners fell into our hands. The way having thus been prepared, the Army of the Potomac advanced across the Rappahannock, Gen. Meade making his headquarters at Culpepper.

September 14th. The cavalry advanced and took possession of the fords along the Rapidan and the Robertson rivers. This was not done without opposition, the enemy defending these important crossings with vigor and pertinacity. The regiment encountered a tremendous shelling at Somerville Ford, on the Robertson.

September 22d. While on a reconnoissance in Madison County, the regiment had quite a skirmish at Brookin's Ford, on the Rapidan.

September 25th. A detachment of the regiment, Captain

Farley commanding, while on a scout, encountered a considerable force of the enemy at Hazel River Bridge, and a sharp skirmish ensued.

October 8th. The regiment reconnoitred along the Robertson river, and met the enemy at Ceighrsville, where a short fight followed, resulting in the retreat of the enemy across the river.

While we were thus picketing and scouting along these streams, living sumptuously on a country that had not yet been impoverished by the march of armies, Gen. Lee, whose army lay mostly south of the Rapidan, crossed the river, moved to Madison Court House, and by a rapid flank movement on our right, compelled us to beat a hasty retreat, which was continued until Gen. Meade's main army occupied the heights of Centreville.

October 10th. In the early morning a heavy force of the enemy came down upon the regiment, picketing along the Robertson river, at Russell's Ford. The flank movement of the enemy was discovered and quick work was required. Swift messengers from officers in high command brought orders to retire with promptness, but in good order, if possible. Our men, in many instances, were compelled to leave their palatable breakfasts of roast lamb, sweet potatoes, fine wheat bread, milk and honey, &c., with which the country abounded, and to attend to the stern and always unpleasant duties of a retreat, with the enemy pressing heavily upon us. A sharp skirmish had taken place at the ford, which was continued at intervals on our march to James City, where a battle raged with fury and slaughter. Though engaged for many hours during the day the casualties of the regiment were not very great.

October 11*th*. Skirmishing was continued to-day at almost every step of our march. On the Sperryville pike to Culpepper, the enemy pressed us closely. From this point the cavalry corps separated, Gregg with his division, falling back by way of Sulphur Springs, Buford by Stevensburg, leaving Kilpatrick on the main thoroughfare along the rail road by Brandy Station. Scarcely had Kilpatrick moved out of Culpepper, when Hampton's division of cavalry made a furious attack on his rear guard with the hope of breaking through upon the main column and scattering it, or of retarding its progress, so that a flanking column might fall upon him ere he could reach the safe shore of the Rappahannock. Gallantly repelling every attack the command moved on, without expending much of its time or material, until opposite the residence of the Hon. John Minor Botts, when a few regiments, including the Fifth New York, suddenly wheeled about, and facing the pursuing foe, charged him with pistol and sabre, thus checking his advancing lines. On arriving at Brandy Station Kilpatrick found his command to be in a most critical situation.

Already Gen. Fitzhugh Lee's division of cavalry held the only road upon which it was possible for Kilpatrick to advance. Stuart, with a portion of Lee's and Hampton's forces, threatened his left flank, assisted by artillery well posted on the hills. Behind him were Hampton's Legions. Buford, having fallen back more rapidly than Kilpatrick, had before passed on toward the Rappahannock, leaving his right flank perfectly exposed, where sharpshooters were already making themselves a source of great annoyance from the woods.

This was a situation to try the stoutest hearts. Nothing daunted by this formidable disposition of an enemy very superior in numbers, Kilpatrick showed himself worthy to command the brave men who composed his division. Forming his force in three lines of battle, assigning the right to Gen. Davies, the left to Gen. Custer, and placing himself in the centre, he advanced with terrible determination to the contest. Having approached to within a few hundred yards of the enemy's lines, his band was ordered to strike up Yankee Doodle, to whose inspiring notes was added the blast of scores of bugles, ringing forth the charge. Fired with a sort of frenzy, and bearing aloft their colors, this band of heroic troopers shook the air with their battle cry, while their drawn and firmly grasped sabres flashed in the light of the declining sun. Gen. Custer, pulling off his cap, gave it to his orderly, and thus led on the charge, while his yellow locks floated on the breeze. Ambulances, forges and cannon, with pack trains, non-combatants and others, all joined to swell the on-flowing tide, before which the Rebel lines broke in wild alarm. Kilpatrick thus escaped serious injury, defeated his pursuers, and presented to the beholders one of the grandest sights ever witnessed in the New World.

His division soon after joined that of Buford, and together they engaged the enemy in a series of brilliant charges, which materially checked his advance. At night they recrossed the Rappahannock in safety.

The cavalry continued its retreat, covering the rear of the infantry, to the old field of Bull Run, where it was expected a third battle would be fought. One night, while the regiment lay bivouacked near Bristoe Station, a caisson was accidently set on fire, causing a rapid explosion of the ammunition it contained. The consequence was a wide-

Kilpatrick's Grand Charge at Brandy Station, Va., October 11th, 1863.

spread alarm, which brought every cavalryman to his horse, ready to meet the foe, who was supposed to have made a powerful attack.

October 16th. The regiment was sent to test the Rebel pickets at Groveton, with whom we had a slight skirmish.

October 17th. The work of yesterday was repeated.

October 18th. A third time the regiment skirmished with the pickets at Groveton and advanced to Gainesville.

October 19th. The Rebel army having spent its time in tearing up and destroying the rail road, refusing to attack, Gen. Meade ordered a general advance. Kilpatrick marched through Groveton and Gainesville, meeting the enemy in overwhelming force at Buckland Mills. Had it not been for great skill and daring his entire command would have been annihilated. As it was, he narrowly escaped, saving all his guns, but leaving some of his men in the enemy's hands.

Before our advancing army, Gen. Lee gradually retreated, receiving a terrible shock at Rappahannock Station, which sent the remains of his army across the Rappahannock. It is quite singular to remark how these great armies have been swinging like huge pendulums during the present season. In June they swung from the Rappahannock, Va., to the Susquehanna, Penn.; then back to the Rapidan; afterward almost to the Potomac, then back to the Rapidan again. It is encouraging to notice that the swing of the Rebel army toward the north, shortens at every move, giving indications of its waning power.

In the early part of November our army laid its pontoons across the Rappahannock, and advanced upon the enemy, driving him from the line he had selected for his winter quarters. Many of their huts, already completed, fell into our hands.

November 8th. The regiment had a spirited skirmish with the enemy, in driving him from Stevensburg.

From a correspondent of a New York daily, we quote the following description of this affair. "I must be allowed to mention, that Kilpatrick's division, or rather Davies' brigade of that division, was engaged in quite a brisk encounter with Hampton's division of Rebel cavalry, on Sunday the 8th inst., in the vicinity of Stevensburg. I allude to it here, because, as yet, it has scarcely been noticed at all in any papers that I am aware of, although it was one of the most spirited and handsomely managed affairs that has occurred during the late movements. There was no very severe fighting, it is true, but the ease with which the enemy was driven from his position, and the short duration of the fight, were mainly attributable to the adroitness used in the disposition of our forces, and the intense eagerness and animation with which our men went up to the attack. A battery of the enemy which occupied a commanding position at Stevensburg, right in the line of our advance, was started off at a double quick, almost without firing a shot, by sending a regiment round to the right, which came in upon it from an unexpected quarter, and threw the gunners into instant alarm for the safety of their guns; and when they had taken up a new position and were busily shelling our troops coming up in front, Major Hammond, commanding the regiment just mentioned, with about twenty of his men, again compelled them to decamp by coming up under cover and unseen to within easy carbine range of them, and thus picking off the artillerists."

The regiment camped among the pines, whence they had driven the enemy.

November 17th. The regiment was ordered to picket along the Rapidan, extending our videttes from Morton's Ford near to Germania.

November 18th. A squad of Hampton's cavalry, dressed in our overcoats, surprised and attacked the 18th Pennsylvania, near Germania Ford, capturing many prisoners, and their headquarters wagon. Capt. McGuinn, Company A, in charge of the nearest reserve, assisted in beating back the Rebels, who fled across the river.

November 21st. The paymaster appeared with his greenbacks, and though the rain has fallen almost incessantly none have been heard to murmur. Whatever trouble or difficulty the soldier has, pay-day is sure to take it all away — at least if his accounts are all right.

November 22d. The men are sending their money home to their friends. Some foolishly squander theirs away, but most men of the regiment put a proper estimate on their earnings.

November 24th. A grand movement of the army toward the Rapidan was commenced, at an early hour. Our division moved toward Raccoon Ford. A heavy rain having set in, the troops were countermarched to their wet bivouacs.

November 26th. The movement commenced and abandoned on the 24th was to-day resumed. Gen. Meade, desiring to cross his main force at Germania Ford, ordered the cavalry to attack the Rebel lines along the upper fords, and, if possible, compel them to busy themselves with us. Our division broke camp early, and reached the river about nine o'clock at Morton's Ford. The fortifications on the high hills along the river swarmed with Rebels. They opened their heavy batteries upon us. The division moved up the river toward Raccoon Ford, most of the time exposed to the artillery fire. Shells fell fast near the solid column, spattering mud all over our Thanksgiving suits, for this was Thanksgiving day. Our flying artillery occasionally replied. This artillery duel was continued all the day, and yet not a man was injured. How wonderful is the preservation of human life on occasions like this! At night we bivouacked in the woods about a mile from the ford. The ground was wet and the weather cold, and we were compelled to make fires sparingly, lest the enemy might discover our position, and give us a Thanksgiving supper of shells, as he had done for our dinner.

November 27th. Early in the morning the division crossed the river at Raccoon Ford, having discovered that the enemy had abandoned his works in the night. Fitzhugh Lee's cavalry, however, was encountered approaching at no great distance from the river, compelling our boys to return after a sharp skirmish.

November 30th. We still continue by the river, exchanging occasional shots, and sometimes volleys, with the pickets on the other side. Now and then the batteries open. Just before sundown the Rebels saluted us with a rapid shelling, which made the woods and hills resound. We bivouac among the pines, when off duty, where moss is plentiful for our carpets. Our fare would be quite pleasant if it were not for the biting frosts of the nights.

December 2d. Gen. Meade is returning from his unsuccessful affair in the wilderness about Mine Run. His expedition has been attended with great fatigue and suffering, and some losses.

December 3d. As was expected, we were relieved from this position and taken back to our old camps, near Stevensburg. Our camp began to assume a delightful appearance, with its rows of shelter tents, and an occasional wall tent, when about 3 P. M. the woods were ringing with bugles, sounding "boots and saddles." Tents were taken down, and the brigade moved out in the direction of the river to meet the enemy, who was supposed to be crossing the river to attack us in heavy force. It proved to be a fright of the pickets stationed along the river. We were soon back in our old spot again, putting up our shelters.

Change is the soldier's life. It marks his daily experience. Now he lies securely in his wood-surrounded home, then he revels in the pomp and terror of the battle; now he suffers from the long march or the extra duty, then he grows weary with long waiting and anxious fears. His life is a moving panorama, which presents every shade of coloring, and every phase of human experience.

December 4th. Quite an excitement was created among the men, by an effort made to ascertain what number of them are willing to reënlist under the orders recently issued by the War Department, respecting Veteran Volunteers.

A large majority of the men present are ready to reënlist for a new term of service. Though they have seen hard service, and long, they are unwilling to return to the quiet pursuits of civil life while the conflict goes on. They want to join in the last conflict and to swell the final shout of victory, over the downfall of this Rebellion. Every one appears to be in the best of spirits.

December 5th. A large mail was received, after a suspension of several days. These are always occasions of great rejoicing, in camp life. Our mail bags are great instruments of power.

December 8th. A large detail of the regiment went out on picket to the Rapidan. A squad of eighteen recruits for the regiment was received this evening.

December 15th. Our boys on picket near Germania Ford are becoming quite familiar with Rebel pickets on the other side the river. Papers are exchanged, coffee is given for tobacco; and visits of the Rebels among us, and of our boys among them, are quite frequent.

December 17th. A cold, freezing rain has fallen all day; and the men, wet, cold, hungry and tired, returned from picket. The pines were lighted up with the lurid light of our fires at night.

December 18th. Moved camp to the hill known in this region as *The Devil's Leap,* where we expect to build our winter quarters.

December 20th. The main portion of the regiment went out on picket.

December 23d. The cold is intense and we are suffering for the want of winter quarters. We have just received orders to build them. We are camped on a crest of hills, which was very thickly wooded with fine timber just before we took possession. The wood had been purchased by the Rebel authorities at a high price, with the hope that this would be *their* winter quarters The forest is quickly disappearing.

December 27th. The men are busily engaged in the work of constructing their log cabins. Every man has suddenly become a mason or a carpenter, and the hammer, the axe and the trowel are being plied with the utmost vigor, if not with the highest skill.

December 31*st.* The Adjutant's quarters are crowded with work. He is making out or giving instructions to others to make out, discharge papers, muster out and muster in rolls for the men, who are enlisting as Veteran Volunteers. A gentle rain fell this morning, and has continued, with some wind, so that all day long the Heavens have wept over the departing year.

CHAPTER VII.

Life in Winter Quarters.— Its Duties and Pastimes.— Its Interesting Scenes.— Dangerous Picketing between the Rappahannock and the Rapidan.— Frequent Attacks by Guerrillas.— Kilpatrick's Second Raid to Richmond.— Col. Dahlgren's Part of the Work.— Full Account by Lieut. Merritt, who accompanied Dahlgren.— Object of the Raid.— General Plan.— Dahlgren's Command.— Successful Capture of Rebel Pickets on the Rapidan.— Honor to Lieut. Merritt's Command.— Capture of a Rebel Court Martial.— Conduct of Prisoners.— The Faithless Negro Guide.— He is Hung.— Property of Mr. Seddon, Rebel Secretary of War.— His Negroes.— Their Depredations.— Our Soldiers falsely Accused of Pillaging.— Henry A. Wise wisely Skedaddles.— Within a few Miles of Richmond.— Coöperation with Kilpatrick Impossible.— Preparation to Attack Richmond. — Nature of the Fight.— Withdrawal.— Casualties.— Terrible Night's March.— Meet a Rebel Ambulance Train.— Crossing the Pamunkey.— The Mattapony.— Marching and Fighting.— The Ambuscade.— Dahlgren Killed.— Road Barricaded.— In Straits.— Ammunition Exhausted.— Preparation to Disperse.— The Party Broken up.— The Cabin in the Woods.— The Surrender.— A Baptist Preacher.— The Parson's Robbery and Apology.— Dahlgren's Remains.— Arrival at Libby Prison.— Casualties of the Fifth New York.— Synopsis of Kilpatrick's March.— The Terrible Tornado.— *January 1st to May 2d*, 1864

After the great excitement of an active campaign with its long marches and almost constant fighting, life in winter quarters seems quite too dull. For some weeks at least, until somewhat accustomed to his new home, the soldier feels more or less uneasiness. However, this life is not without its duties nor its opportunities for employment. Several days are consumed in making our quarters comfortable and convenient. Our northern friends would wonder to see the skill and taste exhibited in the construction and internal arrangements of our cabins.

The day is ushered in with the reveillé, well executed by the bugle corps, which has been reorganized, and drilled for the purpose. At the blast of these bugles we are called to our breakfast, dinner and supper. Roll call is sounded and the men of each company fall into line and are accounted for. The bugle sounds to call the orderly sergeants to assemble at the adjutant's quarters to receive any special orders he may have to communicate. By the bugle the camp guard is assembled, inspected and ordered to its posts of duty. At water call the men lead out their horses to the watering. Drill call sends them to the field to learn the tactics of war.

Thus call after call to duty is sounded at intervals throughout the day, ending with the taps, which calls for the blowing out of lights, and the seeking of rest, which night demands. To these duties and excitements come the days of picketing, when a large detail is sent out, leaving behind a number just sufficient to care for the camp. These are generally men too sick for hard duty, or whose horses are unserviceable.

While in camp checkers and cards afford a pastime to many, but a large number spend their hours in reading and writing. We usually receive a daily mail. Thus our time is filled with some kind of employment, and even our camp life is far from monotonous.

January 1st. The morning was fair and beautiful, but the day ended with the coldest weather ever known to our veterans, while in Virginia. The reënlisted men, numbering one hundred and eighty-one, were mustered in. Others will reënlist before many days.

January 3d. The paymaster has paid his compliments to the veterans, and they abound in greenbacks.

January 7th. Sent out a picket detail of three officers and fifty-six men.

January 16th. The camps of this grand army occupy a large territory, stretching from Stevensburg to two or three miles beyond Brandy Station. The roads are becoming almost bottomless. However, long trains of forage and commissary wagons may be seen passing to and fro with horses and mules in mud from "stem to stern." Cavalcades of mudded horses and riders traverse the camps and adjoining fields in various directions. Large flocks of crows with their high-perched videttes when alighted, or their regular line of march when on the wing, leave an impression upon the soldier's mind. These sights are of daily recurrence.

January 19th. The regiment is picketing near the Rapidan, a little below Germania Ford. A line of pickets extends across to the Rappahannock a little below Fields' Ford. The peninsular territory below this line and between the rivers abounds in thick underbrush and deep ravines, through which guerrillas creep up and attack our pickets. Patrols are sent out daily from the picket reserves, on the main roads to the fords of the rivers, to drive out any force of the enemy that might seek to advance upon us from that direction. To-day our patrol was attacked by a considerable force concealed in bushes by the road side. Under very great disadvantage, our boys defended themselves as best they could, but suffered quite severely. This was near Ely's Ford, Rapidan.

January 22d. Our boys were out again patrolling toward the Rappahannock, and were attacked by bushwhackers near Ellis' Ford. As on the 19th inst., one man was killed, several wounded and captured. Among the latter were several veterans, who were daily looking for their 35 days' furlough promised in their reënlistment. They will have a dreary furlough in southern prisons.

January 31st. Our chapel tent was dedicated this evening by Chaplain E. P Roe, 2d New York Cavalry, who preached an excellent sermon to a large audience.

February 6th. The 2d Corps made a demonstration on the Rebel lines at Raccoon and Morton's Fords, fighting all day. Gen. Hays greatly distinguished himself in some of the charges made on the enemy's fortifications. Meanwhile Kilpatrick's cavalry crossed the river at Culpepper Mine Ford, and reconnoitred along the plank road. At Hampton's Cross Roads a squad of the enemy was encountered and quickly dispersed. A few prisoners fell into our hands.

February 7th. The regiment returned to camp at 2 P. M., after a journey of about 35 miles.

February 13th. Sixty-eight recruits joined the regiment. Our ranks are thus being filled.

February 21st. A large temperance meeting in the chapel, and a large number signed the pledge.

February 23d. A grand review of a portion of the army before Generals Meade, Pleasanton, Kilpatrick and others, took place on the plains between Stevensburg and Pony Mountain. The infantry, artillery and cavalry appeared in their best uniform and with flying colors, presenting an imposing spectacle. The exercises closed with a cavalry skirmish and charge.

February 24th. The paymaster occupies the chapel for paying the regiment.

February 26th. The long-looked-for veteran leaves-of-absence and furloughs made their appearance, but had not been in camp thirty minutes before they were sent for from brigade headquarters. They are doubtless detained for some wise purpose, but many fail to *see the point.*

February 28th. The whole division under Kilpatrick, accompanied by Col. Dahlgren, who was intrusted with a very important position in the expedition, set out on a great raid to Richmond. We append the following full and interesting narrative of the raid, by Major Merritt (then Lieutenant), who accompanied Col. Dahlgren, and was with him at his death.

NARRATIVE OF DAHLGREN'S RAID.

Kilpatrick's second raid upon Richmond was made with the purpose of releasing our officers and men confined in Libby Prison, Castle Thunder and Belle Island, and to destroy the mills, workshops, materials, stores and government property of the Rebels in that city and vicinity, and the rail road communications. The plan also comprehended the capture of Lee's reserve artillery at Frederick Hall Station on the Virginia Central rail road.

In the execution of this general plan, Col. Dahlgren's command, diverging from the main eolumn to the right at Spottsylvania Court House, was to mareh by Frederiek Hall, eapture and destroy the artillery, cross the James river at Columbia Mills, send a party to destroy the rail road bridges where the Danville road crosses the Appomattox river, and move upon Riehmond from the south, in the hope of gaining possession of the bridges spanning the river between Manehcster and the eity by surprise, dash over and release the prisoners, while the main foree under Kilpatriek oeeupied the enemy's attention on the north side of the town.

The expedition of Col. Ulric Dahlgren marehed from Gen. Kilpatrick's headquarters at Stevensburg, Va., on the evening of Sunday, February 28th, 1864. It eomprised detaehments from the 2d New York, 5th New York, 1st Vermont, 1st Maine and 5th Miehigan regiments of eavalry of the 3d division eavalry eorps, army of the Potomae, in all four hundred men. The detaehment of the Fifth New York under command of Lieut. Merritt, Co. K, eonsisted of Lieut. Robert Blaek and forty men seleeted from eompanies I and K. This party left eamp about 3 P. M., being sent in advance with orders to eapture the enemy's videttes at Ely's Ford on the Rapidan river, and, if praetieable, their picket reserve also, the objeet being to seeure the passage of the river and open the way for the march without the alarm's being eommunieated to the enemy.

We proceeded to within two miles of the ford and halted until dark, when Lieut. Merritt, with fifteen dismounted men and two seouts, sent from headquarters, waded the river about one mile above the ford, and, aided by the darkness, the night being stormy, succeeded in approaching and securing the two videttes guarding the ford, and, after much difficulty, ascertained the position of the reserve. A large fire built in a ravine on the banks of the river some distance below the ford, evidently intended to deceive us, caused some delay; but we finally discovered that their picket reserve were in a house some distance back from the river. We proceeded silently to this house, surrounded it, and, rushing in, after a brief struggle, captured the whole party, sixteen men, a lieutenant, and the officer of the day, who had halted for the night on his tour of inspection. His report of the vigilance and efficiency of his picket was probably never made. Only two shots were fired, and no alarm raised, as we afterward ascertained that the enemy were not aware that we had crossed the river until the column had passed Spottsylvania.

Lieut. Black, with the remainder of the men, was left on the opposite bank of the river, with directions to throw out a few skirmishers on the edge of the stream, and move down as close as possible without discovery, and to be prepared either to cross or cover our party as circumstances rendered necessary. Securing our prisoners we returned to the river and found the advance of Dahlgren's column across, we having immediately communicated our success. Twenty-three of our men were sent to the rear in charge of the prisoners. Col. Dahlgren, in recognition of our success, assigned to us the advance of the expedition, which duty we performed throughout.

Taking the Chancellorsville road we passed through Spottsylvania Court House and, bearing to the right, marched without incident, until we came to the vicinity of

Frederick Hall Station, about 3 P. M. Monday. Here we found the reserve artillery, numbering 83 pieces of every calibre, parked, with a small brigade of infantry guarding it. Approaching through the woods with the utmost circumspection, we came within 300 yards of the camp without discovery. A rapid but thorough reconnoissance demonstrated the impossibility of capturing their guns with our small force, and we saw the necessity of withdrawing from the dangerous vicinity without attracting the notice of the enemy. To accomplish this we had to pass around the base of a small hill on the edge of the camp. Here there was a house, and we observed a number of men moving about, and from the character of the ground suspected the presence of a battery also. It was of course necessary to ascertain whether this suspicion was correct, and to capture the men. In order to save the valuable time it would have required to deploy skirmishers, and as the only probable way of preventing the alarm of the camp, our detachment volunteered to charge the hill, Major Cooke, 2d New York, deploying a squadron to cover us in case of need. Separating in two parties we charged on opposite sides of a gorge running into the hill, and approached the small house in such a manner as to surround it. After a few shots, the party who had retired inside the building, when, to their utter amazement they discovered our character, surrendered themselves prisoners, and we learned with almost equal astonishment and no little amusement, that we had captured a court martial, securing the entire party, president, judge advocate, members of the court, witnesses, prisoner, and orderlies in attendance. Among them was a Col. Jones, 1st Maryland Light Artillery, two majors and the usual complement of captains and lieutenants, the whole party numbering about thirty, with several fine horses. The Rebels were engaged in artillery practice when we approached their camp, and the regular and continued discharge of their guns served to inform us that we remained undiscovered.

Nearly all the prisoners subsequently escaped from us during the night, as we were unable to guard them properly, and, in fact, Col. Dahlgren did not desire to be encumbered with them. The judge advocate, Lieut. Blair and another, however, adhered to us most faithfully until the final breaking up of the expedition. Lieut. Blair afterwards visited us in Libby Prison, and tendered his testimony in our favor, but without mitigating the severity of our imprisonment in any way.

The rail road was torn up about one mile from Frederick Hall, and we then proceeded on our march. A heavy storm prevailed during Monday night. The rain fell in torrents and rendered the roads almost impassable. Men and horses were beginning to suffer for rest and refreshment. The woods being dense increased the difficulties of the march, and about three o'clock Tuesday morning, it became necessary to make a brief halt in order to close up the column, which was scattered several miles in the rear, struggling through the mud holes of the miserable swamp road. At the halting place we captured six wagons loaded with forage for Lee's army.

We now learned that we were about three miles from Dover Mills, and ten miles below Columbia Mills. The guide, a negro, had misled us during the night, and, to obviate the delay of retracing our steps, Col. Dahlgren, on the representations of the negro that an excellent ford was to be found at Dover Mills, concluded to cross at that point. After two hours' halt we again moved on, and soon reached Dover Mills, but only to meet disappointment. The negro had deceived us, no ford existed at this point nor any means of crossing the river. He then stated that the ford was three miles below: this was obviously false, as the river was evidently navigable to and above this place, as we saw a sloop going down the river.

This man was sent from headquarters to guide us and was considered faithful and reliable. I afterwards learned that he came into our lines from Richmond, in company with several officers who escaped from Libby Prison by Col. Streight's tunnel, and whom he piloted through. He was born and had always belonged in the immediate vicinity of Dover Mills, was very shrewd and intelligent, and it would seem impossible that he should not know that no ford existed in the neighborhood, where he had seen vessels daily passing. Col. Dahlgren had warned him that if detected acting in bad faith, or lying, we would surely hang him, and after we left Dover Mills, and had gone down the river so far as to render further prevarication unavailing, the colonel charged him with betraying us, destroying the whole design of the expedition, and hazarding the lives of every one engaged in it,—and told him that he should be hung in conformity with the terms of his service. The negro became greatly alarmed, stated confusedly that he was mistaken, thought we intended to cross the river in boats, and finally said that he had done wrong, was sorry, etc. The colonel ordered him to be hung,—a halter strap was used for the purpose, and we left the miserable wretch dangling by the roadside. His body was afterwards cut down and buried by Capt. Mitchell who had remained behind some time to complete the destruction of some mills and grain.

At Dover Mills we halted about two hours on the property of Mr. Seddon, the Rebel secretary of war. No Union troops had ever been here before, and our appearance created great excitement and consternation among the whites,—while the contrabands flocked about us in great numbers, nearly wild with joy. The negroes invariably came with the request that we would visit their master or overseer, and arrest or punish him for his cruelty We of course declined the office of redressers of grievances of this nature.

The ties of affection we sometimes hear about, binding master and slave together under the patriarchal institution, evidently did not exist in Mr. Seddon's neighborhood, however it might be elsewhere.

At this point we destroyed a number of fine mills, several canal boats with army supplies, and a large amount of flour, meal and grain. A lock of the Richmond and Lynchburg canal was also blown up. Besides this, we captured a large number of fine horses. In fact our command had been able to keep well mounted from the number of horses secured up to this time. The barn of Mr. Seddon was burned, whether by accident or design is not known. It was not done by order of Col. Dahlgren. The negroes on this estate, as well as those of a Mr. Morson near by, were greatly excited and exasperated, and invited the soldiers to plunder, themselves setting the example. Some excesses were committed but the officers exerted themselves to the utmost to drive the soldiers from both these houses. The greatest damage was done by the negroes, who seemed frantic for plunder and revenge; it was especially so with the women. They invaded both mansions screaming for silk dresses, breaking furniture, and tearing everything to pieces they could lay hands upon. Pantries and closets were thoroughly ransacked, judging from the appearance of the ground outside the house. They said they were nearly starved, overworked and cruelly beaten without cause, and certainly exhibited a most miserable condition. The extent of the damage I did not observe, having been sent by Col. Dahlgren to search a house near by for Rebel correspondence, upon information given by negroes, and only returned a moment before we resumed the march. But it is certain that nothing of the character charged upon us by the Richmond authorities and newspapers, ever occurred, such as wholesale plundering, wanton destruction of private property, carrying off plate and jewelry, etc. On the contrary the soldiers were restrained to the utmost, and were forced to return such plundered articles as were found in their possession. It was impossible to prevent some acts of disorder being committed upon the property of so prominent a Rebel official as Seddon, especially under the example and imitation of his own house servants; but as to carrying off his plate and his wife's jewelry, I can say that I observed in the possession of one soldier only, anything resembling such articles. One man had a sugar basin, cake basket, and couple of candlesticks, all apparently plaited ware of a very cheap description, of a pattern found in every shop window. These I ordered the man to throw down upon the lawn, and they were left lying there. If Mrs. Seddon's plate and jewelry were all of the same character and value, she will be able to replace them without difficulty and at very slight expense.

Sergt. D. H. Scofield, company K, learned that Gen Henry A. Wise was stopping in the neighborhood, and, after some search, discovered his whereabouts. He went to the place just as the redoubtable ex-governor mounted his horse. Scofield made after him, and quite an exciting chase ensued. The hero of Hatteras Island was not inclined to a personal encounter even with a single man, and, being well mounted, succeeded in making his escape into the woods.

Unable to cross the James, there was but one way open to us — the western pike, running along the river and approaching Richmond from the west. Leaving a small force under Capt. Mitchell, 2d New York cavalry, to burn some mills and stores, Dahlgren pushed rapidly on with the rest of his command (halting only to dispose of the negro guide) until we arrived within seven miles of the city and in sight of the outer line of fortifications. Here we halted about three P M. at a cross road. Kilpatrick had been engaged on the Brook pike, the northern approach to the city, during the morning. We heard his guns for some time, but they had finally ceased, earlier in the day. Dahlgren immediately dispatched scouts to communicate with him; they never returned. We ascertained that the outer line of work in our front was held by a picket only, and made preparations to attack at dark. We had little hope of accomplishing more than a reconnoissance. Kilpatrick had evidently withdrawn, and we could not hope to enter the city with our small party from this direction. The locomotive whistles on the opposite side of the James indicated that reënforcements were rapidly coming in from the direction of Petersburg. But Dahlgren observed that we could gain some information of the ground and character of the defenses which might be useful at a future day, and besides, we were all unwilling to withdraw without at least an attempt to carry out the object of the expedition, however improbable the chances of success. We learned from persons coming from the city, whom we arrested, that Gen. Kilpatrick had retired after the attack in the morning, and the scouts having failed to report Lieut. Reuben Bartley, United States signal corps who accompanied the expedition, was, towards evening, sent out with a party to endeavor to find Kilpatrick or communicate with him. He proceeded across the country to the Brook pike and approached to within a few miles of the city, but without success. He ascertained, however, that a large force of Rebel cavalry was out, and had great difficulty in avoiding several parties. As soon as evening set in Lieut. Bartley endeavored to open communication with rockets but his signals were not replied to.

Before attacking the enemy it was necessary to dispose of the ambulance containing signal rockets, materials for burning bridges, &c., together with the negroes—several hundreds having followed us, on foot and mounted, some with bundles containing their movable possessions, some with an extra horse taken from the plantation in renumeration for services rendered, others barefoot and almost naked, but all happy in the conviction that they were free. They were sent off in the direction of Hungary Station and awaited us near an old church which the signal officer had selected for observations.

Arrangements being completed, at dusk, we moved down upon the enemy's pickets, who hastily retired, evidently in surprise. We pursued them rapidly inside the outer line of defenses — earthworks substantially constructed, but not mounted. The first real opposition we met was near the second line. Here they had rallied a considerable force, and evidently intended to make a stand under the protection of a piece of woods where the road made a bend. Our charge in column was received with a heavy volley, and it became necessary to deploy, to dislodge them. Our men in the advance were quickly formed on the right of the road as skirmishers, and by gaining a position well up on the flank of the enemy, assisted materially in driving them out, which was done after three charges led by Col. Dahlgren and Major Cooke. The Rebels, consisting entirely of infantry, including the Richmond City battalion, broke across the fields for the town. Our men were dismounted and pursued them with the utmost impetuosity. The small column kept mounted on the pike alone maintaining their formation. It was a scrub race,— across fields, fences and stone walls, we pressed after them, rallying, and scattering them repeatedly as they attempted to dispute our advance whenever a wall or house afforded shelter. Between formidable works, over rifle pits, ditches and every obstruction, with a cheer, a run and a volley from our Spencers, we crowded them back to the edge of the city. Here we encountered a heavy force formed in line of battle. It was now dark and the gas lights burning. We were inside the city limits, though the houses were scattered. Many of our boys expected at last to see the inside of the Rebel capitol. But the force in front was soon found to be too great for us to contend with. Formed in skirmish line we could not entirely cover them. Still our men advanced gallantly to the attack, and even forced them back somewhat from their position, stubbornly holding all we gained. Their right rested upon a hill descending abruptly into a swampy flat. This we could not turn in consequence of our small numbers, and the colonel soon decided to withdraw. He said we had gone " far enough "— and indeed had militia ardor been any of the most ardent, we would have found it quite too far. Leaving Capt. Mitchell with a strong party to cover our rear and check either pursuit or attack, Dahlgren proceeded to collect his scattered force, picking up all the wounded we could find in the dark. Having no means of conveyance, the assistant surgeon of the 2d New York was left in charge of them, and fell into the enemy's hands.

We retired leisurely and without the slightest annoyance from the enemy. Their loss was variously stated by their newspapers to be from forty to seventy killed and wounded, including several officers. We had but one officer wounded, Lieut. Harris, 5th Michigan cavalry. Our losses in all could not be ascertained but probably did not exceed a dozen or fifteen.

The route now pursued was in the direction of Hungary Station, on the Central rail road, taking up the signal officer and the rest sent away in the afternoon. We were obliged to force a citizen to become our guide, as the scout, sent from headquarters for that purpose, although assuring us that he knew every foot of ground within thirty miles of Richmond, proved utterly inefficient. No one engaged in that night's march will ever forget its difficulties. The storm had set in with renewed fury. The fierce wind drove the rain, snow and sleet. The darkness was rendered more intense by the thick pines which overgrew the road, and which dashed into our faces almost an avalanche of water at every step. Using unfrequented wood roads we were halted frequently to remove trees fallen across the path, and to trace the course with our hands, for even the sagacity of the horses was often at fault. Tired and exhausted the men fell asleep upon their horses. It became necessary to march by file, and at every turn of the path to pass the word down to "turn to the right" or keep to the left of the tree. It was utterly impossible to see a yard in advance. Slowly and laboriously we toiled through — the jaded animals stumbling and falling down, and when we finally reached Hungary Station, discovered that Capt. Mitchell and his party had become separated from us. They were unable to track us, although following close in our rear, but, more fortunate than ourselves, succeeded, after hiding in the woods all night, in making their way to Kilpatrick, whom they joined next day near White House.

Lt. Bartley had been informed by contrabands, that Gen. Kilpatrick had gone down the peninsula, with a large force of the enemy in his rear. Concluding, therefore, that it was impracticable to join him, Dahlgren, after consultation, decided upon making for Gloucester Point to join Gen. Butler's army. We crossed the Chickahominy at McClellan's bridge, and, soon after, came upon a rebel ambulance train returning to Richmond with wounded from the scene of an attack made that night, upon the 2d Brigade of Kilpatrick's Division. For some time they were not aware of our character, but were loud in their boasts that they had driven off the Yankees — their surprise was ludicrous when Col. Dahlgren informed them that we were Yankees, and asked "if they did not think they were a nice lot of fellows." — Detaining them long enough to enable us to close up our own men, and after conversing with some of our wounded in the ambulances, but failing to gain any information to guide us, we dismissed them,—and anticipating immediate pursuit, proceeded rapidly towards the Pamunkey river. We reached Hanovertown ferry about 8 o'clock A. M. Wednesday. The river was very high, and the flat-boat used at the ferry had been removed, but we discovered it hidden among the bushes on the opposite bank. Several of the boys stripped off their clothing and two succeeded in swimming over and bringing back the boat. The tow rope was found, and quickly stretched across and made fast.— Several hours were consumed in crossing. As soon as all hands were over we continued our march for the Mattapony river, encountering and dispersing several small parties of the enemy.

After driving out a party of Rebels at Ayletts, we crossed the Mattapony about 2 P. M. using the ferry boat, (fortunately discovered some distance down the river), for the men, and swimming the horses. The crossing was effected in about an hour. When half the party had crossed an attack was made upon us, but it was easily repulsed by a few skirmishers.

After crossing the Mattapony until we reached the scene of final disaster, we were engaged in constant skirmishing with the enemy who had collected from every point to oppose our march. But a single road was available, and at every point of woods we were assailed by a volley from shot guns, carbines and rifles. Our flankers were captured almost as soon as sent out. The enemy invariably declined coming to close quarters, scattering before our repeated charges. Notwithstanding the annoyances, our progress, though slow, was steady until about 6 P. M., when we were forced to make a long halt to feed both horses and men, both being utterly prostrated with fatigue and hunger. We stopped soon after crossing the Anseamancock creek, and a few miles from King and Queen Court House. Corn was procured in ample quantity from a barn near by, and the men proceeded to cook their first meal for nearly thirty-six hours. Our party had become reduced to about seventy men. Several had been captured during the day, and a few wounded and left from necessity. Nearly all the effective force was with Capt. Mitchell, and consequently lost the night before. One hundred to one hundred and fifty contrabands still adhered to us. Ammunition was mostly exhausted, the majority of the men having none at all. Some were slightly wounded, or so much exhausted as to be useless, but we still hoped to succeed in reaching Gloucester Point, opposite to which we would find some of Gen. Butler's army. After three hours' rest we aroused the men, not without exertion, and after getting them mounted, resumed the march. The night was again stormy, a drizzling rain falling. The road, as usual, ran through thick pine woods, rendering every object invisible.

The first evidence of the enemy's being in advance was the absence of three men sent upon picket a short distance ahead of our halting place. Very soon after the discovery we were challenged. The advance guard consisted of but six men, all that could be spared from the column. Col. Dahlgren had ridden to the head of the advance guard a moment before we were challenged by the enemy. He was immediately followed by Major Cooke. I responded to the challenge by demanding "who are you?" The word was repeated and the colonel immediately called out, "surrender or we will shoot you"—and snapped his pistol, the cap only exploding. The next instant a heavy volley was poured in upon us. The flash of the pieces afforded us a momentary glimpse of their position stretching parallel with the road about fifteen paces from us. Every tree was occupied, and the bushes poured forth a sheet of fire. A bullet grazing my leg and probably striking my horse somewhere in the neck, caused him to make a violent spring sideways. I was aware of some one dropping beside me, and attracted by a movement upon the ground, demanded who it was. Major Cooke replied, that his horse had been shot. Neither of us knew, at the moment, of the death of Dahlgren, though he was not four feet from us when he fell. A scout who had been somewhat in advance, now returned and reported that the road was barricaded two hundred yards ahead, and was impassable. In a moment a heavy fire was opened upon the flank and rear of our column. Major Cooke desired me to go back and assist the colonel to take care of it. We both supposed he had escaped, as not a groan was heard, and everything was invisible in the darkness. Leaving Major Cooke, who was extricating himself from his horse, I rode back to the column. Dahlgren was not there, and I now knew that he had fallen, as there were but four in the group ahead when the volley was fired

Instantly ordering all who had ammunition to fire into the bushes to check a charge, which would have routed us, the column was moved ahead, until a slight opening in the thick woods enabled us to turn off the road and form into line. The road was graded down about four feet with perpendicular banks supported by cedar boughs interlaced, in a manner frequently seen in Virginia. Ordering the fence thrown down, the men were immediately brought into line, facing the road. Major Cooke had now returned. We soon discovered that we were in a small clearing on rising ground surrounded by the forest. Moving back a few yards for more space, we massed the negroes compactly in the rear, and awaited the enemy. The men stood perfectly firm though almost all of them were utterly destitute of ammunition, and fully aware of the hopelessness of our position. After a time we discovered that the enemy did not propose to attack us. We were aware that two battalions of cavalry were at King and Queen Court House, which we hoped to flank by a road about two miles from the town. We were now cut off from this road by the force ahead and the barricades. There was no other road in the vicinity but the one we had been marching upon. The country was broken up in rough hills, thickly wooded, or dense jungles, rendering it utterly impracticable to make our way across the country mounted. We were also cut off from the rear, and could not retrace our steps, and soon discovered that we were entirely surrounded. The two prisoners, during the confusion, had made their escape, as well as the citizen guide whom we had pressed into service, and the enemy were aware that our ammunition was exhausted. An inspection showed that less than thirty rounds remained in the whole party. I had but a single pistol cartridge myself, which I had reserved for a last recourse.

Under these disastrous circumstances, Major Cooke, after a consultation with Lt. Bartley and myself, decided upon the necessity of breaking up the party in the hope of getting through the enemy's line dismounted, and by spreading out in twos and threes, to baffle pursuit, and accomplish the remaining twenty-five miles which we estimated to be the distance to Gloucester Point. Major Cooke and myself together made a careful reconnoissance, and found that we were closely surrounded by a large force. Their fires could be seen at several points, and so near were they that their voices, in conversation, were plainly audible. The men were dismounted, and ordered to drive their sabres into the ground and picket their horses to them, it being impossible to kill the animals without attracting notice. The Spencer carbines were destroyed by removing and throwing away, or burying the chambers, and breaking the magazine tubes. The men were instructed to take only their belts, revolvers and haversacks, that they might not be impeded by a heavy load which would be soon abandoned, affording evidence of the trail, and assist pursuit. As soon as these arrangements were silently made, we desired them to select companions and to form into parties of three or four, when we gave them the points of direction as nearly as could be determined, and bade them good bye. One of the men made a collection of cartridges and brought me a charge for two revolvers. I shall never forget the kind act.

About forty men departed in this manner, the rest, being too much exhausted, remained on the ground and surrendered themselves next morning. The negroes we had to abandon to their fate. After all who could do so, had withdrawn, Major Cooke, Lieut. Bartley, myself and three scouts, took our departure, which we effected by creeping on hands and knees for about half a mile, between the different parties and posts of the Rebels. We traveled until daybreak when we secreted ourselves in a jungle of young pines, where we passed the day principally in sleep, which we greatly needed. When night returned we resumed our journey. After traveling several miles we concluded to stop at an isolated cabin to procure food. We entered the place and found an old man, overseer of the plantation, and his wife. They consented with apparent willingness to give us supper, and prepare a supply of food to carry with us, for which we offered to pay liberally. The old man built a blazing fire and we all gathered around the hearth to infuse a little warmth into our benumbed limbs. Suddenly the door was opened and before we could grasp our pistols from beneath our clothing, where we had carried them, to keep them dry, the room was filled with soldiers, who demanded our surrender, and we were forced to comply.

The leader of the party was the owner of the plantation, captain of home guards, and Rev Mr. Bagley, pastor of a Baptist church. This gentleman of three-fold calling took us to his own house near by, where a plentiful supper was already prepared for his band, who had been beating the woods all day in search of our fugitives. The chagrin occasioned by our escape from their well contrived ambush had stimulated their exertions, and they had been rewarded with almost complete success, only three of our party making good their escape. The country was completely aroused. Every man, and even women, children and dogs took part in the search.

We were apparently objects of great interest. Numbers came to gratify their curiosity with a view of us. Our captors guarded us most assiduously, pistol in hand, or, while engaged at supper, kept them beside their plates. Major Cooke asserts that the parson said grace with a cocked revoler in his hand. After supper we were removed to the "best room," where shake downs were prepared, and we viewed with great satisfaction the arrangements for a good night's rest. Our slumbers were guarded by five vigilant partisans, sitting cross kneed with leveled revolvers. Twice during the night I was aroused by the ceremony of changing guard, but found them always on the alert, a pistol being brought to bear upon me the moment my eyes opened. They were withal courteous enough, except that they would inflict upon us their views on the secession and war questions, and scoff at the folly of attempting to conquer the South, and while treating us with no small degree of deference, would assert their profound contempt for Yankees universally.

Next morning, after a breakfast the precise counterpart of supper, and which I hold in grateful remembrance to this day, and reverted to in imagination many a time during subsequent days of short commons, the parson politely but firmly demanded our watches, and other articles of personal property, which were handed over with no little reluctance and indignation. Seeming to think that some apology was necessary for conduct so plainly in violation of both clerical and military character, he explained that his loss had been very great, and "that it was his only means of making himself whole." Besides, he remarked, if he did not get the plunder it would be taken from us in Richmond, and he might as well have it as the officials there, who were all thieves and rascals. Well, perhaps the parson was right. He certainly estimated his Richmond friends at the true standard of morality.

From these people we learned the particulars of Dahlgren's fate.[1] His body was found perforated with five bullets, and his death had been instantaneous. One of them, a physician, an intelligent, and in appearanee, respeetable man, assured me that the remains were buried in a decent manner. He said that the best joiner in the neighborhood had been employed to make the eoffin, whieh was of stained wood, the best material available. He also stated that it was the universal wish to give a fitting burial to so gallant a soldier. It was an after thought whieh doubtless eminated from Riehmond, to disinter, and heap wrath and indignity upon the senseless corpse of a dauntless foe. We were subsequently informed that the body had been mutilated before burial by a Lieut. Hart, 7th Virginia cavalry, who severed one of the fingers to possess himself of a valuable ring worn by the colonel; but the act was regarded as so disgraceful, that several soldiers of the same regiment who witnessed the act and informed us of it, said that the scoundrel deserved to be shot.

After breakfast Friday morning, Mareh 4th, we were turned over to Capt. Magruder of the cavalry, who escorted us to Richmond, a distanee of forty miles, where we arrived Saturday evening, foot sore and hungry, to be transferred to the tender mercies of Major Thomas P. Turner, and his

---

[1] As our book goes to press (November, 1865) we find a telegram in the papers, relating to the remains of Col. Dahlgren, which we gladly insert in our pages. The seareh for his remains was long and earnest, and finally sueeessful. "Philadelphia, Penn., Nov. 1st. The remains of Col. Ulric Dahlgren laid in state in Independenee Hall during the night and the funeral took place this morning. Among the distinguished mourners were Admiral Dahlgren, Generals Meade and Humphries and Major Henry."

fellow Samaritan, Inspector Dick Turner, who provided us with a dungeon in the cellar of Libby Prison, where we were considerately informed we should remain until arrangements were completed to hang us.

It would be improper to conclude this paper without alluding to the good conduct of the men of the Fifth New York. Through the entire raid their behavior elicited frequent and earnest commendation from Col. Dahlgren, and reflected credit upon the regiment. But all connected with the expedition did their duty well, and if gallantry or endurance could have won success they would not have failed to grasp it. All entered ardently into the spirit of the enterprise, inspired by the example of the "one legged colonel," whose noble memory no Rebel vandal can ever mutilate or tarnish.

Casualties of the 5th N. Y Cavalry.

Lieut. H. A. D. Merritt, Co. K, captured, escaped from prison, Columbia, S. C., November 28, 1864.

Corp. Alfred Richards,	Co.	I,	captured,	survived,	and	was	exch'd.
Pvt. Charles F. Smith,	"	"	"	"	"	"	"
" John A. Lundin,	"	"	"	"	"	"	"
Corp. George Munroe,	"	K,	"	"	"	"	"
Pvt. John Phillips,	"	"	"	"	"	"	"
" James D. Dowd,	"	"	"	"	"	"	"
" David Howe,	"	"	"	"	"	"	"
" Franz Briell,	"	"	"	"	"	"	"
Sgt. John Hardy,	"	I,	"	died	at	Andersonville,	Ga.
Pvt. Frank Wood,	"	"	"	"	"	"	"
" Herman Harmes,	"	"	"	"	"	"	"
Farrier James Welsh,	"	K,	"	"	"	"	"
Pvt. George Tresch,	"	"	"	"	"	"	"

March 4th. A detail of the regiment for picket remained

here when the raiders left. To-day they were attacked near Fields' Ford, by bushwhackers, and severely handled.

March 11th. Our pickets were again attacked near Southard's Cross Roads, but succeeded in driving the enemy away, after a brief engagement.

March 12th. Just before dark, our weary raiders returned to camp, making the hills resound with their shouts of joy. From them we learn the following particulars. Kilpatrick moved his command rapidly, reaching the fortifications of Richmond in the afternoon of March 1st. A vigorous attack was made on these fortified lines, while the general waited to hear from Dahlgren, who, by the perfidy of a guide, failed to fulfill his part of the programme. At night Kilpatrick withdrew, crossed the Chickahominy at Meadow Bridge, and, in the midst of a drizzling storm of sleet and hail, bivouacked with his weary troopers. Scarcely had the bivouac fires begun to illuminate the darkness of the night, when Hampton's Legions made a desperate attack upon our forces. All that dreary night our men marched, and, continuing their journey the next day, they passed by Old Church, where they scattered the last band of Rebels that hung upon their rear. The march was continued down the Peninsula. Annoyed only occasionally by bushwhackers on their way, our boys finally found safety and rest in the department of General Butler, near Yorktown. The division was brought in transports to Alexandria, whence it marched to its camps at Stevensburg.

March 14th. The veterans left this morning for home on their thirty-five days' furloughs. They were a happy company.

April 22d. Our division of cavalry, with a large force

A H White

of infantry, appeared in review before Lieut. General Grant, on the Plains of Stevensburg. The army is very enthusiastic over its commander-in-chief. Some change has recently taken place in our cavalry. Gen. Kilpatrick has been assigned to a larger command in the west, and Gen. John H. Wilson succeeds him. Gen. Davies is also removed to some other position, and Col. McIntosh commands the first brigade, which is now composed of the 18th Pennsylvania, 1st Connecticut, 2d New York, and 5th New York.

April 29th. Orders were issued early this morning to break up winter quarters, preparatory to the campaign, which is about to open. The regiment moved about half a mile, near brigade headquarters, which are in the house of a Mr. Ross.

May 2d. The day had been fine until about five P. M., with only an occasional cloud, which floated lazily through the sky. At this time a terrible commotion of the elements was observed in the west, and heavy clouds of dust arose from the hills about Culpepper, and swept down over the plains in the direction of our camps. In an incredibly short time from its appearance, the tornado struck us, with a fury and force seldom witnessed. Scarcely a tent was left standing, while pieces of tents, shelters, boards, articles of clothing, papers, &c., were flying on the wings of the wind. At times the dust suffocated and blinded us. Horses broke loose from their fastenings and ran about in wild dismay. Men laughed at each other's calamities or ran to each other's relief. This carnival of winds continued about twenty minutes, and was followed by a cold rain, which fell upon our unsheltered heads. With much difficulty some shelters were replaced, and a tolerable night's rest was enjoyed.

CHAPTER VIII.

Army of the Potomac. — Good Condition. — First Steps of the Great Campaign under Gen. Grant. — The Fifth New York opens the Battle of the Wilderness at Parker's Store.—Detailed at Army Headquarters. — Scenes at the Hospital. — Lines of Battle. — Second Day. — Lee breaks our Lines twice. — Is Repulsed. — Col. Hammond Ordered to Germania Ford. — Is Placed in Command of Provisional Brigade of Cavalry.—Brings up Rear on First Left Flank Movement. — Skirmishes on the Ny and Po Rivers.— Affair at the Mattapony. — Sergeant Sortore Killed.— His Burial. — Battle of Milford Station. — A Stratagem at Little River. — Vast Forests of Virginia. — Battle of Ashland Station — Dark, Muddy March along the Pamunkey — Tedious March in Rear of a Supply Train. — Men Sleep on their Horses. — At Charles City C. H. — Fight at White Oak Swamps. — *May 3d to June 16th,* 1864.

The Army of the Potomac had never been in as good condition as Gen. Grant found it in the spring of 1864. All winter long its ranks had been filling up, and its drill grounds around the camps had been thoroughly trodden. "Numbers and thorough discipline" had been the motto of its masters. The rank and file were largely made up of veterans, who had seen service for three years of hard campaigning, and who had reënlisted for three years more, if their services were needed all that time. This was a great element of power. The supplies from the quartermaster and commissary departments were abundant and generally satisfactory. Great confidence was reposed in our military leaders, who had shown themselves worthy of the positions they occupied. The Lieutenant General, under whose immediate superintendence this army was about to move, was everywhere received with the most enthusiastic applause, while no one doubted but that he could plan a campaign and execute its movements with an ability equal to any general of the age.

Such was the Army of the Potomac on the 3d *of May*, when it received orders to be ready to move at 12 o'clock that night. Day by day, as we had watched the smoke ascending from the camp fires of the Rebel army just across the rapid river, we had gathered fresh inspiration; and we knew that but a short journey would bring us face to face with our confident enemy, whom we expected to drive before us.

The order for preparation to move was obeyed readily throughout our camps, and but a few minutes past 12 at night the bugles sounded "To Horse," and the cavalrymen were ready for the march. The third division moved down to Germania Ford, where it forded the stream early on the morning of the 4th, and the rising sun shone upon its flags, already borne over earthworks which the enemy had used on former occasions, but which we now found deserted. The enemy's plan seems to have been this—to place no obstacle to our advance, and when the army was fairly across the river, and had entered the wilderness country, to fall upon it, break its ranks, and compel a hasty and disastrous retreat. But in this he had mistaken his subjects, as the sequel proved.

The cavalry advanced on the plank road toward Chancellorsville, just beyond Wilderness Tavern, where the plank road from Orange Court House intercepts this. Here the Fifth New York was detached from the division and ordered to proceed to Parker's store, where it was to establish a strong line of pickets. Meanwhile the cavalry corps, now under command of Gen. Sheridan, set out on a grand raid toward Richmond, often meeting and defeating the enemy's cavalry, and killing its chief, Gen. J E. B. Stuart.

May 5th. Occasional shots were fired during the night, and, at the break of day, a heavy column of Rebel infantry made its appearance on our front. The whole line soon became desperately engaged. This was the first blow of the great battle of the Wilderness. For this honor the regiment paid dearly. Having sent word to General Meade that a heavy column of infantry was advancing, and that he would "check them as long as possible," Col. Hammond kept the regiment well in line, encouraging the men with his presence and action. Many of the men were dismounted, and their Spencer carbines made the dense woods ring, and told with fearful effect upon the enemy. Prisoners, afterwards captured from this attacking division, swore that a whole brigade must have been in their front. Fighting with a daring rarely equaled, and compelled to fall back before superior numbers, we nevertheless held them at bay for five hours, until relieved by a portion of the 6th Corps. Our service had been most important to our army, but the regiment had suffered a loss of 13 killed, 22 wounded, and 24 known to have been captured, besides 15 or 20 from whom tidings have never since been heard. They were probably killed. Among those known to have been killed was Captain L. McGuinn, Co. A, a most gallant young officer. A correspondent of the N. Y *Herald* makes his bow to the regiment, on this occasion, and says:

"The Fifth New York Cavalry was detached from Colonel McIntosh's command for duty under the immediate orders of General Meade. This was a compliment well earned by its gallant conduct at Parker's store. It is under the command of Colonel Hammond, one of the best officers in the service."

The regiment having reported to General Meade, was ordered to bivouac just in the rear of the old Wilderness Tavern. But now came the care of the wounded. In ambulances, when they could be secured, or on stretchers, they were conveyed to the hospital, established only about a mile in rear of the line of battle, at a small house in the woods. Some of the poor fellows were fearfully mangled. Private Anson Jones, Co. A, had his left arm completely fractured from the elbow to the shoulder. He died from the amputation. 1st Sergeant Cross, Co. L, had likewise a broken arm. Private Charles Westerfield, Co. B, had a fractured thigh, which, however, was saved from the amputating blade. But the most terrible wound to look upon was that of private John W Slyter, Co. K. A ball had passed through his mouth, tearing it out at least one inch back on both sides, breaking out most of his teeth, and cutting the tongue down to the root, though the end still hung to its place, a helpless appendage. He survived the awful shock, and was afterwards transferred to the Invalid Corps, subsequently known as the Veteran Reserve. But time would fail us to specify even a hundredth part of the mutilation which was presented at the hospital on that terrible day. In the deep wilderness the battle was raging fiercely.

From the battle line to the hospital was constantly passing a train of ambulances laden with our suffering comrades, wounded in every conceivable manner from the crown of the head to the soles of the feet. Occasionally a groan escaped from some poor dying fellow, whose last word or little token of remembrance, such as a daily perused Testament, or cherished portrait, had been deposited with some more fortunate comrade to be sent to friends far away, to testify that even in death they were not forgotten. Remarkable, however, is the stillness of the hospital. How calmly the brave boys endure the wounds received in defense of their beloved country! How cheerfully even they approach the amputating table, to awake from the operation with the painful consciousness of loss of limbs, which no artificer can fully replace.

Now and then there comes from the battle field a wounded man who is able to walk, and who supports with one hand its bloody, mangled mate. At times, two men may be seen approaching, supporting between them their less fortunate companion, whose bloody garments tell that he had faced the foe. By every means possible our wounded were brought from the field of carnage to be cared for at the hospital, but in the vast multitude of disabled ones many were left, who afterwards suffered from fires which broke out and ran far and wide among the dry leaves of the woods.

The line of battle to-day was somewhat in the form of a horseshoe, General Grant having the inner circle. His headquarters, near General Meade's, were well up toward our extreme right. General Lee's attack was mostly on the extreme wings, but with greater fury on our left. Amid the roaring of the musketry, which continued till late at night, the regiment sought rest not a mile from the line of battle, near our left flank.

May 6th. The opening day looked on the renewal of the conflict. Each antagonist, rousing every slumbering element of power, seemed resolved upon victory or death. All day long they struggled for the mastery. So dense was the forest where they fought, that artillery could scarcely be used, and the lines of battle were only a few yards apart. About noon General Lee threw a heavy force upon our left with the design of turning our position. The onset was partially successful. The 9th corps (General Burnside's) received the shock, and was broken; but the repulse was only momentary. Bringing up his reserve and gathering his broken lines, the general hurled them against the exultant foe, driving him back, and regaining the ground which had been lost.

Gen. Lee, having failed upon our left, repeated the operation with redoubled fury, upon our right, just at night. His endeavor, for a time, gave promise of success. The old 6th corps, in which the utmost confidence had been placed by the commanding general, was posted in this important position. Notwithstanding its former prestige, it could not withstand the terrible blows that were dealt upon it. For a time, the rout that followed threatened disaster. General Grant's headquarters were soon within musket range of the advancing Rebels, and doubtless would have been removed to a safer place, had not the general "resolved to fight it out on this line." His band was quickly advanced in the woods as far as possible, where it struck up Yankee Doodle. Inspired by the notes, which sounded clearly on the evening air, our men were reformed, and, with a wild shout of battle, they charged the enemy, and drove him back to his former lines.

The regiment had been ordered from the left to the right wing, just in time to prevent the stragglers from our broken lines passing far to the rear. After our position was reëstablished we rested for the night.

May 7th. Early this morning, the following order was received:

HEAD QUARTERS, 6th Army Corps,
May 7th, 1864.

COL. HAMMOND, Commanding 5th N. Y. Cavalry:

Gen. Sedgwick directs (in accordance with orders from headquarters Army Potomac and General Grant) that you move forward and remain as far as possible near Germania Ford, and report immediately any movements of the enemy. Be sure that no force of the enemy crosses the plank road without notifying General Sedgwick at once.

By command of Major General Sedgwick,

C. A. WHITTEN,
Major and A. A. A. G.

The regiment marched to the ford on receiving the order, and picketed the road, with two other cavalry regiments, which we found posted on arriving. At 2 P. M. an attack was made with cavalry and light artillery, on the two regiments above mentioned. They broke and fled, exposing our left, thus compelling us also to fall back, which we did quite rapidly down the river, nearly as far as Ely's Ford. On our way toward the plank road again, at no great distance from the river, Colonel Hammond received another order.

HEAD QUARTERS, 6th Army Corps,
May 7th, 1864.

Commanding Officer of 22d N. Y. and 2d Ohio Cavalry:

You will report immediately to Lt. Col. Hammond, Fifth New York Cavalry, who is hereby ordered to take command of all the cavalry on the Germania plank road.

By command of Major General Sedgwick,

C. A. WHITTEN,
Major and A. A. A. G.

Having made such disposition of his command as was necessary to check any further advance of the enemy, Col. Hammond moved the regiment, near the spot where we bivouacked last night, arriving late. While we were cooking our suppers by our bivouac fires, suddenly the wilderness before us became vocal with deafening cheers, extending up and down our vast army lines. Lee had been outgeneraled, his lines driven back, his right almost broken, and Grant was prepared for his first left flank movement. Before we slept, still another important order was received.

HEAD QUARTERS, 6th Corps,
May 7th, 1864.

COL. HAMMOND, Commanding Cavalry:

You will please remain with your command near the old Wilderness Tavern, until you are notified by Maj. Gen. Hancock, that his corps and pickets are withdrawn. Gen. Hancock's pickets are to be withdrawn at 2 A. M. (two o'clock A. M.) Upon being so notified you will follow the 2d Corps.

By command of Major General Sedgwick,

C. A. WHITTEN,
Major and A. A. A. G.

May 8th. The night had been occupied in removing the wounded to Fredericksburg. But for want of transportation,—so great was the number of wounded,—a considerable number of the worst ones, who probably could not have borne the journey, and others, were left behind. A surgeon and a corps of nurses were ordered to remain with them. The remains of those hospitals presented one of the most sickening sights ever witnessed. Here were some recent dead, some dying, and some of the most mangled and torn which the battle leaves living. Resigned to their fate we left them to move forward to other scenes of conflict. As soon as we had fallen back they fell into the enemy's hands. About eight o'clock our rear guard left old Wilderness Tavern, and moved on to Chancellorsville, which became our extreme right wing.

May 9th. Sent out on a reconnoissance to Ely's Ford. Returned to Chancellorsville to bivouac at night.

May 10th. Our horses had long been denied their usual allowance,—in fact, we had been without grain for several days. We were compelled to search for the best grazing the country afforded, which we found near Mr. McGee's, on the Fredericksburg road. At night we were ordered on picket at the Old Foundry.

May 11th. Returned to McGee's to graze our horses and bivouac.

May 12th. Moved to Chancellorsville, and found grazing in the neighborhood. The fields and woods show signs of Hooker's great battle here a year ago. Bodies and bones of unburied men, and of those only partially buried, may be found on every hand.

May 14th. All these days the grand army has been fighting

about Spottsylvania Court House. Just at night the regiment marched through terrible mud and dark forests, near army headquarters, not far from Spottsylvania.

May 15th. The regiment was ordered to the extreme left. Grazed our horses near Massaponax Run, and advanced near the church that bears this name, where we had a slight brush with the enemy.

May 16th. Advanced beyond the church, and drove the enemy's cavalry across the Ny river, after a lively skirmish. A heavy force of the enemy was found on our front.

May 17th. The following order in General Meade's own handwriting was received and preserved:

Headquarters, Army of the Potomac,
1, 30 P. M., May 17th, 1864.

COL. HAMMOND, Fifth New York Cavalry:

Colonel: Your dispatch reporting a superior force of the enemy at Guineas Station received. I send you Lieut. Col. Chamberlain, 1st Massachusetts, with 1,200 men from Dismounted camp. You will take command of these men and endeavor to drive back the enemy's cavalry and destroy the depot at Guineas. Also advance on their right flank and ascertain all you can of the enemy's position and force.

Respectfully Yours,

GEO. G. MEADE,

Major General.

Among the men above mentioned were about one hundred and fifty of our veterans. This combined force advanced as ordered, and found the enemy strongly posted on the banks of the Po river. A severely contested engagement followed, in which we lost Capt. Bryant (captured, though at first supposed killed), and others. The main force returned to its bivouac, and the Fifth spent the night on picket.

May 18th. Another reconnoissance was made to the Po, where the enemy still continues in force. A short skirmish followed. Our men returned unhurt.

May 19th. Orders were received this afternoon to be ready to move at eleven at night. The column of cavalry, with a battery of artillery, moved out precisely at the hour, in the direction of Bowling Green. Having gone about four miles, the main column was countermarched, though the Fifth continued to near Fredericksburg, and returned, traveling all night.

May 20th. At noon our mail arrived, the first we have received since the campaign opened. There were at least two bushels of letters! And what eager boys waited for the home messages, as each company's mail was being sorted out! Scarcely a man but had a letter, and some had ten or twelve. A large mail was sent away before night. Orders were received this P. M. to be ready to move for the accomplishment of the task which was abandoned last night.

May 21st. Expecting to move in the night the men had sought an early sleep, as usual, upon the lap of earth, from which they were aroused about one o'clock, and were soon on the march. The night was pleasant. A few shots with scattered pickets were exchanged on the way, until we reached the Mattapony river, at a point below Guincas Station, where the road on which we were marching crosses the rail road. Here quite a force of the enemy made its appearance. The day had now dawned. The Fifth New

BURIAL OF SERGEANT S. W SORTORE.

"From the awful scenes of battle, brother,
You were set forever free :
When your comrades left you sleeping, brother,
Underneath that southern tree"

"Sleeping to waken
In this dreary world no more,
Sleeping for your true-loved country, brother
Sleeping for the flag you bore."

York had the advance. Flankers were sent out, and the advance guard was placed in command of 1st Sergt. S. W Sortore, Company E, who moved boldly forward. Entering the woods, which skirt the river, along whose banks runs the road to Bowling Green, another road was found turning to the right across the river, which the fleeing Rebels had taken. The sergeant advanced to cross the bridge, but found that a portion of it had been removed, rendering it impassable. He had no sooner halted, than a fatal bullet from a Rebel, concealed in the thicket beyond, pierced his manly breast. In less than fifteen minutes he was dead. Wrapped up in his blanket, we buried him under a beautiful swamp willow, only a few of his many friends being permitted to assist in his burial. While this was being done, the bridge had been rebuilt, companies A and B had been sent out to drive the Rebels back and picket this road, and the column had passed on toward Bowling Green. A short halt was made in this pleasant little village; and the column moved again to Milford Station, which was taken after a severe engagement. The regiment behaved handsomely in this fight, which resulted in the capture of six officers and sixty-six privates, and the dispersion of the entire force which guarded the station. In the depot were found some stores of the Rebel quartermaster and commissary, which were readily appropriated.

On the ground whence we had driven the enemy by hard fighting, we built our bivouac fires and rested.

May 22d. About 3 P. M. we were ordered to New Bethel Church, across the Mattapony, where we found excellent grazing for our horses.

May 23d. "Boots and saddles" sounded at three o'clock,

and by daylight the column was in motion, toward Hanover Junction. Not far from the North Anna river, just below Mt. Carmel Church, the enemy in force was encountered. A desperate fight ensued, which resulted in a general engagement, during which the Rebels were driven from their strong position along the North Anna. The battle continued till nine o'clock at night, ending with a terrible cannonade.

May 24th. We were ordered to the extreme right, where, after crossing the North Anna, we had a flying skirmish with the enemy's cavalry.

May 25th. The regiment reconnoitred the enemy's position on the Little river. Fell back from the river to the Virginia Central rail road, which our men are effectually destroying. The fire of the ties, culverts and bridges makes a line of lurid light along the evening sky.

May 26th. We rested in bivouac until about sundown, when we were joined by the division, just returned from Sheridan's great raid, which commenced with the opening of the campaign. At night we skirmished with the enemy at some of the upper fords of the Little river, and made a feint of crossing. To complete the deception, fences, boards, and everything inflamable within our reach, were set on fire to give the appearance of a vast force, just building its bivouac fires.

While we were thus making a feint of lively work on the right, and keeping the attention of the enemy, General Grant effected his third *left flank movement*, which brought his base of supplies at White House Landing.

After the accomplishment of our stratagem we fell back, crossed the North Anna river on a bridge, which we destroyed behind us, and bivouacked, about two hours past midnight.

May 27th. Three or four hours only had the weary boys to rest, and the bugles sounded the advance. Over vast plains, generally thickly wooded, the column passed, and, after seeing the smoking ruins of Chesterfield Station, it halted for another rest. As we travel from point to point over this Old Dominion we are peculiarly impressed with the vastness of its forests, which cover thousands of acres of as fine arable land as can be found upon the continent. How different is this from the impressions we had formed of Virginia when reading of its early settlement, and of its agricultural advantages. But when we look into its system of land owning — wherein we find one individual monopolizing a vast territory,—and into its worse system of labor, we need search no further for the causes of this backwardness in agricultural pursuits. Who does not sincerely hope that the time is at hand when the rich acres of this great state shall be more properly divided among its inhabitants, and, when freed from a burden and curse which has long paralyzed their energies, instinct with new life and enterprise, the people will realize the true dignity of labor. Then will the almost interminable forests disappear, and in their places the industrious yeoman will behold his rich fields of waving grain. Then too, along its now useless streams and swift water courses, will spring up the factory and the mill, whose fabrics will bring wealth and prosperity to the nation.

May 28th. Our march was resumed at an early hour, and continued as usual through vast woods, with only here and there a plantation. For want of forage and rest, many horses gave out by the way. It is wonderful how long these faithful animals carry their riders with their kit, even after overtaxation of muscles has nearly destroyed them. On they plod, fearful of being abandoned by their mates, until strength has entirely departed, and they quiver beneath their load, and would fall, if not relieved.

On a march like this, these "played out" horses are invariably shot, lest they might fall into the hands of the enemy, and, in a few weeks of care, become serviceable.

The column halted for the night at a small settlement called Mangohick, where a good rest was enjoyed.

May 29th. A pleasant march brought us at an early hour to Locust Grove, near the Pamunkey river. Some corn was foraged from the surrounding country for our horses.

May 30th. Gradually, by almost constant fighting, our noble army has been advancing through the enemy's country, until to-day our artillery is plunging its shells very near the door of the Rebel capitol. Our forces have taken possession of Mechanicsville, and established their lines not far from Cold Harbor.

About ten A. M. the regiment was detailed to march to Dunkirk, to guard a supply train, which was expected. The journey was performed and the train brought in before night.

May 31st. We moved early to Dabney's Ferry, where we crossed the Pamunkey on pontoons, and advanced toward Hanover Court House. The enemy's outer cavalry pickets were encountered at Signal Hill, whence they were driven, after a lively skirmish. Gen. Rosser, a Rebel cavalry chieftain, here took a prominent position against us, "fighting," in the language of his friends, "for his altars and his fires." His residence was in the neighborhood. So was also that of Gen. Wickham, another Rebel cavalryman. After scouting the neighborhood, and picketing the main roads, till dark, the whole division was moved toward Hanover Court House.

June 1st. The enemy strongly contested our advance, and quite a skirmish was fought at the Court House. In the early morning this force was driven, and the division moved on to Ashland Station on the Virginia Central rail road. The object of this move was to destroy the two rail road bridges across the South Anna river. The second brigade was sent to do this work of destruction, while the first was to engage the enemy. The plan succeeded, but a fierce battle was fought at Ashland, by the first brigade. Several times our boys were partially surrounded; but the ceaseless fire of their carbines and the grape and canister of the artillery, mowed fearful gaps in the enemy's lines, and strewed the ground with slain. While gallantly riding up and down our lines, directing the operations and encouraging the men, Major White, of the Fifth, received a dangerous wound through the body, which was feared would prove fatal to his valuable life. Col. Hammond received a bullet, which flattened upon his scabbard, but cracked the bone just above the ankle joint. It was a narrow escape. When the force fell back, Dr. Armstrong volunteered to remain with Major White, who could not be removed. This noble act was never forgotten. Crowned with recent victory the division returned to Signal Hill, and bivouacked.

June 2d. After so hard fighting and marching the boys very naturally expected a little rest. Well, they got a little, and a *very little* rest it was. The time for an abundance of that luxury had not yet come. The day was spent broiling under a scorching sun. At 5 P. M., just as rain began to fall, the bugles sounded for another move. Compelled to throw away preparations for supper, which could not be taken, we were soon in line waiting the word to march. The rain fell faster, and a cold wind arose, which made the prospect of a march through mud and darkness rather unpleasant. But wrapped up carefully in our rubber coats or ponchoes, the soldier's invaluable garments, from which rolled the rain drops that pattered upon us, we were kept comfortably dry and in tolerably good humor. However, the march was a hard one. We moved to Dabney's Ferry, and turned to the right down the river, arriving at Linney's, where we stopped, about 12 o'clock that night.

June 3d. About 10 A. M. firing was heard in the direction of Salem Church, and messengers soon announced that the Rebel cavalry had advanced and attacked our pickets. The division was immediately moved to the scene of action, and the Rebels were again beaten and repulsed in a fair open field fight. They had the advantage of some hastily constructed breastworks, from which our men drove them with a charge. In this fight was killed the gallant Col. Preston, of the 1st Vermont; and Col. Chamberlain, of the 8th New York, was wounded. The regiment spent the night on picket.

June 4th. After we were relieved from picket, this morning, we bivouacked on an eminence called Mt. Pisgah. Here a large mail was received.

June 6th. We have passed these few days pleasantly. Our horses are improving on newly brought forage, and the men rejoice in full rations. Bands of music have entertained us with patriotic airs during our evening hours, and we have gained new strength and inspiration for coming labors.

Reveillé was sounded about daylight, and the regiment was marched to Old Church, whence we were sent to picket along the Pamunkey.

June 7th. Continued all day on picket. The lines are quiet and our work is pleasant.

June 8th. Relieved from picket by the 3d New Jersey Cavalry, a regiment that has quite recently been assigned to our brigade. The regiment moved near brigade headquarters, and went into camp.

June 10th. The whole brigade was called out this afternoon to repel an attack upon the pickets. After a brief skirmish, the lines were reëstablished and the brigade returned into camp. A brigade of colored troops occupy Old Church. They have fortified themselves with strong and beautifully constructed earthworks. They are fine appearing soldiers.

June 11th. The brigade was aroused by an early reveillé, and moved out toward Cold Harbor. At Shady Grove the enemy's infantry was encountered, charged and driven into their earthworks. Our boys behaved gallantly in the charge, some of them urging their horses over the fortifications. A few of them never returned. The regiment was in camp again about noon. The few days past have presented signs of another flank movement.

June 12th. We were ordered on picket about three miles from Old Church.

June 13th. We began to withdraw our pickets about two o'clock this morning, and an advance guard was pushed to

Allen's Mill. By daylight the whole brigade concentrated there, and moved on through woods and fields, over deserted camps and fortifications, making but a short halt for breakfast. A few prisoners were captured by our advance and flankers. At noon we halted again a few minutes near Hopkin's Mill on Black Creek. Our march was continued across the Richmond and York river rail road, between Dispatch and Summit Stations, and, about sundown, we crossed the sluggish Chickahominy, on pontoons, at Long Bridge. One can never forget the sombre appearance of the dense and gigantic forest through which we passed, known as the White Oak swamps. This name can never be spoken without a shudder by those who have campaigned it long in these malarious woods.

When night came on we were ordered to be rear guard of a large train. And, Oh! deliver cavalry from such a job as this, especially when the roads are almost impassable, and in the night. Our progress was exceedingly slow, and had it been steady it would have been more tolerable. But it was halt, advance, halt, advance, with this variety occurring at every five or ten rods, and the halts were frequently much longer than the advances. To relieve the tired horses, when a halt occurred, some men would dismount, and sinking to the ground through exhaustion, would quickly fall asleep. With the utmost difficulty they were aroused when the column moved. Others slept in their saddles, either leaning forward on the pommel of the saddle, or sitting quite erect, with an occasional bow forward, or to the right or left, like the swaying of the flag on a signal station. The horse of such a sleeping man will generally keep his place in the column, and the man will very seldom fall; though occasionally this will happen, and the poor fellow awakes only to find himself deep-set into a mud hole, while general merriment is produced among the beholders. As no one is hurt, the man is soon remounted, and the journey pursued.

With all these experiences we traveled until after midnight, and finally bivouacked and sought rest.

June 14th. Four hours' rest was all we got, not half what weary men needed. But to the bugle's shrill call every one must answer. After a very hasty meal the march was again resumed, and we finally halted at Charles City Court House, in sight of the flags and tents of army headquarters. While resting here, by the crumbling walls and chimneys of once opulent and tasty dwellings, we read in the scorched trees and in the general desolation, a few pages of Rebellion's record of sorrow. Having grazed our horses, and received forage and rations, we moved back to St. Mary's church, where we bivouacked about eleven o'clock at night. So near to us were the pickets of the enemy that we were ordered to build no fires, and the boys ate their supper without the usual coffee.

June 15th. The division moved by daybreak toward the White Oak swamps. Just beyond Smith's store, in the edge of the swamps, a strong column of Rebel infantry was encountered. So masterly had been conducted this flank movement across the James river, that the Rebels were deceived as to its object. Expecting that a strong force would advance on Richmond by way of Malvern Hills, on the north side of the James, they had sent a corresponding force to meet it. It was this force which we met. A hotly contested battle followed. Engaged with numbers far greater than our own, and infantry at that, we suffered a heavy loss and were compelled to fall back, which we did in good order, bringing most of our dead and wounded from the field. At St. Mary's Church was established a hospital, and in the fields and woods adjoining, the division went into bivouac. A heavy picket line was thrown out in the direction of the swamps.

June 16*th*. The regiment was detailed on picket this morning, where it remained all day. At night all the pickets were withdrawn, and the division was moved to Wyanoke Landing on the James, where we arrived after a long, toilsome march, a few hours before day.

CHAPTER IX.

Crossing the James River.— Pleasant Scene.— The Wilson Raid.— First Day.— Battle of Nottoway Court House.— The Danville Rail road.— What we Destroyed.— The Contrabands.— Battle of Reams Station.— The Swift Retreat.— Awful Scenes.— The Author's Personal Adventures.— Is Dismounted in the Woods.— Travels by Night and Rests by Day.— Narrow Escapes.— Assisted by Negroes.— Reaches our Lines Safely.— Casualties of the Raid.— The Division Ships for Geisboro' Point, D. C.— *June 17th to August 9th*, 1864.

June 17th. After about three hours' rest we were started on the march again, and about a mile below Wyanoke, and a little above Fort Powhatan, the division crossed the James on a pontoon bridge. This was as pleasant a scene as we had ever witnessed. The broad, smooth river, the crafts of various kinds which had collected at this point and floated so quietly on the water, the long bridge, which, swayed by the current of the stream, formed a gentle, graceful curve, the long lines of cavalry slowly moving to the opposite shore, and, poured over all, the glad sunshine of the Sabbath morning, presented a scene so much in contrast to those rough experiences, through which we had just passed, that every one was delighted. A short rest was enjoyed on the southern bank, during which were issued forage and rations. At three P. M. under a sweltering sun, our march was resumed in the direction of Petersburg. Great destruction of property was visible on the march. People, frightened by the advance of the Yankee army, had forsaken their houses and fled. Such places were destroyed. Had the inhabitants remained at home, the houses, at least, would not have been molested. About sundown we passed Prince George Court House and bivouacked about two miles beyond. With great difficulty the boys obtained water for their coffee, most of them being compelled to take it from the tracks of the horses where they had been led to watering, in the swamps near by.

June 18th. The division moved early, in a southeasterly direction, to the region of the Black Water swamps. The regiment was sent on picket not far from Mt. Sinai Church. As the country abounded in milk, honey, corn, wheat, meat and sorghum, the command lived well.

June 21st. These days have been spent quietly on picket. This afternoon an order was issued to prepare to move early to-morrow morning.

June 22d. About three o'clock A. M. Gen. Wilson's division, reënforced by Gen. Kautz's brigade of cavalry with fourteen pieces of flying artillery, including two mountain howitzers, was ready for a raid. At a rapid rate, principally through by-paths, and unfrequented ways, to avoid any force of the enemy, the command advanced, striking the Weldon rail road at Reams Station. Here the depot and about a mile of track were destroyed. This work was quickly done, and we moved on in a westerly course to Dinwiddie Court House, where we turned our faces northward. At Gravelly Run a short halt was made and our horses were watered. About sundown the Southside rail road was reached a little west of Sutherlands, and destruction of ties, rails, culverts, bridges, &c., began in earnest. The night was soon illuminated by the destroying fires. Our march now lay along the rail road, and was continued as far as Ford's, where we halted about eleven P. M., after capturing two trains, one passenger and one freight. The engines, having been set on fire by means of rails and boards piled around them, made the night hideous with their unearthly shrieks, which continued for several hours, disturbing the rest, which, weary and sleepy, we sought in vain to enjoy.

June 23d. At early light we were on the move again, engaged in the work of destruction. The great heat and drought were very favorable to our enterprise, though men and beasts suffered much for the want of water. A few rails or sticks of wood laid along the track and ignited, sufficed to make the destruction complete. Here and there the road was torn up, the ties heaped together and set on fire, while the iron rails were laid crosswise upon the burning piles. They were thus effectually destroyed. Telegraph posts were cut down, and the wire was twisted and broken. One regiment after another was detailed to perform this labor, and such was the wisdom of the arrangement, that the main column was not impeded in its progress, while the work was going on. Uninterrupted in our progress, we advanced, beyond Blacks and Whites, crossed the Little Nottoway creek, and encountered the enemy in pretty strong force, not far from Nottoway Court House. Intent on harassing our column, the enemy engaged us with spirit and determination. The battle continued until about eleven P. M. The regiment was on the skirmish line and fought with its usual vigor. While the main force of the enemy was here engaged, a feebler attack was made on our rear guard at Blacks and Whites. Meanwhile, Gen. Kautz, who had been detached during the night from the main column at Ford's, had made a successful detour around the enemy, who vainly supposed he was fighting the whole force of raiders at Nottoway, and without opposition, was destroying the junction of rail roads at Burkesville. Thus far Gen Wilson's plans had worked admirably, and success followed in our train.

June 24th. As our object was not to fight the enemy unless compelled to do so for defense, and, having driven him as far from our line of march as suited our purpose, we abandoned this road, and struck out through the country by Hungrytown, and reached the Danville rail road at Meherrin Station about four o'clock P. M. Here Gen. Kautz rejoined the division, and the whole force bent its energies to the destruction of this important thoroughfare. The work was comparatively easy, owing to the peculiar construction of the road. Across the ties a heavy timber, generally of pine, is notched in and fastened, upon which lie the rails,—thin pieces of iron similar to the tire of a heavy wagon wheel. The labor of tearing up and burning could be done in half the time it would take on the ordinary roads. Decidedly encouraged by such advantages, the boys applied themselves faithfully to the accomplishment of their task. Every foot of the road was destroyed from Meherrin to Keysville, where we arrived about eleven P. M. and bivouacked.

June 25th. The Keysville depot and a store near by it were burned this morning. The day has been very warm. Many horses "played out" by the way. They were invariably shot, and replaced by horses and mules captured in the country. Scouting parties and flankers are constantly replenishing the column with installments of fresh, fat animals, which the people have not the time or adroitness to hide from the swift-moving Yankees. This afternoon our advance, commanded by Gen. Kautz, reached the Staunton river, and made a desperate assault upon the force guarding the rail road bridge. For a time there was a promise of success, and our men took possession of the bridge, but before the torch could be effectually applied they were compelled to fall back before murderous discharges of grape and canister from a Rebel battery. The project of destroying this valuable bridge had to be abandoned. In the vicinity of Roanoke Station, the division bivouacked late at night.

June 26th. Up to this time, including Roanoke Station, we had burned ten important stations, and several smaller depots. About fifty miles of rail road track, including several bridges and culverts, had been completely destroyed. Though we had lost many horses, our numbers were made good from our captures by the way. Our column had been reënforced by hundreds of contrabands, who flocked to our banners from the country far and near. Our loss of men had been very slight, and mostly in wounded and captured. Our train had been enlarged by the addition of several fine carriages and barouches, in which our worst cases of sick and wounded were carried. Our *tout ensemble* was encouraging, and though far out in the enemy's country, hopes were entertained of a safe and speedy return. From Roanoke Station the column moved before daylight, in a southeasterly direction, by Wylliesburgh, and thence to Christianville, a fine little village, where was found a great abundance of corn for our horses. From this place our course was directly "facing the east," and about eleven P M. we halted for rest along a nearly dried up stream called Buckhorn creek.

June 27th. Our journey was resumed early, and at ten A. M. we crossed the Meherrin river at Stafford's Bridge. Our course bearing a little to the north, brought us at night, after receiving a refreshing shower, in the vicinity of Sturgeonville, where we halted

June 28th. As usual we were in the saddle before the dawn, and on our march homeward. About twelve M. we crossed the Nottoway river at Double Bridges. Our course now became a little more northward, and contrabands flocked to us in unusual numbers. There was no end of the interesting tales they had to tell, which, at times, excited our admiration, and then incited to tears. To us most of them came destitute of all things, except the *hope of liberty.* This was the circle of all their thoughts. For this the gray-haired slave, bending with the infimities of many toilsome years, was "toting" his grandchild on his arm and on his head by turns, along the column. The mother, with her young babe clinging to her breast, traveled through the woods and brush, the heat and dust, hoping for better days. Young men and maidens, with more of the European than the African in their features and complexion, plodded on their way, happy to be among those whom they recognized as their deliverers.

At night the column encountered a heavy force of Rebel infantry at Stony Creek Station on the Weldon rail road. All night the battle raged fiercely, with only now and then an interval of rest. Those who were not engaged on the battle line were compelled to stand to horse, and to shiver with the cold, which was peculiarly felt in that locality. It was an awful night of fatigue and doubt.

June 29th. Before the dawn of day Gen. Wilson moved forward such a portion of his force as he thought might be spared from the skirmish line, leaving the second brigade to bring up the rear. The enemy made a desperate charge on this brigade, which threatened it with annihilation. A large number fell into the enemy's hands, and the remainder were thrown into much confusion, but escaped. About ten A. M. the whole command was within three or four miles of Reams Station, on ground made familiar by our outward passage just one week previous. It was hoped that assistance would be rendered us by our main army, as we were not far from its left wing. This had been promised us by Gen. Meade. But assistance failed to come in time.

Regiments were deployed to ascertain the position and strength of the enemy. It was soon found that he was not only able to resist our passage, but also to surround and annihilate us if we remained long within his reach. At noon orders were issued to abandon the entire train. Forges and wagons were burned, and the ambulance train was parked near the banks of Rowanty creek, and hospital flags placed over it. All wounded and sick who could ride were mounted; all others must be left behind. It was a sad hour. Never had the boom of cannon sounded more solemnly.

The advance of the retreating column moved about one mile from the ambulances and there awaited orders. The road was literally packed, and for rods in the woods on either side, wherever a man could ride, was a mass of human beings with anxious, throbbing hearts. About three o'clock

Gen. Wilson passed through the column, though it was difficult to make a way for him, and as soon as he reached the front the entire crowd moved forward. What followed cannot be described. Think of such a force of cavalry, at the utmost speed of their horses, over a road with six inches of dust in places, on one of the warmest, sultriest days! There, too, were the contrabands mostly dismounted, men, women and children, who knew that to be captured was death, or worse than death! It was well, perhaps, that the blinding dust should partially hide the scene from view.

No halt was made until we came to Stony creek, a distance of five or six miles from Rowanty. Here the creek is quite deep, and the banks rocky and precipitous. The bridge is very narrow. It was hoped that no heavy force of the enemy had followed us. The scattered fragments of regiments were called together, with design to hold the bridge. The men were almost completely demoralized, at least one third having either thrown away or lost their arms in the flight. Scarcely had the work of reorganization been completed, when the pursuing foe, with cavalry and artillery, came upon us. We were in no condition to resist him, though some men fought bravely. Panic-stricken, nearly all soon broke ranks, and fled as best they could. And such a sight! Down the steep banks of the creek, men urged their weary steeds, until they fell headlong into the splashing water. Some were pushed off the bridge, falling on others in the stream. Men and horses mingled in almost every conceivable shape, struggled to reach the opposite bank, while bullets whizzed among the trees, and shells screamed over our heads. (Diverging from the main tenor of this narrative at this point, the author wishes to give a few days of personal adventures and experiences. He is constrained to do this, as it will represent, in the main, the experience of hundreds of others).

Driving down as far as my horse would go without falling, I dismounted, and, as I knew the animal could not carry me much further on account of exhaustion and lameness, I concluded to leave him. Down the crevice of the rocks near the water's edge, I reached a retreat safe from falling horses and flying bullets, and, for a moment, thought, *I will surrender*. But I had tasted the prisoner's bitter cup, and I resolved to go forward so long as I could put one foot before the other. I stepped into the stream, with water to my waist. Near the opposite bank the water was deeper, and, striking a slimy log on the bottom, I fell prone into it. Struggling toward the shore, the branch of an overhanging tree caught my hat and flung it down the stream. At length upon dry ground I stood, a sorry picture of a sorry Yankee, weak from exhaustion, heavy with water in my clothes and boots, and hatless! Raising my right foot by the toe of my big boot, I poured out the water at the knee, and while endeavoring to do the same thing with my left boot, I beheld a large riderless bay horse, rising from the creek and coming toward me. I seized him by the bridle and mounted into the saddle, joining the column with new hope.

This horse belonged to the 1st District of Columbia cavalry, as I knew by the sixteen shooter that he carried. I had not gone far before I discovered that he was nearly exhausted, and would soon give out. While reflecting on my own wretchedness, I saw a man a little to the left of the column, riding a mule that had neither saddle nor bridle, and the man himself had nothing on but an army shirt! I was compelled to laugh in spite of myself, and soon became willing to be hatless and destitute. I had cut away all the baggage from the saddle, to make the burden of my horse as light as possible. However, on arriving near Sappony creek, he failed me completely. Two men of the regiment, Charles T. S. Pierce, company G, and Oscar L. Barden, company B, were near me at the time. Their horses were nearly in the condition of mine. We resolved to share each other's fate, to leave the column, and on foot, by night marches, to reach our lines if possible. We were in a dense forest. Imploring Divine aid in our hazardous journey, we moved about a mile from the road, and stopped for the night among thick bushes. We heard the rear of our column as it passed Sappony bridge, we also heard the pursuers, who fired into the woods in every direction, but we were quiet and safe.

June 30th. We suffered from the chill of the night. The day has been spent in Wood-tick bivouac, so named from the numberless wood-ticks that have infested the place. Nothing but a wild pig, with which these forests abound, came near our resting place. We are not much burdened with luggage, having but one overcoat, two ponchoes, two haversacks and one canteen. I have a good map, but we have no compass. We have also matches and ink. I carry my journal and Greek Testament, Pierce carries a Bible and Hymn book and Barden has thread and needles. Our store of eatables consists of about a half pint of rice, a quarter pound of coffee and sugar mixed (no cup to cook these in), five pounds of flour and a little salt.

As soon as night came on we began to travel, guided by

the stars, which here and there peeped through the thick foliage of the forest. Our course was northeast. At eleven o'clock we came to Sappony creek, which we crossed yesterday. Bad as was the water, we drank of it freely, having had but one canteen of water since yesterday about seven P. M. Here we mixed about half of our flour into dough. Fearful that if we built a fire we might be discovered by the scouting parties that were hunting for us, we repaired to a deep ravine, skirted with many bushes, where we made a small fire of dry sticks and leaves, on which we laid our dough which was smoked and charred horribly. This was our only staff of life, and all we had to eat for nearly forty-eight hours. Thus ended with us the month of June on the banks of the muddy Sappony.

July 1st. About one o'clock A. M. we crossed the Sappony on a fallen tree. We afterward traveled as rapidly as we could, through swamps, tangled brushwood and briars, occasionally through a field, until daylight, when we sought the shelter of tall, thick-grown brackberry briars, in the edge of a field. At nine o'clock P. M. we came out of our hiding and resting place, and moved on as the night before. Emerging from a thick wood, we came upon a herd of cows in a yard, where we vainly sought to get some milk. As they were doubtless accustomed to be milked by women, as are cows generally in Virginia, we could not approach them. Following a footpath we found a cherry tree with cherries, which relished well. But we had no sooner commenced regaling ourselves, than a tall, heavy, shadowy man dressed in light gray, was moving toward us up the path. On discovering us he moved away rapidly. We traveled on probably quite as rapidly as he, as we soon saw that the neighborhood had been alarmed. Lights were seen at the houses, and dogs made hideous howlings. With terrible pictures of blood-hounds before our thoughts, we quickened our steps. This danger passed, and we were thankful; and our joy was still more increased, when, led by the voice of singing frogs, we found excellent water in a field. On leaving this place of refreshing we entered the woods under a beautiful arch of foliage and soon came to Stony creek. Laying aside our garments, and rolling them up in tight bundles, we crossed safely over. The water was about four and a half feet deep.

July 2d. About three A. M. we came in sight of several picket fires just ahead of us. We flanked them by turning to the left. At daybreak we came into a large field, and sought refuge in a thicket, though not far from a house. We had but just fallen asleep, when we were aroused by footsteps approaching and voices distinctly heard. Soon the black faces of two slaves appeared through the bushes. This gave us hope. One of them afterward disappeared, the other continued coming toward us. Before he had seen us, I spoke at a high whisper, "come here," when his big black eye, with its surrounding pure white, fell excitedly upon us.

"You're not afraid of Yankee soldiers, are you?" I interrogated.

"Oh, no, massa," and he walked up by our side.

"What's your name?"

"Tom."

"Tom what? Have you no other name?"

"Dunno, massa, dey allers calls me Tom."

"Well, who lives here?

"Major Malone, whose son is in the Rebel army."

"How far is it to Reams Station?"

"Two miles an' half."

We now saw that we were in a critical position, within the Rebel army lines, and on the premises of a prominent Rebel. From Tom we learned that Rebel soldiers frequently came to the house during the day, though not generally at night. He promised to get us some bread, which he did, for which we gave him some money. He also promised to guide us at night across a ford of Rowanty creek, by a way that would soon lead us across the Weldon rail road. The time set for starting was nine o'clock. During the day several cavalrymen were seen passing on the road, which, at one point, was visible to us, and, at one time, a cavalryman rode directly toward us, stopping only a few paces from us. We could hear the breathings of his horse, as we lay almost breathless, on the ground. In this condition we longed for the night. It came at length, but with it came no Tom, for what reason we never learned. This was a sore disappointment.

July 3*d*. Having waited for Tom, in vain, until after midnight, we finally started, guided only by the stars. Rowanty creek was soon reached, but at a place so wide and apparently deep, that we durst not undertake to ford. We followed it, until day brought us into a large, muddy dismal swamp. We crossed as we had done at Stony creek. After retiring in the depths of the swamp, we kindled a fire at the roots of an ancient oak, and cooked the last flour we had into bread. Until evening we remained in the swamp, disturbed now and then by the cries of wild hogs, eagles and foxes. When darkness came we moved out of the woods, passed by a farm house, and, having crossed a well traveled road, arrived at the Weldon rail road. This was at a deep cut, where we could not cross. A picket fire could be distinctly seen at our left. Rapidly we followed the road to the right, until, coming to a depression in the bank, we slid down to the track below. We now found the opposite bank too steep and high to climb. Undaunted, we moved on along the track, and found a place, where, by means of bushes and roots of trees, we got out of this dangerous spot. After traveling a few hours the heavens became overcast with clouds, and we were compelled to advance by guess, and finally to stop altogether.

July 4th. We had waited for the morning sun in vain, for clouds so obscured the light as to render the points of the compass very doubtful. However, as we had lost time during the night, we concluded to travel as best we could. Along a swamp we found some ripe berries, which we enjoyed. We had not marched long before two Rebel soldiers were seen advancing in a path that would intersect ours at no great distance. We were quickly hidden under the bushes, which abounded. While the boys slept I made a short reconnoissance, in which I ascertained that we were only a stone's throw from the Weldon rail road again, and near the picket post, whose fire it was probable we had seen the night before. Cautiously we moved out of this place, and continued through the woods to a plantation. In a cornfield a negress was at work. Of her we inquired for direction. Said I, "which way is east?"

"Dunno, massa."

"Which way is west?"

A like answer.

"Well, where does the sun rise?"

"There," pointing with her finger.

Her master's name was John Slay. Beyond that she seemed to know very little.

Our next point of interest was the Jerusalem Plank Road. While standing in the edge of the woods, consulting as to whether it were best to travel much more by day, out rode from the thick forest a cavalryman, whose gingling sabre and accoutrements bespoke danger to unarmed men. He rode quite rapidly by, within three rods of us, and we rejoiced to have escaped his observation. As he disappeared we lost no time in seeking a quiet, secluded spot, where we waited for the night. Night came on with bright stars, and we journeyed joyfully. At nine P. M. we arrived at another plantation. A light was seen through the crevices of a log shanty, and the low voices from within were taken for those of negroes. I knocked at the door, and a voice said, "come in." Opening the low door, I invited a pure African out, and learned that there were none but slaves present. With haste the women began to prepare us some supper, while we waited without. We were soon invited in, and sat down to a dish of fried pork and corn bread hot from the ashes, to which we did ample justice. This was the first meat we had tasted since the morning of June 29th. After supper we paid them well, their eyes sparkling with delight. From them I obtained a hat. The faithful man Alison then guided us through Jones' Hole Swamp, and we crossed the Jerusalem Plank Road near Dr. Proctor's. Alison then left us, wishing us all prosperity, and returned to his master, Fred Raines.

July 5th. We traveled some during the morning at the

right of the plank road, and rested but little during the day. At sundown we made inquiries of some colored people, and of a Union white man, a rare article in that part of Virginia, who informed us that our pickets were only about three miles ahead of us near Lee's Mills, and that the country abounded with guerrillas. We were cautioned to keep in the woods and avoid the road. When darkness came, we advanced. Weary of briars and bushes, on reaching the road, we followed it, carefully watching every suspicious object. Soon something was seen moving ahead of us, which was afterward discovered to be a man. Hoping it might be one of our own men, we quickened our footsteps, and on overtaking him, what was our surprise to find him to be a Rebel soldier, with his musket on his shoulder. My first thought was: this is doubtless a guerrilla, and though alone, by a whistle or other signal, up will spring from the thick bushes along the way as many helpers as he desires. However, I knew that alone he could not harm us materially, as we walked up by his side, so near that he could not take his musket down, before we could seize him. On approaching him, he turned his head about, and said, "You're Yankees, I reckon." We made no reply but walked on in sad silence. On making a turn in the road we came in sight of several fires. I broke the oppressive silence by saying, "There's a Yankee camp, I think." "Yes," replied the stranger, "and there's a Yankee picket just ahead of us, and I am going to give myself up to them as a prisoner." The vail was at once lifted from our prospect, and we entered into a friendly conversation. I found that he belonged to the 2d North Carolina cavalry, and had come from Reams Station, since our fight there. While conversing together, we suddenly came to a stop, at the cry: "Halt! Who comes there?" "Friends," cried I. We were soon safely, with our Rebel friend, within the lines of the 3d New Jersey cavalry, where we found old acquaintances, and received all proper attention.

Almost completely exhausted, we were gladly welcomed to the leafy abodes of our old comrades, where we enjoyed full rations and undisturbed sleep.

July 8th. We reached the regiment, encamped near Light House Point, this afternoon. From them we learned that June 29th, Gen. Wilson retreated south to Jarrett's Station, crossed the rail road, then by an east, northeast, north course, reached our lines after two or three days. Gen. Kautz, more familiar with the country, struck through the woods north of Stony creek, reaching our lines the morning of the 30th. The loss of the command was nearly one thousand men (mostly captured), with the whole artillery and train. Nothing was saved that went on wheels. The loss is less than had been feared, as many, who were accounted lost, afterward came in as did the writer of these lines.

July 12th. As it needed it, the cavalry has been recruiting its energies in quiet camps for several days. However, many of our men were disabled by the raid and have been sent to hospitals, and many dismounted fellows have gone to Camp Stoneman, at Geisboro' Point, D. C. These latter, numbering a little less than one hundred, were engaged in those memorable battles and skirmishes with the Rebel invaders of Maryland and the District of Columbia, commencing with the battle of Maryland Heights, July 6th, and ending with the battle of Kernstown, the 24th, at which time Col. Mulligan was killed.

What remained of the regiment with the division, was sent out at half past three P. M., to picket along Powell's creek at Cooke's Mill, several miles down the river. This duty was very easy.

July 15*th*. We were relieved from picket, and returned to camp again near Light House Point.

July 25*th*. The brigade moved at dusk, to the picket lines at the Gurley House, nearly south of Petersburg. The regiment went on duty, after arriving, establishing its lines nearly parallel with the Weldon rail road. We found the Rebel pickets very quiet and friendly, and a pleasant intercourse was enjoyed.

July 30*th*. The dawn was ushered in with a terrible explosion and cannonade, making the earth tremble beneath our feet. To these was added a rapid musketry. Expecting an attack, the cavalry withdrew its pickets, and made preparation for any emergency. The enemy did not make his appearance on our front. Our infantry lines were engaged for several hours, but the great mine explosion ended very disastrously to our cause, with a loss of many men. We returned on picket at night.

August 1*st*. We were relieved from picket, and went into camp near brigade headquarters.

August 5*th*. For some days the first division of cavalry has been leaving this department, and taking transports for Camp Stoneman, District of Columbia. This morning the third division received orders to march to City Point, where we were embarked on transports, with our horses. This was a slow, toilsome job. It was nine o'clock P. M. before we were aboard.

August 6*th*. The men have enjoyed the day's sail, down

the James, up Chesapeake Bay and the Potomac, to Kettle Bottom, where we cast anchor for the night.

August 7th. We weighed anchor at early light, and about three P. M. we were landed at Geisboro' Point. We went into camp near Camp Stoneman.

August 9th. The boys were made glad by the presence of the paymaster and his greenbacks. Our time is mostly occupied in exchanging our poor horses for good ones, and remounting our dismounted men. This looks like work ahead for the cavalry.

CHAPTER X.

To the Shenandoah Valley. — Exciting Scene in Snicker's Gap. — Battle of Summit Point. — Battle of Kearneysville Station. — Crossing into Maryland. — Old John Brown air in Charlestown. — Skirmishes near the Opcquan. — Battle of Winchester. — Drive the Enemy through Front Royal. — Up Luray Valley. — Raid to Staunton and Waynesboro'. — Cavalry Fight at Tom's Brook. — Battle of Cedar Creek. — Sheridan's Ride. — Unparalleled Captures by the Regiment. — Gen. Custer's Congratulatory Order. — Reconnoissance to Rood's Hill. — Spirited Engagement near Mt. Jackson. — Regiment Detailed Escort of General Sheridan. — The Fruit of Sheridan's Work in the Valley. — *August 12th to December 31st,* 1864.

August 12th. Orders were issued to the division, to be ready to move at sundown to its new field of duty. At the appointed hour the bugles were ringing clearly, and the rested cavalrymen were soon gladly on the march. It was after nine o'clock before these well equipped and thoroughly disciplined squadrons had traversed the streets of the nation's capital, laden with the hopes of every loyal heart. We were now to enter upon a field of operations the glory of which would eclipse all that the cavalry had yet accomplished.

Until eleven o'clock we continued our march up the Potomac to Chain Bridge, where we crossed into Virginia again, and bivouacked about three miles from the river.

August 13th. Before daylight the regiment was detailed

to escort Col. Chipman, a dispatch bearer to General Sheridan in the Shenandoah Valley. Great speed was necessary, and the regiment moved accordingly. The line of march led us through Drainesville, Leesburg, Hamilton, Purcelville and Snicker's Gap. A very brief halt was made near Goose creek, where we forded in pretty deep water. Near Leesburg a slight attack was made on our rear guard by a squad of White's guerrillas, who were easily dispersed

Before reaching Snicker's Gap, we were informed by the inhabitants, that Mosby with a strong force was in the vicinity. We expected to meet him in the gap. It was night, and not a breath of air stirred the heavy foliage of the trees. No sound was heard save the song of the katydid and the heavy tramp of our horses on the hard road. The moon shone brightly, flooding the mountain tops with her silvery beams. The woods wore that sombre, weird appearance, so often spoken of in fairy tales. Our feelings were doubly excited by the expectation, that from the shady nooks or dark crevices of the rocks, would flash the deadly weapons of our enemy. But our passage was performed without meeting him. From the summit of the gap, the Shenandoah Valley, filled with the hazy light of the moon, presented a scene that was perfectly enchanting. We forded the broad, shining Shenandoah river, at Snicker's Ferry. Near Berryville we saw the burning remains of a supply train which Mosby had captured and destroyed that day. We entered within our lines near the Opequan creek, and, tired and sleepy, we halted about three A. M. within two miles of Winchester. This was the longest march ever performed by the regiment in the same time: we had traveled about seventy-five miles in twenty-two hours.

August 14th. This afternoon we moved through Winchester, to Milltown, and camped near the creek.

August 16th. Reveillé sounded before daylight, and, breaking camp, at sunrise, we moved to Berryville. Here we joined the division, with which we moved toward Ashby's Gap, marching till midnight.

August 17th. Moved through White Post, and back to Winchester. Gen. Sheridan's army was falling back from Cedar creek. The third division was detailed to picket the main roads, which centre at Winchester and to bring up the rear of the army. The Fifth was sent on the Romney pike to Petticoat Gap. The picketing was quiet until dark. The Rebels now advanced upon us at nearly every point. From a high hill near Milltown, our artillery opened upon the advancing column of the enemy. In consequence of our line's retreating on the Valley pike, before we could be apprised of the fact, the Rebels entered the town, thus flanking us completely. No time was lost, however, in falling back over the hills, northwest of town, passing through the embankments of Fort Milroy. We rejoined our forces on the plains below, and together we continued retreating toward Summit Point, on a dirt road, east of the pike. About midnight we halted for rest not far from Wadesville.

August 18th. The column was set in motion early, and a heavy rain came down upon us. The division halted at Summit Point, and the regiment was sent back to picket along the Opequan.

August 19th. Our boys on picket were attacked by a strong party of Rebel cavalry, and forced back nearly two miles. Reënforcements were sent out and the Rebel advance was checked.

August 20th. Relieved from picket, and bivouacked near Summit Point. The lines were quiet.

August 21st. As has been so often the case on the Sabbath, it was not possible to pass the day without an engagement. About eight o'clock our pickets were driven in, and at nine a strong force of infantry and cavalry confronted us at the Point. Boldly they came out of the woods into an open field, and flaunted their miserable flag into our faces. But a well directed shell from our artillery, which exploded among them, sent them "kiting" to the woods again. However, a force far superior to ours in numbers compelled us at length to retreat, which we did in good order. We arrived at Charlestown about sundown, but left the village to our right, and halted in the fields almost in sight of the steeples of its churches. Here we found our infantry also falling back, with its main column headed toward Halltown.

August 22d. Our horses, which had stood all night saddled and ready for a move at a moment's warning, were in use with the first light of morning. The enemy's cavalry, displaying a little more daring than was their wont, advanced upon us with considerable show of fight. Their infantry was within short supporting distance. A spirited skirmish took place, and, under the circumstances, we followed the advice of the poet, who sings:

> "He who fights and runs away,
> Will live to fight another day."

We retreated to Halltown, and moved with the head of the column to the left, and finally halted pretty well up the river, opposite Maryland Heights. Within our bivouac was planted the Rebel battery that had killed Col. Miles, commanding Harper's Ferry, on a former occasion. The spot was pointed out to us by a Mr. M., a citizen in the neighborhood, who presented us an anomaly commonly met with in this region of country, of a man making high *professions* of Unionism, and yet earnestly pleading for Secession.

August 23*d*. Under light marching orders, the division went out on a reconnoissance in the vicinity of Duffield's Station, on the Baltimore and Ohio rail road, and engaged a heavy force of the enemy's infantry. The fight was spirited but brief, and our forces returned to camp after a few hours of marching and fighting.

August 25*th*. One day's uninterrupted rest had been enjoyed as a rare luxury; but this morning at three o'clock the hills and woods were ringing with reveillé. At five the division was in motion in the direction of Shepardstown, not far from which we were joined by the first division of cavalry. This united force moved to Kearneysville Station, near which, the enemy, under Breckenridge, was met advancing towards Maryland in heavy force. Seldom are forces so suddenly and furiously engaged. The artillery of both parties was immediately brought into position, and the hills resounded with the rapid discharges of screaming shell and sweeping grape and canister. Before the quick firing of our Spencers, and our swift charges, the enemy's column at first recoiled and gave us a decided advantage over him. But we were at length compelled to retreat before superior numbers, that were lapping around our flanks. In this engagement the regiment behaved with its usual gallantry. Lieut. Greenleaf, in command of Co. A, fell, mortally wounded, but was carried from the field. Nearly all our dead and wounded remained in our own hands, and were taken back with us. We returned to our old bivouac and erected our tents with hopes of a good night's rest. But before dark we were ordered to pack up and make preparations for a night's march.

At ten P. M., the regiment alone, accompanied with a brigade staff officer, moved to the Potomac, which we crossed on pontoons at the foot of Maryland Heights. The division moved also, but by some other route. We marched until three A. M., and halted to rest our weary animals and ourselves at the memorable Antietam creek, near Antietam Furnace.

August 26*th*. At one P. M. we resumed our march to Sharpsburg, nearly every house of which bears marks of the great battle that was fought here in 1862. Turning to the right, the column passed over the main portion of the battle field, and bivuacked a few rods beyond Keedysville. At half past nine P. M., through pitchy darkness, we were countermarched to Sharpsburg. On the way we encountered one of the worst thunder storms ever witnessed. The rain fell in torrents, driven by a strong wind. The frequent lightnings cleft the darkness, and left us blinded and in greater darkness than before. The thunder roared and shook the earth beneath us. Some of our horses became quite unmanageable, and rendered our march perilous as well as uncomfortable. On the wet ground, after this shower, we bivouacked in the fields near the town, having sent out a few pickets towards the river.

August 27*th*. We picketed in front of Sharpsburg till twelve M., and were then sent up the river about three miles, to picket some fords near Mereersville, where we continued till next morning.

August 28th. Sunrise found us with our pickets withdrawn, and in line of march towards Sharpsburg, where we joined the division. Again our faces were turned towards Virginia, and we were soon on its "sacred soil," having forded the Potomac a short distance below Shepardstown. Slowly and safely we advanced to Charlestown, halting by the rail road to allow the infantry to pass through the town before us. With flying colors our brave boys entered this very rebellious village, and the bands struck up the air of Old John Brown, and played lustily as they marched through the streets, where but a few years past gathered the chivalry to witness the execution of Old Ossawatomie. The cavalry at last marched on in rear of the infantry, and encamped in the woods not far from town.

Up to this time our work in the valley had been very discouraging. It had been constant marching and fighting, but always retreating. The Rebels had had things nearly all their own way However, we had prevented their crossing again into Maryland; and now, for some reason, they were falling back to the line of the Opequan creek. Gen. Sheridan, with some reënforcements, was now advancing to make battle in terrible earnest, and to push the enemy, if possible, far from the states he was so anxious to invade.

August 30th. The regiment was made sad this morning by the departure of Col. Hammond from its command. (See Mementos). In a field near our camp, the regiment was formed into a hollow square, and the colonel took formal leave. He undertook to speak a few words, but was choked by emotion. He rode forward to the officers, who were formed in front and centre, and shook hands with them. He then addressed a few parting words to the men, and with three cheers proposed by Lieut. Col. Bacon, he passed out of the square, and left us. The regiment was immediately formed in line of march, and, with the division, advanced to Berryville, where we made an early bivouac.

September 2d. As we have not full feed for our horses, our men are compelled to forage through the country, and occasionally squads of them are attacked and captured.

During the night our position was flanked on the right, and this morning early we retreated on a back road by way of Myerstown, and returned to the pike not far from Charlestown. It was hoped we might here have a few days' rest, and preparations were made for comfortable shelters, but about sundown the woods rang with "boots and saddles." Again we advanced on Berryville, which we reached about ten P. M. We found the place occupied by the enemy, who retreated after a brief skirmish.

September 3d. The division advanced this morning to Millwood and White Post, encountering a heavy force of the enemy a little beyond, from which we retired without an engagement. The rear of the column spent the night near Millwood.

September 4th. The command was made happy this morning with the news: "Atlanta is ours!" The enemy's cavalry, having taken possession of the pike between us and Berryville, we retreated to its vicinity by means of a circuitous route toward the Blue Ridge. On arriving we found that the enemy held the town in force. Our artillery was used quite extensively, the regiment supporting a battery. There was some musketry on the skirmish line, on which the regiment lay all night, having been relieved from the battery.

September 5th. The enemy was expelled from Berryville, and retired to the Opequan. The Fifth New York was sent on picket. A cold rain storm made mud for us and discomfort.

September 7th. The day dawned bright and beautiful, after the storm. The division went out on the White Post road some distance, and turning to the right, proceeded as far as the Opequan, where we had a heavy skirmish with the enemy. Returned to Berryville at night.

September 9th. The regiment spent yesterday and to-day on picket. The division has gone into camp on the north side of the pike. A large force of our infantry is also camped near by; and some of them are busy building earth-works across the pike about one mile east of Berryville.

September 10th. The regiment was relieved from picket.

September 13th. The first brigade advanced toward Winchester on the pike, encountering the Rebel pickets at the Opequan. A quick dash was made upon their reserve, within two miles of Winchester, which, after a short skirmish, resulted in the capture of the 8th South Carolina volunteers. Sixteen officers, including their colonel, fell into our hands, and also their battle flag. The brunt of the engagement was borne by the 3d New Jersey and the 2d Ohio regiments of cavalry.

At the expiration of eight hours from the time the brigade moved out, we were back into our camps. This was one of the most brilliant exploits ever performed by the brigade.

September 15th. The regiment went out again to the Opequan and skirmished with the enemy's pickets.

September 16th. Spent the day on picket

September 17th. At one A. M. several regiments of the 1st brigade made another reconnoissance to the Opequan. The Fifth went mostly through the woods and fields. Crossed the creek at Burnt Factory, where a skirmish commenced and continued, until we returned to the creek, on the pike. We then fell back to camp near Berryville.

September 18th. Regiment on picket.

September 19th. General Sheridan had at length perfected his arrangements for a general move upon the enemy. At one A. M. the "general call" was sounded, tents were struck, and all due preparation made for the march. At two o'clock a splendid force of infantry, cavalry and artillery, was advancing toward Winchester. The 2d New York had the advance, followed by the Fifth. Before daylight the Rebel cavalry pickets were charged at the Opequan, and driven hastily before us. Believing that this was nothing more than a repitition of the many reconnoissances and raids, we had recently made, the Johnnies were scarcely prepared for the onset that was made upon them. Passing around a heavy barricade across the pike, the cavalry waited not for the infantry supports, but dashed up the road, and charged the enemy's fortifications. Before they had fairly time to recover from this unexpected blow, they were struck by the strong lines of our eager infantrymen, and shells from our batteries just in position, fell fast among them. And now commenced one of the most brilliant engagements of the war.

Our first attack, so unexpected and furious, gave us the enemy's first line of works. This was a decided advantage, both in demoralizing the foe, and in giving us a better position. The contestants soon became engaged throughout the entire line, extended for four or five miles across the country.

About ten o'clock, by a persistent effort to keep his army well in hand, and by planting his artillery on the hills and chosen positions in front of Winchester, General Early, commanding the Rebel forces, succeeded in checking our advance. A terrible contest now followed. Forward and backward, advancing and receding, surged those living lines of men like the foaming waves of ocean. But, at length, the cavalry, the first division on the right, the third on the left, succeeded in driving in and enveloping the extreme wings of the Rebel army. At this the centre of their line began to waver, and, ere long, the whole force was in a swift retreat through Winchester, leaving their dead and wounded behind them. The battle had raged from morning till nearly sundown, and the field was strewn thick with the wrecks of recently proud, brave men.

Five distinct charges had the regiment made during the day, four of these against infantry. In one of these charges, Capt. Farley, company C, while gallantly rallying his men, lost his right leg, which was taken away by a solid shot or shell. It was amputated above the knee. In another charge, led by Gen. McIntosh in person, the general received a fearful gunshot wound in the left leg, which was amputated below the knee. We had sustained a heavy loss, the bitterness of which was mitigated by the glorious success which had crowned our effort.

Notwithstanding the fatigue of our horses and men, we were sent in pursuit of the retreating army. Swinging around Winchester to the left, we came up to the pike just above Milltown, and advanced beyond Kernstown, where we bivouacked for the night.

September 20th. The division advanced to Newtown, and, turning to the left, struck the Front Royal pike at Nineveh, which we followed to Crooked Run, where the enemy was met, and a slight skirmish followed.

The command bivouacked early in the grassy fields.

September 21st. The division was early on the move. The morning was chilly and foggy. The North Fork Shenandoah was crossed without opposition, and the enemy was found in considerable force on the South Fork. He was quickly driven from his strong position, leaving his spades and pickaxes in the trenches he was constructing. We pursued him rapidly through Front Royal, and halted to feed our horses in the fine corn fields beyond the town. At three P. M. we moved up the Luray pike to Asbury Church. This road is exceedingly romantic, with the broad, clear river on one side, and the lofty, precipitous rocks on the other.

At the church we halted, and received one of the most fearful shellings, through which we ever passed, from the Rebel batteries posted on a high, commanding hill. Several regiments of the brigade broke before this fire, but the Fifth New York received high commendation for standing firm. We built our bivouac fires by the church at night.

September 22d. In the night the Rebels retreated up the valley, and early in the morning we gave them pursuit. We followed them to Milford creek, where we found them strongly intrenched in an impregnable position. All day we skirmished and fought with them. The Fifth New

York was engaged till night, when the division fell back, and left us on picket.

September 23d. This morning the whole division moved back toward Strasburg, stopping by the river near Waterlick Station, Manassas Gap rail road. Here we received Gen. Sheridan's dispatches announcing his great victory at Fisher's Hill. They were read to the division, and the air was rent with the vociferous cheering of our men. At night we were again advanced up the Luray Valley, halting after midnight near Milford creek.

September 24th. During our absence the enemy had abandoned his strong position at Milford, and was fleeing up the valley. Before sunrise we resumed our march. Near Luray where the valley becomes broad and beautiful, the enemy was encountered in force and driven, about one hundred prisoners falling into our hands. They were all loud in their denunciations of Gen. Early, the "apple-jack bibber," as many of them called him. On the hills beyond Luray we went into camp. But scarcely had we cooked our suppers, when "boots and saddles" hurried every man to his horse, and in an incredibly short time the whole force was in motion. This move was made in hopes of capturing the enemy, who had gone up the mountains toward the Shenandoah Valley, but, finding it occupied by our forces, was compelled to descend to the Luray again. However, night came on too soon, and, in the darkness, the enemy slipped out of our hands. We forded the river, and bivouacked about nine o'clock, in a settlement, called Massanutten.

September 25th. This bright Sabbath morning found us vigorously pursuing our march over the Massanutten mountains, through a gap from which a splendid view is obtained of the two valleys, which this range separates, the Luray and Shenandoah. About ten A. M. we arrived in the vicinity of New Market, where we met our supply train. Commissaries and quartermasters were in great repute just then, as were also the sutlers with their scanty supplies at enormous prices. We were camped a few hours in the woods. Here we received a good mail.

About 2 P. M. the whole command started up the valley, halting near our vast infantry camps at Harrisonburg, about eleven o'clock.

September 26th. This morning the cavalry moved up the valley, reaching Staunton at dusk. Not far from town, on the road to Waynesboro', we bivouacked, after a very fatiguing journey.

September 27th. At ten A. M. the regiment was detailed to escort Gen. Custer to his new command, lately Gen. Averill's, known among us as the Second division. This command was near Port Republic. On the way the regiment had a fearful skirmish with the enemy at Mt. Meridian. However, it succeeded in getting through, with the general unhurt.

September 28th. The boys were early on their way to rejoin the division, which they did at night, just after the battle of Waynesboro', in which a good number of the regiment were engaged. The division was now retreating, and a long, dreary march was before us. We passed through Staunton, and followed the pike down about two miles; then turning to the left, we followed a rough, crooked road that led us to the Glade, a small valley near the foot of the North or Shenandoah mountains. We journeyed all night long, and halted for breakfast at Spring Hill.

September 29th. From this halt the regiment was rear-guard of the column. A slight attack was made on us and repelled. Many of our horses gave out by the way and were shot. The division took possession of Bridgewater about noon. The regiment was on picket till night, when it camped near the town.

October 2d. During our rest here our horses have fared well with the forage, which is abundant all around us, and the men have obtained very comfortable subsistence from the country. Meanwhile, General Wilson has been removed to a large command in the western army, and General Custer has superseded him in the command of the Third division.

At noon the command broke camp, and soon after the enemy's cavalry made a dash on our pickets and succeeded in penetrating the town. They were, however, driven back with some loss. Nearly all the afternoon skirmishing and cannonading have been going on. The regiment had a dark, unpleasant night's picketing along this dangerous line.

October 3d. On picket till five P. M. We then joined the brigade near Dayton and went into camp.

October 4th. In retaliation for the murder of Capt. Meigs, son of Quartermaster Gen. Meigs, near Dayton, by some citizen guerrillas, the regiment was ordered to report to Capt. Lee, provost marshal of the division, to burn every building within a circle of three miles from the scene of the murder. This was the most heart-sickening duty we had ever performed. Splendid mansions in great number, in the vicinity, were laid in ashes; but before the work of burning the town commenced, the order was countermanded. The execution of such orders, however just and right, has a very demoralizing effect upon the men.

October 6th. On falling back from the upper portion of the valley, Gen. Sheridan ordered all stacks or ricks of hay or grain, or the same in barns, to be destroyed by fire. Grist mills were to share the same fate. This precaution was to prevent the enemy's ever returning to subsist his army on this fruitful country. The march of our army could now be traced by the heavy smokes, which rose on the air.

On leaving Dayton this morning two grist mills were destroyed. The enemy followed very closely on our rear. Not far from Turleytown near Brock's Gap, he made a strong attack, in a position very advantageous to himself. By dint of effort and fine fighting he was prevented from doing us much injury. The regiment lay all night on the skirmish line.

October 7th. We continued falling back on the mountain road, and were rejoined by a squadron of the regiment, that was sent to Brock's Gap last evening, was cut off, but succeeded by great exertion and good fortune, to pass unhurt through the enemy's lines. At Forestville our column was attacked by a strong force. During the skirmish we lost seven forges, including ours, several ambulances, and a few men. Here Sergeant Whitney, company F, then in command of the company, lost his life by a fatal bullet, while gallantly struggling to repel the enemy.

We continued our march to Columbian Furnace, near which we bivouacked for the night.

October 8th. As usual we were early on the move. The rear guard was attacked several times on the way. We reached Fisher's Hill before sundown, and were sent on picket toward Tom's Brook.

October 9th. Annoyed by the frequent attacks of the enemy on our rear guards and pickets, Gen. Custer resolved to drive him from the vicinity. So facing about with his division, this morning he advanced upon Generals Rosser and Lomax in a fine position near Tom's Brook. This was a pure cavalry fight, and one of the most spirited of the war. Having properly planted his artillery, and disposed his force as advantageously as possible, the general ordered the bugles on the entire line to sound the *advance*, and leading the Fifth New York in person, he made a dash on the enemy's central position in the road. Our color bearer, Sergeant Buckley, company C, displayed his usual bravery, bearing our flag close by the side, and, at times, ahead of the general's. With a shout and a dash, with thundering artillery and gleaming sabres, with trusty carbines and Yankee grit, our boys scattered the enemy before them, and won a complete victory. On the pike the First division, Gen. Merritt commanding, made a clean sweep of the enemy's cavalry on *their* front.

October 11th. This afternoon we moved to the pike, passed through Strasburg, and camped, after dark, near Belle Grove, Gen. Sheridan's headquarters.

October 13th. The enemy made an attack on our cavalry pickets on Cedar creek. The regiment was sent out to reënforce the pickets. After some cannonading and skirmishing, the enemy withdrew, and the pickets were reëstablished.

October 14th. The regiment went on a reconnoissance to Lebanon church, where the enemy was met, and, after a slight skirmish, we returned to the north bank of Cedar creek.

October 15*th*. Went on picket along the creek.

October 16*th*. We were relieved by the 1st Connecticut, and came back to the brigade, where we went into camp.

October 19*th*. About four o'clock A. M. we were aroused from our slumbers by an attack on our cavalry pickets at the right of our line. This was followed by the discharge of signal guns down the Rebel lines, ending with a fearful and surprise attack on the 8th corps (Gen. Crook's), which occupied our left. Here the men were killed and captured in their tents, and nearly the whole camp, with sutlers' wagons, trains, and several pieces of artillery, fell into the enemy's hands. Driven back in confusion, panic-stricken, the left of the 19th corps (Gen. Emory's), was uncovered and exposed to a withering fire from the exultant foe. Many of our brave fellows fell while contesting this central and important position. But our fortified lines had to be abandoned, and the old 6th corps (Gen. Wright's) came under the flank fire of the advancing columns.

Nine o'clock, and our lines had been driven back about three miles, and disaster had followed us at every step. A deep gloom had settled upon the army. The absence of Gen. Sheridan was deeply felt by all. But about ten o'clock, loud cheering in the rear, taken up by centre and front, announced that the hero of the Shenandoah had arrived upon the field of carnage. His black charger, reeking with foam, and covered with dust, had brought him in quick haste from Winchester.

"The first that the general saw were the groups
Of stragglers and the retreating troops.

> What was done, what to do, a glance told him both ;
> Then, striking his spurs with a terrible oath,
> He dashed down the line mid a storm of huzzas,
> And the wave of retreat checked its course there, because
> The sight of the master compelled it to pause."

The tide of battle immediately turned. Every man became suddenly transformed into two men, and the general's presence gave a foretaste of victory. The meeting of the generals was exceedingly affecting. Hats and caps were thrown into the air, and tears fell from their eyes like rain. Old gray-headed heroes sobbed like girls. Custer, the daring, terrible demon that he is in battle, caught Sheridan in his arms, but was unable to utter a word! It was no time for sentiment. While consulting with his generals the alarming intelligence reached Sheridan that the enemy's cavalry was rapidly moving to flank him on the right.

"Custer, I can trust you with the work of driving back this force," he said, after looking around him for a moment. No time was lost, and the work was successfully performed.

Inch by inch the Rebel lines gave way, until about sunset, when our artillery opened along our entire line with a galling fire. Then came the impetuous charge of our entire force, with the usual war-cry, more terrific than cannon's awful bellowing, and then, too, came the disastrous rout of the enemy. At this juncture the ever-ready Third division of cavalry made a grand dash at the fugacious Johnnies. A glance to the rear showed them closed in a solid body, their sabres flashing dimly through the smoke of that terrible field. No cheering now; nothing but the thundering tread of the columns, announcing our approach to the enemy, as we swept into the fire. The creek had been forded, and only half a mile, before we could reach the guns that were belching shot and shell at our troopers. The bugles again sounded the charge, and with a cheer we rode straight for the foe. It was a maddening time. The Rebels delivered one fierce volley, and the next instant the pitiless sabres of our men and the iron heels of the horses were doing their work. For three miles the charge continued, the bloody ground, the broken muskets, the dead and wounded, told its ferocity. Only the darkness of night put an end to the slaughter. Never in this war was so much gained. Sheridan's victory was complete.

Interesting accounts of extraordinary valor in the regiment may be found in the chapter of registers of companies. The following article, with receipt, from a New York daily, will show how the regiment behaved on this memorable day:

Among the regiments that participated in Sheridan's victory of October 19th, none equaled the success of the Fifth New York Cavalry. The following interesting and important receipt for property, captured by the regiment has been issued:

Headquarters First Brigade,
Third Cavalry Division, Oct. 21st, 1864.

Received of the Fifth New York Cavalry, commanded by Major A. H. Krom, twenty-two pieces of artillery, fourteen caissons, one battery wagon, seventeen army wagons, six spring wagons and ambulances, eighty-three sets of artillery harness, seventy-five sets of wagon harness, ninety-eight horses, sixty-seven mules, captured in action in the battle of the 19th of October, 1864, on Cedar creek, Va.

A. C. M. PENNINGTON, JR.,
Colonel Commanding Brigade.

Adjutant's General's Office, Oct. 25, 1864.
[A true copy.] E. D. TOWNSEND, A. A. G.

To this receipt might have been added two battle flags and many prisoners. The following congratulatory order was issued and promulgated to his division by General Custer:

Headquarters, Third Division, Cavalry Corps,
Middle Military Division, October 21, 1864.

Soldiers of the Third Cavalry Division:

With pride and gratification your commanding general congratulates you upon your brilliant achievements of the past few days.

On the ninth of the present month you attacked a vastly superior force of the enemy's cavalry, strongly posted, with artillery in position, and commanded by that famous "savior of the Valley," Rosser.

Notwithstanding the enemy's superiority in numbers and position, you drove him twenty miles, capturing his artillery, six pieces in all; also his entire train of wagons and ambulances, and a large number of prisoners. Again, during the memorable engagement of the nineteenth instant, your conduct throughout was sublimely heroic, and without a parallel in the annals of warfare. In the early part of the day, when disaster and defeat seemed to threaten our noble army upon all sides, your calm and determined bearing, while exposed to a terrible fire from the enemy's guns, added not a little to restore confidence to that portion of our army already broken and driven back on the right.

Afterwards, rapidly transferred from the right flank to the extreme left, you materially and successfully assisted in defeating the enemy in his attempt to turn the left flank of our army. Again ordered on the right flank, you attacked and defeated a division of the enemy's cavalry, driving him in confusion across Cedar creek. Then changing your front to the left at a gallop, you charged and turned the left flank of the enemy's line of battle, and pursued his broken and demoralized army a distance of five miles. Night alone put an end to your pursuit.

Among the substantial fruits of this great victory, you can boast of having captured five battle flags, a large number of prisoners, including Major Gen. Ramseur, and forty-five of the forty-eight pieces of artillery taken from the enemy on that day, thus making fifty-one pieces of artillery which you have captured from the enemy within the short period of ten days.

This is a record of which you may well be proud, a record won and established by your gallantry and perseverance. You have surrounded the name of the Third cavalry division with a halo as enduring as time.

The history of this war, when truthfully written, will contain no brighter page than that upon which is recorded the chivalrous deeds, and glorious triumphs of the soldiers of the Third division.

G. A. CUSTER,
Brigadier General Commanding.

Official: Chs. Siebert, Captain and A. A. G.

On the 19th of September we gave the Rebels a thorough whipping at Winchester; on the 19th of October we repeated the operation with a double dose on Cedar creek, each time with the 19th corps in the centre of the line, giving us an arithmetical assemblage worthy of remembrance by the American people.

It was quite late at night when the pursuit was discontinued, and the troops returned to their "old camp ground."

October 20th. The division went out on a reconnoissance to Tom's Brook on the mountain road, but captured only a few stragglers. The column returned to camp but the Fifth was left on picket at the Cedar creek neighborhood. Major Boice took command.

October 21st. The 2d Ohio relieved us about sundown, and we came near brigade headquarters into camp.

On the 25th and 31st we took our tour at picketing.

November 5th. The regiment went out on a reconnoissance toward Romney. It returned at night, after a tedious, cold and fruitless march.

November 8th. The whole army broke camp and moved near Kernstown, where it is expected we may build winter quarters.

November 9th. The first brigade was sent out on the mountain road near Zion Church, where a picket line was established.

November 12th. The enemy's cavalry drove in our pickets this morning, and made their appearance very near our camp. The First brigade went out and drove them beyond Cedar creek, after an exciting engagement. Col. Hull, of the 2d New York, while pushing on at the head of his men, was killed. He was a gallant young officer, who had but recently borne the eagle. He was generally lamented.

We returned to our camps at night, after severely punishing the enemy.

November 13th. A reconnoissance was made to Cedar creek, but the enemy was not discovered.

November 21st. The Second and Third divisions started up the valley on a reconnoissance. The whole force bivouacked in and about Woodstock at night.

H. Boice
Lt Col
5th N.Y.

November 22d. The advance, at Edinburg, captured the Rebel outpost of pickets this morning, and as rapidly as possible the whole force advanced to the Shenandoah beyond Mt. Jackson, where a strong picket line was encountered. The Second division was moved across the river, with a portion of the Third division, and advanced in skirmish line near Rood's Hill, where it developed the power of the enemy, who came out in three well-formed lines of battle. To ascertain the position and force of the enemy was all we had intended. Having accomplished this to our satisfaction, all we desired was to escape from this force with the least possible injury. This was not done, however, without a hard-fought battle. In this engagement the regiment performed deeds of the most wonderful daring, preventing a flank movement on the column by the enemy's cavalry. About three P. M. we succeeded in dealing our pursuers such a blow, as to enable us to fall back unmolested. The main force returned to Woodstock, and halted for the night The Fifth, however, was left to picket the rear along Stony creek. The night was very cold, occasioning some suffering.

November 23d. A cold march, over frozen ground, brought us back again to our camp near the sources of the Opequan, about three miles from Kernstown.

November 24th. This evening, after feasting on our Thanksgiving chickens and turkeys, sent us by our friends in the north, the regiment was made doubly thankful by receiving an order from General Sheridan detailing us for his escort.

November 25th. Obedient to the order, we reported to General Sheridan at nine A. M., and were ordered into camp near his headquarters at Kernstown.

Quite an effort was made by some high officials to get the regiment back to the brigade, but the general said, "What I have written, I have written."

As our campaigning is now ended for the season, with pleasure we append the following result of Gen. Sheridan's work in the valley:

Prisoners captured at Winchester (well)	2,200
Prisoners captured at Winchester (wounded)	2,000
Prisoners captured at Fisher's Hill	900
Prisoners captured on the march beyond and since and before the battle	1,500
Prisoners captured at Cedar creek	2,000
Total prisoners	8,600
Cannon captured near Martinsburg	2
Cannon captured on the Opequan	5
Cannon captured at Fisher's Hill	21
Cannon captured in cavalry battle	11
Cannon captured at Cedar creek	50
Total	89
Small arms captured at Winchester	6,000
Small arms captured at Fisher's Hill	1,100
Small arms captured at Cedar creek (say)	5,000
Total	12,100
Caissons captured at Winchester	4
Caissons captured at Fisher's Hill	9
Caissons captured at Cedar creek (say)	12
Total	25
Wagons captured at different points	160
Wagons captured at Cedar creek	100
Total	260

December 1*st.* The regiment escorted the general to Sheridan hospital near Winchester, where we witnessed the ceremony of a flag raising, a flag presented by the Union ladies of the town. There was a large and brilliant assemblage of smiling ladies, and gayly dressed officers, and not a few of our brave boys seated on benches and chairs, who had lost arms, legs, health, &c., for the proud flag, whose floating to-day they cheered with happy voices.

December 14th. We escorted the general to his new headquarters at the Logan mansion in Winchester. The regiment was ordered to build winter quarters, which work was begun near the town on west side of the road to Martinsburg. Nearly the whole army has constructed or is constructing its winter quarters.

December 31st. The old year is dying, with the pure white snow for her winding sheet and the hoarse winds for her requiem. These are solemn hours to the Christian soldier. Memory recalls the terrible dangers through which he has passed and the awful scenes he has witnessed. His heart swells with gratitude to the Great Preserver for the gift of safety, and he prays for courage and strength to be faithful and efficient until his work is done.

CHAPTER XI.

General Sheridan's Last Raid.—Up the Valley—Battle of Waynesboro'.—Many Prisoners.—In Charge of the Regiment.—Rosser Annoys Rear of Column.—Battle of Rood's Hill.—Rosser Defeated.—Fall of Richmond.—Lee Surrenders.—Suburbs of Winchester.—Rebel Soldiers Anxious to be Paroled.—Expedition to Staunton.—Preparation to Muster out the Regiment.—Camp Illumination.—Last Order of Col. White.—Journey to Hart's Island, N. Y. Harbor.—The Fifth New York Cavalry is No More.—*January 1st to July 26th*, 1865.

January 10th. Several of General Sheridan's scouts, accompanied by a detail of the regiment, made a demonstration on the Rebel pickets, near Edinburg, capturing a good number. Returning they tarried too long at Woodstock, where they were attacked by a large force, the prisoners liberated and some of the party captured.

January 22d. An affair quite similar to the above occurred at Edinburg. Our loss was larger than before.

February 23d. The regiment went out on a reconnoissance to Newtown, White Post, Millwood, and returned at eleven o'clock at night, without seeing even the semblance of an enemy.

February 27th. A grand cavalry movement was commenced to-day, the fruit of which will compare favorably with any other movement during the war. Gen. Sheridan, with the cavalry of the valley, moved out toward Staunton about ten o'clock. The regiment accompanied him. The column moved as rapidly as possible up the Valley pike, which is one of the finest highways of the country, and in good condition at all seasons of the year.

March 1*st*. The advance reached the vicinity of Waynesboro', the headquarters of General Early, commanding Rebel forces. Here the Third division again proved itself worthy of the renown it had acquired. With his usual daring Gen. Custer advanced his division upon the Rebel camp. All resistance was fruitless. Our men swept around this ill-starred army and enveloped them like fish in a net. Gen. Early barely escaped, by cunningly dodging into a thicket, pursued closely by the horsemen. His staff officers and nearly his entire force fell into our hands, making a total of about 1,400 prisoners. His artillery, camp and garrison equipage and stores were either appropriated to our own use or destroyed, mostly the latter. This was but the beginning of achievements, which place the name of Sheridan among the first heroes of modern times.

Encumbered by so great a crowd of prisoners, the general concluded to send them to the rear by way of Winchester. This was no small task, to guard upward of a thousand men nearly a hundred miles through a country infested by guerrillas, and by the forces of General Rosser. This task was committed to the Fifth New York, with detachments of other regiments, and a promiscuous lot of dismounted men, and of men whose horses were well-nigh "played out," making a command about one thousand strong.

Retaining with himself such of the regiment as were orderlies for his staff officers, messengers, color bearers, &c., the general pursued his journey over the Blue Ridge, captured cities and prisoners, destroyed rail roads, canals and other public property, eluded the enemy by the swiftness of his motion, and, after inflicting irreparable injury, rested his brave, tired squadrons near White House Landing. But he was ready for the opening campaign near Petersburg, where he covered himself and his men with glory, at Dinwiddie, Five Forks and Appomattox, surrounding the enemy at last and compelling him to a hasty surrender. From this digression we return to the main body of the regiment.

The roads from Waynesboro', cut down by the train, the pontoon wagons and the artillery, and trampled by the long lines of cavalry, were almost impassable. Along these the guard and prisoners floundered, traveling in the fields where they could, and finally rejoiced to have struck the firm macadamized pike near Staunton. Here supplies of flour and meat were obtained in abundance, and the command was prepared to undertake its long, perilous march to Winchester.

At Mt. Sidney a considerable body of Rosser's men made their appearance, and attacked the rear guard. They were repelled after a brief skirmish, during which Edward Morton, company M, had a ball wound his horse and another pass through his canteen full of sorghum, letting out the contents. Occasional shots were exchanged with these pursuers, who hung on our rear, all the way. At Lacey Springs, their numbers having been increased, they made quite a demonstration. This was renewed with new zeal and numbers at New Market, while the force was gathering on every side to contest the passage of the Shenandoah near Mt. Jackson. On the morning of the seventh of March, the command was ready to cross the river. The Fifth was again rear guard. Gen. Rosser, intent on releasing the prisoners, had collected his force, and, coming down Rood's Hill, charged on the column. Col. Boice, commanding the regiment, suddenly changed direction, held his men in good line, each reserving his fire until the enemy had approached within a few rods, then ordering and leading the charge, he fell with a crushing blow upon the enemy. The Johnnies, not expecting such a dash, wheeled about and undertook to fly, but were prevented doing so rapidly on account of the mud of the field where they were. A hand to hand contest of unusual excitement followed, in which the most daring deeds were done. Col. Boice, having emptied every chamber of his revolver, unhorsed six Rebel troopers with the butt. The affair resulted, not in the release of the prisoners as fondly hoped by Rosser, but in the capture of thirty-five of his men, the killing of quite a number, and the dispersion of his entire force. Our boys went on their way rejoicing, and crossed the river unmolested, while a few of the beaten Rebels grinned at them from Rood's Hill, beyond carbine range.

The remainder of the march was quite pleasant, and the arrival of the column at Winchester, the eighth of March, was hailed with a salute from the First Maine battery.

The regiment returned to camp, and the prisoners were sent on to Harper's Ferry. The regiment was now subject to orders from Gen. Hancock, who had the temporary command of the forces in and about Winchester.

March 13th. The regiment went on a reconnoissance to Berryville. Deserters from the Rebel lines are daily coming in our own, and giving themselves up.

March 16th. The paymaster is making us a friendly call, and is relieving himself freely of "stamps," as the boys call his greenbacks.

March 29th. The regiment had the honor of being reviewed by two generals with their staffs, namely, Hancock and Torbert. Gen. Hancock was heard to say, "Well done," on witnessing some swift evolutions, which gave the boys peculiar satisfaction.

April 3d. Swift telegrams announce Gen. Sheridan's victorious battles below Petersburg, and the fall of Richmond! Batteries rend the air with their salutes, and bands of music fill the intervals with joyful airs. The evening has been made luminous with fireworks from the signal tower on Logan mansion, and bonfires in the streets.

April 9th. Midnight! and the booming cannon announce the surrender of General Lee and the army of Northern Virginia. Aroused from their slumbers the soldiers and some citizens rush to Gen. Hancock's headquarters, a happy, almost crazy throng. The Logan mansion shines with an illumination, the signal tower blazes with fireworks, bells ring, bands discourse patriotic music, flags are paraded through the streets, and the multitude grows hoarse with cheering. The whole night is filled with jubilation.

April 15th. All are filled with gloom at the news of the assassination of our beloved President last evening. Thus the bitterest cup is tendered to the lips of the people in the midst of their highest joy over past victories. Freedom's noblest champion, a nation's great chief, falls a martyr to his cause!

April 27th. It has been a busy day, breaking up winter quarters, and removing into a grassy field about a mile from town near the Romney pike. We are now merged into a Provisional brigade of cavalry, under command of Col. Reno. Before leaving sight of Winchester, we should say, that though it does not appear as when first visited by the regiment in 1862, it still presents some objects of interest. Near by it on the Romney pike are the ruins of the mansion of James M. Mason (Mason and Slidell), once the headquarters of Gen. Banks.

On the north side of the town, in an old cemetery, is the grave of "Major Gen. Daniel Morgan, who died in 1808," of revolutionary fame. The marble slab is of poor quality, and has been wantonly broken piece by piece, for the sake of relics, until the inscription is partially obliterated.

To the east of this cemetery is the Union soldiers' sleeping place, a parterre enclosed with a neat board fence, and whose straight rows of graves with their uniform headboards, painted white with black inscriptions, present a scene thrillingly interesting. This graveyard is contiguous to the Winchester cemetery, whose monuments and tombstones show marks of the many battles which have been fought in this vicinity.

April 29th. Fragments of the Rebel army are constantly coming in, even guerrillas, who were scarcely expected to give up their work so soon. They, too, are eager for their parole, sick at heart with the war, and glad to return to more peaceful pursuits.

A salute was fired to-day on the reception of a telegram announcing the surrender of Johnston and his army to Gen. Sherman.

May 4th. At seven this morning the regiment moved out with a brigade of infantry, the whole in command of Brig.

Gen. Duval, on the way to Staunton. The march was performed quietly, resembling more a picnic party, than an assemblage of warriors.

We were everywhere received with cordiality, having nothing to offer but "peace and good will" to all law-abiding citizens. Farmers are in their fields, mechanics in their shops, merchants display their scanty stores, and a new life is manifested on every side.

May 9th. The expedition reached Staunton, and camped in an about the town. It is remarkable how readily paroled Rebel soldiers affiliate with us, and how anxiously those who are not paroled seek their papers. The rank and file of the Rebel army will return to a cordial snbmission to our laws, more readily than the people generally, who have simply looked on the conflict.

May 19th. The regiment went out with two days' rations and forage, under light marching orders, to Lexington, where they captured or arrested Ex-Governor Letcher, and brought him to Staunton, arriving on the 20th. This expedition was quite a relief from the monotonous life, which we are now living. There is not enough to do to keep up our energies. And as the war is over, and we have accomplished the work we came out to do, there is a very general desire that we may be mustered out and sent home at an early day. Several officers and men have sought to dissipate the *ennui* of our situation, by visiting Weyer's Cave, near Port Republic on the South Fork Shenandoah.

June 9th. Under order No. 83, Adjutant-General's Office, mustering out all men whose term of service expires previous to October 1st, we lost quite a large number of our men to-day, who left us for home. It was hard in many instances to sever the attachments that have been formed during our peculiar life and acquaintance.

June 12th. The regiment gladly obeyed orders to return to Winchester. We commenced our march at five P. M., with the design of marching mostly in the cool of evening and night, and of resting during the heat of day. Our march was pleasantly performed, and we reached Winchester about noon of the 15th, and pitched our tents in Camp Hammond, which we had left.

July 15th. Busy preparations are being made and are nearly completed for the *mustering out* of the regiment. Consequently general gladness prevails in camp. This inward joy was manifested this evening by a grand camp illumination. Candles were placed in rows upon the tents and carried up into the trees of the woods where we are encamped. Bonfires were built in the company streets, and torches were carried in procession. Several officers of the field and staff were cheered, and Col. White was called out for a speech, which he made. The entertainment closed by hanging and burning Jeff. Davis in effigy. Those who witnessed the novel scenes of the evening will not soon forget them.

July 18th. This morning the regiment received the last general order ever issued to it.

HEAD QUARTERS Fifth N. Y. Cavalry,
In the Field near Winchester, Va.,
July 18th, 1865.

In compliance with orders from the commanding general the regiment will leave Stevenson's Station this P. M. at three o'clock, en route to New York city, for final discharge.

Transportation will be furnished for officers' horses to place of muster out. The regiment will march for the depot at twelve M. Every officer and enlisted man will be in camp to march promptly at that hour. En route home and until final discharge, it is earnestly hoped the regiment will sustain its good name.

After four years of hardship and honor you return to your state to be honorably mustered out of service and to return once more to a peaceful life among your friends and loved ones. In a few days you will be scattered and the Fifth New York Cavalry will be no more. The hardships you have endured; the comforts of which you have been deprived; the cheerful and prompt manner in which you have always done your duty, and the successes you have met with on the battle field, have won the admiration of every general officer under whom you have served. Surpassed by none, equaled by few, your record as a regiment is a glorious and an honorable one.

May your future lives be as prosperous and as full of honor to yourselves, as the past four years have been to your country, to your state and to the Fifth New York Cavalry.

A. H. WHITE,
Col. Comd'g
5th N. Y. Cavalry.

The regiment was ready to move at the appointed hour, and at three P. M. the train that bore many a happy heart, moved from Stevenson's Station toward Harper's Ferry.

July 19th. Our muster out papers all bear this date. In the City of Brotherly Love at "Cooper Shop," the regiment was entertained with an excellent supper. Cheerfully we pursued our journey to the metropolis, where we tarried not long, and on the afternoon of the 20th, we were neatly encamped on Hart's Island, New York harbor, awaiting our turn with the paymaster. The Fifth Regiment of Cavalry, Fifth Infantry and Fifth Artillery, N. Y. Vols., met together for the first time on Hart's Island.

July 25th. The first and second battalions and Co. I of the third were paid this afternoon and evening, and many of the men took boat from the island for home.

July 26th. The remaining three companies of the regiment were paid this morning, and the Fifth New York Cavalry was no more, except in story.

CHAPTER XII.

Regimental Items. — Tables : Officers at Time of Muster Out. — Commanding Officers. — Non-commissioned Staff. — Exhibit of Strength on Monthly Returns. — Full Statistics. — Former Occupations of our Men. — Their Places of Birth. — Marches of the Regiment — Counties Traversed. — Escort Duty. — Generals under whom we Served. — Burial of Our Dead. — Tables: Engagements and their Casualties. — Men Killed in Action. — Mortally Wounded. — Discharged by Reason of Wounds. — List of Retired Officers.

In passing from the diary of the regiment, we introduce the reader to what may seem more dry and uninteresting, yet not less important, to a vast array of statistics. To any one but a member or friend of the regiment it may seem to have been unnecessary to appropriate so much space to these numbers. Our apology — if indeed any be needed — shall be brief. We look upon such tables as invaluable to correct and full history. Figures often reveal more than narration. Great pains have been taken to present them in an attractive form, and one convenient for reference, and no time has been spared in making them reliable. Not less than three months of hard labor have been consumed in the compilation of these tables, one of them alone — "engagements and their casualties" — having occupied nearly one-third of that time.

Were the historian supplied with such data from each

regiment, which has participated in our terrible struggle, an incalculably interesting and valuable history of this rebellion might be compiled at no distant day. But it is to be feared that in many instances not even the number much less the names, of our noble defenders, who have fallen in the conflict, will ever be known to posterity. While it is a noble thing to die for one's country, it is an ignoble thing for survivors not to chronicle the deeds and names of their less fortunate companions. We have endeavored to do justice to the memory of our comrades in these pages, and if, in any way, we have failed to do it well, let it not be attributed to a want of devotion to them or to the facts of history.

With thoughts like these we are doubtless prepared to enter upon the perusal of the following statistics.

Officers of the Regiment at Time of Muster-out, July 19, '65.

NAMES.	RANK.	RANK AT TIME OF ENTRY.	TIME OF ENTRY.
FIELD AND STAFF.			
Amos H. White,[1]	Colonel,	1st Lieut.	Sept. 26, 1861.
Theodore A. Boice,[2]	Lieut. Col.,	Private,	June 15, 1861.
Elmer J. Barker,[3]	Major,	"	Sept. 19, 1861.
Henry A. D. Merritt,[4]	"	"	Oct. 9, 1861.
Liberty C. Abbott,	"	"	Aug. 26, 1861.
Fred M. Sawyer,[5]	Adjutant,	"	Aug. 22, 1861.
Dewitt H. Dickinson,	Regt. Q. M.,	"	Oct. 18, 1862.
Joseph A. Phillips,	Regt. Comm.,	1st Lieut.	May 3, 1862.
Orlando W Armstrong,[6]	Surgeon,	As. Surg.	Mar. 18, 1863.
Isaac N. Mead,	Ass. Surgeon,	Hosp. St.	Dec. 26, 1862.
Richard H. Goodell,	" "	As. Surg.	May 9, 1864.
Louis N. Boudrye,[7]	Chaplain,	Chaplain	Jan. 31, 1863.
Co. A.			
Frazer A. Boutelle,[8]	Captain,	Private,	June 1, 1861
Michael Hayes,[9]	1st Lieut.,	"	Aug. 15, 1861.
William T. Boyd,[10]	2d Lieut.,	"	Dec. 19, 1863.
Co. B.			
Jabez Chambers,[11]	Captain,	Private,	Aug. 21, 1861.
Samuel McBride,[12]	1st Lieut.,	Hosp. St.	Sept. 23, 1861.
Edward Price,	2d Lieut.,	Private,	Aug. 12, 1861.
Co. C.			
Benj. M. Whittemore,[13]	Captain,	Private,	Sept. 10, 1861.
William Leahey,[14]	1st Lieut.,	"	Aug. 11, 1861.

1. Captured May 23, '62, Front Royal. Wounded in foot June 30, '63, Hanover, Pa. Shot through body June 1, '64, Ashland, and captured.
2. Captured July 18, '62, Barnett's Ford. Again captured Oct. 25, '63, by Mosby, and received five wounds while escaping from captor.
3. Severely injured by falling of horse, in charge, Feb. 9, '63, New Baltimore. Received two grape shot wounds May 30, '63, Greenwich.
4. Received three sabre cuts March 23, '63, Chantilly, and captured. Captured again March 2, '64, near Richmond with Col. Dahlgren. Escaped from prison, Columbia, S. C., Nov. 28, '64, and was 30 days in reaching our lines.
5. Captured July 18, '62, Orange C. H. Wounded in right hand slightly, Oct. 19, '63, Buckland Mills.
6. Remained voluntarily with Major White, who was supposed to be mortally wounded, June 1, '64, Ashland, and captured.
7. Captured July 5, '63. Monterey Pass, Pa. Released Oct. 7, '63.
8. Severely injured by falling of horse, in charge, June 30, '63, Hanover, Pa.
9. Wounded slightly and captured June 30, '63, Hanover, Pa.
10. Captured June 29, '64, Reams Station. Escaped from prison, Columbia, S. C., Nov. 4, '64, and was 21 days in reaching our lines.
11. Captured July 6, '63. Hagerstown, Md.
12. Severely wounded May 3, '63, Warrenton Junction.
13. Captured June 29, '64, Reams Station. Escaped from prison, Columbia, S. C., Nov. 4th, '64, and was 21 days in reaching our lines.
14. Wounded in arm March 23, '63, Chantilly.

Officers of the Regiment at Time of Muster-out, July 19,' 65.

NAMES.	RANK.	RANK AT TIME OF ENTRY.	TIME OF ENTRY.
Patrick Tiffany,.............	2d Lieut.,....	Private,.	Aug. 8, 1861.
Co. D.			
Ransom A. Perkins,.........	1st Lieut.,.....	Private,.	Sept. 26, 1861.
Jeremiah J. Callanan,[1]....	2d Lieut.,.....	" .	Sept. 23, 1861.
Co. E.			
Foster Dickinson,[2]..........	Captain, ...	Private,.	Aug. 26, 1861.
Matthew Strait,[3].............	1st Lieut.,.....	" .	Aug. 31, 1861.
Addison S. Thompson,[4]....	2d Lieut.,.....	" .	Aug. 26, 1861.
Co. F.			
William D. Lucas,[5]..........	Captain, ...	2d Lieut.	Aug. 30, 1861.
Merritt N. Chafey,...........	1st Lieut.,.....	Private,.	Sept. 12, 1861.
John K. Jeffrey,[6].............	2d Lieut., ...	" .	Oct. 6, 1862.
Co. G.			
John H. Wright,[7]............	Captain, ...	Private,.	Aug. 22, 1861.
William H. Knight,[8].........	1st Lieut.,.....	" .	Sept. 1, 1861.
Abijah Spafford,.............	2d Lieut.,.....	" .	Sept. 9, 1861.
Co. H.			
Eugene B Hayward,[9]......	Captain, ...	Private,.	Oct. 1, 1861
Lucius F. Renne,[10]..........	1st Lieut,,.....	" .	Oct. 1, 1861,
Clark M. Pease, ...	2d Lieut.,.....	" .	Oct. 1, 1861.
Co. I.			
Edmund Blunt, Jr.,[11].......	Captain, ...	2d Lieut.	Sept. 26, 1862.
Christopher Heron,.......	1st Lieut , ...	Private,.	Sept. 4, 1861.
William H. Conklin,.........	2d Lieut.,.....	" .	April 8, 1863.
Co. K.			
Laurence L. O'Connor,......	Captain, ...	2d Lieut.	Oct. 16, 1861.
Thomas O'Keefe,............	1st Lieut., ...	Private,.	Sept. 15, 1861.
Nathaniel M. Talmage,.....	2d Lieut.,.....	" .	Oct. 9, 1861.
Co. L.			
George C. Morton,..........	Captain, ...	2d Lieut.	Sept. 3, 1861.

1. Sabre cut in right hand June 30, '63, Hanover, Pa
2. Wounded in left leg June 1, '64, Ashland.
3. Sabre cut on wrist Oct. 11, '63, Brandy Station. Gun shot in thigh March 1, '64, near Richmond. Wounded slightly in hand Sept. 19, '64, Winchester.
4. Captured March 23, '63, Chantilly. Escaped from guards the 24th. Recaptured and paroled the 25th.
5. Captured July 7, '63, near Williamsport, Md. Released March, 1865.
6. Wounded slightly Oct. 11, '63, Brandy Station.
7. Captured June 30, '63, Hanover, Pa.
8. Captured Sept. 3, '64, White Post. Escaped from prison, Columbia, S. C., Dec. 28, '64, and was 18 days in reaching our lines.
9. Wounded in left arm Aug. 2. '62, Orange C. H., and by a shell slightly in the thigh March 1, '64, near Richmond.
10. Slightly wounded by guerrillas in left shoulder May 15, '62, Tom's Brook.
11. Wounded in left ear Aug. 25, '64, Kearneysville Station.

Officers of the Regiment at Time of Muster-out, July 19, '65.

NAMES.	RANK.	RANK AT TIME OF ENTRY.	TIME OF ENTRY.
William H. Whitcomb,[1].....	1st Lieut.,.....	Private,.	Oct. 1, 1861.
Peter McMullen,[2]...........	2d Lieut.,.....	" .	Nov. 18, 1861.
Co. M.			
Wilbur F. Oakley,[3]..........	Captain, ...	Private, .	Oct. 23, 1861.
William G. Peckham,[4]......	1st Lieut.,.....	" .	Aug. 31, 1861.
Justus Travis,................	2d Lieut.,.....	" .	Sept. 20, 1861.

1. Captured May 6, '62, Harrisonburg. Escaped by stratagem. Again captured July 6, '63, Hagerstown, Md. Wounded in neck slightly, May 5, '64, Parker's Store.
2. Slightly wounded in left hand, May 5, '64, Parker's Store.
3. Wounded in head, Oct. 10, '63, James City; again in head Aug. 25, '64, Kearneysville Station.
4. Wounded in breast, June 1, '64, Ashland.

Officers who have Commanded the Regiment.

NAMES	Rank at Time of Relief from Command	Rank at Time of Taking Command	Date of Taking Command.	Date of Relief from Command.
Othniel DeForest,	Colonel,.	Colonel,.	Oct. 1, 1861.	Sept. 10, 1862.
Robert Johnstone	Lt. Col.,	Lt. Col.,	Sept. 10, 1861.	June 1, 1863.
John Hammond,	Colonel,	Major,...	June 1, 1863.	Aug. 30, 1864.
William P. Bacon	Lt. Col.,	Lt. Col.,	Aug. 30, 1864.	Sept. 12, 1864.
Abram H. Krom,	Major,...	Major,...	Sept. 12, 1864.	Oct. 19, 1864.
Elmer J. Barker,	Captain,	Captain,	Oct. 19, 1864.	Oct. 21, 1864.
Theo. A. Boice,	Lt. Col.,	Major,...	Oct. 21, 1864.	Dec. 19, 1864.
Amos H. White,	Colonel,.	Colonel,.	Dec. 19, 1864.	July 26, 1865.

Non-Commissioned Staff, July 19, 1865.

NAMES.	RANK.	RANK AT TIME OF ENTRY IN REGIMENT.	TIME OF ENTRY.	CO. PROMOTED FROM.
Dennis O'Flaherty,[1]	Sergt. Maj.,	Private,...	July 2, 1861,....	A.
William C. Page,[2] ...	Hosp. St.,..	" ...	Jan. 16, 1863,....	B.
Michael Dunigan,[3]..	Q.M. Sergt.,	" ...	Sept. 15, 1861,..	D.
Charles B. Thomas,	Com'y Sergt	" ...	Sept. 21, 1861,...	F.
Stephen D. Green,[4]..	ChiefBuglr.	" ...	Aug. 22, 1861,...	G.
David F. Wolcott,...	Saddler Sgt.	" ...	March 10, 1862,.	E.
Dennis O'Brien,......	Vetr'y Srgn.	" ...	Aug. 22, 1862,...	L.

1. Captured Hanover, Pa., June 30, '63. Again Oct. 20, '63, Thoroughfare Gap. — 2. Captured Oct. 11, '63, Brandy Station.— 3. Captured Oct, 10, '63, Russell's Ford.— 4. For a long time Brigade, and Division Bugler.

The following will exhibit the Non-Commissioned Staff in the order in which they were appointed from the organization of the regiment :—

SERGEANTS MAJOR,—John Greenback, Reg't, from Co. K ; James Seddinger, 1st Battalion, B ; George T. Smith, 1st Batt., B ; Richard C. Stananought, 2d Batt., C ; Warner Miller, 3d Batt., I ; Alexander Gall, 3d Batt., I ; Richard C. Stananought, Reg't ; Alexander Gall, Reg't ; Fred M. Sawyer, Reg't, C ; Lewis J. Gorham, Reg't, H.

HOSPITAL STEWARDS,—Samuel McBride, Joseph Parmelee, Richard Marion, Isaac N. Mead.

QUARTER MASTER SERGEANTS,— ——Simpson, Reg't; W F. Haviland, 1st Batt. ; Fred Paul, 2d Batt. ; Alfred K. Wilson, 3d Batt. ; Dewitt H. Dickinson, Reg't ; David H. Scofield, Reg't, K.

COMMISSARY SERGEANTS,—Miles L. Blanchard, 1st Batt. ; William Banta, 2d Batt. ; Daniel Hitchcock, 3d Batt. ; Merritt N. Chafey, Reg't, F.

CHIEF BUGLERS,—Luke S. Williams, F ; Conrad Bohrer, I ; Julius C. Lamb, I ; Robert Heisser, D ; Louis Erdman, M.

SADDLER SERGEANTS,—John J. Bush, 1st Batt. ; William B. Vincent, 2d Batt., G ; Asahel S. Lohman, 3d Batt., M.

VETERINARY SURGEON,—John Young, B.

VETERINARY SERGEANTS,—James Jelly, 1st Batt., B. ; A. D. Styles, 2d Batt., F ; William G. Edwards, 3d Batt., I.

Whole number on Muster Rolls, as shown by monthly returns of the following dates:

Dates.	Comm. Officers.	Enlisted Men.	Dates.	Comm. Officers.	Enlisted Men.
October, 1861,...	50	1064	October, 1863,...	38	522
January, 1862,...	50	932	January, 1864,...	32	595
April, 1862, ...	47	911	April, 1864,......	36	979
July, 1862.........	35	607	July, 1864,........	32	814
October, 1862,...	39	658	October, 1864,...	25	780
January, 1863,...	36	623	January, 1865,...	38	778
April, 1863,......	44	620	April, 1865,......	46	1007
July, 1863,........	37	534	July, 19, 1865,....	47	954

Statistical Record of the Regiment.

Original number of men	1064,
Recruits added	1074,
Original number of officers	50.
Whole number of officers	124,
Original officers remaining	4,
Officers from the Ranks	36,
" killed and mortally wounded	5,
" wounded	22,
" captured	19,
" died of Disease	4,
" dismissed by Court Martial	10,
" discharged by order War Department	5,
" resigned	37.
" discharged at expiration of term	13,
Enlisted men killed and mortally wounded	75,
Enlisted men wounded	236,
" " captured	517,
" " killed accidentally	18,
" " died in Rebel Prisons	114,
" " died of Disease	90,
Enlisted men discharged by reason of wounds	25,
" " discharged for Physical Disability	295.
" " discharged at expiration of term	302,
" " discharged by order of President	2,
" " transferred to other Commands	103,
" " deserted	325,
" " reënlisted in 1864	212,
Number of Battles fought	52,
" " Skirmishes "	119,
" " Wounds received in action	320,
Men lost in action and never heard from	18,
Men remaining July 19, '65	694,
Original Veterans remaining	167,
Original horses remaining	7.

Former Occupations of its Members.

That the regiment might have constituted a very respectable colony in itself, fully able to go and possess the land and to establish therein the various trades and occupations necessary to progress in all the departments of human thought and activity, may be inferred from the following avocations which it represented, with the comparative number of men belonging to each. Farmers 578, laborers 226, clerks 65, boatmen 54, blacksmiths 50, carpenters 38, sailors 38, shoemakers 29, teamsters 28, mechanics 25, painters 16, soldiers 16, machinists 14, tailors 14, butchers 13, printers 12, coopers 11, masons 9, molders 9, millers 9, bakers 9, students 8, lumbermen 7, tinsmiths 6, harness makers 6, stage drivers 6, showmen 5, hatters 5, merchants 5, engineers 5, hostlers 5, barbers 5, artists 5, stone cutters 5, wagon makers 5, ministers 4, lawyers 4, spinners 4, bartenders 4, wheelwrights 4, mariners 4, book keepers 4, carmen 4, cigar makers 4, tobacconists 3, ship carpenters 3, sleighmakers 3, sawyers 3, peddlers 3, seamen 3, curriers 3, coachmen 3, carriage makers 3, farriers 3, wagoners 3, saddlers 3, wool carders 3, bricklayers 2, wire-workers 2, bloomers 2, waiters 2, sawmakers 2, sailmakers 2, jewelers 2, upholsterers 2, expressmen 2, grocers 2, shoebinders 2, spinners 2, cabinetmakers 2, musicians 2, brushmakers 2, joiners 2, teachers 2, miners 2, veterinary surgeons 2, firemen 1, engravers 1, fishermen 1, papermakers 1, wood choppers 1, roofers 1, file cutters 1, telegraph operators 1, apothecaries 1, clothiers 1, mill hands 1, salesmen 1, burnishers 1, tanners 1, boiler makers 1, grooms 1, brewers 1, lithographers 1, gardeners 1, porters 1, morocco dressers 1, packers 1, jailors 1, locksmiths 1, grainers 1, dressers 1, confectioners 1, cooks 1, druggists 1, doctors 1, travellers 1, coppersmiths 1, colliers 1, iron-masters 1, pailmakers 1, millwrights 1, bookbinders 1, drovers 1, cobblers 1, watchmakers 1, cotton makers 1, caulkers 1, manufacturers 1, hewers 1, currycomb makers 1, minstrels 1, hotel keepers 1, blockmakers 1, gilders 1, axemakers 1, making in all 126 different occupations.

States and Countries represented.

It is not strange that so many men, representing so many and varied walks of life, should have sprung from many different states and countries; nor is it a matter of minor importance to ascertain what regions have contributed thought and muscle for the great work of crushing this gigantic rebellion. The men of the Fifth New York Cavalry had their birth in the following places:

New York 797, Pennsylvania 91, New Jersey 39, Massachusetts 32, Vermont 31, Connecticut 18, Ohio 8, Maryland 4, Michigan 4, Maine 3, New Hampshire 3, Illinois 2, South Carolina 2, North Carolina 1, Mississippi 1, Delaware 1, District Columbia 1, Rocky Mountains 1, Ireland 221, Germany 75, Canada 65, England 62, Scotland 12, Prussia 12, France 8, Switzerland 3, Poland 2, Wales 2, Spain 2, Sweden 2, Australia 1, Italy 1, Belgium 1, Denmark 1, Saxony 1, Nova Scotia 1, New Brunswick 1.

The tallest man ever in the regiment was Jacob H. Ten Eyck, Co. M, 6 feet 4 inches; the shortest, John Catlin, Co. A, 4 feet 5 inches.

Journeyings of the Regiment.

If you take a map of the United States or a good War map, and a pencil, I will enable you to trace the contour of the country in which the regiment has fought its battles and made its marches. Place your pencil on the memorable field of Gettysburg, Pa., and move due east to Hanover, thence southeasterly to the head of Chesapeake bay. Follow the bay to the mouth of James river, and up the river to Fort Powhatan on south side. From the fort, strike a straight line to Jarretts Station on the Weldon and Petersburg rail road, and bearing due west, pass through Christianville, thence a little north of west to Roanoke Station, where the Danville and Richmond rail road crosses the Staunton river. Here you may rest awhile for you are more than half way round. Following the rail road northward to Burkesville, we will go west to Appomattox Court House; strike a straight line to Lexington on the James, west of the Blue ridge and thence north to Moorefield. Now draw your line northeastly through Martinsburg; continue it through Hagerstown, Md., and back again to Gettysburg. The territory inclosed by this line has been traversed by the regiment, and some portions of it many times.

I insert the counties through which the regiment has marched, beginning with those we have traversed most frequently and with which we are best acquainted :—

Fairfax, Va., Culpepper, Frederick, (in these the regiment spent three successive winters,) Clarke, Jefferson, Loudon, Prince William, Fauquier, Madison, Orange, Spottsylvania, Shenandoah, Rockingham, Augusta, Warren, Page, Stafford, Rappahannock, Berkeley, Hampshire, Hardy, Caroline, Hanover, King William, New Kent, Henrico, Charles City, Louisa, Rockbridge, James City, York, Gloucester, Prince George, Dinwiddie, Nottoway, Prince Edward, Appomattox, Charlotte, Mecklenburg, Lunenburg, Brunswick, Sussex, and King George;—Montgomery, Md., Frederick, Carroll, and Washington;—York, Pa., and Adams.

Escort Duty for Generals.

The regiment was appointed escort for Gen. Pope, August 27, '62, and served till Sept. 4, '62. It was appointed escort for Gen. Sheridan, Nov. 24, '64, and occupied the position till April, '65.

Generals under whom the Regiment has served.

Gen. N. P. Banks, commanding Army of the Shenandoah.

Gen. John Pope, commanding Army of the Potomac.

Gen. Heintzelman, commanding Defenses of Washington

Gens. Hooker and Meade, commanding Army of the Potomac.

Gen. P H. Sheridan, commanding Army of the Shenandoah.

Gens. Stoneman, Pleasanton and Torbert, commanding Cavalry Corps.

Gen. John P Hatch, commanding Cavalry with Gen. Banks.

Gen. John Buford, commanding Cavalry with Gen. Pope.

Gen. Stahel, commanding Cavalry Division under Gen. Heintzelman.

Gens. Kilpatrick, John H. Wilson, George A. Custer commanding 3d Division, Cavalry Corps.

Gens. Elon J. Farnsworth (killed July 3, '63, Gettysburg), Henry E. Davies, Jr., J. B. McIntosh (wounded in left leg, amputated, Sept. 19, '64, Winchester), commanding 1st Brigade, 3d Division, Cavalry Corps.

The following Colonels, acting Brigadier Generals, have also commanded us, Wyndham, De Forest, John Hammond, and C. M. Pennington.

Burial of our Dead.

By reference to the table of "Men killed in Action," it will be seen that many of our brave comrades were left unburied on the bloody fields were they fell, many of whose bones have doubtless bleached in the sun and rain, through the wilderness and along the river courses of Virginia. But fortunately we were permitted to perform the solemn rites of burial and pay the last honors to some of them, the memory of whose graves will frequently call forth the sympathetic tear, and stimulate us to the performance of heroic deeds. To thee, O land of our birth! and to thee, proud

Flag of the free, we feel unwonted love, since you have both been bathed with the pure blood of our noble dead!

We have endeavored to indicate the resting places of our companions by rude head-boards with their names engraved or cut thereon, though often nothing has been left to identify the precious remains, except the tree that waved in mournful requiem over them, or the rock that stood as their eternal safeguard. Around those quick-made graves we were often compelled hastily to assemble, and from them, perhaps, more hastily to retire, with no funeral note or word, but not without a purpose. Occasionally the military salute has been fired, the brief eulogium and prayer been pronounced,[1] and we have left our comrades to slumber, *but not to be forgotten*. In some instances we have learned, with satisfaction, that the enemy had given our dead a decent interment, and we are conscious of having often returned the favor. Whenever it has been possible the remains of our comrades have been embalmed and sent home to their friends, to molder by the side of kindred dust.

---

[1] See Burial of Sergt. Sortore, p. 133.

Engagements and their Casualties.

PLACE OF ENGAGEMENT.	NO.	DATE.	NATURE.	Comm. Officers. Killed.	Comm. Officers. Wounded.	Comm. Officers. Captured.	Enlist'd Men. Killed.	Enlist'd Men. Wounded.	Enlist'd Men. Captured.
Fort Republic,	1	May 2, '62,	Skirmish,	..	..	..	..	..	1
Conrad's Store, Luray Valley,	2	May 2, '62,	"						
Rockingham Furnace, "	3	May 4, '62,	"						
Conrad's Store,	4	May 6, '62,	"						
Harrisonburg,	5	May 6, '62,	"	..	..	1	1	1	1
Columbia Bridge, Luray V'y,	6	May 8, '62,	"						
Woodstock,	7	May 14, '62,	"	..	1				
Woodstock,	8	May 21, '62,	"						
Front Royal,	9	May 23, '62,	Battle,	1	..	2	2	15	18
Middletown,	10	May 24, '62,	Skirmish,	..	..	..	1	..	5
Newtown Cross Roads,	11	May 24, '62,	Battle,	..	..	..	1	4	2
Winchester,	12	May 25, '62,	"	..	..	.	..	..	10
Harper's Ferry,	13	May 29, '62,	Skirmish,						
Charlestown,	14	May 31, '62,	"						
Martinsburg,	15	May 31, '62,	"						
Sperryville,	16	July 6, '62,	"	..	..	..	..	1	1
Culpepper C. H.,	17	July 12, '62,	"						
Orange C. H.,	18	July 17, '62,	"	..	..	..	..	..	5
Liberty Mills,	19	July 17, '62,	"	..	..	..	..	..	3
Rapidan Station,	20	July 18, '62,	"						
Barnett's Ford, Rapidan,	21	July 18, '62,	"	..	..	1	..	1	22
Orange C. H.,	22	Aug. 2, '62,	Battle,	..	1	..	2	9	11
Cedar Mountain,	23	Aug. 9, '62,	"	..	..	..	1		
Cedar Mountain,	24	Aug. 10, '62,	Skirmish,						
Louisa C. H.,	25	Aug. 17, '62,	"	..	..	..	..	..	3
Kelly's Ford, Rappahannock,	26	Aug. 20, '62,	Battle,	..	..	..	..	1	
Waterloo Bridge,	27	Aug. 24, '62,	"	..	..	..	..	2	
Centreville,	28	Aug. 28, '62,	Skirmish,	..	..	..	..	1	1
Grovetou,	29	Aug. 29, '62,	Battle,						
Bull Run,	30	Aug. 30, '62,	"	..	..	..	1	..	1
Chantilly,	31	Sept. 1, '62,	"						
Antietam,	32	Sept. 19, '62,	"						
Ashby's Gap,	33	Sept. 22, '62,	Skirmish,						
Leesburg,	34	Oct. 16, '62,	"	..	..		..	..	2
Upperville,	35	Oct. 17, '62,	"	..	..	..	..	..	1
Thoroughfare Gap,	36	Oct. 18, '62,	"	..	..	..	..	2	
Hay Market,	37	Oct. 18, '62,	"						
New Baltimore,	38	Nov. 5, '62,	"						
Cedar Hill,	39	Nov. 5, '62,	"						
Hopewell Gap,	40	Nov. 8, '62,	"	..	..	..	..	..	1
Thoroughfare Gap,	41	Nov. 11, '62,	"						
Middleburg,	42	Nov. 12, '62,	"						
Upperville,	43	Nov. 16, '62,	"						
Aldie,	44	Nov. 29, '62,	"						
Snicker's Gap,	45	Nov. 30, '62,	"						
Berryville,	46	Nov. 30, '62,	"						
Aldie,	47	Dec. 18, '62,	"	..	..	..	1	..	1
Cub Run,	48	Dec. 31, '62,	"	..	..	..	..	..	2
Frying Pan,	49	Jan. 5, '63,	"	..	..	..	..	..	7
Cub Run,	50	Jan. 6, '63,	"	..	..	..	..	1	4
Middleburg,	51	Jan. 26, '63,	"	..	..	..	..	..	1
New Baltimore,	52	Feb. 9, '63,	"	..	..	..	..	..	4
Warrenton,	53	Feb. 10, '63,	"						

Engagements and their Casualties, continued.

PLACE OF ENGAGEMENT.	No.	DATE.	NATURE.	Comm. Officers. Killed.	Comm. Officers. Wounded.	Comm. Officers. Captured.	Enlist'd Men. Killed.	Enlist'd Men. Wounded.	Enlist'd Men. Captured.
Spotted Tavern,	54	Feb. 10, '63,	Skirmish,	..	..	..		..	2
Aldie,	55	March 4, '63,	"	..	..	..	.	1	
Chantilly,	56	March 23, '63,	"	..	1	1	3	2	35
White Plains,	57	April 28, '63,	"	..	..	..	.	..	1
Warrenton Junction,	58	May 3, '63,	"	..	3				
Greenwich,	59	May 30, '63,	"	..	1	..	3	6	3
Middleburg,	60	June 10, '63,	"						
Hanover, Pa.,	61	June 30, '63,	Battle,	1	1	..	4	29	18
Hunterstown, Pa.,	62	July 2, '63,	"	..	..	..	..	..	1
Gettysburg, Pa.,	63	July 3, '63,	"	..	..	..	2	2	3
Monterey Pass, Pa.,	64	July 4, '63,	Skirmish,	..	..	1	..	..	2
Smithburg, Md.,	65	July 5, '63,	Battle,	..	..	..	..	1	
Hagerstown, Md.,	66	July 6, '63,	"	..	2	3	3	8	54
Boonsboro', Md.,	67	July 8, '63,	"						
Hagerstown, Md.,	68	July 11, '63,	Skirmish,						
Ashby's Gap,	69	July 26, '63,	"						
Port Conway,	70	Sept. 4, '63,	"						
Culpepper C. H.,	71	Sept. 13, '63,	Battle,	..	1	..	2	7	14
Somerville Ford, Robertson,	72	Sept. 14, '63,	"						
Brookin's Ford, Rapidan,	73	Sept. 22, '63,	Skirmish,						
Hazel River Bridge,	74	Sept. 25, '63,	"						
Ceighrsville,	75	Oct. 8, '63,	"						
Russell's Ford, Robertson,	76	Oct. 10, '63,	"	..	..	..	..	2	8
James City,	77	Oct. 10, '63,	Battle,	..	1	1	1	1	1
Sperryville Pike,	78	Oct. 11, '63,	Skirmish,	..	..	..	..	3	
Brandy Station,	79	Oct. 11, '63,	Battle,	..	..	..	..	4	2
Groveton,	80	Oct. 16, '63,	Skirmish,						
Groveton,	81	Oct. 17, '63,	"						
Groveton,	82	Oct. 18, '63,	"	..	..	..	..	1	1
Gainesville,	83	Oct. 18, '63,	"						
Buckland Mills,	84	Oct. 19, '63,	Battle,	..	1	..	1	5	10
Stevensburg,	85	Nov. 8, '63,	Skirmish,						
Germania Ford, Rapidan,	86	Nov. 18, '63,	"						
Raccoon Ford, Rapidan,	87	Nov. 26, '63,	Battle,						
Raccoon Ford,	88	Nov. 27, '63,	Skirmish,	..	..	..	..	1	1
Ely's Ford, Rapidan,	89	Jan. 19, '64,	"	..	..	..	1	2	2
Ellis' Ford, Rappahannock,	90	Jan. 22, '64,	"	..	..	..	1	6	6
Hampton's Cross Roads,	91	Feb. 6, '64,	"						
Defenses of Richmond,	92	March 1, '64,	Battle,	..	1	..	..	4	18
Hanover Town,	93	March 2, '64,	Skirmish,						
Ayletts,	94	March 2, '64,	"						
Stephensville,	95	March 2, '64,	"	..	..	1	..	..	6
Field's Ford, Rappahannock,	96	March 4, '64,	"	..	..	..	2	1	5
Southard's Cross Roads,	97	March 11, '64,		..	..	..	..	1	1
Parker's Store,	98	May 5, '64,	Battle,	1	1	..	13	22	24
Wilderness,	99	May 6, '64,	"	..	..	..	..	..	1
Germania Ford,	100	May 7, '64,	Skirmish,	..	..	..	..	..	1
Massaponax Church,	101	May 15, '64,	"						
Ny River,	102	May 16, '64,	"	..	..	..	1	1	
Po River,	103	May 17, '64,	"	..	..	1	..	1	1
Po River,	104	May 18, '64,	"						
Mattapony River,	105	May 21, '64,	"	..	..	..	1		
Milford Station,	106	May 21, '64,	Battle,	..	..	..	3	3	3

Engagements and their Casualties, continued.

PLACE OF ENGAGEMENT.	NO.	DATE.	NATURE.	Comm. Officers. Killed.	Comm. Officers. Wounded.	Comm. Officers. Captured.	Enlist'd Men. Killed.	Enlist'd Men. Wounded.	Enlist'd Men. Captured.
Mt. Carmel Church,	107	May 23, '64,	Battle,	..	..	..	1	2	
North Anna River,	108	May 24, '64,	Skirmish,						
Little River,	109	May 26, '64,	"	..	..	..	..	..	2
Signal Hill,	110	May 31, '64,	"						
Hanover C. H.,	111	June 1, '64,	"	..	..	..	..	1	
Ashland Station,	112	June 1, '64,	Battle,	..	2	3	.	13	17
Salem Church,	113	June 3, '64,	"	..	..	..	..	2	
Bethel Church,	114	June 10, '64,	Skirmish,						
Shady Grove,	115	June 11, '64,	"	..	..	..	2	2	1
White Oak Swamps,	116	June 15, '64,	Battle,	..	..	..	2	8	4
White House Landing,	117	June 19, '64,	Skirmish,						
Blacks and Whites,	118	June 23, '64,	"	..	..	..	..	..	2
Nottoway C. H.	119	June 23, '64,	Battle,	..	..	..	..	2	2
Roanoke Station,	120	June 25, '64,	"	..	..	..	..	..	2
Stony Creek Station,	121	June 28, '64,	"	..	..	..	..	3	6
Reams Station,	122	June 29, '64,	"	..	..	2	3	2	48
Rowanty Creek,	123	June 29, '64,	Skirmish,	..	..	..	1	..	8
Stony Creek,	124	June 29, '64,	"	..	..	..	..	..	24
Maryland Heights,	125	July 6, '64,	Battle,						
Maryland Heights,	126	July 7, '64,	"	..	..	..	1		
Rockville,	127	July 10, '64,	Skirmish,						
Toll Gate,	128	July 12, '64,	"						
Poolesville,	129	July 15, '64,	"						
Snicker's Ferry,	130	July 18, '64,	Battle,						
Kernstown,	131	July 24, '64,	"						
Winchester,	132	Aug. 17, '64,	Skirmish,						
Opequan Creek,	133	Aug. 19, '64,	"						
Summit Point,	134	Aug. 21, '64,	Battle,						
Charlestown,	135	Aug. 22, '64,	Skirmish,						
Duffield Station,	136	Aug. 23, '64,	"	..	..	..	..	1	
Kearneysville Station,	137	Aug. 25, '64,	Battle,	1	3	..	4	11	
Berryville,	138	Sept. 2, '64,	Skirmish,						
Berryville,	139	Sept. 4, '64,	"						
Opequan Creek,	140	Sept. 7, '64,	"						
Opequan Creek,	141	Sept. 13, '64,	"						
Opequan Creek,	142	Sept. 15, '64,	"						
Opequan Creek,	143	Sept. 17, '64,	"						
Winchester,	144	Sept. 19, '64,	Battle,	..	2	..	2	11	2
Crooked Run,	145	Sept. 20, '64,	Skirmish,						
Front Royal,	146	Sept. 21, '64,	"	..	..	..	..	1	1
Asbury Church,	147	Sept. 21, '64,	"						
Milford, Luray Valley,	148	Sept. 22, '64,	Battle,	..	..	..	..	1	1
Mt. Meridian,	149	Sept. 27, '64,	Skirmish,	..	..	..	1	5	9
Waynesboro',	150	Sept. 28, '64,	Battle,						
Bridgewater,	151	Oct. 2, '64,	Skirmish,						
Brock's Gap,	152	Oct. 6, '64,	"	..	..	..	..	..	2
Forestville,	153	Oct. 7, '64,	"	..	..	..	1	4	4
Tom's Brook,	154	Oct. 9, '64,	Battle,	..	..	..	..	4	1
Cedar Creek,	155	Oct. 13, '64,	Skirmish,						
Lebanon Church,	156	Oct. 14, '64,	"						
Cedar Creek,	157	Oct. 19, '64,	Battle,	..	..	..	1	2	1
Cedar Creek,	158	Nov. 12, '64,	Skirmish,	..	..	..	1	1	3
Mt. Jackson,	159	Nov. 22, '64,	"	..	..	..	..	4	

Engagements and their Casualties, concluded.

PLACE OF ENGAGEMENT.	No.	DATE.	NATURE.	Comm. Officers. Killed.	Comm. Officers. Wounded.	Comm. Officers. Captured.	Enlist'd Men. Killed.	Enlist'd Men. Wounded.	Enlist'd Men. Captured.
Woodstock, ...	160	Jan. 10, '65,	Skirmish,..	..	..	..	..	..	3
Edinburg,,....................	161	Jan. 22, '65,	" .	..	..	..	..	..	9
Mt. Sidney,..................	162	March 5, '65,	" .	..	..	..	..	1	
Lacey Springs,...............	163	March 5, '65,	" .	..	..	..	..	1	
New Market, ...	164	March 6, '65,	" .						
Rood's Hill,..................	165	March 7, '65,	" .	..	..	..	1	..	3
Dinwiddie C. H.,.............	166	March 31, '65,	Battle, ...						
Five Forks,..................	167	April 1, '65,	" .						
Sweet House Creek,.........	168	April 3, '65,	" .						
Harper's Farm,..............	169	April 6, '65,	" .						
Appomattox Station,.........	170	April 8. '65,	" .						
Appomattox C. H., ...	171	April 9, '65,	" .						
Casualties with no Engag't...			" .	1	..	1	2	1	32

Men killed in Action.

Number.	Names.	Rank.	Company.	Killed. When.	Killed. Where.	Disposition Made of Remains.
1	Selden D. Wales,......	1st. Sgt.	A,	June 30, '63,...	Hanover, Pa.,.................	Buried in Hanover,..........
2	Luther W. Jones,......	Private,	"	May 5, '64,...	Parker's Store, ...	Left on the Field,..........
3	James Duffey,...........	Corp'l.,	B,	May 23, '62,...	Front Royal, ...	" " " ....
4	Michael Rooney,.......	Private,	"	" " "...	" "	" " " ....
5	Daniel Murphy,........	"	"	May 30, '63,...	Greenwich,.....................	Buried on the Field,........
6	William Walsh,.........	Corp'l.,	"	May 5, '64,...	Parker's Store, ...	Left on the Field,...........
7	Keyes Davenport,......	"	"	June 29, '64,...	Rowanty Cr., Wilson's Raid,	" " " ....
8	James Doyle,............	Private,	C,	March 23, '63,...	Chantilly.....	Sent home,.......................
9	Michael Haley,.........	"	"	May 30, '63,...	Greenwich......................	Buried near Catlett's Sta.,
10	Daniel Hurley,.........	"	"	July 3, '63,....	Gettysburg, Pa.,............	Buried on the Field..........
11	Elijah Jeandro,..........	"	"	March 4, '64,...	Ely's Ford,......................	Buried near Stevensburg..
12	Timothy O'Connor, ...	"	"	June 11, '64,...	Shady Grove,..................	Left on the Field,............
13	Percival Fuller,........	"	"	" " "...	" "	" " " ....
14	James H. Riches,......	"	"	June 15, '64,...	White Oak Swamps,.........	" " " ....
15	George Washburn,.....	"	D,	May 24, '62,...	Middletown,....................	" " " ....
16	John Laniger,...........	"	"	June 30, '63,...	Hanover, Pa., ...	Buried in Hanover,.........
17	James Smith.............	"	"	July 3, '63,...	Gettysburg, Pa.,............	Left on the Field,............
18	Asahel A. Spencer,...	"	E,	May 6, '62,...	Harrisonburg,.................	Buried near New Market,..
19	Elias N. Andrews,.....	Sgt.,	"	Dec. 15, '62,...	Aldie,..............................	Sent home,.......................
20	Elam S. Dye,............	1st. Sgt.	"	June 30, '63,...	Hanover, Pa.,.................	" " ....
21	Samuel W Sortore,...	1st. Sgt.	"	May 21, '64,...	Mattapony River.	Buried on the Field,........
22	Henry Stanton,.........	Private,	"	Sept. 27, '64,...	Mt. Meridian,..................	Left on the Field,............
23	John W Clans..........	"	F,	Aug. 30, '62,...	Bull Run,.........................	Buried on the Field,........
24	William Coulston,......	Farrier,	"	Sept. 13, '63,...	Culpepper C. H.,............	" " " ....

Men killed in Action, continued.

Number.	Names.	Rank.	Company.	Killed. When.	Killed. Where.	Disposition Made of Remains.
25	Pliny A. Graves,	Private,	F,	Jan. 22, '64,	Ely's Ford,	Sent home,
26	Frank W. Carl,	"	"	May 5, '64,	Parker's Store,	Left ou the field,
27	Charles Whitney,	Srg't,	"	Oct. 7, '64,	Forestville,	" " "
28	John Quinn,	Private,	G,	Aug. 2, '62,	Orange C. H.,	Buried on the field,
29	Henry Winfield,	"	"	May 5, '64,	Parker's Store,	Left on the field,
30	S. P Rhinevault,	"	"	" " "	" "	" " "
31	J. Vandermark,	"	"	May 21, '64,	Milford Station,	Buried on the field,
32	John B. Witter,	"	"	Aug. 25, '64,	Kearneysville Station,	Buried n'r Bolivar Heights,
33	Benjamin A. Hulett,	"	"	Oct. 19, '64,	Cedar Creek,	Buried southsideCedar Cr.,
34	Charles Gilleo,	Corp'l,	H,	March 23, '63,	Chantilly,	Sent home,
35	Orlando Drake,	"	"	May 30, '63,	Greenwich,	" "
36	Warren McGinniss,	Private.	"	July 6, '63,	Hagerstown, Md.,	Left on the field,
37	Edward A. Winters,	"	"	" " "	" "	" " "
38	Frank Lafrance,	"	"	May 5, '64,	Parker's Store,	" " "
39	Benj. F. Washburn,	"	"	May 23, '64,	Mt. Carmel Church,	Buried near the Church,
40	Conrad Bohrer,	Bugler,	I,	Aug. 2, '62,	Orange C. H.,	Buried on the field,
41	William Adams,	Private,	"	May 7, '62,	New Market,	" " "
42	Harrison Gale,	"	"	" " "	" "	" " "
43	Samuel Calhoun,	"	"	Jan. 19, '64,	Ely's Ford,	Buried near Stevensburg
44	James Mann,	"	"	May 5, '64,	Parker's Store,	Left on the field,
45	Isaiah H. Lovejoy,	"	"	" " "	" "	" " "
46	James Houston,	"	"	" " "	" "	" " "
47	Jacob Haupert,	"	"	Aug. 25, '64,	Kearneysville Station,	Buried on the field,
48	John Harris,	"	K,	March 23, '63,	Chantilly,	Buried near Fairfax C. H.,

Men killed in Action, concluded.

Number.	Names.	Rank.	Company.	Killed. When.	Killed. Where.	Disposition Made of Remains.
49	Charles J. Smith,......	Private,	K,	Aug. 25, '64,.....	Kearneysville Station,......	Buried on the field,.........
50	Charles R. Petze,......	"	L,	Oct. 10, '63,.....	James City,.....................	" " " ....
51	William Runney,......	"	"	May 5, '64,.....	Parker's Store, ...	Left on the field,............
52	Henry Earle,...........	"	"	" " "....	" "	" " " ....
53	Albert Perry, ...	"	"	Sept. 19, '64,.....	Winchester, ...	" " " ....
54	J. G. Horton,...........	Srg't,...	M,	Aug. 9, '62,.....	Cedar Mountain,..............	" " " ....
55	Hiram S. Graves......	"	"	March 7, '65,.....	Rood's Hill,.....................	" " " ....

Men Mortally Wounded in Action.

Number.	Names.	Rank.	Company.	Wounded. When.	Wounded. Where.	Died. When.	Died. Where.
1	Anson Jones, ...	Private,..	A,	May 5, '64,	Parker's Store,.........	May, '64.	ColumbianHosp., D.C.,
2	Amos Brown, ...	"	"	July 7, '64.	Maryland Heights,.....	July 25, '64.	Sandy Hook, Md.,......
3	Clark Winch,.......	"	B,	June 15, '64.	White Oak Swamps,...	July 15, '64.	Washington, D. C.,.....
4	Martin V Hogle,..	"	"	June 29, '64,	Wilson's Raid,..........	Sept., '64.	
5	Wm. Greenwood,..	"	C,	May 21, '64,	Milford Station,.........	July 7, '64,	Whitehall, N. Y.,......
6	Aaron Wright,.....	"	"	" " "	" "	Aug. 17, '64,	Washington, D. C......
7	Edmund Barber,...	"	D,	March 4, '64.	Ely's Ford,..............	March14, '64	Brandy St., sent home,
8	JohnS.Trowbridge	Srg't,.....	E,	June 30, '63,	Hanover, Pa.,...........	July, '63,	Hanover, Pa., s't home,
9	Curtis E., Pieree,...	Private, .	"	Sept., '64,	Berryville,................	Oct. 11, '64,	Winchester,...............
10	CharlesM.Newton,	Corp'l,...	"	Sept. 19, '64,	Winchester,..............	Oct. 19, '64,	Philadelphia, Pa.,......

Men mortally wounded in Action, concluded.

Number.	Names.	Rank.	Company.	Wounded. When.	Wounded. Where.	Died. When.	Died. Where.
11	Silas M. Atwood,...	Sergeant,	F,	May 24, '62,	Newtown Cross Roads,	Unknown,...	Winchester, ...
12	Elijah Brister,......	Private,..	"	Nov. 12, '64,	Cedar Creek.	Nov. 28, '64,	" ....
13	Ira Brown,..........	"	"	Oct. 19, '63,	Buckland Mills,.........	Dec. 1, '63,	Washington, D. C.,.....
14	Everett A Hawley,	"	"	May 16, '64,	Ny River,...............	June 5, '64,	Unknown,...............
15	Erastus McGowen,	"	H,	Sept. 13, '63,	Culpepper C. H.,.......	Unknown,...	Washington, D. C.,.....
16	Chas. N. Chillson,	Sergeant,	"	June 29, '64,	Reams Station,.........	Sept.24, '64,	Ticonderoga, N. Y., ...
17	Amos Wilkins,......	Private,..	K,	Aug. 25, '64,	Kearneysville Station,	Unknown,...	Unknown,...............
18	Karl Keffer,.........	"	L,	June 29, '64,	Reams Station,.........	" ...	New York City,.........
19	John Fricke,........	"	M,	July 6, '63,	Hagerstown, Md.,......	" ...	Unknown,...............
20	Henry Morris,......	"	"	May 5, '64,	Parker's Store,.........	Dec. 21, '64,	Washington, D. C......

Men Discharged by Reason of Wounds Received in Action.

Number.	Names.	Rank.	Company.	Wounded. When.	Wounded. Where.	Nature of Wound.
1	Edward Graham,......	Sergeant,	B,	May 23, '63,.....	Front Royal,...............	Shoulder,..................
2	David Wilkins, ...	Corporal,	"	" " "	" "	Left shoulder,.............
3	Daniel Shugare, ...	Private,..	"	" " "	" "	Right shoulder,..........
4	Peter H. Fero..........	"	"	Dec. 16, '62,.....	Cub Run, ...	Through groin,...........
5	John S. Smith,.........	Corporal,	"	July 6 , '63,.....	Hagerstown, Md.,...........	Left arm,...................
6	William Youngs,........	Farrier, ..	"	" " "	" "	Arm,..........................

Men Discharged by Reason of Wounds Received in Action, concluded.

Number.	Names.	Rank.	Company.	Wounded. When.	Wounded. Where.	Nature of Wound.
7	Samuel M. Denniston,	Corporal,	B,	May 30, '63,	Greenwich,	Unknown.
8	John Quinn,	Private,	D,	May 5, '64,	Parker's Store,	Left shoulder,
9	Charles A. Morris,	Corporal,	E,	Aug. 2, '62,	Orange C. H.,	Right arm,
10	John Mulligan,	Private,	"	March, '64,	Rapidan River,	Unknown,
11	Joseph Coggen,	"	F,	May 24, '62,	Middletown,	Right shoulder,
12	James De Mott,	"	"	March 4, '63,	Aldie,	Through body,
13	Emile Portier,	"	"	June 30, '63,	Hanover, Pa.,	Through left lung,
14	William Blake,	"	"	Oct. 10, '63,	Russell's Ford,	Right groin,
15	William T. I. Lowe,	Sergeant,	G,	Aug. 2, '62,	Orange C. H.,	Through body,
16	Nathan Vandermark,	Private,	"	June 7, '64,	Cold Harbor,	Left wrist,
17	Charles Wilcox,	Corporal,	H,	July 7, '62,	Sperryville Pike,	Left thigh,
18	Charles W. Curtis,	Private.	"	Oct. 11, '63,	Brandy Station,	Left hand,
19	Joseph Woster,	Corporal,	"	June 29, '64,	Reams Station,	Left side,
20	Warren R. Fuller,	Private,	"	Sept. 19, '64,	Winchester,	Left leg amputated.
21	Thomas Carroll,	"	I,	Aug. 25, '64,	Kearneysville Station,	Face,
22	James Barry,	"	"	May 5, '64,	Parker's Store,	Left shoulder,
23	Frederick L. Hecker,	"	K,	" " "	" "	Right arm amputated,
24	Archibald Fraser,	Q.M.Sg't,	L,	Aug. 2, '62,	Orange C. H.,	Right knee,
25	Anthony Cross,	1st Srg't,	"	May 5. '64,	Parker's Store,	Left arm broken,

List of Retired Officers, Fifth New York Cavalry.

Number.	Names.	Rank at Time of Leaving Reg't.	Rank at Time of Original Entry.	Time of Original Entry.	Time of Leaving Regiment.	Company.	Manner of Leaving Regiment.
1	Othniel De Forest,	Colonel,	Colonel,	July 26, 1861,	March 29. 1864,		Special Order. 131 A. G. O.
2	John Hammond,	"	Private,	Sept. 5, 1861,	Aug. 30, 1864,	H,	Expiration of Term
3	Robert Johnstone,	Lt. Col.,	Lt. Col.,	July 27, 1861,	Dec. 5, 1863,		General Order 104 A. of P.
4	William P. Bacon.	" "	1st Lt. & 2d Batt. Adj.,	Oct. 15, 1861,	Sept. 12, 1863,		Resigned.
5	Philip G. Vought,	Major,	Major,	July 27, 1861,	July 1, 1862,		"
6	James Davidson,	"	"	" " "	June, 1862,		"
7	George H. Gardner,	"	"	Aug. 30, 1861,	Nov. 1, 1862,		"
8	Washington Wheeler,	"	Captain,	" " "	Sept. 26, 1862,	F,	"
9	William P. Pratt,	"	"	" " "	Jan. 30, 1863,	E,	"
10	Abram H. Krom,	"	"	Aug. 1, 1861,	Oct. 19, 1864,	G,	Expiration of Term,
11	John R. Cooper,	Surgeon,	Surgeon,	Sept. 4, 1861,	July 1, 1862,		Resigned,
12	Lucins P. Woods,	"	Asst. Surg.	Dec. 24, 1861,	Jan., 1865,		Expiration of Term,
13	Wm. W. D. Parsons,	Asst. Surg.	" "	Aug., 1862,	June, 1863,		Resigned.
14	E. C. Webb,	"	" "	July 23, 1863,	Sept. 8, 1863,		"
15	Robert R. Thompson,	Chaplain,	Chaplain,	Oct. 1, 1861,	Nov. 12, 1862,		"
16	James P. Foster,	Captain,	Captain,	" " "	Aug. 28, 1862.	M,	"
17	Charles Arthur.	"	"	Sept. 27, 1861,	Oct. 24, 1862,	L,	Special Order.
18	William P. Hallett.	"	"	Sept., 1861,	Dec. 16, 1862,	K,	Resigned.
19	George A. Bennett,	"	"	" "	June, 1862,	I,	"
20	Thomas Coyle,	"	"	Aug. 21, 1861,	Nov. 24, 1861,	D,	Died of Disease.
21	Lyon Isaacs,	"	"	" " "	May 18, 1862,	B,	Resigned.
22	Ira Wright,	"	"	Aug. 8, 1861,	Sept. 22, 1862,	C,	Special Order.
23	Augustus P. Green,	"	"	Aug., 1861,	Nov. 5, 1862,	A,	Resigned.
24	Alfred W. Creamer,	"	1st Lieut.,	" "	Jan. 12, 1863,	E & B,	"
25	William H. Williams,	"	" "	Sept., 1862,	Feb. 7, 1863,	E,	"
26	Levi Curtis,	"	" "	Aug. 30, 1861,	Jan. 22, 1863,	F,	"
27	Samuel Ten Broeck,	"	" "	Oct. 16, 1861,	July 4, 1863,	M,	Died of Disease.
28	Zolman J. McMasters,	"	" "	Sept. 27, 1861,	Sept. 24, 1863,	K,	" " "
29	Augustus Barker,	"	" "	" " "	Sept. 14, 1863,	L,	Killed by Guerrillas at Kelly's Ford.

List of Retired Officers, Fifth New York Cavalry, continued.

Number.	NAMES.	Rank at Time of Leaving Reg't.	Rank at Time of Original Entry.	Time of Original Entry.	Time of Leaving Regiment.	Com-pauy.	Manner of Leaving Regiment.
30	Frank A. Monson	Captain	1st Lieut.	May 3, 1862	July 12, 1864	L,	Resigned
31	Abram H. Hasbrouck	"	1st Lt. & 3d Batt. Adj.,	Oct. 1, 1861	Dec. 26, 1863	B,	Special Order
32	Luke McGuinn	"	2d Lieut.	May 23, 1862	May 5, 1864	A,	Killed in Action at Parker's Store
33	William P. Dye	"	Private	Oct. 1, 1861	Sept. 3, 1864	E,	Resigned
34	William B. Cary	"	"	Sept. 5, 1861	Oct. 23, 1864	I,	Expiration of Term
35	John G. Viall	"	"	Sept. 17, 1861	June 18, 1864	H & M,	Appointed A. Q. M. of Vols.
36	Eugene D. Dimmick	"	"	Sept. 12, 1861	Nov. 6, 1863	M,	Physical Disability
37	James A. Peufield	"	"	Sept. 23, 1861	May 2, 1865	H,	Resigned
38	Seth B. Ryder	"	2d Lieut.	Sept. 29, 1861	May 15, 1865	D,	Expiration of Term
39	Charles J. Farley	"	"	Aug. 8, 1861	Jan. 16, 1865	C,	" " "
40	James Bryant	"	Private	Aug. 28, 1861	Jan. 18, 1865	G,	" " "
41	Thomas Burns	1st Lieut.	1st Lieut.	Aug. 15, 1861	May 21, 1862	A,	Resigned
41	Henry L. Bogardus	"	"	Aug. 8, 1861	June 1, 1862	C,	"
43	David Abohbot	"	"	Aug. 21, 1861	May, 1862	B,	"
44	Wallace M. Boyer	"	"	Aug. 30, 1861	July 1, 1862	G,	"
45	Edward C. Woodruff	"	"	Sept., 1861	April 6, 1862	I,	"
46	Charles C. Suydam	"	"	Sept. 27, 1861	May 6, 1862	L,	"
47	Edward Whiteford	"	"	June 1, 1862	Nov. 12, 1862	C,	"
48	George H. Nichols	"	"	March, 1862	June 11, 1862	D,	"
49	Llewellyn N. Stevens	"	"	Jan. 9, 1863	June 1, 1863	B,	"
50	Henry Wilson	"	2d Lieut.	Aug. 15, 1861	Dec. 28, 1862	A,	"
51	Eugene B. Gere	"	"	Aug., 1861	Nov. 19, 1863	G,	"
52	Edward D. Tolles	"	Private	Sept. 21, 1861	Oct. 29, 1863	F,	"
53	Henry J. Appleby	"	"	Sept. 19, 1861	Sept., 1864	D,	Expiration of Term
54	William B. Pickett	"	"	Sept. 21, 1861	Oct. 15, 1864	F,	" " "
55	Daniel B. Merriman	"	"	Aug. 28, 1861	March 29, 1864	E,	Physical Disability
56	Albert B. Waugh	"	"	Sept. 27, 1861	Oct. 23, 1864	L,	Expiration of Term
57	William Watson	"	"	Sept. 21, '61	July 27, 1863	D,	Special Order

List of Retired Officers, Fifth New York Cavalry, concluded.

Number.	NAMES.	Rank at Time of Leaving Reg't.	Rank at Time of Original Entry.	Time of Original Entry.	Time of Leaving Regiment.	Company.	Manner of Leaving Regiment.
58	Jonas A. Benedict,	1st Lieut.,	1st Lieut., "	Sept. 1861,	Dec. 11, 1861,	H,	Died of Gangrene, from the bite of a man on finger
59	Robert Black,	"	Private,	Dec. 26, 1863,	Dec. 16, 1864,	K & I,	By Reason of Wound, at Winchester, Sept, 19, '64,
60	Phillip Krohn,	"	"	Aug. 26, 1861,	May 15, 1865,	G,	Expiration of Term.
61	Alexander Gall,	1st Lt. & Adj.,	"	Sept., 1861,	June 30, 1863,	I,	Killed in Action at Hanover, Pa.
62	Linson S. De Forest,	1st Lt. & R. Q. M.,	1st Batt. Q. M.,	Oct. 1, 1861,	Oct. 23, 1864,		Expiration of Term.
63	Theodore C. Bacon,	1st Lt. & Adj.,	1st Lt. & Adj.,	" " "	Feb. 13, 1862,		Mustered out.
64	John C. Richardson.	1st Lt. & R. Q. M.,	1st Lt. & R. Q. M.	" " "	" " "		" "
65	George H. Griffin,	1st Lt. & 1st Batt. Adj.	1st Lt. & 1st Batt. Adj.	" " "	" " "		" "
66	Moses Minzesheimer,	1st Lt. & 2d Batt. Q. M.,	1st Lt. & 2d Batt. Q. M.	" " "	" " "		" "
67	Charles L. Frothingham,	1st Lt. & 3d Batt. Q. M.,	1st Lt. & 3d Batt. Q. M.,	" " "	" " "		" "
68	Phillip Dwyer,	2d Lieut.,	2d Lieut.,	Aug. 21, 1861,	May 25, 1862,	B,	Mortally wounded in Action, May 23, Front Royal
69	George F. Clough,	"	"	Oct. 1, 1861,	May 6, 1862,	M,	Resigned.
70	Eugene Sullivan,	"	"	May, 1862,	March 24, 1864,	I,	By Special Order.
71	Edward J. McArdle,	"	"	Feb. 12, 1863,	June 1, 1863,	D,	Resigned.
72	Frederic Von Klitzing,	"	"	May 19. 1863,	Sept. 6, 1863,	B,	"
73	Charles H. Greenleaf,	"	Private,	Sept., 1861,	Aug. 26, 1864,	D,	Mortally wounded in Action, Aug. 25. Kearneysville Sta.
74	Jeremiah Collins,	"	"	Aug. 21, 1861,	Dec, 13. 1862,	B,	By Special Order.
75	Robert Harper,	"	"	Aug., 1861,	Nov. 1, 1864,	C,	" " "
76	Joseph B. Grice,	"	"	Sept., 1861,	May 7, 1863,	C,	" " "
77	Walter C. Smith,	"	"	Sept. 21, 1861,	Oct. 15, 1864,	F,	Expiration of Term.,

CHAPTER XIII.

Mementos to Officers.— Col. O. DeForest.— Col. John Hammond. —Surgeon Lucius P. Woods.— Major A. H. Krom.— Major E. J. Barker.— Capt. L. L. O'Connor.

No pains have been spared by the author to secure documents in which honorable mention had been made of officers and privates for meritorious conduct in battles, but with only partial success. Such as have been obtained are inserted, though many names ought to have been added to this list, whose deeds were glorious, and would embellish the pages of any history.

Colonel O. DeForest.

We have been furnished with an interesting account of the presention of a horse to Col. DeForest, clipped from a New York daily, which we are pleased to give in this place. It is as follows:

"The friends of Col. DeForest met yesterday (October, 1861), in front of his dwelling, No. 97 East Forty-ninth street, and presented him with a very acceptable token of their appreciation of him as an officer, and also of his unequaled efforts in raising the brigade to which he is attached. The present was a splendid light dappled gray stallion, well known as the 'General Jackson' of Cherry Valley. He is seven years old, a noble animal, and was purchased specially for his new owner. About 1.500 men of the brigade almost entirely from the country, fully uniformed, and preceded by their own splendid band of twenty-eight pieces, were drawn up in front of the block in which Col. DeForest resides, the intended present held by a groom, being immediately in front. The Hon. D. B. Taylor then stepped out upon the front steps of the building and formally presented to the colonel, who was standing by his side, the donation, accompanied by the following remarks:

"*Colonel DeForest:* The kind partiality of your immediate friends and neighbors have imposed upon me the pleasing duty of presenting to you in their name something which shall be calculated to keep their memories ripe with you in the midst of the excitements and dangers to which you have so gallantly dedicated your immediate future. * *

"These men, you will in a few short days lead into a battle field such as the good people of this heretofore favored land would give all but their country's life to avoid. But the sad fiat has gone forth; it is a struggle between our country's existence, with all the bright hopes of returning happiness, and its death with the surest certainty of everlasting woe and ruin. Terrible is the issue, but we must contemplate it solely with the stern eye of philosophy, and that, too, quickly. Our independence was achieved by precious blood and countless treasure, and by the same consideration can it now only be preserved. It seems that the tree of Liberty must be nourished by the blood of its subjects; to this conclusion, however sad, must every honest conviction turn. You, sir, will soon lead your column to its position in the long line of battle, and to bear you proudly on, we, whose every pulse beats high with hopes for your success, place you upon the back of this *field horse* and pray that the God of Battles may hold the rein, until victory shall be proclaimed throughout our whole country. Should Providence, in its inscrutable wisdom, cause you to perish in the great conflict before you, we feel a holy assurance that you will fall with your face to the heavens, and your feet to the foe. Go on, then: adieu! but the living God grant that your mission may be fulfilled, and your glorious and happy return give us cause for a day joyous, far more joyous than this; let this be the day of hope, that the fulfillment.

"Col. DeForest then mounted the horse as the band struck up an appropriate air, and when the music ceased, evidently with a good deal of emotion, very happily returned his thanks for the manifestation toward him, and fully pledged himself that if the God of Battles spared his life he would faithfully fulfill the wishes of his friends.

"After the cheering had ceased, a call was made for Sen. Ira Harris of Albany, after whom the Guard take their name. He soon appeared upon the balcony, and, being presented by Mr. Taylor, addressed the officers and soldiers for a few moments with much feeling, telling them that although he was too far advanced in life to join them as a soldier, he felt great satisfaction in being able to send his name. He doubted not it would be seen where rebellion was strongest and treason most defiant, and he was perfectly willing to trust it in the keeping of such officers and such men.

COL. JOHN HAMMOND.

The application of Col. Hammond for muster out was endorsed as follows:

HEAD QUARTERS, Third Cavalry Division,
August 30*th*, 1864.

[Respectfully forwarded, approved].

Col. Hammond is a most valuable and worthy officer and has served with great credit to himself and benefit to the service — but the regiment would be left in the hands of a good officer [1] should he be mustered out, while the reasons urged by Col. Hammond for his leaving service are of so grave a character as to deserve the serious consideration of the major general commanding the department.

J. H. WILSON, Brig. Gen'l.

HEAD QUARTERS, Cavalry Forces,
Middle Military Division,
Charlestown, Va., *Aug.* 30*th*, 1864.

I am constrained to approve this application under the circumstances; but I am pleased to mention from personal observation that he is one of the most accomplished officers I have known in service, and the country can ill afford to lose the services of such an officer at this time.

Respectfully submitted,

A. T. A. TORBERT,
Brig. Gen. Vols. Com'd'g Cav'y.

A few days after Col. Hammond took leave of his command, he received the following letter:

HEAD QUARTERS, Third Cavalry Division,
Near Berryville, *Aug.* 31*st*, 1864.

My Dear Colonel: I am sorry you took your final farewell from the division without letting me see you again; I cannot, however, allow your absence to prevent my sending

---

[1] Lt. Col. Wm. P. Bacon

after you my sincere regrets at losing you, and my best wishes for your prosperity and happiness.

It is no flattery to say, your loss cannot be repaired in this command except by your return to it, and I must earnestly hope for its sake and *the cause*, that circumstances may so shape themselves as to allow you speedily to rejoin us with increased rank and authority

There may be something personal in it, but your absence gives me special pain. Our cause, the country's, needs not only the support of stout arms and brave hearts, but that of every pure and moral nature in the land. When one such as yourself leaves the service, there is, therefore, a double loss, with more than the ordinary difficulties to overcome in repairing it. There are plenty of men who wish to advance themselves, but few that are worthy of the places to which they aspire.

In writing you this letter permit me to assure you the sentiments I express are shared by Gen. Sheridan as well as by every member of my staff.

With sentiments of the highest regard, I am, Colonel,

Very Truly Your Friend,

J. H. WILSON,

Brig. Gen'l.

Shortly after his departure from the regiment, the following letter appeared in the *Essex County* (N. Y.) *Republican.* Its contents were approved by those who had been the colonel's military companions.

It is seldom we are called upon to chronicle as painful an event as that which separated Col. John Hammond from the Fifth New York Cavalry. After so long a term of service with him, we had learned not only to respect, but to love him, while we admired the great virtues which so happily blend in him. It is no wonder that there was not a dry eye among the officers who shook his hand in farewell greeting yesterday, nor difficult to account for the emotion which choked his utterance when he undertook to address us a few parting words.

It is not often we comment upon the private or public virtues of *living* men, but in this case our justification lies in derogating from our general rule.

The early call of our country for patriot soldiers, found nowhere a heartier response than in the heart of John Hammond, of Crown Point, Essex Co., N. Y. Gathering together the young men of his neighborhood, a company of as effective men as ever drew a sabre was formed, known as company H, Fifth New York Cavalry, and John Hammond was chosen its captain and leader. To his men the captain devoted his attention and means. Mutual confidence and respect increased with discipline in camp and service in the field. It was soon discovered that Capt. Hammond was no ordinary military leader. Gradually he rose from one post of trust to another. While a major he had command of the regiment more than a year. At the earliest vacancy he was commissioned lieutenant colonel, and soon thereafter colonel, and no man ever bore the spread eagle more worthily. Had not his term of service expired at a time when the call of his family was nearly imperative, we doubt not he would soon have borne the star. The commendations he has received from both division and brigade commanders, are known to us all, and are such as any man might be proud of. His fame is unsullied and extensive, his record fair and imperishable.

Few men combine in themselves so many qualifications of the *true* man and soldier. His patriotism was not a mere matter of name, as the sacrifices he made for his country fully attest. All who came in contact with him felt that this was the ruling motive of all his action. As a disciplinarian he was strict without being severe, and thorough. In preparation for, and during, a battle, none could excel him.

His plans were quickly made and well executed. His selection of positions, and disposition of forces always exhibited great sagacity and military genius. He held his men in perfect control. His clear voice went like magic through the ranks, while his manly form, always in the thickest of the fight, elicited the warmest enthusiasm. His equanimity of mind was never overcome by his celerity of motion, but seemed to be equal. Rarely is so great prudence found with so undaunted courage. He had an indomitable will that would not brook defeat. The word *impossible* he never knew, when difficulties came between him and duty. He was ambitious, yet humble.

Added to all these mental qualifications was that perfect *physique*, which made John Hammond the model soldier. As an equestrian we have never seen his superior. His power of endurance also was very great. For three long years of active service he has stood with the regiment mid storm and sun, mid fatigue and danger. He was no wanderer from his men, nor lover of ease at the expense of duty. For this the men honored him; and they loved him because in all his promotions he never forgot their wants, nor stood aloof from them. He was always the affable yet dignified John Hammond they had known in days past.

We hope the men of his late command will never forget his last words to them:—"God bless you."

Long live Col. John Hammond, and long be remembered among us his military and social virtues.

SURGEON LUCIUS P. WOODS.

HEAD QUARTERS Fifth New York Cavalry,
Winchester, Va., *July* 10*th*, 1865.

Intelligence having been received of the death of Dr. Lucius P. Woods, late surgeon of this regiment, a meeting was this day convened, and a committee, consisting of Major H. A. D. Merritt, Chaplain L. N. Boudrye and Capt. L. C. Abbott was appointed to prepare fitting resolutions expressive of our sorrow. The following were submitted and approved.

Resolved, That we, the officers of the Fifth Regiment of Cavalry, New York State Volunteers, have heard with most profound sorrow, of the death of our late surgeon, Dr. Lucius P Woods, at Winsted, Conn., May 30th, 1865, and desire to convey to his bereaved wife and friends our sympathy, and to express our sentiments of esteem and respect for the memory of our late comrade and friend. Appointed to this regiment, December 24th, 1861, he shared with us, during three years' active service, its vicissitudes, dangers and privations. Devoted to the duties of his vocation, he added to rare professional skill the most untiring industry. Insensible to fear, indefatigable to alleviate suffering, he was ever to be found where the battle raged most fiercely, ministering to the wounded, shunning not the post of danger, if it were but the post of duty.

Conscious of declining health, and viewing with calmness and resignation the rapidly approaching termination of his life, ne persevered, until strength failed him, in the discharge of his responsible and arduous duties. Finally, enfeebled and dying, he returned to the peaceful scenes of home, and to the loved home circle, to meet the final change. Happily his earnest patriotism was rewarded with a knowledge of the triumph of the cause to which he gave his life.

Resolved, That in the several positions of surgeon of the Fifth New York Cavalry, surgeon-in-chief of the First brigade, Third cavalry division, surgeon-in-chief of the Third cavalry division and medical director of the Cavalry corps, Army of the Shenandoah, Dr. Woods earned the commendation, respect and affection of all who knew him, from the soldier in the ranks to the major general commanding.

Resolved, That as a friend we found in him every quality that could endear him to us and embalm his memory in our minds. To the refinement of the gentleman he added social and Christian virtues rarely equaled, and while his loss will be deplored by all, to ourselves, peculiarly his friends, it is irreparable. We will cherish his memory and strive to imitate his example.

Resolved, That a copy of these resolutions, signed by the officers of the regiment, be transmitted to Mrs. L. P. Woods, to whom we tender our sincere condolence. May "He who tempereth the wind to the shorn lamb," comfort and sustain her; and may the blessed thought that he has given his life for his country mitigate the anguish of her bereavement.

Interesting extracts from Dr. Woods' letters from the army, are here inserted.

"HARTWOOD CHURCH, VA., *Sept. 5th*, 1863."

"I returned yesterday after a three days expedition after

Lucius P Woods
Surg in Chief
1st Brig. 3rd Div

gun-boats![1] We all laughed at the order, sending cavalry after such craft, but I am happy to say, that the object of the expedition was accomplished. We left camp at two o'clock A. M., marched all day and all night, till three o'clock next morning, when we made a furious charge upon Rebel infantry. They ran so fast as to disarrange the general's plan of attack. The morning was so dark we could not see one rod in advance. We captured twelve or fourteen prisoners, and Gen. Kilpatrick gave orders in their hearing to have the whole command fall back, stating that the gun-boats would be alarmed and the expedition be a failure. The general took particular pains to allow half the prisoners to escape and get across the Rappahannock. After falling back two miles, we were counter-marched toward the river, near which we were formed in line of battle. We sat there on our horses waiting for daylight. Then the flying artillery of ten guns, supported by the old Fifth New York and First Michigan, dashed at a full run down to the river bank, wheeled into position and gave the Rebels a small cargo of hissing cast iron, which waked them up more effectually than their ordinary morning call. They soon came to their senses, and for half an hour sent over to us what I should think to be, by the noise they made, tea-kettles, cooking stoves, large cast iron hats, &c. But our smaller and more active guns soon silenced theirs and drove their gunners away, when we turned our attention to the boring of holes in their boats with conical pieces of iron, vulgarly called solid shot. I assure you I can recommend them as first class augers, for they sank the boats in time

[1] See page 74.

for all hands to sit down to breakfast at half past nine o'clock. The repast consisted of muddy water, rusty salt pork and half a hard cracker, termed by us 'an iron clad breakfast.' We were absent from camp three days and had only nine hours' sleep."

"*August* 29*th*, 1864."

"I was quite astonished yesterday at receiving a paper, signed by nearly all the officers of the regiment and approved by Gen. McIntosh, offering me the colonelcy of the regiment. I am now surgeon-in-chief of the division."

"*February* 12*th*, 1865."

"To Colonel Hammond: My official business is done by a clerk and I simply sign my name. The reason: a terrible cough, drenching night sweats, swollen feet and limbs and diarrhœa. Are not these sufficient to palsy the brain and hand? Often have I tried with my will to arouse my system to action and my mind to its duty, but as I crawled to bed I almost cursed the sluggish brain that balked my efforts."

We gladly insert the following tribute to Dr. Woods, in a letter from Col. Hammond to Dr. H. M. Knight, of Lakeville, Conn.

"It will be impossible for me to think of writing anything that would do justice to the memory of one I loved so much. I could but poorly give you an idea of the many trials and hardships as well as incidents of a pleasing character, through which myself and dear friend have passed together.

"His frankness and determination won him a host of friends wherever he went. He was ever quick to appreciate worth and kindness, and ever as ready to resent a wrong or injury. * * * * * * I will close by saying that Dr. Woods was ever in my mind the most perfect type of a man I ever met."

Dr. Woods graduated at the medical college of Pittsfield, Mass., in November, 1855.

CAPTAIN (afterward Major) A. H. KROM.

From the *Owego Times* of May, 1864, we clip the following memorial:

HEAD QUARTERS Fifth New York Cavalry,
Fairfax Court House, Va., *May* 19*th*, 1863.

This has been a high day for the officers and men of company G; and well might it be so, for the boys were about to consummate a noble enterprise, and true merit was about to be rewarded. We may as well tell the story plainly. Capt. Krom had distinguished himself as a man and soldier in camp and in battle. On the 3d instant, during a severe engagement with Maj. Mosby's Rebel band, at Warrenton Junction, Va., Capt. K. narrowly escaped with his life, bearing away two fearful wounds, one in his left leg, the other in the face. His horse was killed under him; but he had used his sabre with terrible effect upon the enemy, as only the man with a brave heart and strong arm can do. From that time he has been a cheerful sufferer in our hospital. He will doubtless recover, as is the strong desire of all his companions in arms. His absence from the company did not obliterate his memory from the boys. They have been busy raising funds among themselves, every man in the company contributing freely, and to-day we see the result—a beautiful *sash, sword and belt* for the captain. At six o'clock P. M. the ceremony of presentation took place. The company were all present, drawn up in line before the captain, who had been brought to his camp quarters on a stretcher, and seated in a large arm chair secured for the occasion. Many officers of the regiment were present, while ladies assisted in making the company complete. The sword was presented by Lieut. Krohn, company G, who read the following address:

"*Esteemed Commander:* The men who have the pleasure and honor of being under your command; men who have learned to respect you for your uniformly kind and generous conduct toward them, who have learned to love you as only soldiers can love their benefactor in the midst of danger and trial; men who now admire you for your tried courage and undaunted bravery in battle; these men have gathered around you to-day to express their deep gratitude to the kind Providence that has preserved your life to this hour, and to present to you a token expressive of their high appreciation of your military genius and valor. And what better could we give to one who has distinguished himself with the sabre in so many engagements, and especially on the 3d instant, at Warrenton Junction, Va., where you valiantly fought, and gloriously fell, bleeding from the wounds that remove you, only temporarily, we trust, from our mdist?

What better could we present to such a hero than this sword?

"Captain, take this: I present it on behalf of these men, who desire never to have a better commander; who pray God to restore you speedily to strength and to command again, that, with you, they may march on to conquest and to victory, and, if need be, to death, scattering the enemies of our beloved country, and bearing aloft the 'Stars and Stripes' in proud triumph."

The captain not being able to respond on account of his wounds, the chaplain of the regiment, who stood by, spoke as follows:

"In behalf and by request of the captain, I wish to make a few remarks in response to the sentiments expressed by the company and the gift presented. He looks upon this as one of the proudest days of his history, and the most memorable since he entered the service of his country. For nearly two years he has been your commander, while the very best of feeling has existed between you and him from the first to the present, only with an increase of respect and affection. He has occasion to-day to entertain the hope that the future, in this respect, will be but a repetition of the past.

"As to his gratitude for your kindness so generously expressed in the gift of this hour, it cannot be told. When a man is overwhelmed with a sense of thankfulness, words are not adequate to the task of uttering the pent-up emotion. And his gratitude is greatly multiplied as he recognizes in this gift an expression, not only of personal regard toward him, but also of devoted loyalty to the cause of the Union, and of attachment to the good old flag, which he feels you are determined to bear forward until it shall wave in triumph over every land and sea. Men, you behold your captain, wounded and disabled; but he wishes me to say to you that he hopes the time is not far distant, when his wonted strength and vigor will return to his now somewhat withered limbs — when again, at the shrill battle-notes of the bugle, he shall be permitted, with you,

20

to leap forward to glorious conflict. *Though wounded he is not killed.* In conclusion, allow me, on his behalf, to bow to you all most heartfelt thanks."

After this ceremony, the numerous guests and all the company were richly entertained with a sumptuous supper, gotten up by the captain. Thus ended an interesting chapter in the annals of company G, Fifth New York Cavalry.

LIEUTENANT (afterward Major) E. J. BARKER.

From one of the April (1864) numbers of the *Essex County Republican*, we extract an interesting account of a sword presentation to Lieut. Barker, at a large meeting, held at Hammond's Corners, Crown Point, when the veterans of company H were welcomed by the people, on their veteran furloughs.

Hervey Spencer, Esq., having been requested by company H, on behalf of the company, presented to Lieut. E. J. Barker a beautiful sword, purchased by the members of the company for gallant conduct in battle, particularly that of Greenwich, May 30th, 1863.

Mr. Spencer, in an able manner, addressed the young lieutenant, giving a short sketch of his gallant and manly bearing since entering the service, reminding him of the due appreciation of his conduct and bravery, by the brave men of his command, and as a testimonial of their love and esteem of him whom they had followed even to the cannon's mouth, presented him with this beautiful sword.

Lieut. Barker, made a short but eloquent reply.

He thanked them for this token of their regard for him. He said he had simply done his duty That without their coöperation he could have done nothing. He again feelingly thanked them for their beautiful present, and assured them that when they returned to the field, that it should be faithfully wielded by him in the defense of his country, as long as armed treason existed within her borders.

The gallant lieutenant was heartily cheered and congratulated for his very appropriate and elegant remarks.

LIEUT. (afterward Capt.) LAURENCE L. O'CONNOR.

WAR DEPARTMENT, Washington D. C.,
April 2d, 1863.

Sir: I am directed by the secretary of war, to acknowledge the vigilance and fidelity with which it is reported, you have in the discharge of your duty, as Provost Marshal at Fairfax Court House, watched contrabandists and prevented or broken up their disreputable and disloyal trade.

Your integrity and efficiency in the discharge of your duties merit and will receive the commendation of this department.

Very respectfully your obedient servant,

P. H. WATSON,
Assistant Secretary of War.

Lieut. O'CONNOR, 5th N. Y. Cavalry,
Provost Marshal, Fairfax, C. H., Va.

CHAPTER XIV

Influence of Campaigning on our Men.— Who can best Resist the Evils.— Means Employed.— The Mail Bag.— The Spelling School.— Literary Classes.— Our Chapel Tents.— Our Temperance Club.— Meetings for Religious Worship.— The Effect on our Discipline.

Many unavoidable influences have a very detrimental effect upon the mind of the soldier. His frequent exposures to the extremes of heat and cold, of hunger and thirst, of fatigue and excitement, with the general wear and tear of military life, debilitate body and mind together. Only men of the most steady habits, and of naturally strong physical constitutions, can at all resist these influences; and even such men are more or less affected. Such influences the soldier experiences on the difficult and dangerous picket; on the long, tedious march, through rain, dust, or snow; in the fierce conflict of battle, and, more emphatically still, in the dreary dungeon, and by the barbarous treatment of the enemy while a captive in his hands. Under the above exigencies, the cavalry suffers more than the infantry — it is more constantly on duty, and, when in captivity, feels more poignantly the effects of the weary *foot* marches to which our prisoners have been so often subjected.

Aside from these influences, affecting the entire mental manhood, are others which have only a moral bearing.

First, and, perhaps, most important of these, *is the removal of the wholesome and normal restraints of virtuous society*, of home and its hallowed associations. These influences may not be entirely forgotten by the soldier, but in few cases only do they control him. Neither must it be ignored that his *business*, in great part, is demoralizing. He is taught and disciplined for one thing — to destroy and kill. Moreover, he is often compelled to execute orders of retaliation for acts of brutality and murder, perpetrated by the enemy.[1] However noble may be the object sought, or wholesome the influence of the chastisement visited upon the evil-doers, these military necessities are far from being promoters of morality in the actors. While we doubt not that the ultimate influence of war is salutary on the body politic and social of a nation, yet it must be conceded that the actors in war,—soldiers in camp and field, are themselves more or less demoralized. And this must be said even of our army, the most intellectual and moral army ever known in the history of nations. Soldiering makes some men; it *un*makes many.

This regiment has had occasion to feel a due proportion of evil influences, which are inseparably connected with active military service. But there has been displayed a strong disposition to resist and overcome them; so that while evils have abounded among us, we are not without some tokens of mental and moral strength, as well as growth and development. These have been manifested, while in camp, through the mail-bag, which carried, on an average, about one hundred and twenty-five letters per day; also in

---

[1] See page 176.

literary classes, established in the spring of 1863, in mental arithmetic, phonography and French, which were kept up as long as camp life permitted, and evinced remarkable application and scholarship. Mention must also be made of what the boys of the Old Fifth will never forget, of the spelling school, which was held regularly once a week, and called out crowded audiences of happy, thoughtful fellows. The following account of "Our First Spelling School in Camp," is drawn partially from my diary and was published in February, 1864, in the *New York Christian Advocate and Journal.*

Efforts had been put forth for several weeks to get the men out to the newly-erected chapel tent for religious services; also for classes in reading, writing, spelling, arithmetic, phonography, etc., but the number secured did not appear commensurate to the occasions. Finally, while repeatedly asking myself the question, "What can I do more?" my mind alighted upon what promised to meet the exigency of the times. Immediately I announced at the meetings, and to individuals whom I met, that on Monday night, Feb. 15th, there would be a spelling school in the chapel. By the sparkle of many an eye I quickly saw that I had pulled on the right string. The appointed time for our first spelling school in camp drew near but too tardily.

The evening was fine and the chapel full. We soon addressed ourselves to the business of the occasion. It was a season of *intense* enjoyment. The "choosing of sides" and the "spelling down," how much they reminded us of schoolboy days! Every one was happy in that remembrance, and joyful in the new throbbings of intellectual life. The short intermission for rest, after the severe conflict, in which troop "A" missed fire eleven times, and troop "B" ten, was spent in social *parley*, and ended with the "Star-spangled Banner," sung with an unusual zest.

Spelling was continued with such interest that the shrill roll-call took us all by surprise, and we dispersed, each feeling that long would be remembered the spelling school, at which our pedagogue was the chaplain, and our spelling-book, the Army Regulations!

I regard this enterprise as a great success in my line of duty as chaplain. For,

First. Anything that will stimulate the mind toward general improvement, must be beneficial. The peculiar trials, habits and labors of the soldier, very naturally benumb his intellect, and, in a great measure, incapacitate him for mental and moral improvement. Hence *ordinary* influences fail to reach him. Something peculiar must be tried. This was furnished by the spelling-school movement.

Second. Memories of childhood's innocence and youth's impressive lessons at the home fireside, at the church and school, are the most potent influences which can be brought to bear on the soldier's heart and conduct. These may be aroused, to a certain extent, by the chaplain's ordinary labor, but to a much greater extent by this novel spelling-school movement.

Third. The chaplain's influence in the regiment is proportionate to his *real* acquaintance with the men. This he may gain by various means: by distributing papers from tent to tent; by visiting the sick at the hospital and at their quarters; by the public services for preaching; by the Sunday school or Bible class, and other social, religious assemblies; but in all these he appears in his *official* capacity, and the soldier who is so disposed, has ample opportunity to prepare himself to repel every approach. Not so when the chaplain comes as the *schoolmaster*, the good-natured schoolmaster of bygone days. The chaplain thus, though not with the intention of the spy, approaches *unawares* to the heart of the soldier, and then has power to do him good. While I do not ignore *any* ordinary means of chaplain's service, I heartily rejoice in the spelling-school movement.

Our second spelling school in camp, Providence permitting, will be held on Monday evening, Feb. 22d, the anniversary of Washington's birthday.

For all these privileges we were much indebted to the U. S. Christian Commission, which furnished us with large flies or paulons and stoves, with which we were able to construct rude, but comfortable chapel tents. These tents were built of large logs or trees, notched at the ends, and thus fitted one on the other, for the walls, while the whole was covered over by means of the flies furnished by the Commission. By a careful application of mud— that Virginia mortar with which every soldier is so familiar— to the crevices between the logs, then by flooring with pine boughs, or boards, as opportunity allowed, we secured places for our public assemblies, resembling those of our pioneers in the western wilds, and rivaling for comfort, if not for architecture, those of our northern homes. In these chapels were also evidenced our moral and religious tendencies. Not only to the classes and schools did the boys turn their attention, but night after night many could be seen wending their way from their tents to the meetings for temperance, and for religious worship. An honorable

OUR CHAPEL TENT,

Near Winchester, Va., 1865.

scroll, superscribed with a total abstinence pledge, contains the names of upward two hundred men of the regiment. On this subject I quote from my diary.

February 21*st*, 1864. It is gratifying to see that notwithstanding the almost universal custom of *dram drinking* in the army, the subject of temperance meets with general acceptation when it is fairly presented to soldiers. On Wednesday evening, the 17th instant, I lectured on the trite subject of the "physical and mental influences of intemperance." A lively interest was awakened. I at once proposed the organization of a temperance society. At least one-half the audience voted for it. A committee was appointed, who drafted the following preamble and pledge:

"We, the undersigned members of the Fifth New York Cavalry, desiring to strengthen each other against the evils of intemperance and to save therefrom our comrades in arms, if possible, do hereby form ourselves into a society to be known as 'The Fifth New York Cavalry Temperance Club,' and agree to conform to the following pledge: I hereby solemnly pledge myself, on the honor of a gentleman and soldier, to abstain entirely from the use of all intoxicating liquors."

This evening our chapel was crowded for a temperance meeting. Chaplain Roe, Second N. Y. Cavalry, gave us a spicy talk on the degrading influences of intemperance. Mr. James H. Bond, of Co. A, followed him, giving us "bits" of personal experience, and deepening the interest already awakened. I then offered the pledge. The invitation was promptly responded to and by greater numbers than had been expected by the most sanguine. Several made remarks as they came up to the noble work. One said, "How glad will mother be when she hears of this." Another, "My wife would rejoice to know what I am doing." Some one asked, "When a soldier deserts the country's cause we shoot him; what shall we do to him who deserts this cause?" "Shoot him," was the almost unanimous reply. One officer came forward, saying, "he could not bear being stumped by a private." The work went on gloriously. Forty-seven names were on our list before the meeting closed; forty-three in the column, "for life," and four, "for term of service."

The meeting was one of intense interest—I think we never can forget it. At a later date I wrote as follows: ninety-five have given their names. Our meetings are large and interesting. A pledge also against *profanity* is being circulated with success.

April 29th, 1864. Before leaving our old camp ground, this morning, the two-hundredth man signed the pledge, in consequence of which, Mr. Doggett, the owner of the place, who was present, changed the name of the eminence from "The Devil's Leap" to "Temperance Hill," a name which it truly deserved and which should go down to history. Some remarkable instances of reform from intemperance as well as from profanity might be mentioned, while the Christian would delight to hear recitals of reforms even more radical and far-reaching. Meetings for divine worship, which have been numerous during winter quarters, whether held in chapels, rudely constructed by our own hands, or under "the clouded canopy or starry decked heaven," in woods or fields, have been generally well attended. These agencies have had no small influence on the discipline and consequent efficiency of the regiment.

CHAPTER XV.

Life in Southern Prisons. — Personal Experience of the Author. — Capture. — Gen. Stuart. — Incidents of March to Staunton, Va., from Pennsylvania.— Libby Prison, Richmond. — Cruelties of Managers. — State of Rooms. — Vermin. — Rations. — The Soup. — Water. — Richmond Papers. — "Skirmishing." — Bone Cutting. — The Debating Club. — "Libby Lice-I-see-'em," (Lyceum). — The Weekly *Libby Chronicle*. — Literary Classes. — Religious Services. — The Author Preaches to our Prisoners in Pemberton Castle. — Wretched Condition of our Men. — Release. — What he Brought with him. — Diary of Sufferings at Salisbury, N. C. — Untold Wretchedness at Andersonville, Ga. — List of Men who Died in Rebel Prisons.

Life in southern prisons presents us by far the darkest picture of the war. The cruel treatment of prisoners during the dark ages of the past, seems but as a pleasant pastime, compared to that inflicted upon our brave men at Richmond, Salisbury, Columbia, Andersonville, and at other places, by the professedly chivalrous people of the south. The statistics of these pages show, that while the enemy killed but seventy-five of our men in battle, he killed one hundred and fourteen in his prisons. Though this proportionate loss may not exist in every regiment which has participated in this struggle, yet the world will stand aghast at the figures, — if a correct computation is ever made, — exhibiting the amount of mortality occasioned by this cause alone.

The outlines of prison life are too well known throughout

21

the country to warrant us in giving more than a brief sketch of personal experience, by men of the regiment. The author, who, with hundreds of others, sojourned for a season in the famous Libby Prison, rejoices in an opportunity of publishing in these records, a few letters, which set forth what he saw, what he did and what he endured while among the Rebels.

NEAR STAUNTON, Va.,
July 17*th*, 1863.

My Dear P. R.: I never wrote you under so embarrassing and peculiar circumstances; nor do I know that my letter will ever be of any avail. I am a poor, wretched prisoner of war! Early Sunday morning, the 5th instant, near Monterey Gap, Pa., during Gen. Kilpatrick's raid on the Rebel train, retreating from Gettysburg, I was surrounded by the enemy and captured. Others with me shared the same fate. It was hard to say, "I surrender." It was Jenkins' cavalry that had done the deed. Being a chaplain and my horse my own and not the government's, it was promised me that as soon as I reached Gen. Stuart's headquarters, I would be released and none of my property would be molested. True as the chivalry are able to be to their promises, on reaching the general, I was immediately released — of my horse and of all hopes of liberty. A personal interview with the general and earnest pleadings were in vain. Gen. S. is a fine looking officer. His features are distinct in outline, his nose long and sharp, his eye keen and restlessly on the lookout. His complexion is florid. He wears a gray plush hat with a black feather; has plain uniform, and a short bowie knife by his side with ivory handle, attached to his person by a golden chain. He seems to trust no man to do what he can possibly do himself. But there is more chivalry in the exterior than in the interior, I fear.

Baffled at every point, dismounted and dispirited, I spent a miserable Sabbath, I assure you, traveling nearly all day over the Catoctin mountains into Maryland.

Monday evening, the 6th, after a dreary day of marching and fasting — for our rations were short and poor, — the column had halted and the prisoners sought sleep on the soft grass. I had just fallen into a doze, when I was roused up by a strange voice, calling "Chaplain Fifth New York Cavalry." Looking up, I beheld a Rebel lieutenant, with whom I had conversed a little during the day, who stepped up toward me with a cup of smoking hot coffee and a fine piece of warm bread. "There, chaplain, I thought you might be hungry, and brought you this for your supper." I was quite overcome with gratitude at an act so unexpected and so rare, and my heart leapt up for joy, as at the sight of the first flower of spring. That, I think, was a noble man, though he was a Rebel, and I have not found another among them like him. On Wednesday, the 8th, we were put across the Potomac at Williamsport. The Rebel army was very much discouraged and demoralized. The officer of the guard on reaching the "Old Virginy Shore," flung his sword on the ground, exclaiming with much feeling, "Lie there, and I never will cross this river again on an expedition of this kind." Many Rebels appeared to feel as he did.

Near Washington Springs, not far from Winchester, we spent two days to rest. There were about 200 officers, prisoners, with me, and about 4,000 privates. While at the Springs we heard of the fall of Vicksburg. An amusing and interesting incident here took place. A little slave mulatto boy, about twelve years of age, was asked whom he liked best, the "Rebs" or the "Yanks?" Scarcely willing to answer, as there were more Rebels around him than Yankees, he hung his head down a little while, but finally looking up with his large, intelligent eyes, he said, "The Yanks." All joined in a hearty laugh over the unexpected answer. I then asked, "Why do you like the Yanks best?" "Because they don't sell me," was the quick and emphatic reply, astonishing us all at his wisdom and understanding.

At Winchester I had an interview with Gen. Imboden. I failed to obtain relief, but obtained a storm of abusive words. With varied experiences I have come up this valley, traveling in all, since my capture, about 200 miles, on an average of twenty miles per day. The soles of my feet are a complete blister. To-morrow we expect to take the cars at Staunton for Richmond. If I ever get a chance, I will send you my letter, if not, I will try to preserve it.

Ever yours,

L. N. B., Chaplain 5th N. Y. Cav.

LIBBY PRISON, Richmond, Va.,
September 1st, 1863.

My Dear P. R: I hope you have received my former letter which I sent secretly by ——, who was more fortunate than the most of us, and got away on a special exchange. On the 23d ultimo, I received two of your letters. Oh! what joy they were to me in my prison house. Every flag of truce boat brings and carries mail, but we have to write only one page for a letter, and it has to be read in the office below, before it can pass. Yours meet the same fate before reaching me. You say you are very anxious to know how we fare. I will tell you. As we expected when I wrote you, we reached this place on Saturday evening, the 18th July. From the depot we were marched to the prison, which stands on the corner of 20th and Cary streets. It is a large brick building, about 135 feet long and 105 feet wide, three stories high on Cary street, and four stories high back on the canal. Next to the street is a row of cells under ground. On the corner of the building is a sign with "Libby & Son," from which the prison takes its name. Two heavy walls divide the building into three nearly equal parts making nine large rooms above ground. By means of openings or doors through these walls, access may be had from one room to the other. You will shudder when I tell you that these rooms are so infested with vermin, that you cannot escape their loathsome presence. The windows around us are mostly barred, though some are not. So much, then, for the *place* where we live, I mean, stay.

I will now give you some specimens of the men who rule over us. On arriving at the prison, we were unceremoniously introduced to Dick Turner, who, having conducted us into the reception hall, fell to pillaging us. I was quickly delivered of my poncho, haversack and canteen. My money was not taken, for what little I had was Confed.; that they did not want. Those who had greenbacks were soon relieved of their burden, unless their treasure was concealed. While this work was going on, Turner took a piece of shell from a lieutenant's pocket, which he was putting in his own. The robbed man said, "I did not know that you had a right to take such things." "No right?" retorted Dick angrily, and at the same time, hit the lieutenant a fearful blow with his hand upon the face, nearly knocking him down, and then ordered him to be put into a cell.

During the warm summer days, the prisoners discovered a scuttle hole through the roof, through which we could climb by means of a ladder, where, in the cool of the evening, we could spend a few moments, freed from the stench and heat of the rooms below, and have an opportunity of looking at the bright sky overhead. Dick Turner, having learned that we could thus obtain a few inspirations of pure, fresh air, came into our rooms furiously mad, and forbade our going on the roof again. They sometimes say they starve us because they have not sufficient bread, but why can't they give us air? The guards who patrol about the prison and live in tents across the way, are generally after the same pattern of Turner. If a man steps near the window, to view the scene beyond, or breathe a purer atmosphere, he is at once told to step back, or is fired on. These are the *men* (if it be proper to call them so), at whose beck we are driven to and fro, and on whose cruel hands we depend for our daily bread.

I will now tell you what they furnish us to eat. In the morning they bring us about twelve ounces of bread and three ounces of boiled beef. At night they bring us about a pint of rice soup, in such pails, and of such sort, that to get it down at all, we must do so without either seeing, smelling or tasting. This is all we have to live upon, not enough to average one meal per day. I have been so weak from hunger, as to be compelled to lie down much of the time, and unable to rise, without a painful dizziness in my head.

One night they brought our soup to us late. It was

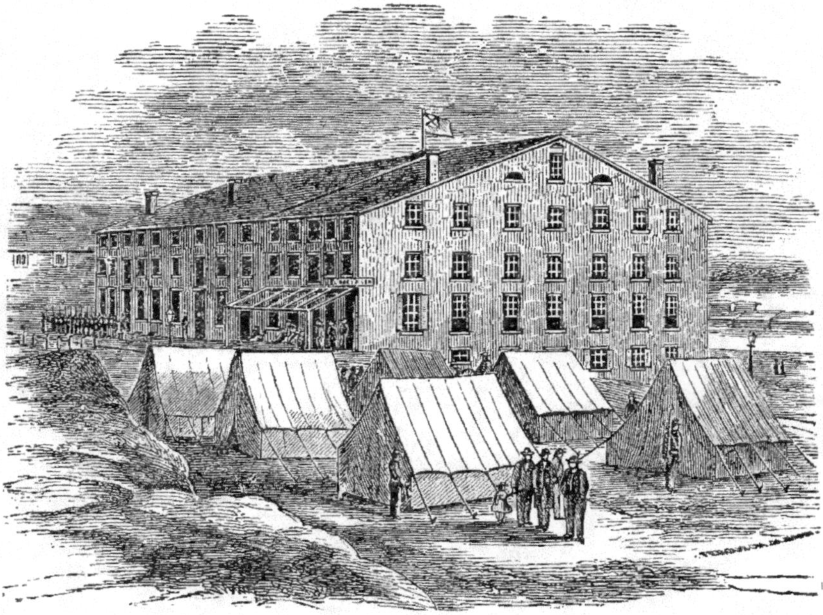

LIBBY PRISON, RICHMOND, VA.

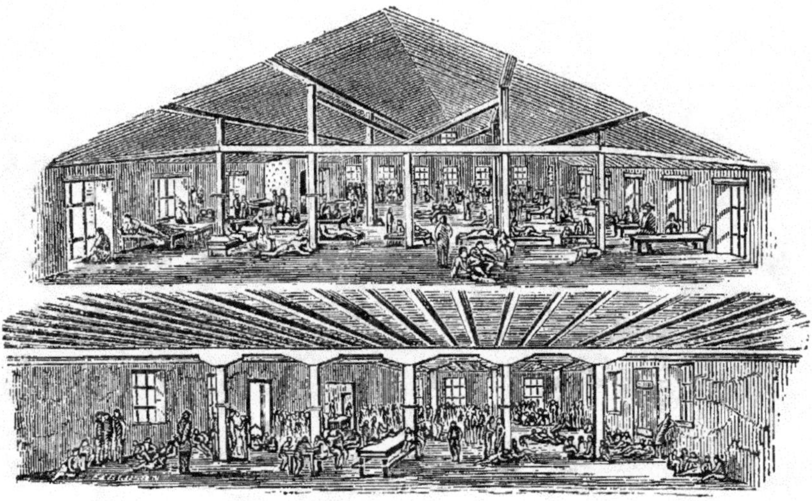

INTERIOR VIEW OF LIBBY PRISON.

Upper and Lower Room.

dark and could not be seen. The next morning wherever a sediment could be found in pails or cups, big maggots took the place of rice. The soup was made of old bacon. Many prisoners were sick at the thought of what they had eaten.

The water we have to drink is from James river, and in consequence of recent rains, it is so roily, that to fill a cup and let it stand an hour, you can find half an inch of mud on the bottom. It is with difficulty we can use it at all.

After we had been in prison about a week, they brought in stoves and wood, gave us our rations raw, bread excepted, added a little salt and vinegar, and we did our own cooking. Though this adds much to the heat of our rooms, we prefer to make our own soup. The prisoners are divided into messes, each using the stoves by turns. A table has also been constructed, with benches along side, which render our meals more acceptable. These are the only seats in our rooms, except in one room, where they have bunks, which are used for sitting and sleeping.

About the last of July an arrangement was made, whereby we could send out money by the prison authorities, and purchase such groceries as we chose. Some had money, and they have been living well. For one dollar greenbacks, we can get from five to ten dollars Confed. Capt. Hamlin had five dollars sent him from home, which the authorities detained, and for which they gave him thirty-five dollars Confed. At this rate of exchange, the enormous figures attached to the things we purchase, are not so very large prices after all. Piles of vegetables, bread and fruit, are brought in about every other morning, and it is estimated that the 600 officers now confined in Libby, expend on an average of $650 Confed. daily. This is a great privilege which most of the prisoners enjoy. However, some have no money, and are compelled to live on their scanty rations.

Yours, at times very lonely,
L. N. B., Chaplain 5th N. Y. Cav.

LIBBY PRISON, Richmond, Va.,
October 5th, 1863.

My Dear P. R.: In my last I gave you a description of our fare, I will now tell you how we spend our time. We are generally roused in the morning by the cry of black Ben:—"All four copies of de morning papers! Great news in de papers!" He finds a ready sale for his insignificant sheets, which are as free of literary taste as they are of truth, though we have to pay twenty-five cents per copy. Between the reading of these and the performance of our toilet, the morning hours pass away. Then comes the work in bones, bones from the beef supplied us. You would wonder to see the crosses, rings, books, boxes, stars, hearts &c., which I have already manufactured with an old jack-knife and a little file. Some of the prisoners spend all their time in this work. In fact, *bone on the brain* is a disease almost as universal as that other which prompts to "skirmishing," a habit the prisoners have of taking off their clothes and picking them. This is done to keep down *animal life*, which, here, is very exuberant. But this mere change between bone cutting and "skirmishing," became too monotonous, and some of us have organized a debating society, which is known as "The Libby Lice-I-see-'em," (Lyceum). In this body grave questions are discussed, besides those that are not so grave, and many moments are whiled away pleasantly. The subject of Mesmerism attracted very able debaters, who entertained us several days with instructive speeches and some amusing experiments. From these debates sprang the idea of mock trials and lectures, which have displayed no little amount of humor, wit and literary ability.

The debating club have also organized a newspaper association, and have appointed me editor-in-chief of the weekly *Libby Chronicle.*[1] This is now the great focus of attraction. Friday morning of each week at ten o'clock, if you could peep into the east room, upper floor, you would see it filled with an attentive audience, while the columns of the *Chronicle* are being read, of course, from manuscript.

To aid in the quickening of our intellectual life, a few days ago, an opportunity was offered for purchasing books from the city, and immediately Libby Prison was converted into one of the highest literary institutions of the south. You will hardly believe me, when I tell you that we have classes in arithmetic, algebra and geometry, in philosophy, history, theology and medicine, while the languages, Greek, Latin, German, Italian, Spanish and French, are each studied with peculiar delight. My French class alone numbers about one hundred members. And last, but not least, comes the class in phonography, which can boast of nearly two hundred. In this we have no books. But by means of a poncho, thrown over a shelf, a narrow blackboard is made, on which, with a piece of chalk, I delineate the mysterious characters, which the prisoners readily learn. Already articles for the *Chronicle* have been received, in phonographic characters.

[1] See Appendix.

You see that many of us are very busy, especially when you add to the above studies and occupations, the hours spent in singing and in religious worship. From two to four sermons are preached per week, alternating between the nine chaplains who are prisoners here. Every evening an hour is devoted to a meeting for social worship in which many take a lively interest. These interesting seasons are often followed by a reunion for singing, during which the prison walls are made to echo with our best patriotic airs, sung with a zest seldom known elsewhere. Chaplain McCabe, one of the most impressive singers I ever heard, generally takes the lead. I have often wondered, that the authorities did not veto this privilege, as the guards around the prison are often heard to curse and hiss with madness, at the sentiments of our songs.

Having thus spent the day and evening, we seek rest upon the hard floor, along which the prisoners lie, close-packed, like sardines in a can. To the hard floor and the "pesky varmints" many sleepless hours are devoted, which, however, are frequently beguiled by the cracking of jokes, and the calling up, by means of catechetical questioning and answering, all the humorous scenes and incidents of the day. Sleep at last comes with dreams of home and better days; but we awake again to the reality of prison life.

Yesterday—which was Sunday—I was permitted to visit Pemberton Castle, across the way from Libby, where I preached to about 1,800 of our brave boys, who were captured at Chickamauga, and whose officers are in Libby. I found these men in the most wretched condition. On being brought here they were stripped of overcoats, blankets, ponchoes, haversacks and canteens. Their rooms are filthy and full of vermin, even worse than Libby. The stench from the rear, unchecked by any doors, floods the rooms with a nausea the most sickening and deadly. These poor, half-naked men, spend their nights walking to and fro in the rooms, unable to sleep from the cold, which, at this season of the year, is quite intense. Their rations are less than those given to the officers in Libby. During my stay in the Castle I found nearly 200 men, so sick, that they were not able to raise their heads from the dirty floor, where they lay without blankets, nor even a stick of wood for a pillow. I was so much affected on seeing them as almost to incapacitate me to preach to them. At the close of the services they brought me a package of about 175 letters for their friends, which the authorities refused to transmit for them, and which I promised to send — a few at a time — through the channel open to the officers. I enjoyed the walk to and from the Castle, and rejoiced on reaching my room in Libby, that my condition was so desirable, compared to that of others.

There are some rumors that the chaplains are soon to be unconditionally released. It may be so.

Yours hopefully,
L. N. B., Chaplain 5th N. Y. Cav.

On Board Flag-of-Truce Boat, New York,
In the James, off City Point, Va.,
October 7th, 1863.

My Dear P. R.: I am free! This morning about three o'clock, the sergeant of the prison guard, entering my room with a candle in his hand, cried out, "Are there chaplains in this room?" I quickly answered in the affirmative. "Pack up, and come down," was quickly said in his usual ly gruff way. Such packing up! it took not many moments. I hastily stuffed the files of the *Libby Chronicle* in my boot legs, carefully secured in my coat pocket 123 letters from the prisoners of Pemberton Castle and of Libby, which were brought me as soon as it was known I was going, put my Spanish grammar under my arm, hid my treasures of worked "bones" in my pants pockets, and drew around me, over all, a shawl which they had not purloined from me. There were fears that we would be searched as we had been upon entering Libby. Those of my friends, who knew how many documents and letters I had on my person, sought to have me leave them, as their discovery by the authorities would cost me prolonged imprisonment, and, doubtless, too, in a dingy cell. But I had promised our poor fellows in the Castle that I would care for their letters, and was bound to do so at any cost, nor was I willing to leave behind me the pages to which I had devoted so many hours of careful study. I ran a fearful risk. We were not searched, and the precious relics are mine. The letters I will seal, put stamps on them, and mail them on reaching Washington. A little before daybreak we bade good bye to our friends and fellow-sufferers, sad to leave them there, and turned our backs on Libby. On passing to the street, the guard were crying out, as was their custom at stated periods of the night, "Post No. 1, all's well," "Post No. 2, all's well," &c. It was the first time we had seen the "all's well" in the light it then appeared.

Only eight of us were released, Chaplains Jos. T. Brown, 6th Md. Vols.; E. C. Ambler, 67th Pa. Vols.; D. C. Eberhart, 87th Pa. Vols.; James Harvey, 110th Ohio Vols.; E. W Brady, 116th Ohio Vols; Geo. H. Hammer, 12th

Pa. Cavalry; O. Taylor, 5th Mich. Cavalry, and myself. Chaplain C. C. McCabe, 122d Ohio Vols., was compelled to remain, sick in the hospital. Before sunrise we left the Rebel capital for Petersburg, where we changed cars for City Point, and at twelve M., for the first time, after many long days of waiting, we beheld our glorious starry flag, floating at mast head on the flag-of-truce steamer. A few moments more and we were beneath its protecting folds and among our friends. Too much cannot be said in praise of Major Mulford, agent of exchange, on board the New York, who sought by every means in his power to make us comfortable and happy. The rest of the story I will tell you when I come, as I expect a leave of absence on arriving at Washington.

Yours, for Home and the Flag,
L. N. B., Chaplain 5th N. Y. Cav.

The following account of prison experience will be found full of interest:

I was captured in the fight at Cedar creek, the 12th November, 1864, by the 4th Virginia Cavalry. They took my horse equipments, pocket book, knife, trinkets, boots and spurs, and marched me off with about 150 other prisoners from our division, to Rosser's headquarters near New Market, where was served out to us a pint of flour each, all we got for thirty-six hours. Here we were stripped and searched. When remonstrance was made, they said they were looking for commissions. Our good clothes were taken from us and we were obliged to take their filthy rags. On the 15th we were sent from New Market to Staunton, a distance of forty-three miles, where we arrived the 17th, almost naked, having been robbed and plundered the whole of the way, even to the cutting off of our buttons. Here we were served with rations, four crackers and one quarter pound of beef to each man, and closely confined in a strong log guard house. The 21st we were put on a freight train and sent to Richmond, being eighteen hours on the cars. Here we were confined in Libby Prison one night. Next morning we were stripped and searched again, meanwhile receiving the greatest abuse. After the search we were placed in Pemberton Castle. We suffered very much for want of food and clothes, it being piercing cold.

December 3d. Served out two days' rations, consisting of one small loaf of bread and one fifth of a cod-fish. Next day we were crowded in freight cars and sent to Danville, where we arrived at eight o'clock P. M., and were confined in the cars all night, without being able to get a drink of water; and some of the men were in the greatest filth.

December 5th. Changed cars. A few others and myself were put in a car with fifty embalmed bodies. Changed cars again at Greensboro', and, at ten o'clock at night, were put on a freight train, with one hundred men in each car, and so closely packed that it was not possible to sit down. Two men died in the night from suffocation. At three A. M. next day we arrived at Salisbury, N. C. and made a stand in the road, mud ankle deep, until nine o'clock, when we were marched to prison. It was once a cotton mill, surrounded by a high fence, strongly guarded, and commanded by three twelve pounders. It is a hard place. Being the last batch, we have no tents nor any kind of shelter yet, and from sixty to eighty dying every day from actual starvation.

December 7th. It rained and froze hard last night, and poor, half-naked men are in a miserable plight. It is heart-rending to see some of them, with their famished looks and mere skeleton forms.

December 8th. The guard (68th N. C. regiment) received orders to fire on any of us seen walking about the yard, or going to the rear after sundown. That night they killed two men and wounded another. In the morning they shot a man in a tent asleep. I reported the sentry to Major Gee, in command. He questioned the sentry about it, whose excuse was, that he had three niggers in line and never expected such a shot again, but he happened to miss them and killed this man. He was praised for the act and received a forty days' furlough.

December 10th. We feel the cold very much. The ground is covered with snow. Men are to be seen almost frozen to death — hands and feet frozen, in several cases — in every direction. A great many died during the night from exposure and want of food. We have been kept seventy-five hours without rations, and in the meantime the Rebels tried to persuade us to enlist, by offering a bounty of fifty dollars, one loaf of bread, and a canteen of whiskey — "the largest bounty," they said, "ever offered in the Confederacy." They got some recruits — men who were afraid of starving to death, and enlisted to save their lives.

December 19th. Several escaped, myself in the number. I got within twenty miles of our lines, was recaptured, and brought back to prison again. We are tunneling, and expect soon to make another break.

January 4th. Eighty-six men in the dead house, who died during the night. Thirty of my men[1] died since I

[1] He had charge of a division of one thousand men.

came here. Four companies of Yanks that were enlisted here, from time to time, and fully equipped, in Florence, killed their Rebel officers, hung their Sergeant Major for interfering, seized four pieces of artillery, and effected their escape to Gen. Sherman's lines.

January 9th. Quarter rations, consisting of meal, made from corn and corn-cobs ground together, and baked into bread.

January 12th. I have several men without any kind of shelter. A great many have dug holes in the ground to live in, working at them with a part of a canteen, a nail, or piece of iron, or any thing they can get, not being allowed any tools. Thirty-nine men died last night. The commissary has nothing to issue to the prisoners, no food of any kind. There is plenty outside the prison, but not for us.

January 18th. Three table-spoonfuls of molasses issued to each man, and one quart of vinegar to every hundred men.

January 20th. One of my men dropped dead while trying to eat some soup, made of rice and water. Another tunnel is finished. Ten of us escape from prison, are seen and fired on by the guard. Three men, with myself, got as far as Morgantown, a distance of eighty-four miles, when we were recaptured and brought back to prison again.

January 28th. A man, sent out to the dead house for dead, comes to life in the dead cart on his way to be buried, and is brought back to the hospital, where he recovers.

January 30th. The Rebs are trying to get more recruits. Last night a man was robbed of seventy dollars in greenbacks and three hundred in Confed. that he was fortunate enough to secure, in hopes of sometime making his escape.

February 3*d*. Two men only allowed to go once a day to bring the allowance of wood for each hundred men.

February 5*th*. Sixty-five men escaped over the fences last night. It is thought the guard assisted them, as some of *them* also are missing.

February 8*th*. There have been, up to this date, five thousand seven hundred and fifty deaths in this prison, out of nine thousand, in less than three months.

February 11*th*. Men suffering very much from scurvy. The small-pox has also broken out. Got one quart of vinegar to each hundred men to-day.

February 14*th*. Capt. Porter, 13th Mass., Maj. Howard, 4th N. Y. Mounted Rifles, and a Capt. of the 146th N. Y. S. Vols., whose name I don't remember, commenced issuing a few blankets the government sent us last November, but were kept in Richmond, until the cold is nearly over, by the Rebel authorities there.

February 18*th*. Three hundred prisoners came here from Andersonville and Charlotte. Pants, blouses and shirts were issued by the above-named officers, one hundred of each to a division, consisting of one thousand men.

February 20*th*. I am making out rolls of the men able to bear a journey. We are going to to be paroled when these rolls are finished.

February 22*d*. Sending sick to Richmond. The rest were fallen in on the square; a parole was read to us and about noon we left the prison, marched to South Atkin, six miles from Salisbury, and camped for the night.

February 23*d*. Marched out early. Passing through Lexington a lady gave me a gingerbread cake that was most acceptable. Four miles beyond the town we camped.

February 24th. Marched along the railroad. A great many men gave out, not being able to stand the mareh. We passed through Thomasville, then on to High Point, where we eamped for the night.

February 26th. Having reaehed Greensboro' we were put on the ears and sent to Goldsboro' by way of Raleigh, where we had to wait until parole papers were made out. I had to pay forty dollars (Confed.) for my dinner there on the 27th. Parole papers made out, we were put on board cars for Wilmington, where we arrived safely. The moment we beheld the Old Glory, three enthusiastic cheers burst from one and all. It was gladdening to think we were under its protection onee more. The dear old flag, may it never lose a star!

On getting into town, the U. S. Sanitary Commission did everything they could to alleviate our suffering.

March 1st. I drank my first eup of eoffee since my imprisonment. It is reported, that when Gen. Sehofield, commanding department, saw our wretched condition from starvation, he gave orders to put the prisoners he took on capturing Wilmington, on quarter rations, and reduce them to skin and bones.

March 3d. Left Wilmington on the Escort.

March 5th. Crossed the Bar and embarked on the Herman Livingston for Annapolis, Md., via Fortress Monroe.

March 10th. Disembarked at our destination, reeeived eompensation money, &c., &c., and got things comfortable onee more. (Extracts from the Diary of John Evans, Esq., of the Fifth New York Cavalry).

Chaplain: You can never know how much we have suffered. Tongue cannot tell nor pen describe the suffering and misery endured by our soldiers at Andersonville, Ga., where I was confined. You would not believe it, if it were told. I would not, had I not been there. But God has been good to me in sparing my life. (Extract from a letter of William P. Smith, company C, Fifth New York Cavalry, dated Parole Hospital, Vicksburg, Miss., April 12, 1865).

The following list of the men of the regiment, who died in Rebel prisons, has been prepared with much care, and must prove intensely interesting to their friends and surviving comrades. These important data were mostly secured from men, who had returned to us, and who had watched their less fortunate fellow-sufferers, as mind and body gave away under the sufferings and destitution of their wretched imprisonment.

Some information was also obtained from official documents from the War Department, at Washington, D. C.

Men who Died in Rebel Prisons.

NUMBER.	NAMES.	RANK.	COMPANY.	CAPTURED. When.	CAPTURED. Where.	DIED. When.	DIED. Where.
1	George Bates,	Private,	A,	May 5, 1864.	Parker's Store,	Unknown,	Andersonville, Georgia
2	Peter B. Laton,	"	"	June 1, 1864,	Ashland Station,	"	" "
3	Alexander Taylor,	"	"	June 29, 1864,	Reams Station,	"	" "
4	Frederic W. Bernhardi,	"	"	" "	" "	"	Macon, Ga.
5	Merlin J. Hopkins,	"	"	Nov. 12, 1864,	Cedar Creek,	Dec. 20, 1864,	Salisbury, N. C.
6	John Rooney,	"	B,	May 23, 1862,	Front Royal,	Aug., 1862,	Belle Isle, Richmond, Va.
7	Robert Christian,	"	"	May 30, 1863,	Greenwich,	Unknown,	Castle Thunder, Richmond, Va.
8	Edward Borst,	"	"	Oct. 19, 1863,	Buckland Mills,	Aug. 10, 1864,	Andersonville, Ga.
9	Simeon A. Hutchings,	"	"	May 18, 1864,	Ny River,	July 10, 1864,	" "
10	John B. Dubois,	Corporal,	"	June 15, 1864,	White Oak Swamps,	Aug. 17, 1864,	" "
11	John L. Morse,	"	"	June 29, 1864,	Reams Station,	Sept. 6, 1864,	" "
12	J. Robert Runciman,	Private,	"	" "	" "	Sept. 11, 1864,	" "
13	Cornelius Gorton,	"	"	Sept. 22, 1864,	Milford, Luray Valley,	Nov. 30, 1864,	Richmond, Va.
14	Laurence Hand,	"	C,	July 6, 1863,	Hagerstown, Md.,	May 15, 1864,	Andersonville, Ga.
15	Edward H. Fitch,	"	"	Sept. 13, 1863,	Culpepper C. H.,	Unknown,	" "
16	James Tench,	Bl'ksmith,	"	Oct. 10, 1863,	" "	Jan., 1865.	" "
17	John Stein,	Private,	"	" "	James City,	May 6, 1864,	" "
18	Matthew Southard,	"	"	" "	Culpepper C. H.	July 18, 1864,	" "
19	Charles L. Church,	"	"	May 5, 1864,	Parker's Store,	Aug. 16, 1864,	" "
20	John Lucha,	"	"	June 29, 1864,	Reams Station,	Aug. 29, 1864,	" "
21	William Jones,	Farrier,	"	" "	" "	Sept. 15, 1864.	" "
22	Robert Taylor.	Private,	D,	July 6, 1863,	Hagerstown, Md.,	Unknown,	Richmond, Va.
23	Patrick Gallagher,	"	"	" "	" "	May 1, 1864,	Andersonville, Georgia.
24	Thomas Lynch,	"	"	Sept. 13, 1863.	Culpepper C. H.,	Oct. 27, 1864,	" "
25	Richard Kenwell,	"	"	Oct. 10, 1863.	James City.	Aug. 31, 1864,	" "
2	Reuben Sanders.	"	"	Oct. 19, 1863,	Buckland Mills,	July, 1864,	" "
27	Cyril E. Scripter	Farrier,	"	" "	" "	" "	" "
28	James Welsh,	Private,	"	Jan. 19, 1864,	Ely's Ford,	Oct. 18, 1864,	" "
29	Charles E. Bingham,	"	"	June 1, 1864,	Ashland Station,	Sept. 29, 1864,	" "
30	Nicholas Washburn,	"	"	" "	" "	Aug. 14, 1864,	" "

Men who Died in Rebel Prisons, continued.

NUMBER.	NAMES.	RANK.	COMPANY.	CAPTURED. When.	CAPTURED. Where.	DIED. When.	DIED. Where.
31	Alfred W. Vanmarter,..	Private,...	D,	June 1, 1864,	Ashland Station, ...	Sept. 10, 1864,	Andersonville, Georgia.
32	O. S. Keyes, ...	Sergeant, .	E,	Sept. 13, 1863,	Culpepper C. H., ...	April 19, 1864,	" "
33	Newton C. Rew, ...	Private,...	"	Oct. 19, 1863,	Buckland Mills,......	Mar. 13, 1864,	" "
34	Andrew Jackson, ...	" ..	"	" "	" "	Aug., 1864,	" "
35	William Jackson,......	" ..	"	June 29, 1864,	Reams Station, ...	Oct., 1864,	" "
36	George McCollon,......	" ..	"	Oct. 6, 1864,	Brock's Gap..........	Dec. 18, 1864,	Richmond, Va.
37	Daniel C. Bixby, ...	" ..	"	Oct. 8, 1864,	Columbian Furnace,.	Feb. 10, 1865,	" "
38	William Hawley,.......	" ..	F,	July 5, 1863,	Monterey Pass, Pa.,.	Dec. 31, 1863,	" "
39	William H. Wells,......	" ..	"	Jan. 22, 1864,	Ellis' Ford,..........	Feb. 15, 1864,	" "
40	Nicholas Zahler, ...	" ..	"	Oct. 11, 1863,	Sperryville Pike,.....	Aug. 18, 1864,	Andersonville, Ga.
41	Hiram H. Earle,.......	" ..	"	Oct. 19, 1863,	Buckland Mills,......	Feb., 1863,	Richmond, Va.
42	Franklin B. Moore, ...	" ..	"	" "	" "	Unknown, ...	" "
43	Peter Engalls,..........	" ..	"	June 29, 1864.	Reams Station,.......	Feb. 26, 1865,	Goldsboro', North Carolina.
44	Waterman Galusha,....	" ..	"	" "	" "	Oct. 7, 1864.	Andersonville, Ga.
45	Daniel Wight,.........	" ..	"	" "	" "	July, 1864,	Salisbury, N. C.
46	John W. Jackson,......	Sergeant, .	"	Sept. 1, 1864,	Berryville, ...	Jan. 26, 1865,	" "
47	Johnson Foster,........	Private,...	G,	July 6, 1863,	Hagerstown, Md.,....	April 27, 1864,	Andersonville, Ga.
48	John Doyle,...........	" ..	"	" "	" "	June 27, 1864,	" "
49	William Turner, ...	Corporal,..	"	" "	" " ...	Aug. 24, 1864,	" "
50	William A. Witter,....	Private,...	"	June 5, 1864,	Old Church Tavern,..	Unknown, ...	Unknown.
51	De Witt C. Overocker,.	" ..	"	June 29, 1864,	Reams Station,.......	" ...	Andersonville, Georgia.
52	Charles Wilcox, ...	Sergeant, .	"	" "	" "	Oct. 24, 1864,	" "
53	Lent H. Towner,.......	Private,...	"	" "	" "	Aug. 16, 1864,	" "
54	John Bidwell,..........	" ..	"	July 1, 1864,	Black Water River, ..	Oct. 10, 1864,	" "
55	George H. Romans,....	" ..	"	Sept. 3, 1864,	White Post, ...	Nov. 12, 1864,	Salisbury, N. C.
56	Almeron Davis,........	" ..	H,	Mar. 23, 1863,	Chantilly,...	Unknown, ...	Unknown.
57	Duransie S. Carr,......	" ..	"	July 6, 1863,	Hagerstown, Md.,....	" ...	Belle Isle, Richmond, Virginia.
58	James Nelson,..........	" ..	"	" "	" "	Dec., 1863,	" "
59	Albert N. Shattuck,....	" ..	"	" "	" "	 1864,	" "
60	Louis Labounty,........	" ..	"	July 7, 1863,	Williamsport, "	Unknown, ...	" "

Men who Died in Rebel Prisons, continued.

NUMBER.	NAMES.	RANK.	COMPANY.	CAPTURED.		DIED.	
				When.	Where.	When.	Where.
61	John Smith,	Private,	H,	Sept., 1863,	Hartwood Church,	June 1, 1864,	Richmond, Virginia.
62	John Redman,	"	"	May 5, 1864,	Parker's Store,	Unknown,	" "
63	John Spaulding,	"	"	June 29, 1864,	Reams Station,	Sept. 16, 1864,	Florence, S. C.
64	Henry Spaulding,	"	"	" "	" "	" "	" "
65	Rufus A. Chaffee,	"	"	" "	" "	Unknown,	Andersonville, Ga.
66	John C. C. French,	"	"	" "	" "	"	" "
67	John Waterman,	"	"	Sept. 27, 1864,	Mt. Meridian,	Feb., 1865,	Salisbury, North Carolina.
68	Wesley Brown,	"	"	" "	" "	Jan., 1865,	" "
69	William Daly,	"	I,	March 1, 1864,	Near Richmond,	July 19, 1864,	Andersonville, Ga.
70	John Hardy,	Sergeant,	"	" "	" "	Sept. 20, 1864,	" "
71	Frank Wood,	Private,	"	" "	" "	July 19, 1864,	" "
72	Herman Harmes,	"	"	" "	" "	Aug. 13, 1864,	" "
73	Joseph H. Bennett,	"	"	May 5, 1864,	Parker's Store,	Nov. 26, 1864,	Salisbury, N. C.
74	William Morrison,	"	"	June 12, 1864,	Mentz Cross Roads,	Sept. 20, 1864,	Andersonville, Ga.
75	William L. Babbitt,	"	"	Sept. 29, 1864,	Mt. Crawford,	Oct. 24, 1864,	Salisbury, N. C.
76	Daniel C. O'Halloran,	Corporal,	"	Nov. 12, 1864,	Mt. Zion Church,	Jan. 19, 1865,	" "
77	George W. Tracy,	Private,	"	Sept. 24, 1864,	New Market,	Nov. 5, 1864,	" "
78	George W. Dinsmore,	Sergeant,	K,	July 6, 1863,	Hagerstown, Md.,	Unknown,	Andersonville, Ga.
79	John Holden,	Private,	"	Aug., 1863,	Thoroughfare Gap,	Oct. 16, 1863,	Richmond, Va.
80	John Mack,	Corporal,	"	Jan. 19, 1864,	Ely's Ford,	Sept., 1864,	Andersonville, Ga.
81	James Welsh,	Farrier,	"	March 1, 1864,	Near Richmond,	Aug. 24, 1864,	" "
82	George Tresch,	Private,	"	" "	" "	July 18, 1864,	" "
83	John Jones,	"	"	Mar. 11, 1864,	Southard's Cross Rds.,	Nov., 1864,	" "
84	James M. Kingsley,	"	"	June 29, 1864,	Reams Station,	Sept. 24, 1864,	" "
85	Robert Jasper,	"	"	Sept. 29, 1864,	Mt. Crawford,	Jan. 12, 1865,	Salisbury, North Carolina.
86	James Shaw,	"	"	" "	" "	Oct. 13, 1864,	" "
87	Lewis Cooper,	"	L,	July 6, 1863,	Hagerstown, Md.,	Unknown,	Richmond, Va.
88	Robert Wharton,	"	"	June 15, 1864,	White Oak Swamps,	Oct. 6, 1864,	Andersonville, Georgia.
89	George Antisdale,	"	"	June 29, 1864,	Reams Station,	Sept. 14, 1864,	" "
90	Thomas O'Brien,	"	"	" "	" "	Sept. 6, 1864,	" "

Men who Died in Rebel Prisons, concluded.

Number.	Names.	Rank.	Company.	Captured. When.	Captured. Where.	Died. When.	Died. Where.
91	Ezra Morse,	Corporal,	L,	June 29, 1864,	Reams Station,	Sept. 6, 1864.	Andersonville, Georgia.
92	Theodore M. Easton,	Private,	"	" "	" "	July 12, 1864,	" "
93	Frederick Tittle,	"	"	July 1, 1864.	Black Water River,	Unknown,	" "
94	Peter Rafferty,	Sergeant,	M,	July 6, 1863,	Hagerstown, Md.,	June 26, 1864,	" "
95	Philip H. Moore,	Private,	"	" "	" "	April 9, 1864,	" "
96	Louis Erdman,	Bugler,	"	Sept. 13, 1863,	Culpepper C. H.,	Unknown,	" "
97	John J. Cole,	"	"	June 29, 1864,	Reams Station,	Aug. 20, 1864,	" "
98	Abram T. Brown,	"	"	" "	" "	Oct., 1864,	" "
99	William Heddle,	"	"	" "	" "	Aug. 10, 1864.	" "

The Following Men Died from the Effect of Prison Life.

Number.	Names.	Rank.	Company.	Captured. When.	Captured. Where.	Died. When.	Died. Where.
100	Thomas O'Connor,	Private,	A,	June 1, 1864,	Ashland Station,	Dec. 4, 1864,	Annapolis, Md.
101	Leonard Owen, Jr.,	"	C,	May 5, 1864,	Parker's Store,	Jan. 1865,	Wilmington, N. Y.
102	John Leiser,	"	E,	June 29, 1864,	Reams Station,	Mar. 13, 1865,	Baltimore, Md.
103	Alonzo Bern,	"	F,	July 1, 1864,	Jarrett's Station,	Jan., 9, 1865,	Trans. *N. Light*, ret'ng fr. prs'n.
104	Irwin W. Jones,	"	H,	July 6, 1863,	Hagerstown, Md.,	Aug., 1863,	Annapolis, Md.
105	Henry Odell,	"	"	Sept. 27, 1864,	Mt. Meridian,	Mar. 10, 1865,	" "
106	Henry Pierce,	Sergeant,	I,	June 29, 1864,	Reams Station,	Dec. 31, 1864,	" "
107	George Scott,	Private,	K,	Unknown,	Unknown,	Aug. 16, 1865,	Ft. McHenry, (Hospital), Md.
108	Franz Briell,	"	"	March 1, 1864,	Near Richmond,	May 2, 1864,	Baltimore, Md.
109	Jacob Swintz,	"	M,	....	....	May, 1865,	

The Following Men are Supposed to have Died in Prison, where they were last heard from.

Number.	Names.	Rank.	Company.	Captured. When.	Captured. Where.	Died. When.	Died. Where.
110	Joseph Latour,	Private,	B,	May 5, 1864,	Parker's Store,		
111	Edward A. Martin,	"	"	" "	" "		
112	Frederick Simonson,	"	L,	March 1, 1864.	Near Richmond,		
113	Louis Holm,	"	"	May 5, 1864,	Parker's Store,		
114	John Hedland,	"	"	May 26, 1864,	Little River,		

CHAPTER XVI.

Our Scout. — With Gen. Stahel. — Guides Cavalry Corps from Fairfax C. H. to Frederick City, Md., June, 1863. — Ordered to Watch Movements of Rebel Army, Marching on its Grand Invasion of Pennsylvania. — In Disguise he Visits Rebel Gen. Stuart. — Captures Rebel Army Mail, with Important Dispatches, at Hagerstown, Md. — Carries Dispatches from Gen. Grant to President Lincoln, during Battle of the Wilderness. — Among the Rebels near Weldon & Petersburg R.R. — Hard Tramp through Woods and Swamps. — The Colored Guide. — Gladly Reaches our Lines Again.

At the time of the Rebel invasion of Maryland aud Pennsylvania, in 1863, I was chief scout of Gen. Stahel, commanding division of cavalry in Defenses of Washington. June 24, 1863, I guided the cavalry from Fairfax Court House on its way into Maryland. We forded the Potomac at Young's Island, two miles below the mouth of Goose creek, and marched to Frederick City. I put up at the Dill Hotel, the headquarters of the general. At eleven P. M. the general sent for me. Obeying the summons, I found him with Major Kephart, Captains Kidd and Chauncey, of his staff, engaged in drawing sketches and routes of the enemy from a large map, spread out before them. Rising from his seat the general bade me a pleasaut "good evening," and added:

"Sergeant, I have a very hard trip for you. If you

think it can be accomplished, I wish you to commence it to-night, for, if it is to be done at all, now is the time."

"Well, general," I replied, saluting him, "I am ready to do all in my power to help the cause, and if we are to commence the work to-night, the sooner we get to business the better."

He then directed me to repair to the Potomac near Williamsport, to watch the movements of the enemy, to ascertain his strength and the routes taken by the different columns, &c., and to communicate all serviceable information to himself, or to Gen. Meade, who had just assumed command. I was to take as many men as I needed, to mount them on horses secured by his order, to take such routes as, in my own judgment, were best, and to return only when I thought the interest of the service so required, or I should receive further orders from him.

My horse was soon ready, and, after receiving the general's order for ten picked men out of Col. Price's brigade, I bade him good bye, and set out to Middletown, near which Col. Price was then encamped. It was ten A. M. when I presented my order to the colonel, with the request that the men should be taken from the 1st Michigan Cavalry, each of ten companies to furnish its bravest and best man. These gallant troopers were soon ready, and, having reported to me in due style, we began our toilsome march over the South Mountain for Boonsboro', which we reached at four A. M. next day.

Here we learned that the Rebels were crossing the river at two points, Falling Waters and Williamsport, but their advance had not yet entered the town. We spent the day riding up and down the river on different roads, watching their movements. At night I left my men at the United States Hotel, kept by a good Union man named Smith, and started for Hagerstown. I soon found that the main body of their army was moving towards Chambersburg, Pa. Having spent the night in the vicinity, I returned early next morning, and dispatched a messenger to the general with what information we had obtained.

These proceedings occupied our time until Saturday night of that week, when Gen. Stuart, commanding Rebel cavalry, came into Hagerstown.

I was very anxious to learn all about his force, and the movements contemplated, and resolved upon a plan to see the general himself, or some of his staff.

Of a Union man I procured a suit of *raglings*, knocked off one boot heel to make one leg shorter than its mate, and put a gimblet, a tow string and an old broken jack-knife in my pockets. My jewelry corresponded with my clothes. I adopted the name of George Fry, a harvest hand of Dr. Farney's, from Wolftown, on the north side of the mountain, and I was a cripple from rheumatism. Having completed arrangements with Dr. Farney, Mr. Landers and other Union men, that they might be of service to me in case the Rebels were suspicious of my character, I hobbled away on my perilous journey, and entered the city, by leaping the high stone wall which guards it on the north side, near the depot, just as the town clock struck one.

It was a clear starlight night, and the glistening bayonets of the sentries could be seen as they walked their lonely beat. Scarcely had I gained the sidewalk, leading to the centre of the town, when the sentry cried, "Halt! who goes there?" "A friend," I replied. "A friend to north or south?" "To south, of course, and all right." "Advance then," was the response. I told him I had come in to see our brave boys, who could whip the Yankees so handsomely, &c., and we fell to discussing the war questions of the day. In the midst of our colloquy, up came the officer of the guard, who, after asking me a few questions, said: "Had you not better go with me to see Gen. Stuart?" "I should reelly like ter git a sight of the giniral," I quickly replied, "for I never seen a reel giniral in all my life." I was soon in the presence of the general, who received me very cordially. I told him who I was and where I lived when at home. "Wolftown?" remarked the general, "have not the Yankees a large wagon train there?" I told him they had, and, turning to one of his staff, he said, "I must have it, it would be a fine prize." I noted his words, and I determined, if I possessed any Yankee wit, to make use of it on this occasion. "Giniral," said I, "*you all* don't think of capterin' them are Yankee wagons, do you?" "Why not? I have here 5,000 cavalry and sixteen pieces of artillery, and I understand the train is lightly guarded."

I told him they came there that afternoon, with twelve big brass cannon and three regiments of foot soldiers, and if he was to try to go through the gap in the mountain, they would shoot all the cannon off right in the gap, and kill all of his men and horses. The general laughed, and said I had a strange idea of war, if I thought so many men would be killed at once, and added, that I would not be a very brave soldier. I replied, that many times I had felt like going into the Confederate army, but my rheumatism kept me out.

After a while the general concluded not to try the train,

and I was heartily glad, for he would have taken 2,000 wagons easily, as they were guarded by not more than three hundred men.

He then gave orders to have the main body of his cavalry move toward Green Castle, and I distinctly heard him give orders to the major to stay in town with fifty men as rear guard, and to send on the army mail, which was expected there about six the next evening. I made up my mind that it would be a small mail he would get, as I proposed to myself to be postmaster for once.

After seeing the general and his cavalry move out of town, I went directly for my horse, which I had concealed in a safe place some distance from the city, and surveyed the ground to see which way I could best come in to capture the mail, and determined to charge the place on the pike from Boonsboro' and made my arrangements to that effect. I got a Union man by the name of Thornburgh to go into the town and notify the Union people, that when the town clock struck six P. M. I would charge in and capture the Rebel mail, at the risk of losing my own life and every man with me. I had now but eight men, two having been sent to the general with dispatches.

I then returned to Boonsboro', and found my men waiting for me. I told them my intentions, and offered to send back to his regiment any man who feared to go with me. But every one bravely said he would not leave me, nor surrender without my order. I ordered them to bring their horses, and we were soon on the road. It was a moment of thrilling interest to us all, as we approached Hagerstown, and lingered to hear the signal strokes of that monitor, in the old church tower. At the appointed time

OUR SCOUT,
With his brave men, approaching Hagerstown.

(we had entered the edge of the town), with a wild shout we dashed into the street, and the major and his fifty braves fled without firing a shot. We captured sixteen prisoners, twenty-six horses, several small arms, and a heavy army mail, which contained three dispatches from Jeff. Davis, and two from the Rebel secretary of war, to Gen. Lee. All this substantial booty we safely carried within our lines, without the loss of a man or a horse.

Many thanks are due to Dr. C. R. Doran, and to Robert Thornburgh, for their kind and timely assistance, and also to Misses Susie Carson and Addie Brenner, who did so much for the comfort of our brave men. I still have in my possession some choice flowers, preserved from a bouquet, presented me by Miss Carson the evening we captured the Rebel mail; and though the flowers have faded, the good deeds done by the giver will ever grow bright through coming time. All honor to the brave Union ladies.

Saturday, May 7th, 1864. I left Gen. Grant's headquarters, accompanied by G. M. Cline, Gen. Meade's chief of scouts, with important dispatches for President Lincoln, Quartermaster Gen. Meigs, Surgeon Gen. Barnes, and others of the Department. The fighting was terrific on the right and left wings when we started. It was two P. M. Crossed the Rappahannock at U. S. Ford. We traveled all night through the enemy's country. We could see their signal rockets, sent up along the line of signal stations, from Belle Plain to Guineas Station, on the Richmond and Fredericksburg rail road. We reached the Potomac at four next morning at Acquia creek. Fearing the guerrillas, should we remain on the Virginia shore, we constructed a raft of drift wood and boards, on which, by great exertion, paddling under a broiling sun, we succeeded in crossing the river, which, at this point, is several miles wide. By traveling afoot about five miles, we met a Union guard, who conducted us to Capt. Russell, company A, First Purnell Legion.

The captain entertained us with a good dinner, which relished well after over twenty-four hours' hard toil, *minus* our rations. After dinner we hailed a schooner, bound up stream, and Capt. Russell sent us out to her in his row-boat. It proved to be the General Hunter of Baltimore. The captain informed us that he had a case of small-pox aboard, and strove to warn us away. But we were too anxious to get to Washington with our dispatches to be delayed by one case of small-pox. Light breezes, or no breeze at all, delayed us, and we did not reach the capital till seven A. M. on the 9th. We were landed at the navy yard, whence we were sent to the War Department in the private carriage of the officer in command.

The authorities had not heard from the army in three days—and eventful days they had been—as Mosby had cut off all communication by way of the Orange and Alexandria rail road.

After delivering our messages and receiving answers, with other dispatches for Gen. Grant, Gen. Meigs sent us down the river aboard the steamer Lizzie Baker. We were landed at night, near Acquia creek, and traveled to Fredericksburg. Seeing camp fires in and about the town, we expected to meet the Rebels, but were gladly disappointed in finding them to be our own.

The next morning, the 10th, we had the pleasure of taking breakfast with Lieut. F. A. Boutelle of the Fifth New

York Cavalry, chief ambulance officer of the division Having secured horses and an orderly, we started for Gen. Grant's headquarters, which we reached about eleven A. M., near Spottsylvania Court House. The fighting was very heavy during the day, and continued through the night.

May 11th, near Spottsylvania Court House. Our men capture eight generals, forty-five pieces of artillery, and seven thousand prisoners.

August 30th, 1864. It had been reported that the Rebels were constructing a cross rail road from Stony Creek Station, Weldon & Petersburg rail road, to the Southside rail road. I was sent to ascertain the fact, in company with James Hattan, one of General Grant's scouts. As neither of us knew the country, we procured a darkey guide. We had proceeded but a short distance from our lines, at a point near Lee's mills, on the Blackwater river, when a squad of Rebels saw us, and gave us chase. Being on foot, we soon reached thick woods, and escaped. We traveled nearly all night, and, getting near our destination, we started for a large farm house, to make some inquiries, when a picket cried out "halt!" As we did not obey him, he fired, and thus aroused a whole regiment, that was soon in the saddle. We took to the woods again. We spent considerable time in trying to cross the Indian swamp, but in vain. Here we lost our guide, who, desiring to visit his wife at her master's, Mr. Dunn, whose house was under Rebel guards, was either killed or captured. By a new route we traveled on toward Stony Creek Station, till daybreak. At this time we sought the nearest ravine, where we crept into a few bushes, and sought rest. Though we were much exposed during the day, much Rebel cavalry prowling about, and, some of the time, very near us, yet from a faithful darkey, whom we saw, we secured both food and drink, and received all needed information about the new cross rail road, which was not yet being built.

Under the darkness of night, we started back for our lines, and crossed the Indian swamp near Mr. Sterling Saunder's farm, and soon arrived at Mr. Charles Kean's, where we found a darkey prepared for a promenade with his Dinah, it being Sabbath evening. He was dressed in grand style, with black coat, white pants and vest, standing collar, and a splendid beaver. He sported a big cane, with a brass knob on the handle. Thus caparisoned, he did not relish the idea of becoming guide. But excuses were useless, and he must show us across the big swamp called Jones' Hole. The night became very dark, and we were compelled to *feel* our way much of the time. This was no easy task, as we were obliged to walk on fallen trees, some lying in the water, and others three or four feet above. By a misstep, Mr. guide went off one of these logs into mud and water. It was difficult to restrain laughter, when the poor fellow crawled out, to think, had it been day, what a sudden change of color his white pants and vest must have undergone. Having reached terra firma on the opposite side of the swamp, we gave the guide a five dollar greenback, and sent him back to his Dinah. We crossed the Jerusalem plank road just south of Captain Proctor's farm house, and reached our lines about twelve M., at Burnt Mills, near the Norfolk rail road. We were furnished horses and an orderly, and made our way to General Grant's headquarters, glad to be within our own lines once more. C. A. P.,

Co. G, Fifth New York Cavalry.

CHAPTER XVII.

Company Registers. — Organizations.— Officers. — Interesting Incidents in Personal Adventures of the men.

In this connection is given only an epitome of each company, in which may be found the dates of the appointments or commissions of its officers; an account of its organization; the leading events of its history, and a brief mention of a few men, who, for special acts of bravery, or for peculiar misfortunes, are deemed worthy of this notice. It would be a pleasure to mention here all those men, who possessed the "stuff of which heroes are made," and who have always performed their duty so well, but the space allotted us will not permit it

COMPANY A.

Officers.

Augustus P. Green, Captain, August 15th, 1861. Resigned, November 5th, 1862.

Thomas Burns, 1st Lieutenant, August 15th, 1861. Resigned, May 21st, 1862.

Henry Wilson, 2d Lieutenant, August 15th, 1861. 1st Lieutenant, May 21st, 1861. Captured, July 18th, 1862, Barnett's Ford. Resigned, December 28th, 1862.

Luke McGuinn, 2d Lieutenant, May 23d, 1862. Captain,

November 5th, 1862. Killed, May 5th, 1864, Parker's Store.

Frazer A. Boutelle, 2d Lieutenant from Sergeant, September 10th, 1862. 1st Lieutenant, December 20th, 1863. Discharged, Expiration of Term, September 1st, 1864. Captain, November 14th, 1864.

Theodore A. Boice, 1st Lieutenant from 1st Sergeant, December 29th, 1862. Captain, Company B, December 20th, 1863.

William T. Boyd, 2d Lieutenant, December 20th, 1863.

Michael Hayes, 1st Lieutenant from 1st Sergeant, November 14th, 1864.

This company formed the original nucleus of the regiment, and was raised by Captain Green, in New York city. It was mustered in the service of the United States, August 15th, 1861, at Staten Island, N. Y., by Captain L. S. Larned, 5th U. S. Infantry. The first recruit of the company was Frazer A. Boutelle, its present captain. It was engaged alone in the first action recorded in our history, May 2d, 1862, near Port Republic. It there lost the first prisoner ever made from the regiment — John Beaumont.

Sergeant C. A. Maguire, August 30th, 1862, distinguished himself as bearer of dispatches from Gen. Pope to Gen. McDowell, having to traverse the enemy's lines between Manassas Junction and Gainesville, compelled to fight much of the way, assisted by only ten men, yet accomplishing his task.

Sergeant T. McGiveran had three horses killed under him, and Sergeant W Murray four. A solid shot taking away the horse's head of the latter, June 1st, 1864, at Ashland, while falling, he coolly exclaimed, " Be jabers, this is a fine way to *dismount* a man !"

Sergeants T. Burke and W Herrick, June 30th, 1863, at Hanover, Pa., captured a Rebel battle flag and several prisoners.

John Catlin, bugler, a boy sixteen years old, March 7th, 1865, Rood's Hill, captured General Rosser's chief bugler, a tall man, and secured his bugle as a memento of the war.

Nearly the whole company was captured, on picket, at Barnett's ford, Rapidan, July 18th, 1862.

Original number of men, at time of muster in, 76; whole number, 183; men killed in action, 2; mortally wounded, 2; wounded, 26; number of wounds, 35; men captured, 58; missed in action and never heard from,[1] 2; died in Rebel prisons, 6; died of disease, 7; veterans,[2] 16; veterans remaining, July 19th, 1865, 12; whole number of men remaining, 63.

COMPANY B.

Officers.

Lyon Isaacs, Captain, August 21st, 1861. Resigned, May 18th, 1862.

David Abohbot, 1st Lieutenant, August 21st, 1861. Resigned, May, 1862.

Philip Dwyer, 2d Lieutenant, August 21st, 1861. Mortally wounded, May 23d, 1862, Front Royal. Died, May 25th.

Alfred W Creamer, Captain from 1st Lieutenant Co. E, May 2d, 1862. Resigned, January 12th, 1863.

Jeremiah Collins, 2d Lieutenant from 1st Sergeant, May 24th, 1862. Left by Special Order, December 13th, 1862.

---

[1] These men were probably killed.

[2] These veterans are men who were originally with the regiment, and who reënlisted in the early part of 1864.

Abram H. Hasbrouck, Captain from 2d Lieutenant Co. G, January 12th, 1863. Left by Special Order, December 26th, 1863.

Samuel McBride, 2d Lieutenant from Hospital Steward, December 13th, 1862. 1st Lieutenant, July 27th, 1863.

Llewellyn N. Stevens, 1st Lieutenant, January 9th, 1863. Resigned, June 1st, 1863.

Frederic Von Klitzing, 2d Lieutenant, May 19th, 1863. Resigned, September 6th, 1863.

Jabez Chambers, 2d Lieutenant from 1st Sergeant, September 1st, 1863. 1st Lieutenant, March 28th, 1864. Captain, December 9th, 1864.

Theodore A. Boice, Captain from 1st Lieutenant Co. A, December 20th, 1863. Major, September 15th, 1864. Lieutenant Colonel, November 14th, 1864.

Edward Price, 2d Lieutenant from 1st Sergeant, December 9th, 1864.

Capt. Isaacs organized this company in New York city, commencing the work in July, 1861. It was mustered into the service of U. S., August 21st, 1861, Long Island, N. Y., by Capt. A. P. Green.

The company suffered terribly with company D, May 23d, 1862, at Front Royal.

These two companies were afterward detached from the regiment, to serve on Crosby's battery, which they did till October 1st, 1862. Meanwhile they were engaged, September 19th, at Antietam.

October 9th, 1864, the company assisted in capturing six pieces of artillery and the enemy's train. October 19th, 1864, it captured four pieces of artillery.

Capt. Chambers, September 19th, 1864, captured seven

prisoners. Sergeant C. Statley was twice wounded and once captured, but escaped from his guards.

John Braden was twice captured, but effected his escape each time, and has had three horses killed under him in action.

Original number of men, 84; whole number, 190; men killed in action, 5; mortally wounded, 2; wounded, 27; number of wounds, 33; men captured, 44; missed in action and never heard from, 2; died in Rebel prisons, 10; died of disease, 2; killed accidentally, 3; discharged by reason of wounds, 7; veterans, 12; veterans remaining, July 19th, 1865, 8; whole number of men remaining, 59

Original horses remaining, 1.

COMPANY C.

Officers.

Ira Wright, Captain, August 8th, 1861. Left by Special Order, September 22d, 1862.

Henry L. Bogardus, 1st Lieutenant, August 8th, 1861. Resigned, June 1st, 1862.

Charles J Farley, 2d Lieutenant, August 8th, 1861. Captain, September 22d, 1862. Wounded twice, October 19th, 1863. Wounded in foot, August 25th, 1864. Lost right leg, and slight wound in head, September 19th, 1864. Discharged, Expiration of Term, January 16th, 1865.

Edward Whiteford, 1st Lieutenant, June 1st, 1862. Resigned, November 12th, 1862.

Benjamin M. Whittemore, 1st Lieutenant from Sergeant, November 13th, 1862. Captain, January 16th, 1865.

Joseph B. Grice, 2d Lieutenant from Sergeant Co. L, September 22d, 1862. Left by Special Order, May 7th, 1863.

Robert Harper, 2d Lieutenant from 1st Sergeant, May 7th, 1863. Left by Special Order 377 A. G. O., November 1st, 1864.

William Leahcy, 2d Lieutenant from 1st Sergeant, November 14th, 1864. 1st Lieutenant, January 16th, 1865.

Patrick Tiffany, 2d Lieutenant from 1st Sergeant, January 16th, 1865.

This company was raised in New York city, by Captain Wright, and was mustered into the service of the United States, September 3d, 1861, at Staten Island, N. Y., by Captain L. S. Larned. It won great praise during the second battle of Bull Run, by carrying dispatches at night through the enemy's lines, from General Pope to General Kearney.

Sergeant McNulty was severely wounded and captured, March 13th, 1864, Ely's Ford, but escaped, saving his money, a considerable amount, in the bottom of one of his boots. The Rebels undertook several times to take his boots from him, as was their custom to do, but he plead successfully on account of his wounds. He was captured again, June 28th, 1864. Escaped from prison, Greensboro', S. C., and was five weeks in reaching our lines.

The following captures were made by the company, October 19th, 1864, at Cedar creek:

Lieutenant Leahey, one headquarters medical wagon; Sergeants Tiffany and Highland, two pieces of artillery and twenty prisoners; Harvey Rickert, one piece of artillery; P. J Geraty, seven prisoners and one wagon; Sergeant W H. Norcott, one caisson and six prisoners; Corporal J. Farrell, one gun and limber and six horses; Sergeant John Buckley, one gun and six horses; the same by James Perry, who was accidentally and mortally wounded, February 27th, 1865.

John Stein was four times captured, and died in prison.

Original number of men, 76; whole number, 188; men killed in action, 7; mortally wounded, 2; wounded, 23; number of wounds, 29; men captured, 43; missed in action and never heard from, 2; died in Rebel prisons, 9; died of disease, 6; killed accidentally, 3; veterans, 22; veterans remaining, July 19th, 1865, 14; whole number of men remaining, 60.

Original horses remaining, 1.

COMPANY D.

Officers.

Thomas Coyle, Captain, August 21st, 1861. Died of disease, November 24th, 1861.

Amos H. White, 1st Lieutenant, September 21st, 1861. Captain, December 9th, 1861. Major, January 30th, 1863. Lieutenant Colonel, September 15th, 1864. Colonel, Noember, 14th, 1864.

Seth B. Ryder, 2d Lieutenant, September 29th, 1861. 1st Lieutenant, June 11th, 1862. Captain, January 30th, 1863. Captured, October 10th, 1863, and a prisoner till March, 1865. Discharged, Expiration of Term, May 15th, 1865.

George H. Nichols, 1st Lieutenant. March, 1862. Resigned, June 11th, 1862.

William Watson, 1st Lieutenant from 1st Sergeant, February 13th, 1863. Left by Special Order, July 27th, 1863.

Edward J. McArdle, 2d Lieutenant, February 2d, 1863. Resigned, June 1st, 1863.

Henry J. Appleby, 2d Lieutenant from Q. M. Sergeant June 1st, 1863. 1st Lieutenant, July 27th 1863. Discharged, Expiration of Term, September, 1864.

Charles H. Greenleaf, 2d Lieutenant from 1st Sergeant, July 27th, 1863. Mortally wounded, August 25th, 1864. Died next day.

Ransom A. Perkins, 2d Lieutenant from Commissary Sergeant, September 15th, 1864. 1st Lieutenant, November 14th, 1864.

Jeremiah J. Callanan, 2d Lieutenant from Sergeant, November 14th, 1865.

This company was formed by Captain Coyle, of men enlisted in the states of Massachusetts and Connecticut, and was mustered into the service of the United States, October 1st, 1861, at Staten Istand, N. Y., by Col. D. B. Sacket, U. S. Army.

With company B, it performed the peculiar work attached to a battery, from June to October, 1862.

Sergeant C. H. Greenleaf, May 23d, 1862, carried dispatches from Front Royal to Gen. Banks at Strasburg.[1] By bravery and skill, he gave timely notice of Stonewall Jackson's flank movement, whereby he saved Gen. Banks' army, which led the general to recommend him for promotion. He was mortally wounded in action, while in command of company A, fighting bravely.

H. A. Smith received four sabre cuts, May 23d, 1862, and was captured. Wounded again and captured, June 23d, 1864, at Nottoway Court House.

Corp. John Walsh, October 19th, 1864, at Cedar creek,

---

[1] See his letter, page 31.

recaptured the eolors of the 15th New Jersey Vols., for which he received the "Medal of Honor," awarded by Congress.

Original number of men, 82; whole number, 161; men killed in action, 3; mortally wounded, 1; wounded, 23; number of wounds, 27; men captured, 59; missed in action and never heard from, 3; died in Rebel prisons, 10; died of disease, 7; killed aeeidentally, 1; discharged by reason of wounds, 1; veterans, 16; veterans remaining, July 19th, 1865, 15; whole number of men remaining, 45.

COMPANY E.

Officers.

William P. Pratt, Captain, August 15th, 1861. Major, July 1st, 1862. Resigned, January 30th, 1863.

Alfred W Creamer, 1st Lieutenant, September 17th, 1861. Captain Company B, May 2d, 1862.

William H. Williams, 2d Lieutenant, November 7th, 1861. 1st Lieutenant, May 2d, 1862. Captain, May 28th, 1862. Resigned, February 7th, 1863.

William P Dye, 2d Lieutenant from 1st Sergeant, May 2d, 1862. 1st Lieutenant, May 28th, 1862. Captain, February 7th, 1863. Resigned, September 3d, 1864.

Daniel B. Merriman, 2d Lieutenant from 1st Sergeant, May 28th, 1862. 1st Lieutenant, February 7th, 1863. Discharged for physical disabillity, March 29th, 1864.

Liberty C. Abbott, 2d Lieutenant from Q. M. Sergeant, June 30th, 1863. 1st Lieutenant, March 29th, 1864. Captain, November 14th, 1864. Major, May 2d, 1865.

Foster Dickinson, 2d Lieutenant from 1st Sergeant, May 21st, 1864. 1st Lieutenant, November 14th, 1864. Captain, June 1st, 1865.

Matthew Strait, 2d Lieutenant from Corporal, November 14th, 1864. 1st Lieutenant, June 1st, 1865.

Addison S. Thompson, 2d Lieutenant from 1st Sergeant, June 1st, 1865.

Major Davidson raised this company in Allegany county, N. Y., and it was mustered into the service of the United States, August 31st, 1861, at New York city, by Captain S. B. Hayman, U. S. Army.

Asahel A. Spencer was the first man of the regiment, killed in action, May 6th, 1862, Harrisonburg.

The company has lost two 1st Sergeants, killed in action, E. S. Dye and S. W Sortore, and their commissions of 2d Lieutenants reached the regiment just after their deaths.

John Leiser deserted from the Rebel army and joined this company. He was a true and brave soldier. (See Table—Men who died in Rebel Prisons.)

Henry W Monroe, June 30th, 1863, at Hanover, Pa., received a gunshot wound through his body, so that stones of cherries he had eaten that morning passed through the wound. He got well.

Corporal Charles A. Miner, October 9th, 1864, Tom's Brook, while pursuing the enemy, emerged from a piece of woods, in sight of eight Rebels. He cried out "Come on boys!" looking back as though he were leading a company of men. Without firing a shot the Rebels fled, leaving a wagon loaded with hay, and six mules. He was killed by the falling of the walls of Union Hotel, Winchester, December 16th, 1864.

Major L. C. Abbott, October 9th, 1864, captured six prisoners, by making a sabre charge upon them.

Lieutenant M. Strait, September 19th, 1864, had a button

of his coat driven into his left hand, by a bullet. He fought bravely, October 9th, 1864, capturing General Rosser's headquarters wagon, and securing the general's private saddle. October 19th, he captured a brass battery of six guns.

S. K. Ford joined the company. August, 1861, but displayed no soldierly qualities until October 9th, 1864. He then captured five prisoners, and October 19th he fought desperately, eliciting general admiration, but was severely wounded through the right lung.

Lieutenant A. S. Thompson, October 6th, 1864, Brock's Gap, had his horse killed under him and was surrounded by the enemy. He managed to secrete himself in bushes until night, though so near the Rebels as to hear them converse, and escaped through their picket line, under cover of the darkness. He has had three horses killed under him. Sergeant S. T. Uptegrove, October 6th, 1864, was captured, stripped of all his clothing, and only old rags replaced, and almost starved. He escaped from Rebels during the fight at Tom's Brook, October 9th.

David F. Wolcott was promoted to Saddler Sergeant, for his fidelity as a soldier and a man.

L. C. Smith had three horses killed under him in action.

Original number of men, 94; whole number, 169; men killed in action, 5; mortally wounded, 2; wounded, 27; number of wounds, 39; men captured, 41; died in Rebel prisons, 7; died of disease, 7; killed accidentally, 2; discharged by reason of wounds, 1; veterans, 36; veterans remaining July 19th, 1865, 31; whole number of men remaining, 60.

Original horses remaining, 1.

Company F

Officers.

Washington Wheeler, Captain, August 30th, 1861. Major, July 1st, 1862. Resigned, September 26th, 1862.

Levi Curtis, 1st Lieutenant, August 30th, 1861. Captain, July 1st, 1862. Resigned, January 22, 1863.

William D. Lucas, 2d Lieutenant, August 30th, 1861. 1st Lieutenant, July 1, 1862. Captain, January 22, 1863.

Edward D. Tolles, 2d Lieutenant from Commissary Sergeant, July 1st, 1863. 1st Lieutenant, July 22d, 1863. Resigned, October 29th, 1863.

William B. Pickett, 2d Lieutenant from 1st Sergeant, January 22d, 1863. 1st Lieutenant, October 30th, 1863. Discharged, Expiration of Term, October 15th, 1864.

Walter C. Smith, 2d Lieutenant from private, October 30th, 1863. Discharged, Expiration of Term, October 15th, 1864.

Merritt N. Chafey, 1st Lieutenant from Regimental Commissary Sergeant, November 14th, 1864.

John K. Jeffrey, 2d Lieutenant from 1st Sergeant, November 14th, 1864.

This company was organized in Wyoming county, N. Y., by Captain Wheeler, and was mustered into the service of the United States, September 21st, 1861, at New York city, by Captain S. B. Hayman, U. S. Army.

George H. Jenkins, May 30th, 1863, shot an English officer, who was working a Rebel howitzer. (See account of that engagement, page 59).

Q. M. Sergeant D. J. McMillan has been six times wounded, receiving three sabre cuts, June 30th, 1863, and three gunshot wounds afterward, one through the left lung, October 19th, 1863.

Eugene Pratt received eight wounds in one engagement, March 11th, 1864, from the musket of a guerrillas three musket balls and five buck shot.

William H. Nieman, captured, October 19th, 1863, was not released till April 28th, 1865.

Original number of men, 92; whole number, 189; men killed in action, 5; mortally wounded, 4; wounded, 23; number of wounds, 34; men captured, 43; missed in action and never heard from, 2; died in Rebel prisons, 10; died of disease, 6; killed accidentally, 3; discharged by reason of wounds, 4; veterans, 9; veterans remaining July 19th, 1865, 8; whole number of men remaining, 66.

COMPANY G.

Officers

Abram H. Krom, Captain, August 1st, 1861. Wounded twice, May 3d, 1863. Major, December 5th, 1863. Discharged, Expiration of Term, October 21st, 1864.

Wallace M. Boyer, 1st Lieutenant, August 30th, 1861. Resigned, July 1st, 1862.

Eugene B. Gere, 2d Lieutenant, August 27th, 1861. 1st Lieutenant, July 1st, 1862. Wounded, August 2d, 1862. Resigned, November 19th, 1862.

Abram H. Hasbrouck, 2d Lieutenant, September 20th, 1862. Captain, company B, January 12th, 1863.

James Bryant, 1st Lieutenant from 1st Sergeant, November 19th, 1862. Captain, December 5th, 1863. Captured, May 18th, 1864. Discharged, Expiration of Term, January 18th, 1865.

Philip Krohn, 2d Lieutenant from Sergeant, January 12th, 1863. 1st Lieutenant, December 5th, 1863. Discharged, Expiration of Term, May 15th, 1865. Three times captured, July 17th, 1862; August 10th, 1863; June 1st, 1864.

John H. Wright, 2d Lieutenant from 1st Sergeant, March 29th, 1864. Captain, January 12th, 1865.

William H. Knight, 2d Lieutenant from Sergeant, January 12th, 1865. 1st Lieutenant, June 1st, 1865.

Abijah Spafford, 2d Lieutenant from 1st Sergeant, June 1st, 1865.

Captain Krom enlisted this company in Tioga county, N. Y. It was mustered into the service of United States, September 30th, 1861, Staten Island, N. Y., by Captain Lyon Isaacs.

John Mooney had five horses killed under him in action, during campaign of 1864, yet was not wounded nor hurt himself.

Sergeant Charles A. Phelps has been employed in the secret service, as scout, by Generals Stahel, Kilpatrick, Pleasanton and Meade.

Sergeant N. W Barnum, at the battle of Five Forks, bore General Sheridan's flag, which was pierced by two bullets, and the standard grazed.

Oscar E. Farnham, captured, June 27th, 1864, made his escape by jumping from cars, while moving at the rate of twenty miles an hour, between Augusta, Ga., and Savannah. He was thirty-four days in reaching General Sherman's army, assisted by negroes, on his way.

P. H. White and R. Dinehart, October 9th, 1864, captured one piece of artillery.

S. Lynch, October 19th, 1864, captured one piece of artillery.

John Evans, March 7th, 1865, had a ball pass through a pack of cards and several plugs of tobacco, lodging against the skin opposite his heart.

Sergeant B. G. Wilmot was captured, rejoined the regiment, and was captured again the same day, May 17th, 1864.

Original number of men, 95; whole number, 155; men killed in action, 6; wounded, 22; number of wounds, 32; men captured, 48; missed in action and never heard from, 2; died in Rebel prisons, 9; died of disease, 7; discharged by reason of wounds, 2; veterans, 27; veterans remaining July 19th, 1865, 25; whole number of men remaining, 56.

COMPANY H.

Officers.

John Hammond, Captain, September 14th, 1861. Major, September 26th, 1862. Lieutenant Colonel, March 24th, 1864. Colonel, July 3d, 1864. Discharged, Expiration of Term, September 3d, 1864. Fore-finger of his right hand broken by a pistol ball, September 13th, 1863; Leg bone just above right ankle cracked by a Minié ball, June 1st, 1864, at Ashland.

Jonas A. Benedict, 1st Lieutenant, October 22d, 1861. Died from amputation of right arm, resulting from the bite of a man on thumb, December 11th, 1861.

James A. Penfield, 2d Lieutenant, October 22d, 1861. 1st Lieutenant, December 11th, 1861. Captain, September 26th, 1862. Wounded by sabre cut in head, and captured, July 6th, 1863. In prison till March, 1865. Commissioned Major, March 29th, 1864. Resigned, May 2d, 1865.

John G. Viall, 2d Lieutenant, December 11th, 1861. 1st

Lieutenant, September 26th, 1862. Captain, Company M, April 2d, 1864.

Elmer J. Barker, 2d Lieutenant from Sergeant, September 26th, 1862. 1st Lieutenant, November 6th, 1863. Captain, March 29th, 1864. Major, November 14th, 1864.

Eugene B. Hayward, 2d Lieutenant from 1st Sergeant, November 6th, 1863. 1st Lieutenant, March 29th, 1864. Captain, November 14th, 1864.

Lucius F. Renne, 1st Lieutenant from 1st Sergeant, November 14th, 1864.

Clark M. Pease, 2d Lieutenant from 1st Sergeant, November 14th, 1864.

This company was organized in Crown Point, Essex county, N. Y., by John Hammond, assisted by C. F. Hammond, Esq., who furnished all the original horses for the company to the number of one hundred and eight. It was mustered into the United States service, October 18th, 1861, at New York city, by Captain Bankhead, U S. Army. It was detached from the regiment, to coöperate with infantry in the Luray Valley, during the early part of May, 1862. While there it participated in several sprightly skirmishes with the enemy.

Lieutenant E. J. Barker distinguished himself, May 30th, 1863, by leading a charge on one of Mosby's howitzers, where he fell wounded with two grape shot.

Abram Folger, June 30th, 1863, captured Lieut. Colonel Payne, Rebel, in a tan vat, where the colonel had fallen.

Sergeant S. J. Mason, with nine men, guarded the neutral ground between the two armies, where General Lee surrendered his army to General Grant, April 9th, 1865, at Appomattox Court House

John P. Durno, O. T. Cornell, D. H. Robbins, all enlisted in this company at Winchester, Va., in the spring of 1862, and were all discharged at the same place, at expiration of term of service, without ever having been wounded or hurt, except that Robbins was a prisoner about five months.

Original number of men, 106; whole number 198; men killed in action, 6; mortally wounded, 2; wounded, 31; number of wounds, 34; men captured, 65; missed in action and never heard from, 2; died in Rebel prisons, 15; died of disease, 12; killed accidentally, 2; discharged by reason of wounds, 4; veterans, 28; veterans remaining, July 19th, 1865, 22; whole number of men remaining, 47

Original horses remaining, 4.

COMPANY I.

Officers.

George A. Bennett, Captain, September, 1861. Resigned, June, 1862.

Edward C. Woodruff, 1st Lieutenant, September, 1861. Resigned, April 6th, 1862.

George C. Morton, 2d Lieutenant, September 3d, 1861 1st Lieutenant, May 6th, 1862. Captain, June 21st, 1862. Discharged by Special Order 70 A. G. O., February 12th, 1864.

William B. Cary, 2d Lieutenant from Sergeant, May 6th, 1862. 1st Lieutenant, June 21st, 1862. Captain, March 17th, 1864. Discharged, Expiration of Term, October 23d, 1864.

Eugene Sullivan, 2d Lieutenant from Sergeant, June 21st, 1862. Left by General Orders No. 7 Army of Potomac, March 24th, 1864.

Robert Black, 1st Lieutenant from 2d Lieutenant, company K, March 17th, 1864. Discharged by Special Order No. 471 A. G. O., December 28th, 1864.

Christopher Heron, 2d Lieutenant from 1st Sergeant, March 29th, 1864. 1st Lieutenant, January 13th, 1865.

William H. Conklin, 2d Lieutenant from 1st Sergeant, January 13th, 1865.

Edmund Blunt, Jr., Captain from Captain company M, June, 1865.

This company was formed by Captain Bennett of men enlisted in New York city, Orange county, N. Y., and in Plainfield, N. J. It was mustered into the service of the United States, September 27th, 1864, at Staten Island, N. Y., by Captain L. S. Larned. It was the escort of General Heintzelman, then in command of Defenses of Washington, from August 27th, 1862, to September 1st, 1863. A portion of the company was in the advance with the lamented Colonel Dahlgren, on General Kilpatrick's raid to Richmond, March, 1864. (See account, page 94).

Bugler Conrad Bohrer, August 2d, 1862, saved the life of Colonel DeForest, who was beset by a dozen Rebels. But Bohrer's horse being shot, he fell, and an enemy thrust him through the body with a sabre. The enemy, being finally beaten and driven, the body of this dauntless bugler was recovered and honored. with a military burial, where he fell.

Robert Campbell, October 20th, 1864, captured fourteen prisoners in a squad near Cedar creek.

Lewis H. Crandall was poisoned, October, 1864, at Harrisonburg, dying soon after.

Original number of men, 90; whole number, 190;

men killed in action, 8; wounded, 6; number of wounds, 8; men captured, 20; died in Rebel prisons, 10; died of disease, 10; discharged by reason of wounds, 2; veterans, 3; veterans remaining, July 19th, 1865, 3; whole number of men remaining, 57

COMPANY K.

Officers.

William P. Hallett, Captain, October 1st, 1861. Resigned, December 16th, 1862.

Zolman J. McMasters, 1st Lieutenant, October 9th, 1861. Captain, December 16th, 1862. Died of disease, September 24th, 1863.

Laurence L. O'Connor, 2d Lieutenant, October 16th, 1861. 1st Lieutenant, December 9th, 1862. Resigned, August 16th, 1863. Captain, March 5th, 1864.

Henry A. D. Merritt, 2d Lieutenant from Sergeant, company L, December 9th, 1862. 1st Lieutenant, August 16th, 1863. Captain, November 14th, 1864. Major, November 14th, 1864.

Robert Black, 2d Lieutenant from Sergeant, September 1863. 1st Lieutenant, company I, March 17th, 1864.

William H. Whitcomb, 2d Lieutenant from 1st Sergeant, company M, May 21st, 1864. 1st Lieutenant, company L, November 14th, 1864.

Thomas O'Keefe, 2d Lieutenant from 1st Sergeant, November 14th, 1864. 1st Lieutenant, June 1st, 1865.

Nathaniel M. Talmage, 2d Lieutenant from 1st Sergeant, June 1st, 1865.

Captain Hallett organized this company in New York city, and it was mustered into the United States service,

September 27th, 1861, at Staten Island, N. Y., by Captain L. S. Larned. It was detailed as Body Guard for General Heintzelman, August 27th, 1862, until September 12th, 1862, and as escort for General Emory, commanding 19th Army Corps, September, 1864, and continued with the general until April, 1865.

Lieutenant H. A. D. Merritt, in command of part of this company, and of company I, distinguished himself with Colonel Dahlgren, by whose side he rode, when the Colonel was killed, on Kilpatrick's raid to Richmond, March, 1864. (See his narrative of the raid, page 94).

Sergeant D. H. Scofield, October 19th, 1864, captured the colors of the 12th Virginia Infantry, for which labor he received from the Secretary of War, the "medal of honor," awarded by Congress.

Michael Kenney has driven a team of six mules since the organization of the regiment, and retains four of the original animals.

Original number of men, 104; whole number, 164; men killed in action, 2; mortally wounded, 1; wounded, 8; number of wounds, 13; men captured, 31; missed in action and never heard from, 2; died in Rebel prisons, 11; died of disease, 5; killed accidentally, 1; discharged by reason of wounds, 1; veterans, 17; veterans remaining, July 19th, 1865, 9; whole number of men remaining, 60.

COMPANY L.

Officers.

Charles Arthur, Captain, September 27th, 1861. Left by Special Order, October 24th, 1862.

Charles C. Suydam, 1st Lieutenant, September 27th, 1861. Resigned, May 6th, 1862.

Augustus Barker, 2d Lieutenant, September 27th, 1861. 1st Lieutenant, May 6th, 1862. Captain, October 24th, 1862. Captured by Mosby, March 9th, 1863, at Fairfax Court House. Killed by guerrillas, at Kelly's Ford, September 14th, 1863.

Frank A. Monson, 1st Lieutenant, October 24th, 1862. Captain, September 14th, 1863. Wounded in arm, May 3d, 1863, at Warrenton Junction. Resigned, July 12th, 1864.

Albert B. Waugh, 2d Lieutenant from Sergeant, October 24th, 1862. 1st Lieutenant, September 14th, 1863. Discharged, Expiration of Term, October 23d, 1864.

George C. Morton, Captain, July 19th, 1864.

William H. Whitcomb, 1st Lieutenant from 2d Lieutenant Company K, November 14th, 1864.

Peter McMullen, 2d Lieutenant from 1st Sergeant, November 14th, 1864.

The original men of this company were mostly from New York city. Captain Arthur organized the company, and it was mustered into the United States service, September 27th, 1861, at Staten Island, N. Y., by Captain L. S. Larned. It has been in all the engagements of the regiment. It was detailed, with companies I and K, as Body Guard for General Heintzelman, August 27th, 1862, reporting to the regiment again, with company K, September 13th, 1862.

John McEwan, on picket near the Rebel lines, accompanied and directed General Lee to the house where he held his first interview with General Grant, and surrendered his army.

Original number of men, 79; whole number, 164; men killed in action, 4; mortally wounded, 1; wounded, 9;

number of wounds, 12; men captured, 39; missed in action and never heard from, 1; died in Rebel prisons, 10; died of disease, 12; discharged by reason of wounds, 2; veterans, 12; veterans remaining, July 19th, 1865, 10; whole number of men remaining, 44.

COMPANY M.

Officers.

James P. Foster, Captain, October 1st, 1861. Resigned, August 28th, 1862.

Samuel Ten Broeck, 1st Lieutenant, October 1st, 1861. Captain, August 28th, 1862. Died of disease, July 4th, 1863.

George S. Clough, 2d Lieutenant, October 1st, 1861. Resigned, May 6th, 1862.

Eugene D. Dimmick, 2d Lieutenant from 1st Sergeant, May 9th, 1862. 1st Lieutenant, August 28th, 1862. Captain, July 4th, 1863. Wounded in right hand, July 6th, 1863. Discharged by reason of wound, November 6th, 1863.

Edmund Blunt, Jr., 2d Lieutenant, September 26th, 1862. 1st Lieutenant, July 4th, 1863. Captain, November 14th, 1864. Transferred to company I, June, 1865.

Wilbur F. Oakley, 2d Lieutenant from 1st Sergeant, July 4th, 1863. 1st Lieutenant, November 14th, 1864. Captain, January 12th, 1865.

John G. Viall, Captain from 1st Lieutenant company H, April 2d, 1864 Appointed Assistant Quartermaster of Volunteers, June 18th, 1864.

William G. Peckham, 1st Lieutenant from Sergeant company E, January 12th, 1865.

This company was raised by Captain Foster in New York

city, and in the counties of Greene and Columbia, and it was mustered into the service of the United States, October 31st, 1861, at Staten Island, N. Y., by Captain A. H. Krom. It was escort for General Banks, from August 28th, 1862, till September 21st, 1862, when it reported to the regiment.

E. B. Warner had five horses killed under him in action, in one day, September 19th, 1864, at Winchester. He was not hurt himself.

Sergeant W H. Whitcomb had two horses killed under him in action, and six mortally wounded.

Original number of men, 86; whole number, 186; men killed in action, 2; mortally wounded, 2; wounded, 11; number of wounds, 14; men captured, 26; died in Rebel prisons, 7; died of disease, 9; killed accidentally, 3; veterans, 13; veterans remaining, July 19th, 1865, 10; whole number of men remaining, 77.

CHAPTER XVIII.

Complete Roster of the Regiment; each company given alphabetically.

The following abbreviations are used:—Veterans, by small CAPITALS; Prisoners of War, by the letter *a*; Died of disease, by the letter *b*; Killed accidentally, by the letter *c*; Missed in actiou aud never heard from, by the letter *d*; Number of wounds received in actiou, by the figures 1, 2, 3, &c.

Company A.*

Allen, Solomon,
Allison, John,
Avery, Edward,
Bolt, James V., 1.
Brandt, George,
Bahby, Justin, *a*
Bernhardi, Fred. W., *a*
Burke, Thomas,
Beaumont, Johu, *a*
Bond, James H.,
Bro, Joseph,
Barwick, Thomas,
Branch, Ruthvin L.,
Brown, Amos, 2.
Boyd, William T., *a*
BOICE, THEO. A., 5. *a*
Bates, George, *a*
Bradford, Landon,
Buckman, Augustus
Brittell, Erwin,
Bradley, Peter,
Bibhins, John E.,
Burns, Michael,
Boutelle, Frazer A.,
Calvin, Henry,
Cavanaugh, James,
Chadwick, William,
Crowley, James,
CATLIN, JOHN, *a*
Clark, William,
Coon, Samuel C.,
Crandall, Charles A.,
Chaffee, Alpheus, *b*
Chadwick, Francis B.,
Clooney, John J., 1.
Cooper, Edward,
Clinton, Robert,
Donohue, Patrick,
Donohne, James,
Duncan, Alexander,
Dougherty, Charles,
Day, Edgar, *b*
Douglass, John,
Eldridge, Thomas,
Flemmings, David,
Flagg, Hubert,
Freeman, William,
Farley, James, *a*
Goodwin, Rollin C., *a*
Gallagher, James H., 1.
Glodell, John,
Going, James, *a*
Gillespie, Patrick,
Golden, Charles, *a*
Geho, Edward,
Goodrich, Calvin J.,
Gregory, George A.,
Halpln, Joseph,
Hall, Benjamin F., *a*
Hare, Cornelius,
Hacket, Uri,
Hay, Asa,
HAYES, MICHAEL, 1. *a*
Hennessey, William,
Hathaway, Charles A.,
Holloway, William H.,
Hanherry, John,
Hassett, William,
Hallenheck, Tunis,

* This Company had in all 183 Men.

HALEY, PATRICK, *a*
HERRICK, WILLIAM, 1.
Heinsler, Henry,
Heiler, John, *a*
Hopkins, Merlin J., *a*
HODGKINS, JOHN,
Hopkins, William H.,
Isdell, John B.,
Innells, Robert,
Irwin, Robert,
Jones, Anson, 1.
Jones, Luther W.,
Jones, Julins,
Johnston, Robert, *a*
Jenks, George E., 1.
Kenney, Thomas S.,
Kelley, John,
Lampert, John H., *a*
Leary, Daniel,
Leddy, Bernard,
Lively, William H.,
Longeway, Antoine, *a*
Lord, William E.,
Lappan, William H.,
MURRAY, WILLIAM, *a*
Malley, John, *a*
MCGEARY, BARTLEY,
Michaels, Charles A., *b*
Marron, John, *b*
McCarron, William J.,
Moon, John,
MCGIVERAN, THOMAS, *a*
MAGUIRE, CHAS. A., 2.
McKeon, Arthur,
McNeve, Patrick, 1. *a*
MARTIN, DANIEL, *a*
MCDONALD, JER., 2. *a*
MERRILL, CHAUNCEY,

Mnller, Charles,
Morehouse, Edward A.,
Merrill, Henry,
Morgan, William,
MORGAN, CHARLES,
Milspaugh, William,
Mohan, James,
McCanley, Robert, *a*
McCormick, Michael, *a*
McCormack, William,
McDermott, Thomas,
Murphy, William,
Neil, Arthur, 1. *a*
Norman, Merritt,
Nealon, Patrick, *a*
O'SHAUGHNESSY, PAT.,
O'DONNELL, PATRICK,
O'Connor, Thomas, *a*
O'Farrell, James,
O'FLAHERTY, DENNIS, *a*
O'Brien, John,
O'Connell, James,
Otis, Henry,
Peck, Jeremiah,
Pierson, William H.,
Pulcipher, William P.,
PETERSON, JOHN,
Phillips, Christopher, *d*
Pierre, François,
Plunkett, Robert,
Peet, Edward D., *b*
Rickey, James,
Ritchie, Thomas, 1.
Rodgers, William,
Romaine, Constantine,
Ryan, Peter,
Reed, Alexander E.,
Ryan, Thomas,

Ryner, John,
Stickney, Moses,
Simmonds, Chas. F., *b*
Schreidner, George,
Sinclair, Donald,
Smith, Charles A.,
SCHNEIDER, CHARLES,
Stevenson, John H.,
Sullivan, John,
Sntherland, Charles,
Sinclair, Robert,
Smith, David,
Salter, Alexander,
Spargi, Francis,
Taylor, William, *a*
Taylor, Alexander,
Thompson, James,
Tripp, John,
Tappan, William H.,
Terbush, Launcelot B.
Tyrrell, Seth, *d*
Taylor, Abel T.,
Van Kirk, Thomas W.,
VAN WERT, JAS. C., *b*
Van Osdale, Lewis, *a*
Williamson, George,
Wandell, Andrew, *a*
Wetmore, Dennis,
Wales, Selden D.,
Wilbur, George F., *a*
WYNN, JAMES, 1. *a*
WALKER, GEORGE,
Winchell, James N.,
Wilson, John,
WHITMORE, ALEX.,
Woods, William,
Woods, John,
Zimmerman, Baldwin.

Company B.*

Avist, Henry P.,
Alderdice, William,
Ahel, Fredrick, 1.
Billings, Calvin,
Brown, William,
Bradshaw, Gust's. W.,
BUTTERWORTH, THOS.,
BEERS, CHARLES,
Borst, Edward S., *a*
BRADEN, JOHN, *a*
Brown, George,
BROWN, JOHN,
Burnap, Tracy,
Balcom, Myron B.,
Burt, Edmund, Jr.,
Barden, Oscar L.,
Buffington, Henry P.,
Buffington, Nathan H.,
Bonxcries, John,
Bradshaw, John,
Barrilla, Francis,
CHAMBERS, JABEZ, *a*
Cooney, William,
Criddle, William, *c*
Coleman, Michael,
Christian, Robert, *a*
Chaffee, Hanson G., 1.
Chaffee, Otis H.,
Chaffee, Edwin E., 1.
Cole, Orlando, 1.
Cole, Avery,
Corhin, Levi H.,
Cortes, William,
Cann, Edward, *b*
Crum, Henry,
Coffin, German,
Caraher, Peter,
Carlos, John,
Collins, Jeremiah,
Dyke, John,
Dewey, Matthew,
Dillon, John,
Driscoll, James,
Denniston, Saml. M., 1.
Davenport, Keyes,
Dongherty, William, *a*
Decker, Charles,
Day, Michael,
Duffcy, James,
Dana, Henry L.,
Duhois, John B., *a*
Depew, Job, 1.
Ducat, Joseph, Jr.
Dubois, Henry,
Ellis, Charles,
Eddy, Alhert,
French, James,
Ford, William V., *a*
Feeney, Thomas,
Freeman, Hugh,
Fergnson, John H.,
Fowler, John A.,
Fero, Peter H., 1.
Goggans, John,
GARDELLE, GEORGE, 1.
Gorton, Cornelins, *a*
Graham, Edward, 1.
Green, Jackson,
Green, John,
Hayes, Charles,
Huller, Christian,
Hank, Edward,
Hogan, James,
Horr, John,
Hutchins, Simeon, A., *a*
Hogle, Martin V.,
Hay, Wellington,
Hay, William,
Hannau, James,
Isaacs, David,
Jones, Joel,
Jelley, James,
Kelley, James, *a*
King, Louis,
Leech, Thomas S.,
Lamarsh, Peter,
Leno, Thomas,
Laven, John,
Latour, Joseph, *a*
Latour. Solomon, Jr.,
Lathrop, Mervin, 1.
Lewis, Cyrus B.,
Lewis, James, 1. *a*
Lynch, John,
Lanney, Patrick H.,
Levy, Bernard, 1.
Laguna, Mignel,
Miles, Silas, *a*
McChale, Michael,
McCormick, Robert,
McNalley, Edward,
McChale, James,
McCaw, John,
McManns, John,
McCarty, James,
Miller, Amos,
Morse, John L., *a*
Mills, Francis,
Martin, Edward A., *d*
Major, Benjamin,
Murphy, Daniel,
More, Adam,
Mowhray, William R.,
Moran, William,
Manning, Mortimer F.,
Mahar, Rohert,
Morrissey, John, *c*
Newland, Francis,
Northaway, Erastus,
Neddo, John B.

---

* This Company had in all 190 Men.

O'Blenis, Charles,
O'Connell, Lewis,
O'Donnell, James,
O'Connell, James,
Page, William C., *a*
Putnam, Charles E.,
PRICE, EDWARD,
PARLOW, EBENEZER E.,
PERRY, JOSEPH,
Place, Armstrong B.,
Pray, John H.,
Quinn, Joseph,
Reeves, William P.,
Reed, John,
Reed, Gorman H.,
Rosenbrock, Joseph,
Richards, Samuel,
Roach, James M.,
Rix, Silas A., *a*
Runciman, John R., *a*
Richards, Thomas,
Richards, Herman, *a*
Rooney, John, *a*
Rooney, Michael,
STATLEY, CHAS., 2. *a*
Snyder, Edward,
Sheardown, J. M., 1. *a*
Smith, John S., 1.
Stewart, Charles,
SAMPSON, WILLIAM H., *a*
Surprise, Nelson, *d*
Scafe, Robert,
Smith, Amos B.,
Stafford, John, 1.
Scully, William,
Son, William M.,
Strong, Harvey J.,
Smith, George T.,
Smith, Edmund,
Seddinger, James,
Scherry, Jacob,
Sauerwein, Albert,
Shugare, Daniel, 1.
Tunnerhill, James,
TIERNEY, PATRICK,
Updyke, John R.,
Ward, Edward,
Walsh, William,
Waghorn, John. 2. *a*
Whalen, James,
Wood, Oscar,
Wilkins, David, 1.
Welsh, Andrew,
Waggoner, George,
WALSH, JAMES,
Whaley, George T., *b*
Winch, Clark, 1.
Wilbur, Willis, 1. *c*
Whipple, Elisha W.,
Whipple, Frank,
Wheeler, Elias W.,
Williamson, William,
Whitaker, Aaron,
Walsh, James,
Wayne, William,
Walker, Charles H.,
Westerfield, Charles, 1.
West, William,
Young, John,
Young, William, 1. *a*

Company C.*

ANDERSON, ROBERT S.,
Adams, James,
Bateson, John,
Bakeman, William H.,
Brothers, Charles, *a*
Bissell, Abner,
Billings, Calvin,
Bureau, Joseph B., *a*
BURGESS, A. D., 1. *a*
BUCKLEY, JOHN, 1.
Brennan, William, 1.
Bogue, Fred S., *a*
Barry, William.
Bigelow, Ephraim, *d*
Bigelow, Henry, *b*
Beardsley, William P.,
Brown, Charles,
Curtis, B. N.,
COFFEE, MICHAEL,
Clarke, James W.,
Conklin, Gardner, 1. *a*
Creighton, William,
Cooper, Louis,
Caldecott, Joseph,
Church, Charles L., *a*
Campbell, Levi C.,
Cavanaugh, Joseph,
Caple, Elijah,
Clare, Simon,
Duvall, Robert H.,
Doty, George W.,
Douglass, Joseph,
Dailey, Anthony,
Doyle, Cornelius,
Doyle, James,
Driscoll, John,
Donohue, Florence,
Devoe, John,
Dudley, John,
Durand, Ferdinand,
Desilctz, Felix, 1.
EVANS, JOHN W., *a*
Flitchard, George,
Farrell, James,
Fuller, Percival,
Fitch, Edward H., *a*
Fairchild, Henry,
FRENYER, THOMAS,
Ferris, Almon F.,
Finau, Patrick, *a*
Finley, Martin, *b*
GRAHAM, ROBERT W.,
GERATY, PHILIP J.,
Gaffney, Philip,
Greenwood, William, 1.
Gregoire, Simia,
Gardner, John,
Haley, Michacl,
Halley, Michael,
Hodge, Charles,
Hogan, Philip,
Hickok, George C., 1. *a*
HARPER, ROBERT, 1.
Hogan, Patrick,
HOWARD, MICHAEL, *a*
HIGHLAND, JAMES,
Hayes, Timothy, *c*
Haley, Michael,
Hurley, Daniel,
Holdridge, William,
Hickey, William,
Hand, Laurence, *a*
Hill, Henry,
Hughes, Michael,
Harrington, Philip,
Johnson, Charles,
Jones, David,
JONES, WILLIAM, *a*
Jeandro, Elijah,
Keefe, Edward,
King, Theodore,
Kistner, John, 1.
Ketchum, Charles, *b*
Kelley, William,
KANAHAN, PATRICK, *a*
Kenney, Patrick,
Leeney, George, *a*
LEAHEY, WILLIAM, 1.
Lconard, Bartholomew,
Lincoln, Patrick Q., *a*
LUCAS, JOHN C.,
Lauray, George C.,
Lucha, John, *a*
Lahue, Napoleon, *a*
Murphy, Michael, *c*
Meagher, John,
MARTIN, EDWARD,
Michaels, James, *a*
Morrell, Isaac,
Mornement, Mark D.,
Meade, Sylvester, 2. *a*
Montgomery, Thomas, *c*
Manor, William, *a*
Miller, Rockwell D., *d*
Moore, Orlando, 1.
Moran, Edward,
Mead, Edward, *b*
Mitchell, Thomas,
Mack, Michael,
Marshall, Milton C.,
Mason, George,
McCormick, William,
McCoy, Allen B.,
McComb, James, *b*
McKissick, David,
McCAULEY, OWEN, 1. *a*
McNULTY, OWEN, 7. *a*
McGlade, Joseph,
McLane, John,
McDade, James, 1.

* This Company had in all 188 Men.

McNearney, Charles,
McGrath, William,
Norman, Adcodat,
Norman, Edward,
NORCUTT, WILLIAM H.,
Newton, Horace,
Nolan, Thomas,
O'Meara, Daniel,
O'Connor, Timothy,
O'Connor, Patrick,
Owen, Leonard, Jr., *a*
Pease, Henry W.
Perry, James, *c*
PYRES, HENRY, *a*
QUINLAN, PATRICK,
Rickerts, John B.,
Rickerts, Harvey H.,
Rensing, Egnetz, 1.
Raymer, Fredrick, *a*
Riches, James H.,
Roach, William,
Reynolds, Thomas,
Rock, John,
Riley, Martin, 1.
Riche, Louis, 1.
Stananaught, Richard,
Smith, Sherman H.,
Smith, John,
Smith, John,
Smith, William P., *a*
Smith, George W.,
Smith, James,
Stinson, George,
Sackett, Edmund, *a*
Southard, Matthew. *a*
SAWYER, FRED M., 1
Shea, John,
Stein, John, 1. *a*
Snyder, John,
Shalley, Thomas,
Spaulding, Nelson W.,
Soper, Briggs,
Schoolcraft, Perry, 1.
Shaver, Samuel M.,
Skelton, John,
Sullivan, James,
Tiffany, Patrick, *a*
Taylor, John W.,
Tench, James, *a*
TILESTON, ARTHUR T.,
Titus, William H.,
Touhill, John,
Van, Nicholas,
Vreeland, James,
Wright, Aaron, 1.
Willard, Charles W.,
Wilbur, George H.,
Wilter, William,
Whittemore, Benj. M., *a*
Wissells, George,
Williams, Charles,
Weaver, Charles,
Whalen, Michael,
Withers, John, *a*
Williams, John,
Wescott, Erastus,
Wood, James,
Whitney, George,

Company D.*

Alherty, James F.,
Armstrong, James H.,
Angeline, Michael,
Allen, Alonzo F.,
Appleby, Henry J., 1.
Adams, Joseph,
Bush, Thomas,
Billings, Henry C.,
Bellows, George H.,
Ballard, George W.,
Bingham, Charles E., *a*
BOWLER, PATRICK, 1.
Barher, Edmund, 1.
Bakeman, William H.,
Bennett, Edwin,
Bunn, George A.,
Brooks, Renhen,
Collins, Thomas,
Courtney, John C., *a*
Curran, John C.,
Chaffee, Wilson, *b*
Cady, Michael,
Chapman, Tarquin, *a*
Critchley, Edward,
Cadwell, Jerome,
Cole, John P.,
CALLANAN, JER. J., 1.
Cinnamon, C. M., 1. *a*
CINNAMON, PETER,
Cook, Ira J.,
Caroli, Frederic,
Cringer, David E., *b*
Cardelle, Samuel,
Davis, Henry,
DUNIGAN, MICHAEL, *a*
Duren, Henry M.,
Devoe, Cornelius, *a*
Elliott, John H.,
EASTMAN, CHARLES R.,
Faneier, Thomas,
Fox, Thomas,
Geary, Michael,
GREELEY, S. H., 1. *a*
Gallagher, Patrick, *a*
Grosvenor, Charles H.,
Goyette, John,
Garrow, James,
GREENLEAF, CHAS. H.,
Hurlbert, Ira O.,
Hams, John G., Jr.,
Hathaway, William,
HEISSER, ROBERT,
HURLBERT, GEORGE E.,
HOKIRK, GEORGE R
Higgins, Peter, *a*
Hearn, Joseph,
Hastings, Edward, *a*
Hazleton, Norman, *a*
Hurd, Henry, *a*
Jordon, Walter,
Jandrew, Francis, 1
Kenwell, Richard, *a*
Kelley, Patrick,
Lee, James,
Lester, Charles F.,
Laspen, Germania,
Lindee, Francis, *d*
Latham, Joseph,
Langdon, John,
Lanigar, John,
Luther, Allen D.,
Lynch, Thomas, *a*
Marshall, William H., 1.
Matthews, Peter,
MOFFATT, JAMES,
Mahoney, Dennis, 1. *a*
Matthews, Charles, *a*
Murphy, Michael J..
Malone, Edward,
Morchouse, Frank, *a*
McDermott, John,
McGinley, Jas. A., 1. *a*
McCarthy, Patrick, *b*
McSweeney, Eugene, *a*
McGovern, Peter, 1. *a*
McNeil, John T.,
McDougall, Horace,
McCoy, Thomas,
Newell, Nelson M., *a*
Ortman, Henry,
Preston, Edwin, *b*
Preston, Heman,
Perry, Abraham,
Prehle, Clark,
Pitcher, William,
Pinkham, Andrew, *a*
Pierce, Henry C., 1.
Perry, Arthur, *a*
PELLETT, HENRY H.,
PERKINS, RANSOM A.,
Parris, George W.,
Quinu, John, 1. *a*
Riley, Thomas,
Ross, Thomas H.,
Rhiuevault, Orman, *a*
Riley, Patrick,
Randall, A. M.,
Reed, James W., *b*
REYNOLDS, THOMAS,
Rogers, Harman, *a*
Shearer, Sanford L., *a*
Stone, Heury, *a*
SMITH, HIRAM A., 5. *a*
SULLIVAN, MICHAEL, *a*
Smith, James, *d*
Smith, Nelson,
Smith, Henry J.,
Scripter, Cyril E., *a*
SULLIVAN, JOHN, *a*
Saunders, Reuben, *a*, *b*

* This Company had in all 161 Men.

Sheehey, William, *a*
Stone, Fred. B., *a*
Schermerhorn, E. L., *a*
Schermerhorn, Peter, *a*
Schultz, Henry, *c*
Stone, Gardner,
Tuffield, Labare,
Terhune, John J.,
Tracey, Ezra B.,
TIERNEY, JOHN, *a*
TOBIN, MICHAEL, *a*
Tanner, James H.,
Taylor, Robert, *a*
Tucker, John, *a*
Trendon, John B., 1
Tuel, David,
Tainter, Charles,
Thomas, Highland, 1. *a*
Underhill, Frederick,
Van Valkenburgh, G.,
Van Orman, William D.,
Van Marter, William W.,
Van Marter, Alfred A., *a*
Vaughn, John,
WALSH, JAMES, *a*
WALSH, JOHN, *a*
Washburn, Albert, *b*
White, James,
White, Joel J.,
Wright, Charles,
Williams, John P., *a*
Watkins, William W.,
Wyatt, David K.,
Watson, William, *a*
Watson, John, 1.
Washburn, Nicholas, *a*
Wheeler, Garry D.,
White, Addison D., 1. *d*
Wales, Russell,
Warner, Ebenezer,
Welsh, Thomas,

Company E.*

ABBOTT, LIBERTY C.,
AUSTIN, ROYAL G., *a*
Austin, Frank,
ALEXANDER, B., 1. *a*
Adams, Leouard,
Aldrich, Anson,
Andrews, Elias N.,
Beardsley, Charles B.,
Barunm, Godfrey, Jr.,
Balgard, Edward,
Bixhy, Daniel C., *a*
Boyle, James,
Blood, Augustus C.,
Bronson, Lafayctte,
Berdan, Albert,
Bennett, Lyman H.,
Bennett, Milton H.,
Beardslcy, Charles W.,
Brown, Eli P., *b*
Brown, George R., *b*
Brown, Heury C.,
BYINGTON, R. N., 1.
Burke, John,
Brouson, Frank,
Boylston, Edgar C.,
Brennan, John,
Bernard, Jules,
CHASE, JAMES H., 1.
Camphell, Dennis, *a*
Cuff, Charles,
Crowley, James,
Clark, Fred J., *a*
Crawford, Rochester W.,
Camphell, Owen,
Dragon, Frank,
Davis, Leroy F.,
Dcvanna, John H.,
Dolph, Aaron,
Dolph, Joseph,
Dickinson, D. R., *b*
Dye, William P.,
Dye, Elam S.,
DICKINSON, FOSTER, 1.
DAVIS, WILLIAM H., 1
Davis, L. Uberto,
Dillon, Michael,
EATON, AARON C.,
EATON, WILLIAM A., *a*
EHMAN, CHRISTIAN, 1.
Ehman, Fred J., Jr., *a*
Ehman, Jeremiah,
Elliott, William J.,
Euber, Lcwis,
Fitch, John P.,
Fisk, Frank, *b*
FILKINS, ISAIAH V., *a*
FORD, SHERMAN K., 1.
Gould, Adelhert E.
Gallup, Joseph O.,
Gallup, Gordon,
Gleason, Jonathan,
Gordon, Jefferson T.,
Grauger, James,
Hams, Edward, *b*
Heady, John, 7.
Hahue, John,
Hiles, Francis,
Huestis, John,
Hall, Archihald, 2.
Hall, William,
Hamilton, John S.,
Husscy, John,
Howard, William,
Johnson, Erastus,
Juhert, James,
Jacksou, William, *a*
Jackson, Andrew, *a*
King, Joshua,
King, Renhen T.,
Keyes, Orson S., *a*
KILMER, SUMNER E.,
Kennedy, John C.,
Leslie, William J.,
Laromy, Bartomie,
Lawrcnce, Hiram M.,
Litynski, Joseph,
LAMB, GEORGE W.,
Lollis, John E.,
Lamarsh, Charles,
Leiser, John, *a*
Long, George,
Marsh, Daniel W.,
Merriman, Daniel B.,
Merriman, D. W.,
Morris, Charles A., 1.
MINER, CHAS. A., 1. *c*
Miner, Henry, *a*
Miner, Coruelius W.,
MORGAN, JAMES K., 1.
Mouroe, Henry W., 1.
Morris, Edward L.,
Maloney, Michael,
Montz, William,
Mulligan, John, 1.
Mortimer, Henry, *b*
Magai, Johannis,
Mahla, Charles, *b*
Mackey, Patrick, *c*
Masten, Paul,
Myott, Oliver,
Moran, John, 1.
Machling, Dehold, 1. *a*
McMULLEN, CHARLES,
McELHENNEY, A. J.,
McGroigan, Charles,
McCallon, George, *a*
NEWTON, CHAS. M., 1.
Nash, Malcom M.,
Olmsted, Franklin,
Oshorn, Joseph R., *a*

* This Company had in all 169 Men.

Porter, John C.,
Palmer, Alonzo,
Pierce, Curtis E., 1.
Penner, Francis,
PECKHAM, W. G., 1.
PACKARD, LOREN F., 1.
PADDOCK, ROSWELL A., 1.
PARCELLS, T., 1. *a*
REW, MILTON D., *a*
Rew, Newton C., 1, *a*
Rathbone, John,
Rasey, Lorenzo L.,
Robertson, J. Eliphalet,
Ryan, John A., *a*
Richards, Godfrey,
Richards, Thomas B.,
Robertson, Alex. L.,
Staunton, Henry,
SORTORE, SAMUEL W.,
SORTORE, HANFORD H.,
Sortore, John D.,
Sortore, Elisha,
SWART, FRANKLIN S.,
STRAIT, MATTHEW, 3. *a*
Snow, Andrew J., 1.
Seaman, Henry,
Sherrer, Henry,
Spencer, Asahel A.,
Smith, Lafayette C.,
THOMPSON, A. S., *a*
THRALL, EDWIN, *a*
Thrall, Ira,
Trowbridge, John S., 1.
Tourrillon, Adolph,
UPTEGROVE, S. T., 2. *a*
Vanderville, John, 1.
Whipplo, Walter,
Woodward, Jacob,
WOODRUFF, JOHN B.,
WORTHINGTON, L. M., *a*
WOLCOTT, DAVID F.,
WATERHOUSE, W. H., *a*
Walsh, Michael,
Wood, John L.,
Well, John,
Wells, Richard M.,
Wemette, Paul, *a*
Williams, Edwin C.,
Willis, James,

Company F.*

Austin, Merritt, *a*
Arnold, Corrington F.,
Axtell, Joseph,
Ackley, William F.,
Aiken, Horace,
Atwood, Silas M., 1.
Aylesworth, C. De F.,
Aiken, William,
Arnold, Addison C.,
Baker, Samuel,
Bush, Amos,
Bates, Samuel,
Beuton, Thomas,
Butler, Samuel,
Brand, Charles,
Bloor, Charles,
Babcock, Samuel,
Bern, Alonzo, *a*
Baldwin, Lyman,
BROWN, WILLIAM J.,
Brown, Ira, 1. *b*
Brown, John,
Bernard, John W., *a*
Brooks, Henry J. *a*
Bennett, Wiuaut H., *a*
Brady, John R.,
Brink, Perley,
Brister, Elijah, 1.
Brister, Ira,
Bagley, Avery E.,
Bostwick, Judson,
Blake, William, 1.
Bullock, Samuel,
Briggs, William E., *b*
Bensou, Peter,
Bagley, Daniel E.,
Cummings, Nelson E.,
Coulon, John, *a*
Carney, Philip, *a*
Clark, Theodore,
Carl, Frank W.,
Catlin, Thomas N., 1.
CHAFEY, MERRITT N.,
Clark, Nelson,
Craig, John,
Churchill, Homer,
Coggen, Joseph, 1.
Claus, John W.,
Coulston, Willam C.,
Craig, John,
Clough, Clarence M.,
Curtis, Henry, *c*
Davis, William,
Dodge, George W.,
Donlon, Thomas, *a*
Devanua, John, *a*, *d*
Davies, William J.,
De Mott, James, 1. *a*
Dennis, George W., *b*
De La Losa, Ysidro, *c*
Earl, Hiram H., *a*
Epsal, Gabriel F.,
Engalls, Peter, *a*
Edwards, Albert,
Ensign, Nelson,
FULLER, COLONEL,
Freeman, Peter E.,
Fowler, Hickson A.,
Fowler, William H.,
Freeman, James,
Ferris, John P.,
Gregg, John, *a*
Galusha, Waterman, *a*
Griffith, Lucius,
Galpin, William, 1.
Goodale, Ezra M.,
Graves, Pliny A.,
Hogan, James,
Hanley, Michael,
Hooper, John,
Hayes, John W.,
HAZLESWARTH, P., *a*
Hutton, William B., *a*
Hawley, William, *a*
Holmes, John,
Hawley, Everett A., 2.
Harrington, Charles H.,
Hurlburt, Riley A.,
Huestis, Frank,
Hall, Warren A.,
JONES, JOHN B., 1. *a*
JACKSON, JOHN W., *a*
Jeffrey, John K., 1.
Jenkins, George H., 1.
Jackson, Francis A.,
Knowlton, Clark C., *a*
Kinney, Edward,
Kimball, Horton, *a*
Leek, Horace F.,
Logan, Charles H.,
Lawrence, George D.,
Luther, Asa, *a*
Lewis, Charles,
Leilous, Henry,
MCMILLAN, D. J., 6.
McMillan, John, B., *a*
McGowan, James,
McDonald, Bernard,
Morey, William C.,
Morey, Homer A.,
MOORE, JAMES,
Moore, Wallace, 1.
Moore, Franklin B., *a*
Maddon, John,
Meade, Alonzo H., 1.
Mullen, William,
Metcalf, A. Judson,
Metcalf, George,
Morton, Henry A.,
Moore, Viceroy,

---

* This Company had in all 189 Men.

Mapes, William W.,
Morgan, Daniel,
Masterson, James,
Miller, Jacob,
Nieman, William H., *a*
Nourse, Alfred W.,
Norton, Samuel E.,
Nichols, Wallace,
Nash, Orvin D.,
Osborn, Calvin W., 6. *a*
Ogden, William,
Oliver, Judson S., *a*
Olney, Marvin,
Prinz, Ewald,
Palmer, Henry,
Peterson, Mahlon J., 1.
Perkins, Samuel S.
Pettis, Ralph, *b*
Prince. Henry A.,
Pickett, William B.,
PRATT, EUGENE, 8. *a*
Porter, Charles H.,
Pettis, Zephaniah,
Pinney, Henry A..
Parks, William H.,
Pratt, Gardner, 1.
Partridge, Hezekiah D.,
Portier, Emile, 1.
Poyer, Henry,
Roff, John F.,
Richardson, Charles H.,
Riley, John,
Rogers, Edward A., 1.
Rathbone, George D.,
Rhodes, Julius D.,
SOWERSBY, WM. W.,
Smith, Victor D., *b*
Smith, Peter W.,
Smith, Walter C.
Stewart, Hosea B.,
Sayles, William J.,
Stevens, Victor M.,
Stiles, Addison D.,
Stearns, Rollin A.,
Sumner, Byron, *a*
THOMAS, CHARLES B.,
Tuthill, James H.,
Tracey, Walter J.,
Tolles, Edward D.,
Tolles, Ralph N., *c*
Tallman, Frank,
Updyke, Nelson,
Waite, Darwin,
Wickham, James B.,
Whitmarsh, Erastus, *b*
Wight, Marvin, *a*
WIGHT, DANIEL, *a*
Wells, Miles,
WHITNEY, CHARLES, *a*
Whitney, Elisha,
Whitlock, Thaddeus K.,
Williams, Luke S.,
Wells, George, *a*
Wells, William H., *a*
Wilcox, Charles F.,
White, Andrew J., *a*
White, Henry,
Waterman, Nelson E., *d*
Youngs, Silas A.,
Zahler, Nicholas,

Company G.*

Adams, William, *a*
Arnts, Frederic D.,
Adderley, James,
Byron, Theophilus,
Bowden, William,
Bailey, David, *a*
Bailey, William V., *a*
BRYANT, JAMES, *a*
BUTMAN, WILLIAM,
BOVEE, RODNEY,
BARNEY, ALLEN,
BARNUM, N. W., 2. *a*
BRAINARD, H. E., *a*
Barnes, Eugene B., *c*
Benner, Philip R.,
Brookins, Fred O.,
Buffington, Chauncey,
Bidwell, John W., 1. *a*
Billings, James D.
Case, Houston L.,
Courtwright, Richard, *a*
CADWELL, EGBERT B.,
Conlon, Peter, *a*
Camphell, Philip,
Clark, David A.,
Cox, Augustus,
Curry, John,
CAMP, W HARRISON,
CARPENTER, RYRON R.,
Culver, Lewis J., 2.
Dunn, Michael,
DINEHART, ROBERT,
DINEHART, JAS. A., 3.
Devine, John,
Davis, Heury T., *a*
DAVISON, EGBERT,
DOOLAN, TIMOTHY, *a*
DOREMUS, THEODORE,
DINGMAN, JOHN,
DANIELS, JOHN L.,
DEYO, CHAUNCEY, *b*
DE THOMPSON, GEO. E.,
Doyle, John, *a*
Dingman, Ahram,
Fverett, James H.,
Evans, John, 2.
Fox, Jefferson, 1.
Fairchild, Mason A.,
FARNHAM, OSCAR E., *a*
Fuller, Corydon,
Forsyth, Augustus,
Foster, Johnson, *a*
Farnham, Charles F., *a*
Gatefield, Edmund M.,
Grant, James,
GREEN, WHEELER C., 2.
GREEN, STEPHEN D.,
Gordon, Samuel, *d*
Green, Calvin E.,
Goodwin, Edward H., *a*
Horgan, John,
Hihhard, Edward,
Hoyt, Audrew J., 1.
Hayden, Albert B.,
Hunt, James,
Hulett, Benjamin A..
Hulett, Abram H., *a*
Hazen, Alfred B.,
HAZEN, JOHN M., *a*
Johusou, Horace P.,
Knuppenhurg, John, 1.
KNIGHT, WILLIAM H., *a*
KROHN, PHILIP, *a*
Knapp, Joseph, *b*
Lane, David, 1.
Lane, Cherter J.. 1.
Lloyd, John,
Lowe, William T. I., 1. *a*
Lynch, Stephen,
Markham, Chester C., *b*
Mooney, John, 4.
Moran, William,
McBride, John,
Markell, James,
Marikle, James,
Mallory, James, 2. *a*
Meddaugh. George,
Mallory, Warren, 1. *a*
Noble, Asa S.,
NORTON, CYRUS B.,
Narsh, Marvin A.,
Narsh, John W.,
Overocker, DeWitt C., *a*
Osborne, Richard,
PIERCE, CHARLES T. S.,
Payne, George, *a*
POLLARD, JAMES M., 1.
PHELPS, CHARLES A.,
Phelps, John H.,
Phelps, Jeremiah W.,
Phelps, Theodore A.,
Prince, George M.,
Quinn, John,
Rowley, James,
Roberts, Lucius, *d*
Rush, Richard,
Ryan, Philip, 2,
Roberts, Philemon,
Rhinevault, S. P.,
Romans, George H., *a*
Russell, Ralph L.,
Rogers, Martin S., 1. *a*
Steele, Seth A., *b*
Smith, Schuyler F., *a*
Smith, John,
Shaw, William,
SPAFFORD, ABIJAH,
Sullivan, Daniel, *b*
Snow, George W.,
Spencer, Nathan O.,

---

* This Company had in all 155 Men.

Southwick, George,
Taylor, Benjamin F.,
TIERNEY, JOSEPH, *a*
TRIBE, JOHN, *a*
Thorn, John,
Turner, William, *a*
Towner, Lent H., *a*
Thompson, Isaac M.,
Vincent, William B., *b*
Van Marter, F. W.,
VAN MARTER, J. C., 1.
VANDERMARK, LUCAS,
Vandermark, Nathan, 1.
VANDERMARK, JOHN,
VAN WINKLE, C. O.,
WRIGHT, JOHN H., *a*
WILCOX, CHARLES R., *a*
WILMOT, BYRON G. *a*
WEISS, JOSEPH, *a*
WHITE, PETER H., 1.
WHITE, LORENZO,
WHITE, HENRY P.,
White, Barney H.,
White, Charles,
White, Amos,
White, Squire,
Wilson, John A., *b*
Williams, John A.,
Witter, John, B.,
Witter, William A., *a*
Witter, William,
WINFIELD, HENRY,
Weston, Nathan, 2.
Wiggins, Frank,
Wright, William,

Company H.*

Andrews, Thomas,
Brislin, Patrick,
Bottomly, William,
Beebe, Calvin L.,
BARKER, ELMER J., 2.
BRYDEN, JAMES, 1.
BAKER, GEORGE A., 1.
BAKER, RUSSELL W.,
BROWN, WESLEY, *a*
Barrows, William,
Bondrye, Charles A.,
Barton, William H.,
Baker, Fayette H., 1. *a*
Baker, Caleb C.,
Barrett, Alvin, *a*
Barber, William N.,
Barher, George D.,
Black, George,
Bigelow, Amos,
Brittell, Guy,
Baker, George W.,
Benedict, Jonas A., *b*
Burlingame, Henry H., *b*
CAMPNEY, JAMES,
CURKENDALL, WALTER,
Curtis, Charles W., 2.
Cornell, Oliver T.,
Chillson, Charles N., 1.
Cook, William H., 1.
Culver, Coolidge B.,
Carr, Dnransie S., *a*
Connor, John, *d*
Chaffee, Rufus A., *a*
Conway, John,
Conway, John, Jr.,
Cronk, Ahram,
DAVIS, WILLIAM,
Dickerson, Nelson H.,
Decatur. Samnel O.,
Dawes, Orson J.,
Durno, John P.,
Durno, George C., *a*
Du Chene, George C., 1.
Dunlap, Robert A., *a*
Dolbeck, Cleophas,
Darling, Truman,
Dwinclle, Nehemiah B.,
Daniels, Andrew J.,
Drake, Orlando,
Davis, Almeron, *a*
Edwards, Robert W.
Ellis, Richard R.,
Elliott, Robert,
Fuller, Nelson, *c*
Ferby, John,
FULLER, WARREN R., 1.
FRENCH, JOHN C. C., *a*
Folger, Ahram, 1. *a*
Finney, Thomas, 1.
GORHAM, LEWIS J.,
Griffin, Henry,
Graves, Horace,
Gilleo, Henry, *b*
Gilleo, Charles,
Glidden, Stephen T.,
Gillett, Mark,
Hildreth, Charles H., *d*
Hildreth, Hartwell H.,
Howland, Arthur,
HOWLAND, WARREN,
HANCHETT, ELBERT E.,
HOLCOMB, CHARLES H.,
HAYWARD, EUGENE B.,
Hayward, Monroe L.,
Hart, Frank, *a*
Hoyt, Irvin F., 1.
Hammond, John, 2.
Howe, Lowell E.,
Hayes, Elun,
Howke, Phineas,
Hayford, Edwin T., *b*
Holden, Ira E.,
HASCALL, ELISHA F.,
Ives, George,
Jackson, Richard,
Joiner, Henry M.,
JORDAN, CARLOS A., *a*
Johnson, Walker E., *a*
Johnson, Perry,
Johnson, Warren,
Johnson, Henry F.,
Jordan, Alfrado,
Jones, Irving W., *a*
Keach, William H., *b*
Kilmer, Reuben,
KNIGHT, JABEZ, *a*
KELLEY, WILLIAM E.,
Lane, Zadoc F.,
Laverty, William,
Laverty, Allen,
LETSON, THOMAS,
Lamb, Joseph J.,
Lafrance, Frank,
Lamson, William P., 3.
Lyford, Erskine W.,
Lively, James,
Lively, William, 2.
Labounty, Lonis, *a*
Leach, George W.,
Maloney, Nelson,
Mead, Abner B.,
Moncrief, Albert,
Miller, David B.,
MILLER, HARMON C.,
Murdock, James A.,
Marshall, Charles E., *b*
Moore, Viceroy,
Moore, Orville J.,
MOORE, ALPHARIS H.,
MINER, JOHN J., JR., *a*

* This Company had in all 190 Men.

MASON, SILAS J., *a*
MCCARTY, TIMOTHY, *a*
MCCAUGHN, PATRICK,
MCMANUS, EDWARD, *a*
McConley, John, *a*
McKenzie, Walter J.,
McGinniss, Warren,
McGowen, Erastus, 1.
Nelson, James, *a*
Ozier, Joseph J., 1.
Odell, Henry, *a*
ORR, HORACE, 1. *a*
OAKS, NELSON S., 2.
Ober, William,
Oliver, Edward A.,
Oakley, John,
Payling, William,
Porter, Zely W.,
Palmer, Allen,
Perkins, Isaiah, *b*
Perkins, Gilman, *b*
Porter, Robert W., 1. *a*
PEASE, CLARK M.,
Penfield, James A., 1. *a*
Pierce, Amos, *a*
Potter, Allen L.,
Peasely, Henry, *a*
Page, Benjamin F., *a*
Parmenter, George, *b*
Palmer, Peter W.,
RENNE, LUCIUS F., 1.
Raine, James H.,
Robbins, David H., *a*
Redman, John, 1. *a*
Rush, John, *b*
Sickler, Isaac,
Smith, George E.,
Smith, Henry V., *b*
Smitb, George W.,
Smith, George W.,
Smith, Charles, *a*
Smith, John, *a*
Swift, William W.,
Shepard, Edgar C., *c*
Sherman, Abram,
Starling, Edgar,
Sartwell, William, 1.
Starks, John E., 1., *a*
STACY, JAMES, *a*
Spaulding, Henry, *a*
Spaulding, John S., *a*
Spaulding, Joseph W.,
Shattuck, Albert N., 1. *a*
Stone, Harry L.,
SCHENK, CHARLES,
Town, George L.,
Town, Simon,
Thrasher, Orlando F.,
Todd, Henry D.,
UNDERHILL, HIRAM,
Underhill, Charles,
VIALL, JOHN G.,
Van Wert, James E.,
Wescott, Joseph J., 1.
Westcott, Jonathan,
WELLS, CHARLES,
WYMAN, HENRY E.,
WATERMAN, JOHN, *a*
Washburn, Benj. F.,
Woster, Joseph E., 2.
Warner, Samuel S.,
Wells, Edgar J.,
Wells, Nathaniel,
Wiley, Henry A.,
Winters, Edward A., *a*
Wright, Abner Z., *b*
Wilcox, Charles H., 1.
Warren, Joseph R.,
Woodward, Zephaniah,

Company I.*

Adams, William,
Adams, Henry,
Anderson, Robert S.,
Arnold, George,
Beylan, John,
Brooks, John,
Bell, Richard,
Baurer, August,
Bahhitt, William L., *a*
BARRY, JAMES, 1.
Barry, Edward,
Banker, George R.,
Barlow, Nathaniel A.,
Banfield, Michael, *b*
Bennett, Joseph H., *a*
Behrendt, John,
Blauvelt, John H.
Boland, William,
Bohrer, Conrad,
Boyer, John,
Boyle, Michael,
Bly, Reuben,
Battles, Isaac D., *a*
Calhoun, Samuel,
Cary, William B.,
Carroll, Thomas, 1.
Carpenter, George A.,
Clarkson, James B.,
Cleeland, William,
Coddington, Joh,
Conroy, Frank,
Conway, Jacob,
Connolly, John,
Conklin. William, H.,
Crandall, Lewis H., *b*
Crawhuck, Richard V.,
Cnnningham, Thomas, *a*
Crooks, Jacoh C.,
Clynton, William H.,
Clinton, Robert,
Cummings, Rohert B.,
Camphell, Robert,
Drake, William,
Douglass, John,
Dempsey, Charles,
Dowdy, James,
Daly, William, *a*
Darsy, Nicholas, 1.
Day, Patrick,
Dow, Edward S.,
Duuu, William B.,
Dnnn, Joseph, *b*
Dunham, Raudolph, *b*
Edwards, Isaac,
Edwards, Charles,
Edwards, William G.,
French, James,
Fairweather, John B.
Fennely, Martin,
Frazer, Lewis A., *b*
Ferguson, John H.,
Freeman, Alhert S.,
Flynn, Laurence,
Fuller, Ira W.,
Gall, Alexander,
Gale, Harrison,
Garvin, Frank E.,
Gardner, David, *a*
Grist, John P.,
GRAHAM, ELLIS J.,
Gray, Asa,
Green, Robert,
Garrigan, James,
Garanger, Stephen,
Hughes, Francis,
Harding, Alonzo,
Havens, Ransom W.,
Henderson, William,
Hand, Laurence,
Hill, Henry,
Haney, George H.,
Harris, George H.,
Harris, George W.,
Hart, Joseph,
HERON, CHRISTOPHER,
Harmes, Herman, *a*
Haupert, Jacob,
Heck, Henry,
Howe, Lowell S.,
Havens, Thomas,
Harder, John, *b*
Herriman, Edson,
Houston, James,
Jordan, Christopher,
Johnson, Daniel R.,
KING, CHARLES,
Koch, John,
Klette, Henry,
Lowrey, Harvey,
La Fountaiu, Gabriel
Lnndin, John A., *a*
Lewis, George C.,
Lovejoy, Isaiah H.,
Lamb, Julius C.,
Lynch, James,
Maun, James,
Meeken, Henry,
MILLS, WILLIAM, 1.
Miller, George,
Miner, Peter,
Morrison, William, *a*
McNallen, James,
McMinn, Samuel,
McDonald, James,
McKenney, Edward,
Mundrane, John,
Moulther, Charles,
Moore, J. Buel,
Mattison, Dwight L.,
Miller, Warner,

---

* This Company had in all 190 Men.

Mack, James D., *b*
Moore, A. B.,
Norman, Adeodat,
Nickerson, Daniel,
Noonan, Edward,
O'Halloran, Daniel C., *a*
O'Reily, William,
O'Meara, Daniel,
Olmsted, John A. H.,
Olmsted, Orman B.,
O'Mellie, Matthew,
Pierce, Henry,
Parsons, Thomas C.,
Phillips, John,
Phillips, Edward,
Poulson, Jacob C.,
Port, John H.,
Peaseley, Amasa M.,
Randolph, Jonathan D.,
Randolph, William M.,
Richards, Alfred, *a*
Roach, Charles,
Riley, Martin, *a*
Ryan, Patrick,
Runyon, Augustus,
Reardon, Daniel,
Stimpson, George B.,
Scott, John J.,
Santabar, Francis, *a*
Shiffer, Morgan, *a*
Snow, John, *b*
Schwartz, John,
Shay, James,
Smith, Charles F., *a*
SMITH, JOHN W.,
SOULE, PETER, 1.
Spencer, Robert, 1.
Springsteen, John,
Southard, Asahel,
Shalley, Thomas,
Sabring, Alfred, *b*
Tracey, George W., *b*
Townsend, Thomas,
Titus, William H.,
Townsend, N.,
Tool, John,
Timmons, Stephen,
Van Iderstein, Peter J.,
Van Gorden, Eli,
Van Allen, Benjamin F.,
Vasbinder, William H.,
Vreeland, Stephen K.,
Vreeland, John T.,
White, William,
Wedding, William,
Wermetzter, Francis,
Wiltse, Isaac,
WILTSE, W. KELSEY,
Wiltse, Robert L.,
Wood, Frank, *a*
WRIGHT, JAMES O., *a*
Whitfield, Nathan A.,
Westervelt, Benjamin,
Wolfe, John,
Wilson, William,
Wool, Luther,
Woodward, Philander,
Young, Abner S., *a*
Yates, Henry,
Zimmerman, Herman,

Company K.*

Aldrich, Aaron,
Ahhey, Alanson L.,
Batey, John,
BLACK, ROBERT, 1.
Briden, Dominick,
Brown, Leonard,
Briell, Franz,
Beach, Henry C.,
Butts, Horace D.,
Barher, William,
Bailey, Amos, *d*
Coles, William P.,
Conners, John,
Cullion, William,
Coleman, John,
Clark, John,
Clark, John C.,
Conners, Michael,
Currier, Andrew,
Conway, Jacob J.,
Carter, Rollin W., *b*
Campbell, Ed. A., 1. *a*
Cole, George W., *b*
Coggins, Thomas E.,
Concilyea, Edward,
Ducat, Moses,
Daly, Philip,
Dinsmore, George W., *a*
DOOLING, JOHN, 1.
DONALD, JOHN,
Dowd, James D., 1. *a*
Doty, William,
Dougherty, John,
Daley, Timothy,
Deegan, John,
Dubois, Henry,
Dikeman, George R.,
Erregger, Charles,
English, George C.,
Flaherty, Thomas, *a*
Fox, John,
Fuller, Robert,
Fealey, John,
Griffin, Patrick H.,
Garroty, James,
Greenback, John,
Gleason, Patrick, *a*
Galen, Michael,
Geshaw, Dennis,
Holden, John, *a*
Howard, Abraham, *a*
Howe, David, *a*
Hemble, Michael,
Hecker, Frederick L.,
Howard, George,
Howard, Charles W.,
Hastings, Chester C.,
Holden, Thomas M.,
Harper, James,
Haley, Michael,
Hohart, Albert,
Head, William,
Hoover, Samuel,
Herriman, Reuhen D.,
Hall, James A.,
Henley, Frederick, *c*
Harris, John,
Jasper, Robert, *a*
Judah, Theodore,
Jones, John, *a*
KENNEY, MICHAEL,
Keeley, Michael,
Kennedy, William,
Kelley, Patrick,
Kingsley, James M., *a*
Keeler, Horace,
Latterall, Charles,
Lahiff, James,
Lockwood, Edmund,
Mack, John, *a*
Monroe, George W., *a*
McCullough, William,
McDonald, Edward,
McCue, Alonzo,
McIntyre, James,
Martin, Joseph,
Mooney, Terence,
Myers, Joseph D.,
Maddon, John,
Martin, Thomas,
Maddon, James,
Mallory, Thomas,
Maxfield, George,
Mahan, Benjamin, *d*
Merton, Robert R.,
NOONAN, JEREMIAH,
NEALON, JAMES,
Nadow, Michael,
O'KEEFE, THOMAS,
O'NEIL, MICHAEL, *a*
O'Brien, John,
O'Reilly, William,
O'Connor, Henry,
Otis, Horace,
PHILLIPS, JOHN, *a*
Perry, George W.,
Perry, Alamanza,
Perry, Antoine,
Porter, Marvin B.,
Parsons, Nelson R., 1.
Parker, Lewis B.,
Palmatier, Daniel,
Pecot, Eugene,
Pecot, Joseph,
Pease, William H.,
Quinn, Francis, *a*
Quern, Carl,
Rouse, Peter,
Rouse, Alvin,
Rhodes, Lucius,

* This Company had in all 164 Men.

Reed, John,
Russell, Warren,
Reynolds, Edward D.,
Stanton, Amos,
Staves, Anthony H.,
Staves, Peter,
SCOFIELD, DAVID H.,
Schaffer, Charles,
Stockton, Thomas,
Stafford, Thomas,
Sherwood, Nathan,
Slyter, John W., 1.
Shaw, James, *a*
Schaeffer, Frederic
Scott, George, *a*
Suddard, David H.,
Smith, Charles J., *b*
TALMAGE, NATH'L M.,
Talmadge, Oliver, *b*
TOMS, GEORGE W.,
Telfer, James.
Turley, William.
Truesdale, Lucius,
Tresch, George, *a*
Tyrrell, Patrick,
Van Valkenburgh, R.,
Vilandre, Theodore, 1.
Watson, George,
Williamson, James,
Wilcox, Edward, *b*
Wilson, William J.,
Willis, Charles H.,
Ward, Richmond,
Weatherwax, John, *a*
WRIGHT, HORACE,
Wilkins, Amos, 1.
Walker, Charles H., *a*
Wilkins, James, 1. *a*
Walsh, James,
Welch, James, *a*
Whitmore, James,
Young, John,
Young, Willett,
Young, Henry Y.

Company L.*

Aikens, Hugh,
Allen, Henry M.,
Alexander, Charles,
Ames, James F.,
Akers, Charles,
Avery, Horace G.,
Antisdale, Frederick, *a*
Antisdale, George, *a*
Barton, Joseph,
Bowen, Eseck,
Booker, Joseph,
Brown, Henry,
Brown, William,
Boyd, James,
Boyd, John,
Brady, Thomas, *b*
Brennan, John,
Bridges, Charles D.,
Boate, George, *b*
Companion, Edward,
Camel, William,
Crane, Frank,
Compton, Lewis,
COLLESKIE, JOHN, 1. *a*
Cross, Anthony, 1.
Cooper, Lewis, *a*
Coles, William T.,
Carman, Archibald,
Comes, William,
Cooley, Horatio C.,
Cameron, Eli, *a*
Connell, Dennis, *a*
Clark, Job D.
Connor, Thomas,
Crow, Benjamin,
DAVENPORT, H. L., *a*
Driesens, Julius,
Dunn, John, *b*
Darling, Thomas,
Dorsey, Edward,
Dorman, James,
Earle, Robert,
Earle, Henry,
Eineson, Richard,
Easton, Theodore M., *a*
Fraser, William,
Fraser, Archibald, 1.
Fohs, Gottlieb,
Fitzpatrick, Cornelius,
Fitzsimmons, Patrick,
Gartland, John,
GORDON, JOHN, *a*
Genard, Auguste, *a*
Gorth, Henry,
Grieser, John,
Grice, Joseph B.,
Gable, Michael,
Gerock, Charles,
Harvey, Frederick, *b*
Hicks, Frederick M., *a*
Holm, Louis, *a*
Hedland, John, *a*
Hegeman, William,
Haines, John Y., *b*
Hatch, Orrin S., *b*
Holm, Martin,
Hambleton, William,
HENRETTY, MICHAEL, *a*
Hewitt, James,
Hurd, Joseph,
Holford, William,
Hibbard, Gardner,
Hedrich, Ferdinand,
Jockum, Adolf,
Keer, Charles,
Keffer, Karl, 1.
KILBEY, JAMES,
Kernon, James,
Klotz, Julius,
Kellett, Robert J.,
Knapp, Theodore M.,
Keefer, Frank,
Lindsay, James,
Leigh, James D.,
Lee, Henry R.,
Lavoisier, Frederic,
Lockwood, Sidney B.,
Lalor, Finton,
Lamb, George, *a*
Lang, George,
Lehman, Henry,
Lawrence, Edwin C.,
McMULLEN, PETER,
McKnight, Mortimer,
McEwan, John,
McManus, Hugh,
Merton, Curtis,
Merritt, H. A. D., 3. *a*
Marland, Charles, *d*
Miner, John S.,
Metzler, Joseph,
Mahoney, John,
Morse, Ezra,
Nelson, Peter,
Needham, William,
O'BRIEN, DENNIS,
O'Brien, Thomas, *a*
Perry, Albert,
Perry, Alhannan,
Plude, Henry, *b*
PURDY, JESSE,
Porter, Claudius,
Pratt, Albert Y.,
Place, Philip M., *a*
Petze, Charles R.,
Quest, John P., *b*
Rooney, Daniel,
Runney, William,
Riley, James,
Robinson, Calvin,

* This Company had in all 164 Men.

RUSSELL, WILLIAM P.,
Rugg, Silas,
Richards, Frank,
Reynolds, Charles J.,
SMITH, JAMES G., *a*
Smith, John, *a*
Smith, David A.,
Sythoff, Henry A.,
SENE, PETER A.,
Stevens, George,
Simpson, Benjamin,
Sparks, Elijah,
St. Clair, Nelson, *a*
Sandispree, Paul, 1.
Simonson, Frederick, *a*
Schlapfer, John,
Strutz, Charles O., *a*
Stone, Nelson J.,
Scott, William J.,
Sweeney, John D.,
St. Clair, Joseph,
Starks, William, *b*
Taft, Henry,
Tardy, Auguste, *a*
Trainor, Michael, *b*
TURNER, BENJAMIN,
Tittle, Fredcrick, *a*
Townsend, Samnel, *a*
Taylor, John,
Utter, James,
Unwin, Edward, *a*
Watson, William,
Wells, Alfred,
Waugh, Albcrt B.,
Walders, Charles, *b*
White, Charles H.,
Williamson, James,
Walker, Albert G.,
White, Isaac,
Wallace. Matthew L., *a*
Wharton, Robert, *a*
Yagle, Joseph, 1. *a*
Yontz, William, *a*
Zimmerman, Baldwin,

Company M.*

Anson, Jedediah B.,
Akers, David,
Aret, Martin,
Alger, Alonzo,
Acker, De Witt,
Acker, Wallace,
Birdsall, Chester K.,
Bogardus, George A.,
Bogardus, Jeremiah,
Bogardus, William H., 1.
Burns, James, 1.
Bishop, Walter J.,
Blunt, Edmund, Jr.,
Bebon, Joseph, *a*
Brown, Abram T., *a*
Brown, John,
Blanchard, Henry B.,
Barton, Ezra,
Brando, Lewis,
BRIDGEMAN, ANDREW,
Crans, William, 1.
Cole, John J., *a*
Coon, Alfred,
Cole, John,
Clough, George S.,
Clough, Jeremiah J.,
Chapman, William,
Crandall, Edwin,
Conine, William H.,
DE WITT, ORLEAN, 2. *a*
Dougherty, John, *a*
Davis, Michael,
Duvall, John W.,
Daines, Arnold P.,
Deitz, Arthur M.,
Deer, Jacob,
Dimmick, Eugene D., 1.
De Long, Ira,
Dennis, William H.,
Delano, Charles,
Depew, Moses,
Driscoll, James,
Depew, James,
Dowling, Henry,
Erdman, Louis, *a*
Edwards, James,
Edwards, William H.,
Fricke, Charles,
Flemming, Samuel,
FRANK, GODFREY, *a*
Frazier, Francis H.,
Feen, John, 1.
Fryhoon, James H., *a*
Freeling, John, *c*
Fulton, Philip S.,
Foster, James P.,
Finlay, James,
Fenner, Charles,
Fenner, James,
Fiero, James,
Gardner, Leslie,
Goodsell, Timothy M.,
Graves, Hiram T.,
Garvey, James,
Heddle, William,
Hoover, James,
Haines, John H., *b*
Howe, Ralph, 1.
Hoover, Augustus,
Holman, Melvin,
Horton, J. Goodrich,
Havey, John,
Heckerman, Thomas,
Hollenbeck, Eugene,
Hawes, Leroy, 1.
Hollenbeck, Charles W.,
Haley, John F.,
Haney, John D.,
Hoyt, William F.,
Hayes, Peter,
Jones, William A., *a*
Jackson, John,
Johnson, William H.,
KIVILAND, HENRY, *a*
Keeler, Egbert,
Kuhn, Bernard,
Knhn, Daniel, *b*
Lewis, Oliver C.,
Locke, John,
Luth, Charles,
Lewis, Jocob S.,
Lawrence, Nathaniel,
Lohman, Axel S.,
Lowe, Abraham,
Lucklow, Philip,
Lowe, Levi F.,
Lee, John H.,
Lee, George S. W.,
Lucas, Charles B.,
Lynch, John,
Moore, Philip H,, *a*
Moore, Franklin,
McCann, John F., *a*
McAllister, Peter, *a*
McGrady, James, *b*
McGready, Hugh,
McCarthy, Daniel,
Morton, Edward,
Myles, John,
Markham, William D.,
Murray, Thomas,
Morris, Henry, *b*
Magher, John,
Morse, Harrison,
Marston, Erastus D.,
Mahue, John,
Matthews, George A.,
Matthews, Laurence A.,
Mead, William H.,
Mickle, Peter,

* This Company had in all 186 Men.

Minnerley, Charles,
Mahar, John,
Martin, Hawley, *b*
Morrison, William,
Neef, Philo,
O'Rourke, Patrick,
Odell, Oliver,
OAKLEY, WILBUR F., 2.
Osborn, George C., *b*
Poultney, Robert,
Plimley, George P.,
PAINE, OLNEY,
PITCHER, SAM'L T. B.,
Pfister, Samuel, *a*
Quimby, Ephraim,
Rafferty, Peter, *a*
Root, George O.,
RIZER, WILLIAM,
Rowell, William,
Reynolds, John C., 1.
Ryan, Michael, *b*
Rice, George P.,
Rainey, James,
Ryan, John,
Rowe, John,
Rockafellow, Horace,
Rugg, George, W., *a*
Reeves, William, *c*
Shepard, Charles,
Smith, Charles D., *a*
Smith, Henry, 1.
Smith, Frank,
Smith, Charles R.,
Sharkey, Edward, *c*
Scott, Elisha B.,
Straut, Jacob,
Swintz, Jacob, *a*
SPAHN, JOHN,
Shoemaker, John W.,
Saunders, Carmine,
Spencer, Andrew K.,
Seaman, Samuel,
Swan, Thomas M.,
SHONESAY, JAMES, 1
Schadler, Louis,
Ten Broeck, Samuel, *b*
TRAVIS, JUSTUS, 1.
Thornton, J. Chauncey,
Ten Eyck, Jacob H.,
Ten Eyck, Edward,
Tripp, Levi.
Van Ness, Harmon B.,
Van Loan, Jacob H.,
Van Gorder, Elias,
WHITCOMB, W. H., 1.*a*
Winnie, Peter,
Wallace, Edward,
Wait, Richard, B.,
Warner, Edward B.,
Warner, William,
Werner, William,
Williams, Samuel,
Woodbridge, Henry N.,
Waldolph, William P.,
Yence, John E.,
Zimmerman, Fred,
Zimmerman, Jacob.

NOTE 1.—Great labor has been bestowed upon this Roster. Should inaccuracies occur, or some men fail to recive due notice of their casualties, it must be attributed to the want of documents for reference. In some instances,—as in Gen. Banks' Retreat from Strasburg,—company papers were lost. However, it is to be lamented that full documents were not kept more generally.

NOTE 2.—Many of the men marked VETERANS, were not originally with the regiment, but joined it after having served two years or more, in some other organization.

APPENDIX.

Yielding to an urgent desire and request of my many subscribers and friends, I append to these Records the following selections from the files of the weekly journal, which I published or read, to the prisoners, while confined in Libby Prison. It may serve to illustrate more clearly than it has been done in the body of the work the *tout ensemble* of that dark period in the history of thousands of our soldiers.

The Libby Chronicle.

DEVOTED TO FACTS AND FUN.

Vol. I.] *Libby Prison, Richmond, Va., August* 21*st*, 1863. [No. I.

PROSPECTUS.[1]

The *Libby Chronicle* will be issued weekly, from Prisoner & Co.'s steam press of thought. Such will be the equalization of labor among those engaged in the enterprise, that this publication can be afforded at very low rates. Price of subscription, weekly, one —— moment's good attention, in-

[1] Eight numbers of the *Chronicle* were issued.

variably in advance. These terms being complied with, the paper will be forwarded postage free.

With such facilities before the public for obtaining useful knowledge, it is needless to state that we expect an extensive patronage. Our adherence to facts, which are always the most stubborn arguments, and to the motto that

"A little nonsense now and then,
Is relished by the wisest men,"

is a full guarantee to our patrons that they will ever obtain an ample equivalent for their subscription price. We cannot very well forbear mentioning that the contributors to our columns are among the most eminent of the land, including the skillful lawyer, the sedate judge, the erudite priest, the amusing comedian, the renowned legislator, and scores of others from the various walks of life, whose connection with our periodical places success beyond a doubt.

As we make our humble bow to the public, we hope that progress may mark our course in every department of our work, until the *Libby Chronicle*, its editor and publisher, its friends and patrons, will find themselves sailing toward the North Land of liberty and civilization.

KANSAS BRIGADE'S VERSION OF JOHN BROWN.

John Brown's body lies mouldering in the grave,
While weep the sons of bondage whom he ventured all to save,
And though he lost his life in struggling for the slave,
His soul is marching on.—CHORUS.

John Brown was a hero, undaunted, true and brave,
Kansas knew his valor when he fought her rights to save,
And though the grass grows green above his northern grave,
His soul is marching on.—CHORUS.

He captured Harper's Ferry with his nineteen men so few,
And frightened "Old Virginny" till she trembled through and through;
They hung him for a traitor — themselves a traitor crew,
But his soul is marching on.— CHORUS.

The conflict that he heralded he looks from heaven to view,
On the army of the Union with her flag, red, white and blue,
And heaven shall ring with anthems o'er the deeds we mean to do,
As we go marching on.— CHORUS.

O soldiers of Columbia, then strike, while strike you may,
The death-blow of oppression in this better time and way,
And the dawn of old John Brown will brighten into day,
As we go marching on.— CHORUS.

CAPTAIN.

"SOUTH WINDOW," LIBBY PRISON, RICHMOND, VA.
No. 1.

Mr. Editor: Who among your hearers have not felt as the writer feels to-day, weary and worn out with the dull monotony of prison life? There is no future here; night and day succeed one another with but the same scene, the same fruitless longing for liberty. Even these more than precious letters, brief mementos of the dear ones at home, make the bitterness of captivity but the deeper. Many, if not all of us, have faced death on the battle field and are willing to do so in our Country's cause again; but who, once released, would yield to see the walls of Libby Prison once more? True, that some have been unfortunate enough to now be prisoners of war a second, and, in one instance, we believe, a third time, — such are entitled to our sympathy. They are indeed sufferers.

Am I harping, Mr. Editor, on a threadbare theme? I crave pardon. A fit of the blues is on me to-day, and what I write partakes of it. Even the heavens are overcast with clouds.

> "The autumn days have come
> The saddest of the year.—"

We take a sidelong glance from our "south window," and see away off in the distance a portion of Belle Isle, occupied by thousands of our brave men. Poor fellows! There lot is, while it lasts, even worse than ours.—

Hark, what sound breaks from the depths below our feet? "Mess No.——, dinner." We go, Mr. Editor, we go. Sorrowfully we lay our pen aside, hoping when we write again, to reach a more cheerful result.

Au revoir. Black bean soup awaits us.

CAPTAIN P.

CONUNDRUMS.

Q. In what respect do the officers confined in Libby resemble Dives in the parable?

Ans. They are looking to Abraham for comfort.

Q. Why is an elephant like a pile of brick?

Ans. Because neither can climb a tree.

Q. Why is our soup in Libby like the stuff of which dreams are made?

Ans. Because it is a body without substance.

CASTLE THUNDER.

PART I.

On Cary street, in Richmond, there is a mongrel den
Of thieves, sneaks, and cowards, mixed up with gentlemen.
Oh, it is a shame to huddle in together
Men and beasts, wild and tame, like birds of every feather.
The Reb. authorities scared up this living wonder,
Made it a prison, and named it Castle Thunder.
Here they tumble in characters of every hue,
Reprobates steeped in sin with the Christian and the Jew.

Conscripts by the dozen, at daylight and after dark,
Come pouring in the Castle like animals in the ark;
Some are small, some are great, some show pluck, some white liver,
Some from Mississippi state and "Goobers" from Tar river.
Substitutes and deserters come in in sorry plight,
And sub-gents, too, are here quartered for the night.
Blockade runners, also, are shut up for a warning,
But seldom leave, as promised, early the next morning.
While on Potomac's banks both parties try to nab 'em,
If they escape the Yanks, old Jeff. is sure to grab 'em.

So-called spies are castled here, who think it real hard luck,
They are all from Yankeedom, excepting one Kennuck;
Disloyalists are also here, and one for being a guide,
The boys call him Doodlebug, for piloting Burnside.
We also have an oyster man, who the officers discover,
Was Union on the York but Secesh on James river.
Part first tells you where the Castle is and who are there,
Part second will disclose the manner of our fare.

PART II.

We have a dozen rooms or more, and in some two or three,
The boys wear handcuffs, balls and chains — Confederate jewelry,
Some rest on cots, on boards, with blankets, some without them,

And when they get to sleep the big bugs often rout them;
They never sleep in quiet though ever so much drowsy,
For the vermin are so thick and big, the lice themselves are lousy.
We have eighteen kinds of food, though 'twill stagger your belief,
We have bread, beef and soup, and bread, soup and beef;
Then we separate about, with twenty in a group,
And get beef, soup and bread, and beef. bread and soup;
For our dessert we obtain, though it costs us nary red,
Soup, bread and beef, and beef, soup and bread.

The bread we usually get is of a very good sort,
True, it is the staff of life, but our staff is rather short.
Our beef's so lean and dry, that, swallowing, it will bound back,
Unless we recollect afore, to try to grease the track.
It is too tough and strong, for our noses or our knives,
The cattle were so poor and thin, were killed to save their lives.
The hides are made up into shoes, the sinews into strings,
The marrow into soup, and the bones in pretty rings.
Our soup is much too weak, to please a very high liver,
'Tis made of beans, bugs and rice, and extract of James river.

Now I've told you what we eat, whether we're well or sick,
What we drink is never strong though sometimes rather thick.
Our drink is rarely river water, except to save from death,
And then for want of whiskey we smell an officer's breath.
Meat and drink are now so scarce as to raise a serious doubt,
Whether the Confederacy is not about played out.
Number one and two you've heard, and now in division third,
I will say a word about the way we are officered.

PART III.

Military officers of the very meanest stuff,
For every local post, are considered good enough.
In officering Richmond they varied not the general rule,
To appoint a drunkard, a tyrant, a coward or a fool.
It is plainly to be seen that in a little while
When Satan scoopes his jewels up, in Richmond he'll get a pile.

At the head of Richmond post they've placed a Marylander,
And like the devil in regions lost there sits General Winder.
He snaps and snarls, he rips and swears, whether sober or tight,
The old villain's heart's as black as his head is white.
All through this vicinity they hate him as hard as they can,
Nor ever slander him with epithet of decent man.
However mean, he's a patriot, that may be understood,
For when he left the Yankee land, 'twas for his country's good.

We come to Major Griswold, who is our Provost Marshal,
He's a little prejudiced, which makes him rather partial;
But when compared to Winder he seems no virtue to lack,
As green is almost white by the side of jet black.

And there's Judge Baxter, who also is a queer old case,
He has so large a centre he can hardly change his base.
He says whiskey's a dangerous thing to have about the town,
So, with all his might, he's for putting whiskey down.
Whiskey is fifty cents a drink, and of the meanest sort,
The Judge, to get his money's worth, swallows it by the quart.
I will slyly tell you, boys, if your money you begrudge,
How to get your whiskey cheap — step up and tap the judge.

In the door of the castle, like a stopple in a jug,
To shut the prison's mouth, they've stuck a Baltimore plug;
It is Captain Alexander, who is so cross and spunky,
He is certainly not fit to command an oyster pungy.
The captain is such a case as may be often seen,
Who thinks he's very smart, but is invisible green;
He is a thundering blower, but would not dare to fight,
As dogs that bark the loudest are seldom known to bite.
Yet he has streaks of good, as well as mean, mixed for relief,
The first are scarce and thin like fat in Confederate beef.
He also came from Maryland, and mean as Nick can make him,
And the reason why we keep him is because the devil won't take him.

Allen is a smooth old rat, that is truthfully said,
He shines with black from boots to hat, his face shines with red;
He pours down whiskey double-quick, there is no doubt of that;
Sometimes he makes believe he's sick but it's a brick in his hat.
Old Allen is a villain of the very darkest stripe,
He'll go home to purgatory as soon as he is ripe.
And if he does not blow off steam and soon shut down the brakes,
In a dream of delerium he'll find his boots are full of snakes.
He has an oily tongue and face full of deceit and evil.
And should Old Nick miss that scape-grace, there's no need of a devil.

A PRIVATE.

FACTS AND FUN.

I am one of those who have derived much information from the facts which have been demonstrated, and much amusement from the fun which has been generated in the columns of the *Chronicle*. We have been favored with statements and demonstrations of facts pertaining to almost every subject of public interest. Creeds of religion and political faith have wisely been excluded from the *fact department* of this association. No one could consistently with the objects of the association and the courtesy due individual members thereof, lead off with a bigoted or partisan statement and denunciation, which would necessarily be offensive to others, and would, if replied to in the same spirit, lead here as elsewhere, to recriminations, disputes and disunion.

We are gratified to observe that this principle has commended itself to all, and that such questions have not been obtruded upon ground sacred to instruction.

Success to the "stubborn" department of the Lyceum, and may matters of personal experience, travels, history, science with its innumerable branches, extending from the depths of the earth to regions above and beyond our ken, the arts and graces, Christianity and patriotism, never lack for able defenders and expounders, and the meetings of the association will not lack in interest, nor the speakers or readers for appreciative listeners. In the stubbornness of fact is found a self-supporting dignity.

Fun, on the contrary, is apt, inside and outside of our circle, to degenerate into folly. The harmless play of seven and eight P. M. has, at nine or ten, degenerated into profanity and obscenity, which wisely await darkness before coming forth to disturb the sleep and sensibilities of the majority of the officers here confined. Inside our circle great care is necessary lest the joke grate too harshly on rough edge or straight edge.

Of this food so healthful for body and mind we should seek the highest and best, by keeping watch and ward over our unruly members, and carefully analyzing and examining those specimens which are recognized models of wit. When well executed the burlesque is, perhaps, the happiest style of wit. May our *fun* never grow less in quantity or quality. *Vive la Bagatelle.*

MAJOR P.

NEWS OF LIBBY.

Monday, September 28th, 12 M.

Rumored that the exchange commissioners did not meet yesterday as was expected.

Four P. M. Rumor says that the United States commissioners, having heard of Spencer Kellogg's execution, immediately returned without awaiting the arrival of the Confederate States troop, and that there will be no exchange of prisoners soon.

September 29th. As a result of yesterday's news the spirits are drooping in all, except those of the huxtering fry, who seem to have renewed their diligence.

September 30th. We have news from a reliable source, that all the Federal officers are to be paroled and sent north on the next truce boat.

Three P. M. Since receiving the above telegram we have received information that no exchange or parole is to occur, as the exchange agents have not acceeded to any propositions yet offered, and that the next truce boat will bring blankets and clothing for the Libby family.

October 1st. The huxtering fry say they will allow fruit to be conveyed down Red Lane pike, if the teamsters will allow them a profitable remuneration.

Latest from the hospital, four and one half P. M. A United States gun-boat brought dispatches that no exchange even of privates would be allowed until the case of Kellogg is satisfactorily explained.

Still later, nine P. M. The commissioners are to meet on the 3d October. The United States commissioner will bring six gun-boats along to protect the white flag.

Yours,

JACK RUMORTRAP.

"SOUTH WINDOW."

No 2.

Shall I tell you why, Mr. Editor, that ensconced in this out-of-the-way corner, close to this cross-barred frame, why I call it my South Window? Because memory reverts to another scene and time in by-gone days, when a fair bright face oft watched adown the road, the first to welcome the toiler home. I wonder if she sits in that "south window" now and waits the wanderer's return?

Ah, Mr. Editor, whose heart so cold it would not warm with thoughts like these? Ever as memory goes back to those fast-growing far distant hours I picture my happy home. Situated a few miles away from the busy hum of the metropolis on a little bay, nestled among a magnificent grove of chesnuts, hid by them from the sight of the passer by, is my home.

There at night, after the work of the day, have I retired in keen enjoyment of the comforts of a happy home, surrounded only by those who love. Such a life is almost the poet's dream of Elysium. There in the early mists of the morning have I mounted my horse for a ride along the seashore, or through the clover fields; or in the moonlit summer's evening have unfurled the sails of my "Bonny" yacht and glided on the smooth surface of the bay, hour after hour, happy in forgetfulness of all save the present. This, in all its wide meaning, is home.

And here, Mr. Editor, the oft-repeated prayer arises, may the day soon come, when you and I, and all of us, shall leave our prison abode, and be permitted to clasp our loved ones in a warm embrace, when the dismal clouds of war are scattered, and the sunshine of peace shall fall upon a reunited land.

Once more, *Au revoir*.

CAPTAIN P.

(Written expressly for the *Libby Chronicle.*)

THE LIBBYAD.

"Of Libby's lice to us the direful spring
Of woes unnumbered, heavenly muses sing."

Homer modernized.

Think not my theme so trifling, none you can mention,
Receives in Libby half so much attention.
A phonographic class of half a dozen score,
In one short week, falls off a half or more;
French, too, and Spanish, as all can plainly see,
Lose their students in the same degree;
But who so lazy, so busy, or so nice,
Neglects to give an hour each day to lice,
Will be beset with troubles great and small,
And have hard scratching to get along at all.
If poets write of battles 'twixt frogs and mice,
Why not of skirmishes 'twixt men and lice?
And while these verses rude we are enditing,
Look 'round to see the different styles of fighting.

Watch Pugilisticus, he in a trice,
Pulls off his dirty shirt to fight his lice;
His muscles thus of cumbrous duds bereft,
See with what science he "puts in his left"
Upon the bodies of his luckless brood,
And Pugilisticus has gained "first blood."
With double fury he "puts in his right,"
And Pugilisticus has "won the fight."

And there's Historicus, with scabby back,
Would trace their history as he hears them crack;
Wonders if these lice bear the same description,
As those once scratched by Pharaoh and the Egyptians.
He tries, in vain, from facts and from analogy,
To thread their lineage and genealogy.

He learns, however, with very little pains,
The proudest blood of Libby is flowing in their veins.
He marks, too, that the death of these, his little foes,
Is not as ignominious as thoughtless men suppose.
Sisera, a great warrior, was slain by Jael,
With those unwarlike weapons, a hammer and a nail,
While to slay these, so very much abused,
Although there be no hammer, *two* nails are always used.

Mark now Gallantricus, that nice young man,
With taper fingers made to wield a lady's fan,
Much disgusted, see him hunting, half ashamed of being seen,
Thinks it "very unpretty," lice should stay in shirt so clean.
See now his handsome visage, what contortions and grimaces!
As if to scare the nasty things, by making ugly faces.
What would she think, his would-be, future spouse,
To see him strip and squat and grin and louse?

Behold Theologicus, with reverend face,
Peering with care in every hiding place.
And while his little flock crawls 'round through heaps of slain,
Such thoughts as these come crawling through his brain:
What if 'midst all the creeds and doctrines which so stagger us,
That should be true announced by old Pythagoras!
That after death men's souls instead of going
To heaven or hell according to the showing
Of orthodoxy teachers, simply go forth
To inhabit birds and beasts, insects and so forth
Base or noble as their lives may show forth.
Most in this prison, if I judge aright,
Will live in noble beasts and birds of lofty flight.
But some there are, who'll live again as hogs,
Some skunks, some asses, some as snappish dogs.
A very few have souls so small and base
That even such as these they would disgrace.
Crammed in this loathsome prison, scorned like slaves,

Insulted, starved by coward traitor knaves,
The men who in our suffering have betrayed us,
And fawn on those who brutally degrade us,
Even such small souls, will find a fitting nice,
And live hereafter, in loathsome Libby's lice.

There's Philosophicus, with thoughtful brow.
Who knows the "why" of everything, the "what" and "how."
He watches his louse to learn each secret habit,
Before with bloody fangs he proceeds to grab it.
Sees it in its cozy nest recline,
Marks it making love and observes it dine.
With wise discrimination he can trace
The differcnec 'twixt the louse and bedbug race—
But I'll cease scratching lines and scratch "Scotch-fiddle" tunes,
At something crawling in my pantaloons.

LIEUTENANT COLONEL W.

Libby Prison, Richmond, Va., September 26th, 1863
To His Excellency, AUGUSTUS W BRADFORD,
Governor of Maryland,

Sir: We, the undersigned officers of your state, now suffering the privations of prison life, though conscious that we are not forgotten by you, would nevertheless urge upon your consideration the importance of making a personal effort for our release, should such effort be found practicable. Our imprisonment has become almost intolerable. Deprived as we have been, so long, of the sweet sunshine and pure air, also of our accustomed diet when free, we have gradually sunken under the debilitating influence.

Scrofulons and dropsical diseases have already manifested their alarming symptons among us, and will doubtless prove fatal in many cases. unless we are soon released. Our fellow-sufferer, Major Morris, but recently fell a victim to our wretched condition. Others will probably soon follow him. Can anything be done for us? Our prayer is brief, but earnest.

We are, respected Sir,

Your obedient servants, &c.

(Signed by many officers of the state of Maryland).

WHO IS RESPONSIBLE FOR NON-EXCHANGE OF PRISONERS?

BY LIEUTENANT COLONEL N.

It is with much regret that we announce the fact to the readers of the *Chronicle*, that there are those among the officers now confined in this delectable (?) locality, ycleped Libby, who are uttering curses, "not loud, but deep," against our government, for permitting them to remain here so long. These officers evince more of the spirit of spoiled children, than of that manly courage and patience which should characterize the actions of the American officer and soldier.

The officer who utters complaints against our government for his continued incarceration, shows that he does not understand the principles involved in the controversy, in relation to the exchange of prisoners, or else he is prompted by motives altogether selfish and unpatriotic. The exchange of officers was suspended in consequence of the unfair proceedings of the Rebel authorities, about the first of June, in retaining certain officers in an unjust and arbitrary manner. Among those thus retained were Colonel Streight's officers, Captain McKee, of the Fourteenth Kentucky Cavalry, and Lieutenant Conn, of the Second Virginia Cavalry. Our commissioner, on discovering this injustice, respectfully informed the Rebel commissioner, that all exchange of officers would be suspended, until the Rebels would exchange officer for officer and man for man, according to rank and to date of capture.

The Rebels, at that time, were anticipating a series of successes, which they have not realized, though they persist, with a dogged obstinacy, in the unjust course which they had marked for themselves. Instead of removing obstacles which they had thrown in the way of the cartel, they continue to increase those obstacles, by high-handed acts of injustice and cruelty, and make the affair more complicated. All that is necessary, is to return to the cartel and proceed as formerly. When the Rebels do this, our government is ready to exchange, but until then, it acts properly in refusing to exchange. A partial or special exchange would leave many an unfortunate prisoner, exposed to even worse insults and indignities, than now. The suspension of the cartel will doubtless continue until the Rebels are willing to conduct the exchange on fair principles, and every patriotic officer should submit to his sad fate with manly fortitude.

Our government has not forgotten us, but, on the contrary, it is pursuing that course which will result to our advantage. Should partial exchanges be made, a portion of the officers would be held as hostages, confined in wretched cells, and reserved for hanging or shooting, for the amusement and recreation of the chivalry. Such exchanges would add to the comfort of some, but would increase the sufferings of others. What officer is so devoid of humanity as to be willing to accept his personal liberty at such expense? If there be any such in Libby, they had better tender their "immediate and unconditional" resignation, as soon as possible, and retire to *their own place.* But, in the language of Holy Writ, let us "endure hardness as good soldiers," trusting in the God of battles to deliver us; assured also that we are not forgotten by father Abraham, who is evidently doing all that justice and mercy can prompt him to do for our relief. While it is well for us to invite the aid of our influential friends in the north, in this matter of exchange, it is equally proper to bide our time with patience and resignation.

"SOUTH WINDOW."

No 3.

October, 1st, 1863.

Amidst the excitements of "fresh fish"[1] (and this is ever a fishy place) and exchange, there has been little time of late to write, and even now your correspondent knows of little that will interest your hearers. "Changing, forever changing; so runs on the petty pace from day to day," says the poet, and how has its truthfulness been proven during the few weeks past. Victory and defeat have hovered o'er our country's banners, and as we watch to see the smoke of battle roll away, we see the red result—a result which we, men of war, have seen but too often.

[1] Whenever a company of prisoners was seen approaching Libby, the cry, "fresh fish!" "fresh fish!" was made within, followed by a rush to the front windows, to get a glimpse of the new comers. As they generally had friends in the prison, and were bearers of the latest reliable news from the army, on being introduced into the rooms, they were surrounded by an eager throng, and a shower of questions was rained upon them. Those were seasons of great excitement.

Vast armies, numbered by their tens of thousands, go crashing together; steel clashes against steel, fire responds to fire; the one recoils, and again amid the whistling ball and hurtling shell, the scene is reënacted, until the one, weaker and worn out, is hurled back, whipped, defeated, routed. They, who were brave men an hour before, on losing hope, fly for safety under some impregnable fortress. Thus, though, Mr. Editor, has it not been with our valiant army of the Cumberland.

Forced into a battle without position, what did our brave Rosecrans? With numbers small in comparison to those of his foe, we see him day after day stubbornly fighting. At length his lines are driven back, for they cannot resist the force that is hurled, confident in their weight of numbers, against them. Back, back they fall, and, in a few moments more, all will be lost; but see! a form, well known and loved by each of that gallant army, dashes forward, scarcely an hundred yards from the advancing foe; and there, amid a storm of bullets, which they who were there tell us they never saw equaled, right in the jaws of death, between the two combatants, their leader rides; his hat is raised aloft, and he shouts, "Forward men! Will you let Rebels drive you back? Forward! Give them the bayonet!" And they did; the day was saved.

Night came on apace, and, so quietly that the enemy knew it not, he fell back to Chattanooga, where Braxton Bragg, with all the appropriateness of his name, will not attempt to attack him. Better far, and none know it better than he, to be content with what he may call a victory,—a victory indeed in one sense, but certainly a very barren one.

AN OFFICER AND A GENTLEMAN.

BY LIEUTENANT COLONEL S.

It still runs in the memory of many, when to be an officer of the American army, was to be as a consequence, a gentleman and a man of honor. The claimant to official rank, of whatever grade, was ever the recipient of marked attention. The announcement of his arrival was paraded in the journals of the day, and the blandest smiles of mine host, and the cosiest chamber of "mine inn," were instantly at his command. From the great, the learned, the wealthy and the fair, hospitalities, invitations and favors of every kind were tendered him, and his sojourn in town or country, was a continuation of fête days, culminating in intensity as his leave of absence drew near its close.

"All men revered him, all women loved."

To impugn his character, or to doubt his honor, subjected the utterer to the closest investigation, or to the stern arbitrament of arms, while, to him, to fall from his high position, was a descent second only to that of Lucifer. In camp, courteous to his subordinates, he was ever respectful to his superiors; and in the field, he faced the foe, because the path *to* glory is *through* the field of danger.

For his associates, with whom he had encountered many vicissitudes "through field and flood," he entertained an affection dearer than the ties of relationship; and was ever ready to aid, support and defend them at all hazards. Such were the life, character and attributes of an American officer at the commencement of this contest; and whether enrolled in defense of constitutional right and a just government, or engaged in marshalling the ranks of the disloyal and the traitor, to this day he retains, in an eminent degree, most, if not all, of these virtues.

Let us now turn to the volunteer. Called to arms by his country's need, the gifted, the honored, the brave, throwing off the lethargy of peace, donned the uniform of his government, and, pledging his life and his sacred honor, rushed to the defense of a time-honored flag, and the beloved institutions of his forefathers. A hearty volunteer in a glorious cause, he brought with him the enthusiasm of the patriot, and the loyalty of the citizen; accustomed to comfort and nurtured in luxury, he endured the privations of the camp and the bitter experiences of martial life, with cheerfulness and obedience; proud of his cause, his country and his uniform, he strove so to guide his steps, that each and all might be honored by his advocacy. Acquainted with the amenities of civil life; filled with the recollections of the social distinctions accorded to the officer of former days, and a firm believer in the attributes of the chivalric soldier, he naturally turned to his immediate associates in arms, for an exhibition of those characteristics, which have garnished the pages of history and peopled the world with heroes.

The child which nightly awakens the denizens of Libby by its eager search after the paternal Teet;[1] to whom the knowledge of light, air, and impalpable being, is but a thing of yesterday, is yet old enough to chronicle the downfall of these expectations; and could he answer, young as he is, his youthful visage would rival, in intensity of color, his spanked extremity, after a severe flagellation by his irate

[1] Captain John Teed could imitate the crying of a little child so perfectly, as to render detection almost impossible. Hours of intense merriment were occasioned by this thing alone.

ancestor, while recounting the reverse of the picture. For, did he speak truly, he would tell of the lie bandied, in lieu of the sacred word of honor ever implied; of the act and gesture of filth and indecency, in place of the manly joke and good humored repartee; of the blasphemous response to the authorized command of the superior, instead of the graceful obedience of the subordinate; but, worse than all, he would tell of the rights invaded, the property purloined, and the pocket rifled of one officer, by his fellow.

Mr. Editor, had such a statement been made in any journal as respectable as your own, previous to my advent to Libby, I would have deemed it my duty to hunt the anonymous slanderer from his secret lair, and nail the calumny to his forehead; but now, alas, a short but painful experience in a military prison, has revealed to me, that an officer and a gentleman are no longer synonyms; that the uniform of the soldier may cover the carcase of the sneak, and the shoulder straps of the officer may serve to conceal the brand of the thief. Dare any one deny this? If any such there be, let them dispassionately investigate the record of the past two weeks, and, ere venting their virtuous indignation, inquire of the first officer they meet of *his* experience; or, better, let them consult the official announcement, affixed to these walls, proclaiming the loss, by theft, of one hundred and eighty dollars, within the past fortnight; or they may be enlightened by the recital of innumerable petty larcenies, minor scoundrelisms and sneaking pilferings, unworthy the talents of the meanest thief that ever graduated from the Five Points. Even the honor which obtains among rogues, is forgotten, for we have it on record, that thief has robbed thief, and the sneak preyed upon his brother. And yet, forsooth, these miscreants bear a commission, hold a command, and, by my manhood, even sport a sword. Of such men the immortal Shakespeare has written thus:

"He will steal, sir, an egg out of a cloister. He professes not keeping of oaths; in breaking them he is stronger than Hercules. He will lie, sir, with such volubility, that you would think truth were a fool. Drunkenness is his best virtue, for he will be swine-drunk, and in his sleep he does little harm, save to his bed clothes about him; but they know his conditions and lay him in straw. I have but little more to say, sir, of his honesty; he has everything that an honest man should *not* have, what an honest man *should* have, he has nothing."

I would not have it understood, Mr. Editor, that a majority, or even a tenth of our number, are open to these charges. The bad among us are, I am proud to say, numerically small, but that they are skillful and proficient their present concealment evidences. Brought from the various armies of the north and west, we are, in a degree, total strangers to a large number of the present inmates of this prison. The very man who shares our plank, is unknown to us, by name or state, and may be, for all we know, the mirror of knighthood, or the veriest poltroon.

A sufferer by the peculations complained of, we turn in querulous haste, with jealous eye, upon the first comer, and are more likely to suspect the innocent, than to detect the guilty; and we ourselves, while seeking our despoiler, are in turn suspected by a fellow-sufferer, who deems the eager looks of the loser, the preying scrutiny of the thief. For our own sakes, then, let us combine to purge our body of this moral blot, to rid our profession of this novel stain

To one or the other, the condition and opinion of each and every man are known. The knave and the coward, under a close surveillance, must inevitably be discovered, while the brave and the honorable can rarely be misunderstood. Mark then every man, by his words and actions. Scan closely the unguarded movements and desultory remarks of the suspected. Meet cunning with stratagem, and ply the rogue to his ruin. The cause we advocate and the uniform we wear, demand that we should expose the unworthy and unmask the dishonest; and it is the duty of every honest man, to bring the recreant thief to that justice he so much needs and fears.

Written expressly for the *Chronicle*).

THE IRRUPTION.*

BY LIEUTENANT N.

'Twas night, and Rebel Libby, wrapped in sleep,
Was hushed to quiet, weird, sublime and deep:
Along the floor the moon's pale, flickering beam,
Athwart each visage, shot with fitful gleam,
As if in pity she did stoop to bless,
And cheer each prisoner with a fond caress.

And what a sight that moon-lit floor displays!
In each pale face, upturned to meet her rays,
She shines resplendent, and paints in colors bright
A cheerful soul within, content and light;
Yet through its workings, now in fit and start,
Unfolds the sorrows of an anguished heart.

---

* This poem was written soon after the arrival of our officers, captured at Chickamauga.

From scene like this we turn our weary head,
To court unwilling Sleep to bless our bed;
When, hark! upon the stillness harshly breaks
A sound, that to the base old Libby shakes;
Like to the war of billows, tempest-clad,
That beat old Ocean's shore, in foment mad,

Or cannon's thunders loud, when heard afar,
In battle's dreadful strife, "grim-visaged war."
It nearer, louder comes. "What can it be?"
Each wakened dreamer cries, and starts to see.
And what a sight meets their astonished gaze,
By light of moon and candle's flickering blaze!

The vandal Yankees, in "irruption" bold,
In numbers seventy and one all told,
Are in a horde dark Libby's cells invading,
And 'long its files with stealthy tread are raiding;
Their guide a contraband: deceitful black,
To thus direct the cunning Yankees' track.

Surprised, awaked by the in-coming foe,
The inmates rise to strike a mortal blow:
Aloft they rise in majesty so grand
These dreamers, this incarcerated band;
With mingled cries of joy, of fear and rage,
They quickly haste the coming fight to wage;

When, lo! above the din cries out a wag:
"'Tis not the vandals, only Braxton Bragg,
Who comes to reënforce the garrison,
With gobbled troops of Teuton Rosy's men"

CPSIA information can be obtained
at www.ICGtesting.com
Printed in the USA
LVHW101936050422
715402LV00003B/71

9 783752 588491